PRAISE FOR ANDREZ BERGEN &

DEPTH CHARGING ICE PLANET GOTH

While having the perfect pitch for witty dialog and cultural references, and characters that are fascinating people you'll want to hang out with, Bergen also creates some of the most wildly imaginative places ever encountered in fiction.
Chris Rhatigan, editor of *All Due Respect* and *Pulp Ink*

Marked by a surreal quality reminiscent of Haruki Murakami — here far more brutal — Bergen's additional eye for detailing the mid '80s world, set in a sham city named Nede (but actually Melbourne) is a stunning journey.
The Pulp Braggart

A coming-of-age novel set in Australia in 1986, narrated by a sixteen-year-old girl named Mina. That's a challenge by itself, with Bergen more than up to the task — but at the same moment this manages to be a compelling crime novel with a touch of magical realism.
James Reasoner, author of *Dancin*

Mad genius at work.
Book Reviews by **Elizabeth A. Wł**

There are mutiple intriguing layers here and, as with Hansel and Gretel, Bergen provides numerous breadcrumbs to follow. This author has a style all his own, giving the text a different sound — both perky and quirky — from other writers... and that was one very clever ending. Need I say that I loved it?
McDroll, author of *Feeling It*

If you've read any of his previous work you'll know what a magpie eye Andrez has, with influences ranging from Soviet propaganda to Dashiell Hammett to Charles Dickens.
Eva Dolan, author of *Long Way Home*

Picture *Dogs in Space* banging heads with *This Boy's Life* in the back seat of a classic roadster — one erratically handled by Jimmy Stewart's best friend Harvey. A riveting ride taking unexpected curves.
Catachresis & Co

He's done it again! The Magical Mystery Tour through the mind of Andrez Bergen continues with his awesome fourth novel. I love it!
David Walden, Nerd Culture Podcast

Nobody else today writes with the same dark wit, style or mad creativity.
Christopher Black, Available in Any Colour

The most wildly inventive teenage-girl-grows-up book you're likely to read.
John Rickards, *The Nameless Horror*

Depth Charging
Ice Planet Goth

Depth Charging
Ice Planet Goth

Andrez Bergen

PERFECT
EDGE
BOOKS

Winchester, UK
Washington, USA

First published by Perfect Edge Books, 2014
Perfect Edge Books is an imprint of John Hunt Publishing Ltd., Laurel House, Station Approach,
Alresford, Hants, SO24 9JH, UK
office1@jhpbooks.net
www.johnhuntpublishing.com
www.perfectedgebooks.com

For distributor details and how to order please visit the 'Ordering' section on our website.

Text copyright: Andrez Bergen 2013

ISBN: 978 1 78279 649 7

A CIP catalogue record for this book is available from the British Library.

Design: Lee Nash

Printed in the USA by Edwards Brothers Malloy

We operate a distinctive and ethical publishing philosophy in all
areas of our business, from our global network of authors to
production and worldwide distribution.

CONTENTS

Also by the same author:

TOBACCO-STAINED MOUNTAIN GOAT
ONE HUNDRED YEARS OF VICISSITUDE
THE CONDIMENTAL OP
WHO IS KILLING THE GREAT CAPES OF HEROPA?

For the nobodies of the world

"All those supernatural vampires, ghouls and bogeymen...
The only real monsters are people."
— *Dr Christopher Stein, MBBS, Kentigern Regional Hospital*

In the Beginning, the Word

Before a further piece of wisdom I poke the chromed muzzle of my .45 calibre Auto-Ordnance into the front angle of her neck, between jawline and a noticeable laryngeal prominence.

"You know only six-point-two percent of women have them?"

"Have what?"

The brunette's return comes out surprisingly confident despite the question mark. For my money, I reckon I'd be all croak if the positions were reversed. Examining her pretty face for signs of nerves leaves me impressed. Only the blue eyes let her down — the long-eyelashed lids blinking faster than usual.

Then again, some people do that.

"Have a prominent Adam's apple," I say.

Ought to pull the trigger now and have done with it. Shame to mess up the good-looks, but worse things do happen.

"Gets me in trouble," she muses, gazing straight back along the barrel.

"How?" The query pops out before I think.

"Well, the odd paramour gets to thinking I'm a man in drag."

"You're kidding me?"

Heart's hammering. Voice isn't much better than the croak I mentioned earlier. She's a looker, no matter the Adam's apple.

"Sadly? No kidding. Some men get frightened."

That's not what frightens me. It's the weakness enveloping my limbs while I take in the red, Cupid's-bow mouth and a lot of perfect skin that clings just right.

That mouth purses, almost a pucker, like she's mulling over something and blowing me a kiss at the same time.

Before I know what's happened she's wrapped her right fingers around the pearl-handled pistol, gently removes it from my fist, twists the thing about, and has it pointed into the front angle of my neck — between the jawline and a likely bulging Adam's apple.

The pout becomes a smile as she uses her southpaw to straighten the collar of her shirt to better cover the throat, and then the gun presses hard into mine.

"You know a hundred percent of men have them?"

"That so?" I mumble, flummoxed.

"Yep." Her eyes now narrow, a breeze of grievance winging my way. "Forbidden fruit, my arse."

I kick back on the bed, overlooking the page before me. Hanging as it does just inside the typewriter paper fingers, the type guide a centimetre beneath 'arse'.

Nothing like a silly, hardboiled yarn to start off the day, firearm info plagiarized from my dad's *Complete Book of Pistols and Shotguns* — blame the episode of *Mickey Spillane's Mike Hammer* I'd watched on the box the night before — with my best friend Sarah cast as unwitting femme fatale.

She'd never read this anyway.

The unnamed narrator? Definitely my brother.

And then, right then, I remember the time.

Shit!

Version 1611, Part 1 of 10

Optimistically designated the International Year of Peace by the U.N., for most people 1986 mattered because it was the year Swedish Prime Minister Olof Palme was assassinated on his way home from the cinema, Chernobyl's nuclear power plant disaster happened in the Ukrainian SSR, and the American space shuttle *Challenger* disintegrated over the Atlantic.

I remember that last one in particular because here in Nede (pronounced 'Needy') our big city department store, Amand's, neglected for several weeks thereafter to remove a 1/25 scale plastic model of the *Challenger* from public display.

For me, 1986 meant a final skirmish with secondary school misery — that February I was locked in to set about Year 12 at Mac.Duagh Girls' High School.

While the spelling of Mac.Duagh should've meant we called it 'Mac.Dawg' or 'Mac.Darg', apparently back in the old country (Scotland or Ireland, I forget which) they went with a relatively spooky 'Mac.Dark'.

And what was with the full stop between the Mac and the Duagh?

Regardless, the pronunciation and the punctuation were drummed into us from scratch, the moment we got accepted into a shady place once upon a time ranked sixth in Australia's top ten girls' schools — but ranked by a right-wing newspaper I barely trusted (*The Sun News-Pictorial*).

Age-wise I was on the cusp of seventeen and had spent the previous three years embedded at the art-deco premises of this school, a place all straight lines, unadorned brickwork, white sills and complete lack of ornamentation that was located off Kings Way, next to Addlebert Park Lake.

Like its sibling school Nede Boys' High, which my brother Patrick attended, Mac.Duagh was a four-year affair (Years 9 to

12) that had a deluded belief of itself as on par with private schools in the country, when in fact this was a perfectly reasonable public school that didn't need to aspire to such dubiously lofty heights.

Direction hung alien to me even before the year began.

Future plans were amiss, career intentions M.I.A., and I'd simply cherry-picked subjects I liked — hence dropping sciences and maths like the sizzling hot potatoes they'd become.

Went instead with humanities (English, German, cinema studies, visual art, English literature, European history, token 'science' geography) and believed my mother would have concurred at least with English lit if she were alive to do so.

Two months.

It'd been hardly two months since she died.

Felt like another life. Not that I behaved like she was so recently ripped out of mine. I'd felt isolated even while Mum was here. Once she was gone things didn't exactly change. I cried a bit when the news came in from her hospital, but hardly shed a great flood of tears — I'm sure I wept more that time I was tied upside down.

Initially my father took note.

Looked at me strangely, asked if I were bottling things up. The only answer I could give was a shrug, since I had no idea. Knew I should experience more pain than I did, and was vaguely horrified by my lack of a reaction.

But most of all? I felt nothing. Life was rotating, twisting and turning about me, full of emotional ups and downs for everyone else, and yet I appeared to be transfixed dead centre, where feelings were frigid.

Aside from family, not a single one of my friends knew. About Mum, I mean.

Helped that she'd died just after summer holidays began, a week before Christmas. Didn't have to lug the baggage to school for seven weeks, by which time I believed I was cured.

Besides, from Santa I'd got a new Sony Walkman (weighing in at just 300g) to help me forget any woes — and other residual aches.

Six weeks post-Walkman delivers us to a particular weekend before the school recommencement ceremony, the last Saturday of freedom prior to brainwashing kicking back into gear.

Not that we weren't indoctrinated in other ways.

A date had been set, memorized and circled (in HB pencil) on the water lily-ridden fifty-cent shop Claude Monet calendar. This hangs at an angle in our downstairs toilet.

Organized by Sarah, with pencilling by me to ensure I remember to meet our posse.

Should've left the reminder in the upstairs loo as well — I got so caught up writing away in my room that I forgot the time.

Therefore hurry along Ackland Street, late again. Breathe in a heady aroma of seaweed breeze and continental cakes, assailed by the sound of late summer cicadas.

Next to a restaurant called Adán's Ribs and an electricity pole sloppily painted with seven Ps — both convenient landmarks — I detour to the right and push through heavy plate-glass doors into Deveroli's, our favourite Italian café-cum-restaurant in St. Kilda — a place fully modern, with chrome fixtures, pastel walls, and Simply Red's 'Fake' playing on the in-house soundsystem.

The date memorable because it marked the first time Animeid had left the house, even if the excursion is an uninvited one and I have no idea at the time.

Clair, Hannah, Sarah and Nicole are already in the place, seated around a square wooden table next to a simple square pillar, close by the front window.

The four of them have left me very little room to muscle in. I go borrow a chair from another table and tow it over to a vacant corner of unclaimed territory, a space about six-inches wide. Can fit only one elbow on the pine surface to lean in.

Nothing strange about this. I always existed on the outer.

The other girls are talking all at once in excited tones that border on hysterical, each trying to outdo the other — actually, I lie. All of them except for Clair, who's quiet and docile (like me) and occasionally glances my way with a tenuous smile. Kindred spirits and all that jazz.

Mention of school, personal issues, the private past, or bodily functions — such as a certain time of month — was taboo. Anyone breaking this tribal rule fated to suffer scowls from the collective whole.

Sarah and Hannah are now holding court. They speak, gasp and shriek at a hundred-point-two miles per hour, while Nicole interjects very occasionally. Otherwise she sits preening with ramrod posture, the outcome of ten years' ballet.

By contrast Clair slumps in her chair, sipping cappuccino, elbows stuck to the table. No matter how I try, with space for only the one elbow I can't compete.

It's in precious moments like this that I can zone out to other places, start conjuring up depraved new worlds — or return to silly flights of fantasy I'm currently writing.

"It was *unreal!*"

Sarah has spoken, bringing me back to the here, the now. Chuck Berry having replaced Simply Red with 'Oh Baby Doll'.

Hadn't been tuning in, so it doesn't really matter what earned the over-oiled tag 'unreal' — or the 'baby doll' one on the stereo. We lobbed the former word about with the kind of desperate abandon appreciated by topless bathers at the beach nearby, while Chuck's 1950s song seemed to be waxing nostalgic for old school days.

Nodding along with the others, I pray there'll be no pop-quiz, but otherwise the rhythm of the song and the conversation are pretty easy to slip back into.

In this case, by conversation I mean listening — to Sarah.

Sarah Murray held down the post of ringleader, organizing

hoops the rest of us needed to jump through in order to play catch-up. Strong-willed and pushy (as all benevolent tyrants need to be), she was captain of the Mac.Duagh tennis team. I knew she was far stricter in that capacity since I'd been a member for twelve excruciating months before getting the flick.

Also she was class captain and one of the most popular girls at Mac.Duagh.

Possessed of a healthy tan, Sarah had a sporty, nicely rounded physique and straight, black hair that fell past her shoulders. Long lashes, a vaguely prominent Adam's apple. Had a Cupid's-bow mouth that softened the prevailing attitude and allowed her to get away with murder.

She figured as my best friend in the world.

Assuming the role of brutal *aide-de-camp* was Nicole Milton, class vice-captain, who doubled-up as resident style critic. Like Sarah she boasted long hair, tied back, hers almost reaching to the waist (thanks to subtle extensions) — chocolate-brown without a follicle askew, a dead-straight fringe above arched eyebrows and deep-set hazel eyes.

Courtesy of the acne she'd had in her mid-teens, there were some permanent pockmarks to the upper face that she carefully covered with make-up. Barely noticed till you got up close.

Nicole often broadcast mixed messages back-to-back, scathing one moment of basic fashion faux pas and the next smitten by what she deemed 'ace' in the field of global haber-dashery.

Blessed with the wealthiest parents, she had a budget to kill for and the heftiest Chanel purse, yet never cared to share these ill-gotten ducats. Instead Nicole played complete miser when it came to splitting bills.

Hannah Satana, a part-time model and brown belt in the Japanese martial art *baritsu* — with blue eyes, ears that stuck out a little, and bouncy, blonde hair styled like Marilyn Monroe's in her prime — one time featured in an inset photo on the front cover of *Dolly* magazine.

She not only pushed tallest in our group but also most visually dazzling, blessed with the loudest voice.

Funnily enough, much of what Hannah said meant little and fell by the wayside within seconds and she had the tendency to go along with whoever had the upper hand — but then so did I. Nicole had christened her 'D.D.', a nickname that stuck. While Hannah believed this came from an American comic book called *Daredevil* and liked anything with twin letters (M.M. and B.B., for instance), Nicole told the rest of us the nickname's true meaning: Dumb & Ditzy.

Our shortest member was Clair René, who additionally edged plump — a bob-cut redhead with the kind of personality that made her radiate in spite of deference to others. She was genuine, sweet and caring; boasting the best husky laugh I'd ever heard.

Good reason I called her Clair-Bear — even if Nicole used the epithet 'Goodwife René' because of Clair's strict Calvinist upbringing.

She also had a brain. Clair was the one we got all the cheat-notes from whenever there was a maths or science assignment, not that I'd be needing them with my choice of subjects in Year 12.

Otherwise?

I barely knew any of these people, not even after three years living out of each other's pockets and badgering Nicole for her share. Funnily enough, I have no memory of actually meeting them, of wandering up, shaking hands or nodding or however people are supposed to introduce themselves. It felt like I'd landed in their midst and that was that.

Don't know why I got accepted in the circle — I was like the stray peanut in a deluxe packet of shiny cashews. But I didn't doubt my luck. Couldn't remember any friends from my previous school.

Me. Christ, where should I begin that won't be disappointing? Shoulder-length, dirty blonde hair, my mum's over-large green eyes, baby fat to an inconsequential face dusted with light-coloured freckles. Thick black eyebrows (Patrick'd always called them my caterpillars) and forgettable other facial features aside from a small, round mouth that looked like I was pouting or sulking — choose your tangent — even when I didn't mean to do either.

Skinny arms and legs that were too long, made me feel awkward in my own skin. Body straight, few half-decent curves. And why those eyebrows I mentioned were black when all the other hair on my body was off-blonde is a question I can never answer.

Wilting under any spotlight, found it difficult to say a single sentence to anyone I didn't know, let alone friends. Hated celery.

The only prize?

A long fringe I could always skulk behind.

No memorable hobbies that'd make me rich, famous, the envy of anyone else. I liked sneaking a peek at old films, scribbling silly pictures while burrowing into comic books, and chopped together stories no one read aside from my sibling — Patrick was a fan, I'll give him that much. We had a history of sharing fiction.

Guessed I had a nickname too, but no one told me what it might be.

"Kid Pathetic jumps to mind."

The sixth person at the table this time round surprises me, if not the others — probably because they couldn't see her.

Animeid.

Don't quote me, but I first became aware of this particular bird girl the time my brother Patrick hung me from our rotary clothesline.

I dangled in the backyard upside down like a leg of *jamón* beneath a ballooning Daisy Duck skirt, and had been in that position about four hours. Happened when I was also aged four — knowing my inventive brother (then six), the synchronicity of time/age would've been planned.

Patrick had lashed my ankles to one of the four prime metal spokes of the Hills Hoist, using fishing line rustled up from the tool shed. Tied a series of impenetrable knots to a pulley system learned in Cub Scouts.

Upside down as I say, I pointlessly bawled, skull pounding, until eventually a surreal kind of dizziness gripped me. There I was, swinging with head two feet from summer scorched grass and a coil of dog poo, when something passed close by, falling from above. I cut the snivelling to look below and spied said object — having skewered the dung, it stood to flagpole attention.

A liquorice-coloured feather several inches in length.

Twelve years later I was stuck with the owner.

"So the gang's all together," Animeid now whispers in my ear, outside peripheral vision and barely a rustle. She tended to be shy in front of others even if invisible.

"Shhh," I breathe, lips barely moving. I'd had lots of practice, but never before in public.

"*You* shush."

"What're you doing here?"

"Investigating the hoi polloi."

She's in the other ear now, a speedy traveller, and I can almost — almost — make out her dark profile beside me before turning away.

"Nice to see you and Clair know your place, scraping the barrel of this week's pecking order."

I refuse to look at her. "Who cares if we're stuck at the bottom of a step-ladder?"

Keep this quiet-like, but really wouldn't matter if I spoke in a louder voice — Hannah, Sarah and Nicole wouldn't notice with all their intense chatter, while Clair busily rearranges cutlery like she's doing some kind of sacrament.

"And dressed for the occasion," says Animeid.

"Eh?" The comment makes me suddenly imagine Clair in a

choir smock.

"Not just her. *All* of you."

She isn't wrong.

Though we aren't in school uniform — summer at Mac.Duagh meant identical A-line dresses, charcoal-colour blazers (with red and green trim and the school emblem), white knee-high socks, straw boaters, and black leather lace-ups — the other four girls and I insisted on wearing matching clothes.

Garden-variety replicas of one another.

And on today's menu?

Over-large, black cotton Witchery jumpers, puffball skirts, long black socks and patent leather, Succhi brand pointed-toe, flat-sole shoes (again in black).

Some accessories — rings and bracelets (only a minimal number), plus a watch or two — allowed to differ, but we had the same style gold hoop earrings, between six and eight centimetres in diameter.

Make-up minimal — we were pushing, or just past, seventeen — but hair and nails required precision maintenance and an exceptionally neat finish.

"Your social uniform is a tougher call than the stupid school's," Animeid huffs, and she gets a partial smile from me.

"Feels like it sometimes."

"Feels like *what*?"

Oops. Sarah again — she eyeballs my way, over and above a small beige tablecloth and Clair's carefully arranged knives and forks.

"Um," I hedge, darting behind bangs in a rather pathetic attempt to diminish the other girls' scrutiny. "What you guys were just talking about."

The corners of Sarah's Cupid mouth turn upward. "Mina, we're talking about how dreamy Rob Lowe was in *Oxford Blues*."

"Ah."

"So, what d'you mean by 'Feels like it sometimes'?"

I shrug. "Missed the boat?"

"You did. Landed completely in the water. Honestly, don't you ever listen properly?"

"Sorry."

"Rob's still dreamy," Clair interjects, saving my bacon from a possible collective roasting. "I liked him in *St. Elmo's Fire* and —"

"Are you kidding, Clair?" Blowing out cheeks as she shakes her head, Nicole looks at each of us around the table, eyes challenging. "Do they even have a video club in the church cloisters? Andrew McCarthy was *way* cooler in *St. Elmo's*. Have you seen the preview yet for *Pretty in Pink*? Wow. Andrew blows Rob away. And he's a better dresser. So stupid."

Ignoring Nicole's thrown gauntlet, Sarah still gazes my way — I can see that through a gap in my fringe. "What do you say, Mina?"

So typical of my friend, drawing me into the fray when least prepared. She knew I had opinion on very little, at least none I was keen to share about. Nervously battening-down by pushing the hair back behind my ears, I finally shrug again. Old habits die hard.

"I'm not really into either of them. Still, I don't think Rob will age so well."

Having briefly shared amazed eye contact, Hannah, Sarah and Nicole burst out laughing. Even Clair has a silly grin.

"Age well," Sarah finally manages to say as their mirth subsides. "*Age* well? Mina, you're absolutely *unreal*."

"Oh, I like her," Animeid decides. "She's funny."

While my face is likely beetroot-red, I can make out Animeid's shadow close by my left (I doggedly wouldn't look), hear her breathing and the scratch of wild feathers on vinyl.

"Shut up," I whisper — right at the point when there is a lull in the group laughter.

This triggers another stare from Sarah, an agitated one. "Say again?" she demands in a voice curiously off-key.

I chew my lower lip, contemplating a diabolical lack of escape clauses.

"Nothing?"

"Ye gods," tut-tuts Animeid. "How unbelievably wet."

Sarah's mouth has lost its charm, becoming a taut straight line as she glares. But it's Nicole who speaks.

"You know what? You can be *such* a freak."

"Oh, that's just mean." Animeid pushes forward. "Can I gut her now?"

"No!"

Error #3.

When everyone's eyes flick straight back to me and silence prevails, I play it cool and suave — shrug again.

"So. *No* one is having another coffee?"

"I think you've had enough to last a lifetime," Nicole mutters.

She doesn't notice Anim attempting to set fire to her hair with two sticks.

Anyway, having ordered a second drink, a flat white this time, and the spotlight losing intensity, I sit quietly. Try to cause no more fuss by keeping my mouth full of coffee while listening to 'School's Out' by Alice Cooper on the restaurant stereo.

"Best friend, huh?"

Animeid could be persistent.

"See how much she loves shooting you down in front of the others? Keeping you in your box. Tamed and trained like a performing seal. Let's toss you a kipper."

Shut up, birdbrain, I think, face unmoved.

"Oh, hurrah!" Animeid responds. "Keep the avian wordplay flying." Apparently annoyed yet unaware of the pun she's additionally inserted.

Never realized I could ruffle her feathers.

"Will you stop it?" she adds, hovering behind me. I hope she doesn't still have those sticks.

"What's this?" Nicole now demands to know, holding up an

ancient library book that Clair had apparently brought along. Titled *The Wonderful Tar-Baby and Other Antiquated Uncle Remus Riffs*, with a hand-drawn picture of Br'er Rabbit talking to the Tar-Baby of the title.

"It's interesting," speaks up Clair, albeit in deferential tone.

"Isn't it supposed to be racist?"

"I don't know. Haven't got that far in."

"Too busy occupying yourself with the religious references?"

"Nicole. Shush." — Sarah again.

Seconds later Nicole has moved on from my case and Clair's to make derisive comments regarding the wardrobe of a fellow patron in the café, and the girls again guffaw.

Takes me a moment to warm to their laugh track but within seconds I've rejoined the fold. The mutual mirth, even forced shrieks such as these, appear to banish Animeid — a form of Kryptonite I'd never previously noticed.

I can feel she's gone.

New Order's synth-ridden song 'The Perfect Kiss' commences thumping over the in-house system. We smile — our collective favourite for the moment and I actually did like it as much as my friends.

Other officially cleared group tuneage came from Wham!/ Style Council backing vocalist Dee C. Lee, Cyndi Lauper and Kids in the Kitchen, as well as Whitney Houston's self-titled debut album.

Wasn't a fan of these things aside from Cyndi, much as I protested otherwise.

As the tune hits its groove a new waiter — one tall, dark and outrageously handsome — is busy serving the next table and Hannah has noticed.

"Omigod — he is *so* gorgeous!" she declares with glee, voice loud enough to make it over to the man's ears. "I'm in love!"

Sarah rolls eyes at this proclamation and whispers something in Nicole's ear — leading the other girl to grin, fix hair that doesn't need repair work, and raise her hand to summon over this waiter. Upon arrival, in her most sophisticated, dawdling of tones, Nicole asks for... a spearmint milkshake.

Hannah blushes and stares down at her lap. I notice Sarah pinching her under the table the entire time the waiter's there taking Nicole's order.

Likely well aware of the teenage infatuation at play, Tall, Dark and Handsome delivers up an urbane smile, bows, and heads for the kitchen.

Looking like she is going to faint, Hannah groans. "Omigosh."

"Oh, D.D.," Sarah says, followed with a sigh.

On the way home that afternoon I pop into Record Paradise and buy my first New Order album: *Power, Corruption & Lies* (Factory, 1983) — the title of which was based around some German artist's protest graffiti.

Honestly? I picked up the vinyl in the shop because of the sad-sack still-life cover of flowers with a strip of colours down the upper right-hand side.

Didn't know this was New Order till I looked at the back.

End up playing both sides over a dozen times that night — I'd never before heard anything so mesmerizing and beautiful coming out of one speaker. And while Bernard Sumner's vocals may not've been crash hot, tonight they make my heart sing along with him.

In smothered fashion, needless to say, while clattering away on the typewriter.

6 plus 4 ends up being 10

At around eight p.m., beyond Bernard's voice, I hear the familiar engine roar of Dad's BMW entering the garage, followed by a squeal of rubber as he hits the brakes.

He'd performed the same trick every evening for years, a kind of tradition of heading in too fast and stopping before slamming into the bricks.

Thing is, this wasn't just any BMW — it was a silver-painted 328 Touring Coupe "designed by the great Fritz Fiedler, with a top speed of 220 kilometres an hour," as my father loved telling bamboozled people without a clue. I didn't have one either, but heard the speech often enough. Apparently this reconditioned jalopy raced Le Mans with good results in 1939 and won the 1940 Mille Miglia. I didn't know where on the map to look for Mille Miglia.

Also in the temperature-controlled garage was a powder blue, open-roofed 1950 Simca Gordini T15s — with the number 67 painted on its sides — that Dad never drove.

Anyway, the sound of the brakes and possible impending disaster used to make my mother jump every single time. I'm sure she hated it, but said nothing. Mum's tradition — rocking no boats.

Actually half-asleep, hardly in the mood to socialize, I rise from the bed and close the door. This will likely be the sum total of my exercise routine for the night, since I lie down again. Diplomatically reduce the volume of the record.

Above electronic instrumentation I can make out the sounds of Dad's entry into the house. The front door shuts. He announces he's home (no one answers — that was also Mum's job). There're footsteps and the occasional creak on the staircase.

I hear my father's voice again, diffused this time, secretive. It's promptly pursued by a diminished female laugh.

Ah.

The two of them have reached the landing, where more whispering takes place. As a pair of feet head along the passage to my father's bedroom, there's a light rap on my door.

I sit up, the door opens a fraction, and Dad's head peers in. He has a big smile creasing his salt-and-pepper beard. Asks how I am, if I've eaten, the standard formalities. He's already thinking ahead, I can see that — pays no attention to my answers.

"Ciao for now, sweetheart."

He closes the door and I'm alone again.

Hadn't eaten dinner — I lied. Easier that way.

Around midnight I suffer an attack of the munchies.

Push aside the paperwork, take the stylus off the LP — giving Bernard a rest for the first time in hours. Venture down to the kitchen. I have a plan, a simple Vegemite sandwich and a mug of strong coffee. Stuff didn't give me insomnia anyway.

The house is silent while I wait for the kettle to boil.

Having pushed aside a magnet holding an overdue electricity bill, I lean back against the fridge. Close my eyes, try to come up with a solution for the latest round of fisticuffs with writer's block.

There was half an unfinished A4 page stuck in the typewriter upstairs, and I hadn't got past a particular sentence for almost an hour. Six words, shocking ones for me: "She's gone and gotten her period." Actually seven, if you prefer to be pedantic and separate she/is.

Thing was, how to proceed from there?

Having never entertained this kind of conversation with anybody — when I was younger Mum failed to explain away the basics of the menstrual cycle — I found myself hanging. At a loss for written words, which was never usually a problem.

The more I thought about it, the less I could focus.

So maybe a stomach lining would help.

The water has almost reached boiling point and I wait for the sounds of bubbling before switching it off.

At that point, about to lean forward and stop the power, I see it.

In the corner of my eye, over by the kitchen doorway, someone my mother's height, wrapped in her favourite cloud-design dressing gown.

Sleepy as I am, so wrapped up in the writing, my stomach grumbling, I react in a way that scares me.

"Mum?" I say, even as I look over properly and see this isn't her.

The woman in my mother's gown shakes brown hair cut into a Princess Diana 'do.

"No — sorry to startle you. I'm Wendy. You're —?"

"Mina."

"Mina. Beautiful name."

She has an attractive smile, on a face pushing thirtyish. I'd never seen her before, and doubted I'd meet her again. This one was young.

Wendy's gaze falls onto the kettle, which is now funnelling steam.

"Great minds think alike. I felt like a hot drink too — chilly tonight, right? Autumn is kicking in."

"Guess." I turn it off.

"You're having coffee at this hour?"

"I love coffee."

"Oh boy, no." The woman laughs softly. "Keeps me up all night. Do you have any herbal tea?"

I reach up into the cupboard above the sink, find there Mum's dried chamomile flowers, precisely where she always left them. Haven't been touched since she died. Also hand the woman one of Dad's prize, antique Kobayashi Porcelain china cups, a set he never allowed anyone to use.

After that I leave her to the chore. Have my coffee and

sandwich to prepare. While I'm spreading Flora margarine I notice the odour, know precisely what it means.

I turn slowly; examine this stranger in my mother's clothes, drinking Mum's tea in Mum's kitchen, smelling of my dad. Instinct tells me to leave. Quickly. Abandon the coffee in the sink, forget the sandwich.

I rush straight past, headed for the stairs — which is when this woman Wendy calls after me.

"Mina? Is anything the matter?"

A feather drops, not a penny. And I mean that literally. There's a black feather on the floor at my feet.

Something snapped then.

Before I know what I'm doing, I've swivelled on my heel to face the intruder. I'm yelling sweet nothings her way at the top of my voice, insults I mostly don't recall. I *do* remember asking why she was fucking Dad in my mother's bathrobe.

The woman wilted under my verbal assault, fiddled with the lapels of the gown — like she wasn't sure whether to toss it off or pull the thing up over her head.

"Mina! Mina, that's enough!"

This was my father's booming voice, coming from above me on the tenth stair up. He's wrapped only in a towel with cartoon penguins on it. His face and the purple flush on the throat show how furious he is.

I don't care.

I glare straight back, several seconds' worth, and then take off up the stairs, shoving past him, in the direction of my room.

"You come back and apologize this instant!" I hear him shout; precisely the moment I slam shut my bedroom door.

Stand there against it, panting, trying to come to terms with everything running roughshod through my senses.

After a long while I understand my dad will make no attempt to enter, no efforts at redress, reconciliation or apology. I hear hushed tones the other side of the door, too low to make out, and the closing of Dad's bedroom door.

Didn't move from where I stood for about an hour. Stared around the room like I failed to recognize it — and actually did.

All day Sunday I spent alone in that alien place, trying to lose myself in reading comics, writing and music.

For February the cold weather had kicked in obscenely early, and that last Sunday of holidays I sat on icy grass that fringed the sand at Helwood beach.

Observing seagulls.

The sky was overcast and threatening rain. A stiff breeze whipped past, occasionally making my scarf flutter. It would've been about one in the afternoon and my stomach grumbled since I'd skipped lunch.

I'd wrapped myself in my grey, cashmere coat and the scarf I mentioned — a green, blue, red and white Mackenzie tartan thing Mum had picked up in Scotland when she was young, before she got married. Had gone over there to rediscover hereditary roots.

Anyway, here I was at the beach, watching those gulls. Get bored after half an hour and so head for a nearby playground. Deserted place, which suits me. Plonk myself on a wooden swing and sway from side to side. Feeling chilled to the bone, and my left elbow hurts, but I don't care. Don't think I care about anything right now.

Bliss.

Occasionally I kick at the small puddle of mud beneath me, and then try to twist the swing, on its chains, in circles — but it refuses to go far and immediately rights itself, making me somewhat dizzy.

So I kick off back and forth, setting the swing in its natural course. Begin to pick up speed and height as I go. It's exhilarating. Forgot how much I loved doing this.

My legs kicking up, tucking in, kicking up.

The world around taking on extreme new angles.

Anim's shadow in the branches I glimpsed on my sixth birthday, after Patrick shoved me off a higher section of our big ghost gum, and then smothered yells of pain with one hand, hissing — with spit that flecked across my face — to shut up.

The wraith weaved through leaves like a wizened old magpie, watching the diorama beneath, listening perhaps, too, as Patrick spun an expert story to tell our parents, one that would explain away my sprained ankle and five red finger marks on my face. One involving him as saviour rather than scoundrel.

But the first occasion I actually saw Animeid was during a beating from my brother when I was ten.

Pinioned to the floor on my back, with each of Patrick's knees on one of my shoulders and his butt deposited on my tummy, my brother had started out singing a song.

"I found a cocoon that a caterpillar made, fastened to a leaf, hanging in the shade."

He then made busy by slapping my cheeks as he lovingly strung frothy saliva across my face.

Patrick had this down to a fine art, somehow invading all available orifices like ears, nostrils, and my tightly closed mouth. The eyes he allowed to escape spittle since part of the joy was allowing his victim to witness this travesty-in-motion.

As I watched his freckled face thirty centimetres away and that taut, white mouth puckered up for another strafing run, I winced — at which point a peculiar dark halo formed behind Patrick's head.

Spit dangled above my nose while a pair of huge black wings unfurled beyond his crushing bulk.

That was when Patrick sucked in and licked his lips. "I ought to bust every stupid bone in your body," he decided.

"Now, now."

This was a female voice, blasé, pushing careless, close by and yet the sound travelled from behind my brother.

"Why don't we break one of yours instead?"

Those wings I mentioned — which were in actual fact long, skinny arms covered in midnight feathers just like the one stuck in the dog poo six years before — went around Patrick's upper skull, and then yanked it sideways with a snap.

I blinked quickly several times.

Contrary to recent events Patrick's head was in its correct position while the black plumage and accompanying limbs had vanished — precisely when my brother decided he'd had enough for the day.

"This is no fun. You're vagueing out on me." Having stood up, he wiped his chin. "You tell Mum or Dad and you've had it. Now go clean yourself up, you little shit."

And so Animeid engaged in repeat appearances at our house thereafter — not that any of this was continuous.

There were gaps in my memory, like someone had got a pair of scissors and Sellotape, and edited a 35 mm movie reel.

The rest of my family appeared not to suffer from this scattershot form of amnesia, though it was hard to tell. We rarely talked about the past at all. The four of us collectively trod only recent history, keeping one another at arm's length — even if Patrick's connected once in a while.

Anyway, I could never make out this outsider's face since there was a weird shimmer that rendered any features out of focus. She hovered mostly sight-unseen, a favourite hiding place behind Patrick as he went through the motions of punishing me for misdemeanours I never understood.

With the bird-girl there to distract me, king-hitting my assailant and cooing sarcastic nothings — well, ineffectual she may've been but her presence made the routine a fraction less oppressive.

Before school officially started at 8:30 a.m. that Monday, I had a 7:45 appointment with our principal Paula Cook.

I couldn't recall ever sharing a single sentence with the woman and never before set foot in her office.

I do so now with my father.

The room is dark and mouldy-smelling. It has little in the way of furnishings, like maybe Miss Cook expected to be asked to leave her post any given moment.

Seated behind a barren desk, Paula was a small woman in a grey box-suit that overwhelmed a washed-out complexion, faded red hair tied back severely in a bun, and pale grey eyes that would've attracted any wolf on the prowl.

Wise words, commiseration and abstract advice follows, much ado about dealing with my mother's loss. The ageing school counsellor Glenda Matlock, who was eighty-odd, puts in a brief appearance to add some — I don't know — authority?

As we leave the principal's office I see my form teacher Mrs Williams waiting her turn. She looks like she's been compressed into an ugly canvas captain's chair over by the secretary.

A solidly built woman in her forties with a thick neck, Mrs Williams had also been our 11E head honcho in 1985. And while she wasn't ever Nicole's instructor, our friend insisted on calling her Dame Slap — some obscure Enid Blyton reference to a domineering school ma'am.

With the change of numeral before the E (to 12) this part-time ogre insisted the students now call her Roslyn.

"You're young adults," she announced to us on the final day, last December. "Next year you may refer to me by my first name."

Doubt she realized how difficult it would be to break the shackles of eleven years' indoctrination, or that most people didn't care. And for all her protests about us now being on a level playing field, Mrs Williams was the first to kick the soapbox from beneath our feet, and thereby remind us exactly who was in charge.

The way she presented herself was deceptive enough.

Always gift wrapped in floral blouses and loose trousers, the woman insisted on slapping a brown vest over this ensemble, no matter if it was summer or winter. In summer — like now — wet sweat marks soaked the vest beneath her armpits.

She nods to me while squeezing out of the chair, staggers a moment, and disappears into the principal's office.

That's when I say goodbye to my dad, who has to go to work. There's been no word about my performance on Saturday night. He doesn't gift a hug or kiss my forehead or tussle hair. P'raps he thinks I'm too old. Doesn't even shake my hand like he does Patrick's, sometimes. There's an awkward moment, and then he's strolling away. No way he'll look back to wave.

Quarter of an hour later, when I file into class with the others, we have a surprise.

Lucky for me this isn't Animeid — apparently she'd left school off her busy agenda. Instead, Mrs Williams is chatting at the front of the room with a student I'd never before set eyes on.

After finding our desks — Sarah's behind mine and Clair's to my right; Nicole and Hannah lived in 12D, the class next door — we settle down and face front.

The girl standing before us on the slightly raised teacher's platform is tall enough already — a lanky individual, obviously uncomfortable in her brand new A-line dress. Below this, a white sock sits in its proper place on one calf while the other has fallen — bunched up round the left ankle. Her shoes? Chunky black, six-hole Doctor Martens boots.

A silver crucifix, dangling from a chain, had fallen outside the neckline of her uniform.

Above that she had short, black hair cut elfin style, shades of Jean Seberg in *Breathless*, with three silver sleepers puncturing each ear. Detracting from these ornaments were enormous brown eyes verging on black and a puckered, playful mouth. Overall, a strong, unusually pretty face that looked like it had trace elements of Scandinavian in there, and the palest skin I think I'd ever seen.

A name was written with white chalk in bold caps across the blackboard behind her: ANGELICA.

"Girls," Mrs Williams announces in her deep, resonant voice — Nicole once tried to convince us she was a guy in drag — "We have a new member. This is Angelica Aire." Our teacher points at the blackboard just in case anybody is stupid enough not to be able to spell the first name. I find myself more curious about the spelling of the second.

"Actually," this newcomer suddenly speaks up in a surprisingly relaxed manner, "sorry, but I spell it with a K. D'you mind?"

She swivels, takes the chalk from Mrs Williams, and with her finger smudges out the C. Writes a flowing replacement that looks far prettier than the boxy print already on the blackboard.

"It's the Czech spelling. Angelika — with a K."

After returning the chalk, this girl turns to face us with a smile creating two dimples beneath high cheekbones.

"Hey, everyone."

Our scattered, lacklustre response fails to smother those dimples or the smile.

"Very good." Mrs Williams breathes out through her teeth, an old habit — makes her sound like she's deflating. "Well, now, Angelika-With-a-K, you can have that empty seat three rows back over there. See?"

Now pointing at the forlorn stall immediately to my left, one deserted the previous year when Candie Delmar was hospitalized. Bulimia, the rumour-mill decreed.

Perhaps distrusting her new charge's eyesight, Mrs Williams personally delivers her to this location while the rest of us fiddle in awkward silence — the only reassuring sound that of the overhead ceiling fans.

Angelika sits. Her smile lingers.

Still standing beside this intruder's newfound enclave, Mrs

Williams makes to clear her throat.

"Angelika, dear, before I forget – I'll have to ask you to remove the earrings. Students at Mac.Duagh are not allowed to wear jewellery."

Angelika's hand instantly goes to the exposed crucifix, but our teacher shakes her head.

"I'll make an exception there. You'll need your parents also to purchase more appropriate footwear. School regulations, and all that silly nonsense."

"That's all right. I'll tell Mum."

"Good girl."

Instead of returning to the front of the class, Mrs Williams props herself on the corner of my desk, forcing me to peer up at her from beneath my fringe. She smiles.

"How are you doing, Mina?"

"I'm okay."

"I was really very sorry to hear the news."

"It's okay." I wish she'd drop the subject.

"You know, if ever you feel the need to speak to someone, you can always come visit me in the teachers' room."

"Thanks."

"Anytime."

"Okay."

"Oh, and I noticed that you're going to share three subjects this term with Angelika. Would you overly mind showing her the ropes? The layout of the school, and what-not."

"Sure, Mrs Williams."

"Roslyn, dear." The woman pats my shoulder, and then launches herself back toward the front of the room.

"Psst!" Sarah has leaned over as far as she can manage. "What was *that* all about?"

"Nothing."

"Didn't sound like nothing."

I look past her, out through the window at the blue sky and

little fluffy clouds on the horizon, and shrug shoulders.

"Hi."

Broken out of my detachment to glance to my left. At *her*. Into those incredibly big, black/brown eyes.

"Hi," I say. Easy enough.

"Mina, right?"

"Mmm."

"I'm Sarah," my best friend announces, reaching over me to wave hello and kind of pushing me out of the way.

I immediately look down at the scarred wooden surface of the desk before me, at the graffiti dug into it by some prior resident.

I LUV BRUCE.

I wonder who Bruce could be, whether he was worthy of the engraving. Zone out on the brief conversation between Sarah and Angelika before Mrs Williams calls the room to order and reads the roll.

At lunchtime, instead of hanging with my friends atop our scenic bench seat overlooking the lawn and sports ground, I have to play tour guide. I might've lacked a flag to usher along my charge, but successfully erect a cold-shoulder behind my bangs, never once look her way, and point out facts and figures about Mac.Duagh — as we wander around the premises — in a bland manner that would make Arnold Schwarzenegger's Terminator proud.

The moment Angelika detours into the toilets I bolt.

Step outside to find the others have all gone, bar Sarah.

Though it isn't cold, there's a breeze that makes her hair flutter. Seated with consummate posture on the bench — a glowing advertisement for Mac.Duagh girlhood — while apparently watching hockey practice on the oval.

Deigns to notice me anyway.

"We missed you at lunch," says she in greeting, chirpy as usual, but I don't believe the words that come out.

"Had to play chaperone," I mutter, sitting beside the girl and slouched over in accidental contrast to her perfection.

"Really?"

"Mm-hmm."

"Everything okay?"

"Sure." Taking this moment to peer sideways, I frown. "Why're you still here?"

"Waiting for you." Sarah smiles.

When I get home that afternoon and gallop upstairs, through a thankfully empty house, I discover Animeid in my room. Seated at the dresser, doing her nails.

"Met someone today at school," I announce, flinging my bag onto the bed.

"Do tell — I thought there were nine hundred and fifty other students there."

"No, I mean someone different."

Animeid pauses mid-manicure. "Hmm?"

"She's a little off."

"By 'off', how d'you mean?"

I raise my considerable eyebrows. "Don't know."

"Well, does she have feathers?"

This conversation is making me tired. I sit on the edge of the bed, in front of the bag and beside my ancient soft-toy Basil Brush. "No."

"There's a shame."

"The whole world doesn't revolve around you, Anim."

"Doesn't it?" she murmurs, preoccupied now applying varnish. "There's a shock."

"I just mean she was — different."

"And different is a bad thing?"

"No." Thinking, *yes*.

"Chucking round words like 'off' infers it is."

"Oh, whatever."

"You know, if you smiled more you might be happier."

"I don't like to smile."

I pull off my shoes, climb out of school uniform and cross the carpet dressed only in undies and bra — being home by myself (aside from Animeid hanging about, but she didn't count and I certainly don't feel a prude in front of her) was one of the best things possible.

I know the disclosure will hang in the air like a silly cliché and/or an off smell, but this bedroom was sanctuary, a personalized sandbox in which no one else was allowed to play. Had my own set of plastic tools (books, manual typewriter, TV, radio-cassette player, bed, lava lamp, turntable with a five-cent coin sticky taped to the needle so it wouldn't jump) — and thereby could bury myself there out of view of the world. All that was missing was a video to record the late-night movies on Channel 9.

To emphasize the great escape, I usually had my Moomin-character curtains drawn.

The main wall across from this floor-to-ceiling window peppered with faux hippopotamuses was the only one with wallpaper, boasting a Noah's Ark of animals done in Paul Gauguin style (Mum and Dad had chosen this when I was in kindergarten).

The bed was pressed against this wall, and above that — continuing the kingdom Animalia theme — hung a large, framed publicity poster for a 1965 film titled *The Tomb of Ligeia*, starring the great Vincent Price.

This was a depiction of a black cat's head (with menacing yellow eyes) shaped like a downward-pointing arrow. The slogan above the head read "Even on her wedding night she must share the man she loved with the 'Female Thing' that lived in the Tomb of the Cat!" A birthday present from my mother when I was fifteen, by which time it'd become clear I loved cinema and had a penchant for '60s gothic horror classics.

On the wall to the right I'd Blu-Tacked a collage of oddball and sometimes-tasteless postcards (the Eiffel Tower being knocked over by a bowling ball, a dingo with a baby in its mouth).

About a dozen cut-out pictures of a young Brigitte Bardot, Louise Brooks and Mitzi Gaynor — my hush-hush icons, Brigitte in particular since I longed to believe we shared mouths.

These interspersed with Hollywood blondes like Jean Harlow, Marilyn Monroe and Lana Turner, and actors Kirk Douglas, Vincent Price, Peter Lorre, Charlton Heston and George Peppard.

Had stuff torn out of magazines *Dolly*, *i-D* and *The Face* — people such as David Bowie, Sade, Molly Ringwald, Patsy Kensit and the members of Swing Out Sister and New Order.

There was a collection of good-looking boys too: Andrew McCarthy, Rob Lowe, Matt Dillon and Michael Schoeffling, pin-ups I thought my friends would approve of if ever they deigned to visit or I actually bothered to invite someone — which was never.

Beside the boys was a narrow pine bookcase, the two top shelves jammed with novels, the usual rambling childhood fodder like *Anne of Green Gables* and its five sequels, *The Wishing-Chair Again*, *Pippi Långstrump*, and *Pollyanna* — tempered by more recent grabs (*Wuthering Heights*, *The Works of John Donne*, Longfellow's translation of *The Divine Comedy*, the Penguin Classics version of *Tristan* by Gottfried von Strassburg).

Had other books I didn't much care about shoved under the bed.

The next shelf, a roomier one, boasted thick tomes on the Pre-Raphaelites, 1960s horror movies, Shiseido advertising art in roaring '20s Japan.

A collection of worn out thirty-year-old comic books (*Science Fiction Space Adventures* and *Outer Space*, with illustrations by the great Steve Ditko — both sets'd belonged to my uncle, also a fan, who found a kindred spirit in his niece) along with incomplete sets of *Miss Fury* from the 1940s and Jack Kirby's 1976-77 take on

2001: A Space Odyssey.

I'd compiled that last series all by myself when I was about eight.

Dad was less than impressed with the comics, but since he still dabbled with assembling Airfix models of World War One airplanes, well, he couldn't exactly bellyache.

Beneath these books and 'zines, on the two lowest shelves, was a growing collection of VHS cassettes and records.

The wardrobe, beside the door, was an antique Victorian number jammed with clothes, some dating back to childhood. A lot of cutesy pinks and powder blues.

Finally, the dresser — where Animeid currently preened — was cosmetics chaos, most of the stuff a half-empty inheritance from Mum.

There was also a brush and two pairs of TweezerPro, since I'd taken to trimming those eyebrows Patrick still insisted upon calling caterpillars. Didn't have the heart to diminish them too much, since there was every possibility I could chuck a Samson and lose any remaining strength.

I switch on the TV, find Madonna's 'Dress You Up', wince, and turn it straight off. Think better music instead.

On the carpet beside the dresser, with its detachable mono speaker, sat the pop-yellow/orange Portable Phillips 133 vinyl player.

Dad had got this beauty over a decade before, apparently with family picnics in mind since it conveniently folded up as a little suitcase with a handle that could be carried outdoors — intended also to turn heads with its garish '70s colour scheme. The thing ended up collecting dust in the garage until I requisitioned it.

I slide *Power, Corruption & Lies* out of its sleeve, thence to squeeze Side A of the record onto this tiny turntable and lie back on bed to listen to 'Age of Consent'.

Consider dragging out the Olivetti and notes to continue the story, but I don't feel in the mood for that particular yarn. I grab fresh paper, sit cross-legged on the bed, and embark on a new tale — something intended to be shorter, lighter-weight and silly.

How I got here was not important.

The way in which I removed myself mattered, especially given my position — hanging upside down from a leather strap that was loosely coiled around the shin of my left leg, the other end snagged in a two-inch-thick scrub plant that grew out of a cliff face. The cliff continued in a straight line down to rocky terrain about a hundred and fifty foot away.

So, while extraction was my principle concern, I also had to hang docile and move as little as possible. The ring-in bonsai up there could snap at any moment, and then it'd be sayonara Angelika.

I stop typing.

Had meant to insert our heroine's name as Valeria or Valeska or something exotic. Don't know why 'Angelika' popped out via the keys. I guessed with the K it was vaguely outlandish.

I'd started out the story with a particular caricature in mind: A rough-and-ready Hyrkania-born warrior maiden in the Frank Thorne/*Red Sonja* comic-book mold, with bee-stung lips and flowing, flame-coloured hair, lots of make-up around blue eyes, leather gauntlets and a chainmail bikini.

But now, in my head, I see hair cut very short and dyed midnight black, her eyes have turned brown, and there are bonus extra earrings — along with a pair of six-hole Doc Martens.

Well, why not? At least this made her deviate from Robert E. Howard. I'd think of a different name later.

Thank somebody-I-can't-think-of-at-the-moment for the belly dancing lessons.

A couple of years ago I wouldn't have been able to do what I now did — lift up my torso, using my stomach and back muscles alone —

so that the world flipped the right way round, and my eyes were parallel with my knees. The belly dancing had been done to sneak into a palace and steal a treasure. I hadn't expected fringe benefits.

That was precisely when the bonsai shook and dirt tumbled—

"What're you writing?" This is Animeid again, interrupting the flow.

I pause, my finger above the D-key. "Stuff."

"Why so mysterious?"

"Not mysterious. I just can't explain it so well. Haven't finished yet."

Anim snorts, not the prettiest of sounds, while turning back to her nail polishes. "I can always read it when you're not here."

This concerned me. "Do you do that?" I ask. "Go through my stories?"

"Wouldn't you like to know?"

"I would, actually." It's then that I decide she's bored and baiting me, so I turn away to focus again on the story before I lose momentum. Rest my finger on the D, then press.

—down.

I froze, not an easy thing when you've bent yourself up into a U-shape and every fibre of your body squabbles for release. This is the kind of moment when how you got here does become important, and in my case it was the fault of a man. Always was; always would be.

This man's name was Lord Paimon of Blackwood.

"That's nowhere near Whitewood, is it?"

Animeid is now beside me, apparently attempting to co-author.

"No — it's not. Go away."

"Temper, temper."

With that, the girl hops up and over to the dressing table again. I scrutinize the feathers on her back. Well, okay, then.

33

"That's nowhere near Whitewood, is it?" I remarked, when I first encountered the effete, rake-thin uppercruster in an arranged meeting at an inn.

Paimon frowned and wobbled his unattractive head, crown and all. Yes, he had a crown. "I haven't the woolliest."

No sense of humour though.

In case you haven't figured it out, I was more enamoured with this man's jewel-encrusted headwear (and no doubt hefty purse) than any screaming loud physical attributes or a snappy personality. He had none of these things. But his crown — ahhh, his crown. It dazzled me.

"I hear tell that you are rather the good swordswoman."

"Swordsman," I said. "I'm better than any man, other woman or diabolical pell you might decide to match me up with."

Paimon, several inches shorter, an effeminate face and with that shimmying skull, walked slowly around me there in the yard of the inn. "Tall, full-bosomed—"

"Excuse me?" My sword was out of its scabbard and at his narrow throat in less time than it took for him to finish his irritating appraisal.

"—Err... devilishly fast with a blade, I'll give you that. Kudos, my dear. Also large-limbed, compact shoulders — yet still overtly feminine."

"So, I do have charms." I slotted the sword home. "Ta. What's the ruckus?"

"Ruckus?"

"You know, the racket. Swindle."

"I have no idea what you are talking about."

"The job."

"Oh! Oh, yes, I see. Well, I want you to be my wife."

What now?

Gazing at the ceiling above for a while, thinking I-don't-know-what, eventually I take out *Science Fiction Space Adventures* issue

12 and flip through the pages. I can just make out the sounds of my roommate fussing with her manicure.

And then a real din commences on the floor beneath.

My brother had started drinking, so far as I knew, when he was sixteen. Dad had discovered a dozen empty bottles tucked under Patrick's bed and chucked a hissy fit, but that was never going to deter him. While I didn't exactly care what Patrick did with his life, the problem here was that my brother turned into an angry drunk, and invariably took out this grumpiness on me — like the time last year he broke up with some girlfriend called Kerry.

Having bulldozed home with furious tears in red, bleary eyes, he didn't so much as knock on my door but instead knocked me down. Seized my old RCA Deluxe portable black-and-white TV set, hefted it while it was still plugged in, and screamed at me.

I remember a rerun of late '70s show *The Incredible Hulk* was dancing across the rounded screen. The telly lifted high in the air while I lay there, paralyzed. Animeid yelled at him but I said nothing, unable to move yet still shaking all over. Silently watched as Bill Bixby warned somebody that they wouldn't like him if he got angry.

I don't know how Patrick stopped from crowning me. Maybe he fretted about other people's opinion — these things mattered more to him.

From the sound now as he comes in the front door, Patrick is obviously drunk and disorderly. Something crashes, perhaps breaks, there is much swearing, and then a heavy, uneven footfall on the staircase.

I think I stop breathing — I certainly stop reading the comic — but my heart beats so hard it hurts. "Fuck, *fuck*... What should I do?" I mumble aloud, having sat up and wrapped myself in my arms.

"Be brave — and go hide in the wardrobe?"

I blink several times, fast. "He knows that trick."

"So he does. Then get dressed."

"What?"

"Mina, get dressed — now."

The urgency in Animeid's tone kick-starts my brain and possibly also the stupid diaphragm. I swing my legs over the side of the bed, fetch back the school dress, and put the thing on.

Meanwhile the footsteps rear closer and louder, but the amount of time Patrick is taking to reach the landing makes me wonder if Escher had miraculously redesigned our staircase.

"Oh, God," I put out one more time as I frantically smooth the material over my thighs, fingers clenching and straightening, clenching and straightening, my teeth chewing at different parts of upper and lower lip while I wait. Can taste the blood. "What'll I do?"

"You could kill him."

I swing my head to take in Animeid at the dresser. She's finished placing caps back onto various bottles of nail polish and holds feathered arms up before her to inspect.

"He's stronger than me," I whine in return.

"He's blotto." I sense her eyes now on me, even if I still can't make them out.

"I'm scared."

Animeid stands, black feathers ruffled about her like some wispy taffeta ball gown, and she comes to the bed once more. Sits beside me.

"You're going to have to one day. Kill him, I mean. Before he kills you."

"I can't."

"Won't?"

"Can't." I briefly close my eyes. Open them as I hear my brother stagger closer.

I think Anim and I both push surprised when Patrick chooses that moment to appear in the doorway in his dishevelled Nede High uniform. His solid form sways, a lopsided grin on the face and absolutely no venom whatsoever.

"Hi, sunshine. How was school?" he inquires, all manners —
tempered by a slur.

Takes me a few seconds to react, I'm so surprised. "Good. It
was good. And you?"

"Fantastic. Off to bed now. 'Night, sis."

"Goodnight."

"Sweet dreams."

Don't tell him the time is 4:30 in the afternoon. Say nothing
more as he trudges down the passage, singing a distorted dirge,
and closes his bedroom door — either to flop onto the bed or
play a rowdy game on his Nintendo prior to passing out.

It's Animeid who states what we both think. "He obviously
got laid."

I laughed when I heard this. The other option was bringing out my
blade again and sticking the fellow for real, but he did tickle my
funny bone.

"Laugh away," Lord Paimon muttered in an annoyed fashion.

He dusted down a log and sat there. "I don't mean a bona fide
bride, just someone to pretend being one."

After my chuckles subsided, I felt sorry for the loser and sat next
to him. "Why?"

"I need a bodyguard for a trip from this town to my villa."

"What kind of body guarding are we talking?"

"Really, now."

"How far is it?"

"The villa? A day's ride."

"You're expecting trouble?"

"I will be carrying a shipment of jewels. Word has leaked out and
about."

"Iffy."

"I suppose."

"And the sham spouse?"

"I believe a 'wife' would be a wonderful disguise. No one would suspect."

"Well, I think some might, given your personality and habits."

"How dare you!" After a momentary head sway, Paimon slapped me with his glove. I'd have said it hurt, just to make the fellow feel better, but it merely tingled. I wasn't in the mood for fabrications to make a potential employer happy. That cost extra.

"Look, how much are you prepared to pay?"

This man's vitriol was a quick-burning beast. The rage vanished, and he was suddenly counting out gold doubloons into both my hands.

"Enough?"

"With this, I'd marry you for real."

There was a reason Patrick was still wearing his high school uniform the final year I was going to do so.

For all his bluster and bravado, his athletic prowess excelling at judo (he was a brown-belt), cricket (star all-rounder) and Roman rings in the gym, Patrick wasn't particularly tall and the way I was sprouting it looked like I'd outstrip his height any day now.

I don't know that he had a hang-up per se, but he had started to wear shoes with a taller heel and I caught him a couple of times in the bathroom studying his stocky physique in the full-length mirror, clad only in briefs while on tiptoe.

Anyway, his sporting successes had begun to diminish once he started at Nede High School in Year 9. He likely found the competition far tougher than at Gardenview Central, our previous school, plus he'd discovered a social life – along with alcohol, as I mentioned.

Patrick had inherited our father's Irish genes and was a redhead with a lot of freckles, but these started to diminish in adolescence and he appeared to believe he cut a dashing figure so far as the opposite sex was involved.

All that partying meant he failed Year 9, repeated, and then failed Year 12 and was forced to repeat that as well. So in 1986 we were both set to finish our HSC on equal footing – leading to more regular intimidation with or without a tipple.

My only form of revenge was spitting on his toothbrush occasionally, so while he cleaned those crooked teeth – he openly despised mine for being straight – I got some semblance of satisfaction.

"Oh, no need." The blueblood's frigid gaze washed over me. "Of course, we will have to get you a change of clothes. Breeches, boots, that scabbard and a chainmail brassiere better worn by pirates of ill-repute are not appropriate."

"Aren't all pirates people of ill-repute?"

"Even so, this wardrobe is hardly becoming for the spouse of someone as important as me — or even some low-ranking fool, for that matter."

"Keep the compliments coming," I sighed. "I feel like we're married already."

Which was why, the next day, I was embalmed with an extremely tight bodice — stiffened with whalebone — that cut off half my blood circulation, and my legs smothered beneath three different voluminous skirts that dragged on the ground when I dared walking. My hair was braided and twisted up into a top-knot beneath a silk veil that hampered my peripheral vision, and I ended up riding my horse far more than usual if only to avoid accidents.

"You look a vision," Lord Paimon was gushing as he trotted beside me astride a camel he insisted on calling a dromedary. I couldn't see the difference. We'd followed the road to a high bluff around the hillside.

Paimon's crown wobbled more than usual, catching the light and making me careless.

"I look like an upscale dimwit," I decided.

"Like me?"

He had a smirk so I smiled back.

"Like you."

In the midst of the sweet nothings, while my eyes were affixed to his tiara, the ambush took place.

Think ruffians with poor dress-sense swinging down from trees to our left, jumping out of bushes and from behind trunks. The place was full of the buggers. I counted at least twenty as I clutched for the rapier that was hidden somewhere in my skirts, but this took too long — and then I was knocked from my nelly.

A group of men surrounded me, boasting an assortment of dangerous instruments that ranged from a primitive garden hoe to an overdone mace.

Having finally freed my sword, I dealt with these five, and was straight after leaning against my horse — breathless, dizzy and wheezing. I had to get the corset off. Hacking at the strings, I ripped it free and tossed the garment as I swung around to face another dozen fiends. I couldn't see Paimon or his camel anywhere close by — likely he'd scarpered, and good for him, but I missed the pretty gems.

Another four men dropped to my sword before I misjudged my place on the edge of the cliff, tripped on skirts, and took an unhealthy plunge.

Which was how I wound up here, upside down in a tricky situation.

A lucky one, I'll give you that — I should have ended up on the rocks far below, where the bodice I'd cut off even now lay. The problem was how to untangle myself from the leather strap, get a decent grip on the vertical rock, and climb the six feet to stable terra firma.

"May I give you a hand, fair maiden?"

I spied Paimon gazing over the edge, a large grin on his face.

"Fair maiden, my foot. You know your disguise very nearly killed me?"

"That was the plan."

I stared up at him. I figured the smile wasn't so friendly after all.

"Go on. You have a captive audience down here."

"Why, that's very kind of you."

"I've learned how much the villains of the piece like to wax boring."

"Well said."

"Not particularly. Anyhow — what's afoot?"

Paimon pouted in a triumphant kind of way. I noted that his head had stopped bouncing. The crown was perfectly still.

"I spread the rumour around these parts that my new bride would be carrying all my worth, given to her as a sign of my absolute devotion. When those cretins attacked, they went straight for you, and I was able to slip away. I knew either you would kill them or vice versa, and to be honest I didn't care which outcome transpired. I could ride home safely with my fortune."

"You took a risk coming back, then, to see what happened."

"I was going to lie," he chuckled, "but in this position I see there's no need."

"Wrong."

While we'd been indulging in honeymoon talk, I'd got a decent grip on the rocks, untied the leather strap, and tethered it to a strip of cloth from my dress. This I had fashioned into a rough lasso and I swung it around and up, over the man's narrow, girlish shoulders, before his lordship knew what to expect. Then I pulled — hard.

"You won't be needing this," I muttered, tearing the crown from Lord Paimon's head as he flew past.

He certainly screamed like a lady. It was embarrassing.

After I heard the crunch of bones far below, I focused on climbing the rock face, inch by precarious inch. It took me half an hour to reach the top. When I got there, I flopped over onto my back and looked up at a beautiful blue sky I hadn't noticed before.

"God, I'm sick of men. Always doing the wrong bloody thing."

I sat back up, laughed, and shook my hair free of the veil. Then I lobbed it and focused on the tiara on the ground beside me.

"Oh, well. Time to go shopping."

Next morning I had my first class with Angelika-With-a-K.

English lit, so luckily Sarah was there also and her presence meant I didn't have to speak more than your basic monosyllabic stuff to either the new girl or our teacher, Mr Osterberg.

I mean, I liked the guy a lot, one reason I opted for literature — though I know Sarah swayed me most. Trouble was he always tried to motivate us to greatness, and while doing so the man had a disturbing style of referring to himself, when carried away, in the third person — all "Jimmy this" and "Jim that". Didn't help matters he had the same first name as my dad.

He was also apparently once a beatnik. There were no giveaways like a beret or a goatee, but occasionally he recited oddball, pseudo-hepcat poetry, like one that went "City. Pizza. Hot chocolate. Books. *Love*."

I tended to hide behind Sarah to conscientiously take notes.

Also knew straight away that Sarah had taken a dislike to Angelika.

The clues were right there in front of me, just like Sarah: My friend snubbed her when the new girl nodded from her desk, and then she kicked me when I responded.

"What're you smiling at?" she muttered.

Don't know why Sarah bothered. My smile was adequately repressed anyway and most people would never notice.

I doubt Angelika did.

While initially busy writing in a notebook at the beginning of the lesson, she eventually dropped her pen, placed elbows on the desk, deposited her chin into cupped hands, and sat transfixed.

Mr Osterberg had started to gesticulate wildly like he was playing up King Lear to a packed crowd at the Royal Shakespeare.

The book we'd started on was anything but Shakespeare — it was our token Australian novel for the year, *My Brother Jack*.

Patrick's favourite read. Yawn.

The class straight after, Sarah and I went our separate ways. She had Maths II in a beautiful new classroom while I had to travel to the ends of the earth — well, to a side annex of Mac.Duagh — where our facilities were fifty years out of date. Visual arts were given exceptionally short shrift in a school famous for its mathematics and science graduates.

Clair was supposed to be doing this class with me, but had bailed to focus also on maths, since we needed the subject to get into most major courses at university. The fact I'd dropped all mathematics would be a cross against my name once we started applying. I'd been advised against doing so by Miss Matlock, but hated mathematics and probability and all that other stuff. Didn't care either way whether or not I went to uni.

So there were eight members in the art class, most girls I'd never before bothered to speak to — as well as Angelika-With-a-K.

She breezes into the large space like she owns the place and when glancing my way delivers up a charming, easy-going smile. My debonair response is to blush and twist awkwardly on my heel. Could hardly tell her she'd starred in a sword-and-sandals romp courtesy of my imagination.

Our art teacher Victoria Perks — or 'Miss Vicks' as she preferred to be called (I think it was a play on the brand of cough, cold and flu medicine) — was a born-again hippy child at age sixty who loved listening to Peter, Paul & Mary.

She'd also been my art teacher in Year 11.

Usually got around in flared pants and a suede poncho, dyed-orange hair permed into madness. She had a habit of talking to herself aloud in the middle of a lesson, head nodding or shaking from side-to-side depending upon the nature of this internal debate.

"Anything important I should know about Miss Perks?"

My eyes shoot to my right, where Angelika has positioned herself barely thirty centimetres away. In that moment I notice we're the same height. I swallow, or at least try to do so without making it obvious. Which probably makes the process more so.

"She likes to be called Miss Vicks," I say in a voice that seems to belong to someone else — a person tonally awry, barely audible.

The new girl has obviously heard. Maybe she has good ears. "A fan of the '70s, I take it," she muses while gazing at her own feet, to a pair of shiny, new lace-ups that rendered her more like the rest of us, if that were possible.

"Yes," I agree.

Since Angelika is busy scrutinizing those shoes, eyes off me, I can safely lay mine on her. There are three tiny holes in the closest ear, where the sleepers had been the day before. She has perfect skin, not a blemish nor freckle in sight.

I want to tell the girl about Miss Vicks' tendency to talk to herself, but I don't have the stamina for longer sentences, and already feel hypocrite enough.

"Mina, can I ask you something?"

Angelika's big browns whip back before I can think to avert my gaze, and she's now looking straight at me. I think my mouth has fallen open and I forget to breathe.

"What?" I manage.

The girl puckers her lips, twists them to the right, like she's debating something inside, mindless of body language. And then she grins. A real expression, something to treasure that's bookended by dimples either side, a sparkle to her eyes.

"Oh, nothing. I'm just being silly," she says. "So, I don't think we've been properly introduced even though you were coerced into playing tour conductor."

Angelika sticks out her right hand.

I look at it a few seconds before thinking to respond. We shake hands there in the midst of art class, while Miss Vicks mutters to herself over in a corner by the blackboard.

"Angelika," the new girl reminds me.

"With a K." I actually smile too, something of a coup.

"You remembered."

"Hard not to."

"You'd be surprised." Angelika rolls eyes.

"Anyway, I'm Mina. With a Y."

"A Y? Wouldn't that mean we pronounce it *mye-nah*?"

"Oh, yeah. Oops. Guess it fits — minor. Huh."

I notice the girl's crucifix poking out again from under the neckline of her dress.

"Um. Can I ask *you* something?"

"Shoot away."

"Are you a Catholic?"

"What, this?" Angelika tugs the silver ornament into the air. "No, I use it to ward off vampires." She laughs. "They can be pesky buggers."

I like the quip, so try to come up with one of my own. "I suppose, then, you also carry round a pistol loaded with silver bullets."

"What, for a werewolf? Everyone knows there's no such thing as werewolves."

Before I can respond, Angelika has winced. Placed a hand over her lower stomach.

"Are you okay?"

"Yeah — I've gone and gotten my period."

I think I back up a step or two. Wasn't counting. "Oh."

"Not that big a deal," the girl goes on obliviously, "aside from the stupid aches and pains. You know how it is."

I did, since I currently had mine, but would never tell anyone that.

"Hence the crucifix to fend off vampires who've caught the scent," she says in a confidential tone.

To this I nod, struck dumb.

"Anyhow, I tend to forget things when I get it – like thanking you for showing me round yesterday."

"That's okay." The comment comes out rushed, unsettled. "I don't think I gave you the chance."

"Late for an important date?"

"Huh?"

45

"Can't say I've ever seen anyone move so fast!" Angelika laughs.

"Oh. That. I kind of had to go somewhere."

"So I noticed. You trying out for the sprint club?"

"No, I – *um* – I just had to be somewhere. Sorry."

"Hey," Angelika lightly shakes her head, "I'm not trawling for apologies." She still has a warm smile, not the mocking kind I usually duelled with. "I was impressed. Wish I had that kind of speed."

Miss Vicks has started to speak at the front of the class, to us this time, and I remain mum the rest of the lesson. Since Tuesday's lesson was the art history side of things and basically a fifty-minute lecture, all the easier.

But Thursdays would be a double period of art prac, meaning over an hour and a half's interaction between we students.

I dread the thought.

When I get back to the house that afternoon, I'm surprised to find Dad home early.

First indicator is in the downstairs loungeroom, located near the front door — he has his second-favourite Steely Dan recording, called *The Royal Scam* or *The Royal Flimflam*, spinning on the upright Recordio Stereophonic/Hi-Fidelity reel-to-reel in the bookcase next to stacks of black Betamax tapes.

Even above this pop-rock/disco I make out the sounds of my father and brother in the kitchen, gabbling at the top of their lungs. The staircase began just after the entrance to that room, so I'll have to walk past. I stop to listen and gauge the topic of conversation, but it's impossible to get the gist in another room.

Better to get this over with.

I wander to the kitchen doorway, offer up a hello once the two men notice from their places at the breakfast table. There are several brown longneck bottles of Victoria Bitter between them. Dad has a beaming smile, one that pre-existed my arrival, and I make scarcely a dent.

"Mina, darling — Patrick broke the drought!" Dad exclaims, truly happy for the first time in what feels like months. "Your brother scored a century today! A hundred and thirty-three not out! Can you believe it?"

Patrick, seated on a back-to-front Series 7 dining chair over by the wall, is still dressed in cricket whites, but I guess that's not so unusual before five p.m. What *is* unusual is the amount of alcohol they've consumed — together. Without making it obvious, while I go through the motions of smiling, pushing hair behind my ears and congratulating Patrick, I do a speedy tot-up of the bottles. Nine.

Likely more lived in the fridge.

Patrick is nineteen now. This is his privilege, I guess. No way I'm going to be offered a glass, and no way I want to join them anyway, but there are formalities to follow.

As he natters on about the big sporting accomplishment, I inspect Dad's face and neck. Flushed skin above a beige pinstripe business shirt. I don't like seeing this side of him, nor of my brother who is vaguely pink — not sure if that's because of the alcohol or an afternoon in the sun. My eyes wander further. Red smudge marks on the white material around Patrick's crotch.

This is the moment I realized an all-rounder bowled as well as batted.

"I'm bursting to go to the toot," Dad abruptly announces, laughing at himself before he heads out of the kitchen. "Neither of you two move — I'll be straight back."

Once the toilet door slides shut, I glance down again at Patrick. "Really. Congrats."

Surprisingly, he's lost the look of someone who ought to be celebrating. He fidgets in his seat, takes a big swig of beer, and looks away.

"I lied," he says to the wall. "Scored thirty-three, fell leg before wicket, after five hours of struggling out there on an easy wicket. My highest score in two years. I couldn't tell him that, Mina. It'd break his heart."

Patrick turns back to me, a plaintive look now consuming his face.

"Don't tell him."

"I won't."

After that I head upstairs, before Dad returns. If he missed me I couldn't hear it — within thirty seconds the two drinkers are cheering and toasting one another.

In my bedroom Animeid has flown the coop.

I sit on the end of the bed, switch on the TV, and flick channels.

A rerun of game show *Blankety Blanks* hosted by Graham Kennedy, American soapie *Another World*, commercials, and some documentary on the upcoming Commonwealth Games in Edinburgh — a speech in London from Maggie Thatcher makes me duck for cover. On SBS? *Mobile Suit Gundam*, this anime with big, fighting mechanized robot suits. Actually does keep my attention for a while, but then it ends and the news kicks in — with interstate election results.

So I turn off the telly again, bored.

"You here, Anim?" I ask aloud. No response. I push myself up against the wall, legs crossed, and think about my roommate.

Funnily enough, the bird lady really made herself known to me about six months before, when I was sixteen-and-a-half and attacked. No, not by Patrick — instead by a mouse.

Had been home alone, downstairs in our ill-lit loungeroom, late at night.

Kneeling on a counterfeit Persian rug (a better sitting position than the icy slate floor) to watch a 1970s Karen Black telemovie called *Trilogy of Terror*. This was scripted by a fave author of mine, Richard Matheson — yep, horror. In the middle of the show, just as a native voodoo doll attacks our heroine, I started hearing noises in the hallway, minute ones I barely made out above the sound of the TV.

Swore I saw a tiny movement in the corner of my eye and swung around to face my very own native voodoo doll.

Precisely at that moment something shot across the floor and took flight — straight into my long hair. I jumped up, screaming, shrieking, shoving hands about to shed the unexplained menace.

A grey mouse tumbled to the carpet, shook itself, and then was crushed beneath a small bare foot that belonged to a complete stranger.

The black feather girl was there, semi-naked aside from those feathers, and she peered at me from a face I still couldn't properly fathom, bathed as it was in oddball shadows. A mop of wild black hair surrounded that gloom.

"Grow a back-bone," was all she said, followed by: "Jesus."

After this strange visitor pulled one of her magician-friendly disappearing tricks, I cleaned up the mess caused by blood and spilled out internal rodent's organs before Dad got home from the hospital.

Next morning she'd graffitied the dresser mirror in my bedroom, using one of my mother's ruby-red lipsticks. 'ANIMEID' was scrawled there in a childlike hand, with the N, E and D back-to-front.

The lipstick, Clinique, lay on the floor.

Once I picked up the thing I pressed it against my chest. God, Mum.

Anyway, that's how we met. Now I can't get rid of the thing.

I actually go open the Moomin curtains (horror!), and then the window to allow in some fresh, late afternoon air.

Get changed into an old, tight lemon-coloured *Empire Strikes Back* t-shirt and a pair of cut-off denim shorts.

No one's going to see me here.

Hop onto the bed with some of my fiction folders (I had dozens more beneath the bed) and the red Olivetti portable-manual typewriter.

Sit there cross-legged again, just like every other evening with bits of scrap paper (scrawled notes and vignettes) everywhere, flicking through these, thinking up a tangent, and starting to clack away on the keys.

Occasionally ripping out a page with too many errors in order to start afresh, and other times adjusting the ribbon.

Page after page manually cranked from the Olivetti, the majority destined to remain accidentally encoded after being shoved into different folders with a filing system I didn't understand.

The medicos threw in an abortion, gratis, the very same day. Was sick, some disease she don't know the name of, would no doubt have died as well, but they cured her — though choice never entered into the equation.

She had no notion of why they did that, not initially; yet gradually put two-and-two together, in between medicine hits supposed to keep her zapped out. Leverage, that's what she was, nothing more to it. Being kept alive meant she could be flaunted as a bartering tool, just like the other 'lucky' patients she met, the survivors, the ones who stayed round.

The others who disappeared or died — they had no such use.

At first she submitted to all the pain and humiliation, the abuse, the medication. Hid in the recesses of the mind, far back as possible, but eventually they hacked through. Was a time, a black spot, when she lost any sense of self, of awareness. Didn't know how or why she started swimming against the current. Once she did, though, she made it duty-bound to wipe clean every remaining morsel of whom she was and what she'd been.

The few memories clung to — being a wife, almost having a child — she kept to torment herself at the lowest depths.

Thursday.

The day before Friday — best day of the school week — makes me ill. Means that double art prac lesson with Angelika, alongside eight other girls I barely knew.

I woke in the a.m. feeling ill, tried to convince my father I had a fever. Didn't exactly suck my thumb, but thought I play-acted pretty well. Dad wasn't impressed. He stuck a thermometer under my arm, announced I was fine, and sent me packing.

When I enter the 12E classroom at 8:31 — late again, though this time by a single minute — Roslyn Williams frowns. Roslyn has a terrific frown, visible from the opposite side of large open spaces. She'd been writing my name under the absentee list on the upper left of the blackboard, and now has to backtrack through the effort of erasing all four letters.

After apologizing, conscious of a classroom of people rubber-necking my way, I allow my fringe to fall as I plough in the direction of my desk. This means I don't have to look at Sarah or Angelika, not even Clair.

I pull out the chair more noisily than I intend, slump onto the cushion, and gaze straight ahead through the veil of my bangs. Vaguely make out Mrs Williams like she's in some strange dream, wading through tall grass. An explorer in deepest, darkest Africa. All she needs is a pith helmet.

Don't know when I become aware of the small, scrunched-up piece of paper taking up space next to my pencil case. As our form teacher makes a series of hardly important announcements to which I'm blissfully able to tune out, I unfold the paper.

It's a note, all caps, that says:

ARE YOU OK? X

I stare at the handwriting, know it straight off the bat.

Sarah's.

What does she mean? — *'Are you okay?'* plus that single kiss mark? I fret the moment I read the words.

An obscure form of apology?

She'd barely spoken to me all day Wednesday, aside from

basics that came across snappy. But why should Sarah apologize? She wouldn't feel she'd set a foot wrong. I knew her that well, at least.

Something else then. The words linger before me.

Are you okay? x

Gnawing again at the inner right side of my lower lip, I begin to wonder. Does she know? What if she's found out about my mother?

I brush something imaginary off the surface of the desk, think about feathers. Midnight plumage, just like liquorice.

Slightly turn my face to the left, away from Clair — feeling at a loss, scared of the sensation, trying desperately to keep everything together in a neatly wrapped package in my gut or my brain or wherever it's supposed to be tucked away.

My fringe has fallen to one side, and I find Angelika peering my way with those enormous browns.

There's no silly grin on her face. No shock, horror, revulsion or scorn. I find myself searching out that old favourite, pity, or its close-cousin sympathy, but both are amiss.

Wasn't sure what I looked at. Some kind of exceptional form of understanding, empathy I guess — but I didn't know that at the time. Don't think I'd ever encountered it before.

Angelika then erects a tiny smile, disarming and honest at once.

This is a creature no one else sees, and at the same time she nods in my direction. An equally miniscule gesture, mostly imperceptible.

I don't know how but I find myself able to scale the abyss just for that moment, to return both expressions, and then we face front again to truly listen to what Roslyn has to say.

I can feel Sarah behind me.

Later.

I skip art prac that morning.

Go instead to the school nurse to complain, for the first time in my life, of period-pains and cramping.

Kick back for the two lessons on top of a relatively comfy white cot in that small, Spartan, gloriously empty room, reading *The Mists of Avalon*.

That is, until Animeid pops head in. And the rest of her.

Thought I was free of the girl at school, but she saunters in like she owns the place, shams an inspection of the hygiene posters on one wall, and then leans over more annoyingly to read the title of the book I'm pretending to read.

Her verdict?

"Airy-fairy stuff. Hope the narrator's better than you."

Course she gets my attention. I place the open book on my lap. "Meaning?"

"Well, I think it's obvious — you're unreliable. You have a chronic inability to fathom what's going on right before your field of vision; you deceive yourself, me, and anyone else you care to include. Have no idea of how you feel and refuse to try. Selfish and somewhat self-indulgent."

"Well, that's unfair."

"Think about it, Mina. You need an imaginary bird-woman to spell out home truths and tell you what you really ought to do — not that you listen anyway. If this were a novel or a play and you were the narrator, I'd be concerned."

"Well, then, lucky it's not. And aren't you tired? I don't believe I've ever heard you talk so much."

I lift the novel, flip a page, try to concentrate — but can't. That's when I glance at her again.

"Look, who says there needs to be one single narrator? This book's already had two different ones and I'm only a third of the way through. Plenty of time yet for you to muscle your way into pole position."

"Oh, hurrah," she says, waltzing out.

That afternoon, feeling guilty, I go visit Miss Vicks in the art department. She asks after my health, and then pauses, eyes watery.

"Now, I know you don't want people making a hoo-har," says she, taking both my hands in hers, "but I was so utterly sorry to hear about your mother Mary. A lovely lady."

Coming from Miss Vicks this sympathy wasn't so oppressive as the dose Roslyn had delivered up. I'd grown attached to my art teacher; felt we shared a lot in common — such as having the odd grand confabulation with ourselves. Besides, no one else was here.

"Thank you."

Her fingers squeeze mine. "Is there anything I can do?"

"This is enough." I squeeze back, and straight after drop the hands to my sides. "I'm doing okay. Think I just need to stay busy."

"Which brings me to our first project!" Miss Vicks abruptly announces, tears and sympathy tossed by the wayside.

She goes to fetch a square, dark brown piece of linoleum, about thirty-by-thirty centimetres in size. Gives that to me as she natters further. "We're doing linocuts, same as last year — do you still have the tools?"

"At home. Least, I think so."

"Well, fingers crossed and fear not — I know you can catch up. So, your homework is to sketch out your subject and try to get most of the cutting done before next week's session. We're going to start printing them up on Thursday, and the following week there will be a new project."

"Any particular theme?" I ask.

Miss Vicks smiles, taps the side of her head. "Imagination. In here. No real life, and especially no still-lifes. You know how much I abhor my rancid plates of fruit."

"I do!" I laugh — precisely when Miss Vicks grabs at my hands again.

"You're blessed with such beautiful laughter, Mina. That's where you need to focus now. The laughter, the joys of life and living. Peace will find you."

I nod.

It's the right thing to do. Don't want to tell her that the gushing makes me uncomfortable.

Next day was Friday.

The aforementioned best-day-of-the-educated-week, but also my third class with Angelika-With-a-K — cinema studies.

Luckily, a subject handled with aplomb by our brand new teacher, requiring no conversation at all.

Mitchell Brenner was a former journalist with *The Argus* newspaper, unmarried, an obvious playboy, and the owner of a yacht down at Bodega Bay. In spite of these trappings, not only did this mid-forties, openly gay man have a deep brown tan, salt-bleached hair and calloused fingers, but his knowledge of motion pictures put mine to shame — and (till then) I believed I was pretty darned good.

Straight away in this introductory lesson the three of us (Angelika, Clair and me) grab three seats in a row at the centre of the room, and kick back to the screening of the first half of Alfred Hitchcock's *The Birds*.

Mr Brenner had assured us that the last hour would be screened next Friday.

Having never seen the film before, I find it riveting — yet still notice in the corner of my eye how Clair ducks and covers in the more suspenseful sequences.

The crows in the playground make me think straightaway of Animeid.

That afternoon, after school, I walk to the tram stop with Clair and Sarah.

While Clair and I unusually gush about the plot of *The Birds* along with Rod Taylor's looks — well, me doing most of the gushing and Clair listening — by contrast Sarah is quiet.

Of course Clair and I both notice.

We share conspiratorial looks while speaking, and I actually wink at my friend. The three of us had had plans to go into the city together, but Sarah makes a snap decision to catch the old wooden W-Class tram headed in the opposite direction.

"Don't worry about her," Clair assures me. "I'll come with you."

Not really paying attention, but this is fine by me since I want to go to a comic-book store (a small place called Gorgon, down a narrow shopping arcade in Chinatown) to buy a picture book by artist Frank Thorne, collecting together his *Red Sonja* run at Marvel Comics from 1977 to 1979.

Had most of those issues stored under the bed, but this was a glossy version.

While she was indifferent to comic-book charms, Clair was also patient. Hating the medium, Sarah would literally stamp her foot and demand immediate evacuation.

So being just Clair and me was convenient.

Anyway, having picked up said book, the two of us had a quick cappuccino at Pellegrino's Espresso Bar on Hare Street — a relatively famous family business where an old guy with a dreaded beard, Indian-style regalia, rings on all his fingers including two inset glass eyes, and bracelets galore assailed us.

He lugged along a big, handmade staff with a sheep's skull atop. A nice enough gentleman but had a booming laugh that kept drawing attention our way.

That's why we indulged in the *quick* cappuccino I mentioned.

Once I finished my cup in a rush, I nudged Clair, and we said goodbye — to him as well as each other.

Since Pellegrino's was up the top end of Hare Street, I detoured via Gaslit Records to rummage through the growing alternative section, even if they'd mislabelled it as 'Alternative Music'.

Found my second and third scalps for the day: Joy Division's LP *Unknown Pleasures* (Factory, 1979) and a seven-inch version of 'Love Will Tear Us Apart', slipped inside a simple sleeve that had an image of the title engraved in marble, along with the record label (Factory again) beneath that.

Thanks to an article scoured in *NME*, I'd backtracked New Order to their earlier incarnation (Joy Division) before lead vocalist Ian Curtis committed suicide in 1980.

Apparently 'Love Will Tear Us Apart' was that band's best-known song. Yet I was also curious about *Unknown Pleasures* since it had a track titled 'She's Lost Control'. Felt it somehow fit me like a glove — so bought both records.

Then caught the train toward home from Flinders Street Station.

This was a Red Rattler, an ancient locomotive painted pillar-box red — hence the nickname — constructed sometime after 1910, all wood-panel finish with an open saloon layout and bench seats. Said saloon divided by partitions into a number of smaller areas, decorated with brass fixtures and old framed photos of Victorian tourist spots from the '20s.

Time? Six p.m.

Carriage? Fairly crowded.

Me? Positioned perfectly in a seat by the window, making sure my fringe hangs diplomatically so that I can then scan other passengers in anonymity.

Subject #1: An elderly, haggard-looking man the next seat over, dressed in a crumpled slate-grey suit covered in suspect stains.

I can smell the stale alcohol and urine four metres away. Snoring, apparently asleep, or this is a sham to deter ticket inspectors. If so, no need — the stench is deterrence enough.

Subject #2: A younger guy closer to me, much better repair, clad in a navy, linen-material double-breasted suit, garishly accessorized by a fat, pink-and-white polka-dot tie that threatened to blind other passengers.

Ostensibly browsing a copy of *The Financial Times*, this man occasionally glances over right shoulder-pad at his hobo-counterpart, disgust planted on his mush, and he sighs aloud. On repeat.

Subjects #3-7: Further down the carriage sits a group of Nede High School boys, likely new recruits in Year 9, fourteen or fifteen years old.

They look like primary school kids stuffed into oversized uniforms, huddled together as the topic switches from *Dungeons & Dragons* to the latest Timelord (Colin Baker) in *Doctor Who*.

Every now and then one of them, the tallest, a blond kid with a nice smile but still very young-looking, glances over my way. I find the attention disconcerting; didn't care if I was guilty of the same pastime.

Subject #8: Seated to the left of the Nede High kids is a boy in his early twenties, seriously cute.

Wardrobe consisting of a bleached denim jacket that'd been worn to absolute death, a pair of old jeans in similar state, and tattered Nike runners — that 'over abused' look, so popular now, that still hung somehow cool.

Wish the rule applied to me.

Anyhow, he flicks through *Rolling Stone* magazine while I continue to peer and feel uncomfortable. Yes, he's attractive — I like his forehead (steep) and nose (subtle), but in this position I can't check out his eyes and am determined not to let him see mine.

So I break contact, pulling my fringe further forward, and gaze out the window at fly-by factories and warehouses and homes. Past the sprawling Rosella factory, the Birrarung River, and then the castle-like battlements of Nede High.

Not long later the train pulls in to Flahan Station.

Tempted as I am to alight then and there to embark on a pilgrimage down Grevillia Street to Chapel — and the goodies in shops lining that street all the way through to South Birrarung — fact is I'm alone, unchaperoned, spent most of my money on this heavy art book I carry in my schoolbag and the records next to my leg.

Behind me, at the other end of the carriage, a set of doors is manually cranked open, and then I make out loud, cheery voices. Casually I glance over my left shoulder to evaluate these newcomers.

Yes, I was being snoopy.

Yes, I was bored.

The four people I spy — Subjects #9, #10, #11 and #12 — nip both indulgences in the bud, dressed as they are (mostly in black) and carousing my way. I know the type and panic.

Swing my head straight, eyes a little wide, force attention to the graffiti outside the window — something rushed in ugly big letters that says 'Little Nobody was here, unseen, got depressed, went there!' and above that a more elegant, hip creation in geometric purple capitals: 'ERE SAW DOG'. Okay. Whatever. It'll do. Distracting enough.

Should've known this rowdy new crew would make themselves at home between me and the agitated businessman with that offensive pink tie.

The train shudders and lurches forward, an elderly set of carriages in a cantankerous mood, leaving graffiti behind.

"Hey, excuse me."

A girl's voice. Close-range. Nice enough — no threat there.

I continue to eyeball the window, shamming fascination with passing back yards, overgrown foliage, rusted swing-sets and ancient sheds.

"Hey — Goldilocks. Can you hear me? Hello?"

That voice again, far too close.

Something brushes the right lapel of my school blazer, making me understand I will not be allowed to continue the bluff. Biting my lower lip (again) I turn.

Two guys, likely late-teens, all black, sit across from me. Next to Pink Tie.

They resemble identical twins guilty of impersonating Robert

Smith from The Cure. Wrapped in woollen winter coats and tight black jeans, with fingerless leather gloves, pointed-toe shoes, ebony hair wildly teased and spiked in every direction.

Preoccupied with kicking one another, all madcap abandon, I doubt Tweedledum or Tweedledee have noticed me and their well-dressed neighbour — he who now recoils, fending off the boys with his newspaper, while pretending to read.

But seated right next to me are two girls.

The far one I can't see clearly since the nearest plays interference.

This closer girl has leaned forward my way, her left elbow propped on left thigh, chin in left palm. She watches me from just twenty centimetres distant — eyes so heavily made-up (in black, of course) that it takes me a moment to fathom where the irises really reside. Makes me think of Elizabeth Taylor in *Cleopatra*, bastardized by silent film actress Theda Bara.

"So — you're alive," this hybrid girl decides aloud.

Are *you*? I wonder, keeping my trap shut.

Don't want to get into any kind of trouble with these people. Nod instead. When the girl rolls her eyes, as she does now, the whites become glaringly obvious.

She isn't wearing much other make-up, aside from thickly drawn black eyebrows — above which rest a head of hair mostly lilac, punctuated with streaks of darker purple, cropped short on the right side. This hair isn't quite so teased as the boys opposite, but shaped in such haphazard fashion I start to wonder if Vidal Sassoon might've cut and coloured it in his sleep.

"What's your name, hon?"

My heart is beating fast. I want to make up something, a lie, but the truth slips out before I realize.

"Mina."

"Cute. I'm Margaret."

"Nice to meet you."

"*Aw*. So polite."

"I try."

This comment also slides out unchecked. Astonished as I am, I regret the thing the moment it's uttered.

"A smart-arse too?"

This girl Margaret lifts her chin from the hand, sits up straighter, and appraises me in a manner that's intimidating. I fret she may clock me right there on the train, but instead the girl beams.

"Cool. Okay. Hope you don't mind me asking, but reckon I recognize the uniform — you go to Mac.Lark, right?"

"Mac.Duagh."

The other girl again sizes me up, grin this time dead in the water and face otherwise expressionless. Of course I quail.

"Yes," I add, meek as.

To which Margaret breaks up. She has trouble controlling wild peals of laughter in order to be able to speak again.

"Oh, wow. Don't worry — hah! Just messing with you. I know its real name."

Still chuckling, this lilac-haired girl swivels to her companion on the other side of the bench seat, leaving me relieved.

"See? Told'ja. Two bucks, pay me later," I hear her say — but then she's straight back in my face, leaning close again with chin in hand, elbow on thigh.

I whiff perfume this time, something beyond the hobo's smell, a combination of ginger and sandalwood. Takes me longer to recognize the third new scent: hairspray. A sticky, pungent aroma of industrial polymers and alcohol — just like my grandmother used to deploy.

"You won me two bucks — ka-ching. Cheers! Thing is I'm broke and could do with the money. Rent and food and bills and all that shit."

Oh crap, I think, she's going to ask for money.

"But I have another Q&A, this time worth nothing. Curiosity, all that nonsense of killing cats. I don't believe that, do you?

Anyway I have this question, hon, figure I should ask, no harm done — that okay too?"

While she babbles, relieved as I am that she doesn't appear to be sponging for cash, I do a speedy glance-over from behind my fringe, executed in two seconds flat.

This girl's wearing a short, pleated tartan skirt bordering on a mini, under which are opaque black tights — ripped up and held together by safety pins — along with knee-high, black leather boots boasting high heels and pointed toes.

Up top, beneath an open black cardigan, sits a surprisingly hot-pink t-shirt, one size too large, holes and tears and the words 'Thrush and the Cunts' emblazoned across the front.

This is all way too much for my small, very narrow mind and me.

"The question," this girl repeats, like I'd missed something.

I had good practice pretending I got things I'd only tuned in to part of the way, so I honed on these two words. *The question.*

"Ask away," I say.

"Cool. A friend of mine goes to Mac.Duagh — she's in Year 12, doing HSC."

"Same as me," I muse, internally flicking through the roster of faces in all five classes. No way was this possible. No one to bookend this girl. Unless — Angelika?

"Doubt you'd know her." Margaret is dismissively final. "The two of us were drummed out of this stupid little Christian school called Star of the Sea a couple of years ago. Actually, not that little, but still. Something to do about the way we looked. Something like that. Those people were anuses. Glad to see she's stuck it out. Girl's too bright to drop out of school. Not like moi."

"You don't go to school?" I ask. Have no idea why I'm surprised, given her makeover and wardrobe, but she looks around the same age as me.

"Nup. Fuckit. Merrily on the dole now."

Her gaze drops then to the plastic Gaslit Records bag by my leg.

"Anyway, enough about me. What's in there?"

"Nothing." Can't believe I'm saying this. Of course there was something.

"You often carry round bags of empty air?"

"Sometimes." *Shut up, Mina!*

The other girl smiles from only one side of her mouth, a half-hearted thing that borders on menace. Meanwhile, she leans forward, left hand reaching toward the bag.

"D'you overly mind?"

Think my expression gives the game away.

"Don't worry, I'm not going to steal anything. Huh." A second later the bag is on her lap and she's checking the recorded contents. "My, *oh* my — you actually have half-decent taste. Not bad for empty air, unless these're for someone else?"

"No. Me."

The other girl frowns. "Favourite song?"

I head out on a limb, committing musical perjury. "Prob'ly 'She's Lost Control'."

"Really?"

"Mmm."

Not sure this girl believes me.

"Okay, then. Neat." She puts the vinyl back and passes back the bag.

That's when one of the male twins across from us, Tweedledee I think, stops kicking his partner and from a coat pocket extracts one packet of Dunhill.

He leans over to Margaret to say something in a low voice I can't make out (and don't exactly try — I think I still have delusions of escaping through the window next to my shoulder). Even so, I do observe as the girl's fingers, covered with silver rings and embellished by purple nail polish, pluck a cigarette from the pack. The movement — somehow — comes across graceful.

Pink Tie watches also, from over his *Financial Times*.

"Excuse me. You're not allowed to smoke on public transport."
"So?"

Margaret stares or glares at him — I can't tell from my angle — and if she expected a response she was to be disappointed. The businessman twirls away, pokes his nose deeper still inside the newspaper.

The girl definitely has a smirk when she glances back to me. "Some people," she murmurs with counterfeit disdain. "Listen, d'you have a light on you?"

"A light? You mean, a lighter?"

"Or matches. Either will do."

"No. I'm a schoolgirl."

"So was I, four months ago."

While Margaret gazes thoughtfully at the cigarette between her fingers — perhaps trying to summon up Hellfire — I have a chance to properly see her face.

An attractive girl in spite of all the eye make-up, reminding me in profile, especially with the slightly upturned nose, of my fave Hammer Films actress Ingrid Pitt. Don't know what I expected to find. Probably that she'd painted over some hideous defect.

After more noise and theatrics, Margaret and her troupe alight at the next station.

Next weekend my father headed off for a romantic forty-eight hours holed up with some new piece of tail. Left Patrick in charge, so I tried to make myself scarce.

Spent Saturday morning in my room, door barred, slaving over the typewriter while listening to Joy Division, since they'd usurped New Order. Played Side B of *Unknown Pleasures* several times over — funnily enough 'She's Lost Control' was my favourite after all.

Loved the darker music here, Peter Hook's minimal bassline, Bernard Sumner's crisp guitar, the mechanical drum beat, but mostly I adored the lyrics. Confusion in her eyes saying it all?

God, right on.

Just after lunch Sarah rings.

"We're having a session later this afternoon," she says. "Bet you miss those."

I pull a face, one I'm glad she can't see down the line. "The three-hour special?"

"If the players aren't up to scratch, I might just push it to four."

"Ouch," I say.

You might've noticed I do tend to be more effusive on the phone, since it's impersonal. Also get to doodle on a pad beside the rotary dialler, and am currently sketching a caricature of Sarah beneath a Native American chieftain's headpiece of feathers.

"Any good players in Year 9 this year?" I muse, touching up the cherubic mouth.

"Well, I won't know till this afternoon, will I?" There's a crackle in the reception — a poor connection despite this being a local call. Sarah sounds a million miles away. "I *do* miss having you on the team, M."

Nice of her, but I find that impossible to believe. "Yeah, right. Breaking tennis racquets with every second serve."

"Actually, I seem to remember it was your first that did the damage. The second was the safe, reliable lollipop. That first one was an ace every time."

She does manage to get me laughing.

"But I only managed to get five percent of them over the net and between the lines," I mutter in between. "Never guaranteed to earn me sponsorship from Slazenger."

As I say, I'm more relaxed with a telephone. Placing the receiver in the crook of my neck, I pin the finished penmanship on a corkboard we're supposed to use for messages.

Then I lean over a little to enjoy sunlight streaming in through the loungeroom window. "Remember? The other ninety-five percent maimed doubles partners."

"And broke racquets." Sarah returns the laugh, a breezy sound that fades. "You won't come."

"Think I'll sit this one out."

"Oh, ace."

"Are you having a go still about my hack service?"

"Never! As I say — you'll be missed."

Don't know why but I'm somehow more talkative than ever. I even stretch myself by continuing a conversation that's in the process of wrapping.

"What're you doing after tennis?" I ask.

"Sadly, I have to go into the city to the State Library — I reserved a translated copy of the *Malleus Maleficarum*."

"And that should mean something to me because..."

"You know, *The Hammer of the Witches*."

"Ah-hah!" I say, liberal with the sarcasm, and then think twice. "Actually, that does ring a bell — think I heard about it in a Vincent Price movie. *Witchfinder General*, maybe?"

"You're the film buff — don't ask me!" Sarah again laughs. "But apparently, according to Mr Hopkins, the book contributed to the witch craze in medieval Europe and later in Salem. He put me onto it so I'm doing an essay on the thing."

"Then you're busy with witch stuff."

"Looks like it — will have to get myself a coven together. You up for membership?"

"Does it come with a fancy glossy card?"

"Embossed and all."

"Okay. So, I'll see you on Monday? With your broom, I mean."

"Okay. Ciao."

That afternoon, only three of the chain gang meets at Deveroli's: Hannah, Nicole, and me.

Sarah, as I mentioned, had tennis, while Clair was committed to some theological goings-on at her local church. The duo's absence means I arrive to enough available table space to plant both elbows.

Hallelujah.

Right away I hail over a waitress, order an espresso, and slump.

"Strong stuff," Hannah remarks.

Me: "I need it."

"Where's Sarah?"

"Busy with witch stuff."

"Huh?"

I toss her a shrug. "Tennis practice."

Seeing Nicole was surprising since she had ballet lessons three or four times a week and allowed these to rule her social schedule — as well as often ours.

I mention this in more diplomatic terms.

"Teacher's got herself sick," the other girl says in irritated fashion. "Speaking of sick, how were your lessons last week with the newbie freak?"

I know straight away who she's reffing to. Comes as no surprise, but my mood chills in an instant.

"How does that relate to sick?"

"I don't know," muses Nicole in a playful, singsong way that still comes across worrisome, "she seems to me like something pretty broken. You heard she was expelled from Star of the Sea?"

Hannah, who'd been zoning out to comb her blonde hairdo, reengages. "What's *that*?"

"A posh private Irish Catholic girl's school down in Brighton."

I glance at my friend. "How do you know about it?"

To which Nicole does my trick — she shrugs. "Have my sources."

"Why? Why was she expelled?" asks Hannah, excited and eager to hear the gossip.

Of course Nicole leans close, all conspiratorial and the corners of her mouth turning up — the beginnings of a savage smile — but for the first time in our friendship, I cut in.

"Nic, you shouldn't talk about stuff like that."

Both sets of eyes lock on mine. I can read every shred of disbelief there.

"You're kidding?" Nicole demands to know.

I shake my head.

Can't believe I look so fixedly in return, don't back down, duck and cover, or give up the ghost. My heart is racing and I feel words will likely fail me, but I'm determined — God knows why — to make a stand.

"If Angelika wants to share the gory details, let *her* tell us."

This comment makes Nicole bristle. "What, are you two best friends now? Why doesn't that surprise me? Miss Weird, meet Miss Weirder."

Just for a second I have a feeling I now know my nickname.

"It's okay!" Hannah suddenly interrupts in a loud voice.

I'm not sure if the girl does this to break the stressful impasse between two of her best friends, or just because she feels she can turn it into another game.

"I can try to guess, can't I? Mina, let me, please — I can take pot shots to see if I guess the reason. Nicole doesn't have to tell me at all. Can I?"

Nicole momentarily seems taken aback, and then nods, pleased. "There's an idea. Means I'm not breaking any of Mina's newfound humdrum rules."

"Whatever," I mutter. I'd leaned away from the two of them, needing distance.

"Okay," Hannah goes on, relishing this opportunity. "So... I do like her initials — double A — but, um... maybe she's a commie? A spy! That's it! Isn't her first name Russian?"

This time Nicole shakes her head. "She says it's Czech."

A comment that makes our comrade confused. "Like in the chess game?"

"No, no, D.D. — not 'check'... '*Czech*' — as in Czechoslovakia, the country."

"Oh, well that's alright, then — they're good guys."

"No. They're communists too," Nicole sighs, her gossipy intrigue shelved.

"Really? That close to Madagascar?"

"Madagascar?" Battling perhaps not to roll eyes or tear hair, Nicole heads for condescending instead. "Mm-hmm. That's right, dear."

She might've sounded just like Mrs Williams, but wasn't as cluey as our teacher — totally missed the annoyed look on Hannah's face.

While I was out, Patrick decided to throw an obligatory party at our house, no doubt influenced by American frat boy flicks he'd indulged in like *Risky Business* and *Weird Science*.

Dad would've thrown a wobbly if he'd been aware of the shenanigans, and Patrick let me know he'd beat the living daylights out of me if ever I blabbed.

So I ended up helping him blow balloons, fold serviettes and top up paper plates with potato chips, peanuts and sliced kabanosy sausage. Guess he wanted to demonstrate his hosting prowess since a few girls came — acquaintances I didn't know from Mac.Duagh, as well as Caellainn Girls Grammar School — but eighty percent of the one hundred or so guests were boys from Nede High.

Most were smashed before they set foot in our house, which was open to the public from six p.m. on, and several carted in beer slabs of twenty-four cans.

Tobacco smoke and marijuana fumigated the furniture and drapes despite the windows being open, but worse still was the music — mixed cassettes arranged by identical twin, second-generation Pakistani brothers Gad and Raz Shaytan.

These boys were in Year 12 at Nede High too, same class as Patrick.

They boasted surprisingly pale skin, were mad about cricket

(always wore white V-neck jumpers and were star spin-bowlers in the Nede High School Eleven), had matching Brylcreemed rocker quiffs, and sounded more Aussie than any other Australian I knew.

The two of them had strung together the likes of Dire Straits, John Cougar Mellencamp, Divinyls, Johnny O'Keefe, Bryan Adams, Midnight Oil, Australian Crawl and Hunters & Collectors.

Some of it I didn't mind, but compressed in this manner — selecting tracks I'd heard way too often on *Countdown*, WJAD FM and Patrick's stereo — made the tapes a form of torment.

By nine o'clock, when I finally venture down to get something to eat from the kitchen, the place is a pigsty.

Bottles and cans, filled with used butts, roll around in overturned piles of nibblies. Discarded wine corks and filthy napkins litter the floor. Still-life drunks and listless conversationalists dressed in electric neon colours stand in my way.

Patrick and his best friend Nicholas Shahan are in the hallway, far more animated, rambling in loud voices over the sound of AC/DC's 'Shoot to Thrill'. Though he's wearing Ray-Ban Aviator-style sunglasses inside, at night — a poor-man's Tom Cruise — my brother somehow deems to spot me by the kitchen.

Leans in to his mate and whispers something that makes Nick burst out laughing.

Probably they're picking on my bedroom choice of wardrobe: An oversized, pink t-shirt — bearing a watercolour of a lotus flower — that comes down to my knees, above brown-and-tan striped legwarmers. The tee keeps slipping off one shoulder to reveal a beige bra strap, and I keep awkwardly adjusting it.

Anyway, I turn away from those two to fetch a big green rubbish bag from the pantry, start throwing in everything that clutters up the kitchen. Wish I could squeeze Patrick in there.

Head out the back door to throw the bag in the bin, and see a boy in white tongue kissing a full-length looking glass.

Takes me time to understand there's no mirror — this is Gad and Raz, necking in our back yard.

One of them, I don't know which, breaks away from the other to glare at me.

"Whaddaya want, sheila?"

"Um... Nothing."

"Then cut the bloody starin'."

"Hard not to. You were kissing your brother."

"So?"

"Okay then."

Spinning on my heel, I go back inside to relative sanity. That was disturbing.

Afterward I'm further blessed to hear Brian Johnson growl something about letting him put his love in someone while I scoff down two slices of bread.

Almost reach the stairs when a pair of strong arms encircles me and I'm lifted off my feet, to the tune of "Mina-Mina-Mina!" — and both of us come close to falling.

Having put an emergency hand on the rail, I stare at Patrick's friend Nick since he's parked himself between the staircase and me. Intentionally.

The guy rubs his chin as he studies me closely, and he's sporting a harebrained grin.

Same age as Patrick (nineteen), I'd seen Nick on and off over six years — they started Nede High together. These days at Blamey Uni studying business, tonight Nick has chosen to model a casual, peppermint green shirt underneath an expensive-looking white suit jacket with roomy, padded shoulders.

He has brown hair above that, cut shortish at the back and sides but left longer — slicked with gel — on top. Hasn't shaved in a few days, this dark growth framing a strong, athletically handsome face and a pair of the most piercing, pale blue eyes I've ever seen.

Had noticed them before, somewhat smitten.

"Hey, Nicko, catch!" shouts someone in the kitchen, after which an unopened can of Carlton Draught flies straight into Nick's hand. I'll give him points for fielding ability. Patrick should take pointers.

Leaning against the wall, still obstructing my path, he pulls the ring top and offers the can. "You want a sip, Min?"

"No, thanks. Don't drink."

"Really? I heard apples don't fall far from trees."

Fact is I'm finding it a little difficult to breathe. Not sure if this is caused by all the cigarette smoke, or proximity to this admittedly devastating university boy two years my senior.

"Meaning?" I squeeze out.

"That Pat drinks like a fish."

"Does he?"

"Crap, yeah. You know we call him Tipple Fish?" Nick leans closer now, the grin fading, replaced by something else. "He's nowhere near cute as you, either."

I manage to laugh off the comment, albeit via a nervous titter that sounds forced, when the guy catches me unawares — pitches forward to kiss my mouth. It's a quick manoeuvre, like a Stuka dive-bomber. Once he's dropped his load, Nick ducks back to have a victory swig from the can of beer at his lips.

Now I really have lost my breath. Feel like I'm frozen to the spot.

After paying an inordinate amount of attention to his drink, Nick remembers me, smiles, and touches my cheek with fingers wet and cold from the can.

"Hey, wow. The face angels would sing about..."

That's where Nick loses me.

Completely.

I mean, even *I* wasn't that much of a twit. Doesn't help his cause that 'Working Class Man' — a song I loathed — is on the record player in the lounge room and a whole group of drunken boneheads are warbling along with Jimmy Barnes.

Nick is another of these boneheads, making a play at his best friend's hopeless younger sister.

Without further dialogue I squeeze past him, take steps three at a time, head to my room, slam the door. Sure, downstairs such dramatic flourish will be lost, but I feel better already.

It is relatively dark in here — only a small night-light in a corner by the bookcase — but I preferred subtle illumination.

First up, I peel off the legwarmers.

Now to drown out the vacuous, so-called working-class Aussie rock below.

I stick on David Bowie's orchestral 'Sense of Doubt' (off my father's LP *Heroes*), with the volume cranked up high to enhance the piano motif and that eerie, foreboding synth line. Trouble is the track being too minimal and spacey to succeed, especially coming out of only one speaker.

So I switch records to The Cure's *Faith* album.

Their song 'Primary' — all bass, no guitars — attempts (gloriously) to conquer the first-floor din but also fails.

Only one thing for it.

I go grab the beaten-up cassette of my childhood hero Suzi Quatro. *Can the Can*. Slip that into the tape player, and press play on '48 Crash'.

Perfect.

Nothing like classic femme rock 'n' roll to drown out the boys.

I've hopped onto the bed with my typewriter and a bottle of liquid paper, ready to squint and write in the inadequate light, pages spread out across the bed before me. Just as the next track ('Glycerine Queen') kicks in, I notice the door opening.

Nicholas' silhouette is there, slicked-back hair unsettled, with tufts sticking up either side of the skull. This shade walks in uninvited, shuts the door behind.

"Hey," I hear his voice say, "saw your light on, thought I'd drop in."

Heading straight to my bed, he picks up and places the

Olivetti on the desk, and then pushes the paperwork onto the floor.

"Unfinished business," he's announced.

Stands there a few seconds more, taking me in. I can't see his face at all.

"No."

My single word pops out hardly louder than a whisper.

"C'mon, don't be like that. *Mina, Mina, Mina.*"

A white suit jacket drops to the carpet.

"No." This time it comes stronger.

"That's not what your eyes said downstairs." He pushes somewhat clumsily against the mattress. "Was it?"

I can now smell beer and cigarettes.

"Know you dig me. Hey? What's not to dig?"

My body is unresponsive, jelly, as this man slaps one of his knees onto the end of the bed, and then leans forward and the other leg appears.

In seconds he's pushed up the t-shirt from around my waist, fumbling fingers of his right hand pulling at my Antz Pantz while, with his left hand, he's unhooking white suit trousers.

Like downstairs, I feel frozen to the spot — though this time the sensation isn't related at all to chemistry or charm. Instead there's nothing, a vacuum. Realize I lie there docile, just like my brother taught me, waiting for this person to tire and move on.

Now on top of me, having forced my legs apart. Pushing and shoving but missing his target as this intruder head-bangs to the sounds of Suzi's 'Shine My Machine'. How drunk *was* he?

Haven't thought of Animeid till she makes her presence known — slides up behind Nick as she flicks open a straightedge razor.

Where'd she score that?

Dad used an electric shaver. I'd seen only one of these instruments before, the theatre prop for a school production of *Sweeney Todd* — an all-girl affair in which Clair was supposed to co-star as

Mrs Lovett before her parents withdrew her from rehearsals. Something to do with the profane nature of said musical.

Anyway, Anim has one in her right fist and — with one quick movement — gives Nick the shave he'd forgotten, slicing open his thick neck.

"Whoa. I like that," I decide on the spot — far more gleeful than I ought to be.

In response my saviour sits back on her haunches, inspecting the handiwork. "Sweet, huh? And I do have a nice recipe for a pie."

Nick breaks the moment. Between huffing asks, "You like it?"

Kneeling over me still, he has a liquored-up grin that pushes self-satisfied — despite the fact he's mislaid the mojo to insert a seriously drooping penis. Inexplicably, this smile of his mirrors an upward-turning line of the bloody slit across the jugular beneath.

"Not you, you moron." I sigh. "I mean seeing your throat cut ear-to-ear."

Half-hearted humping ceases. Immediately. Animeid has scarpered — as has her dramatic act of mutilation.

Staring down with wide eyes, Nick slides back to his feet, pulls up his undies and trousers. Looks panicky.

"Christ," he mumbles.

I don't move. Don't speak.

Remain splayed on my back on the bed, tee bunched up around my bust and Antz Pantz hanging off the left ankle. Otherwise naked. My head is on the pillow, so I can see every-thing — no matter the half-darkness.

The dismay on Nick's face is priceless as he swings on his jacket.

Not sure if that's because the guy's sobering up — realizes what he just tried to do — or alternatively that he didn't get to go further. Had a bucket of ice lobbed his way by an otherwise passive, easy mark.

After he walks to the door, Nick pauses to lob back one last nugget: "Fucking freak."

I guess he was feeling the latter rather than the former.

Door opens, I hear Cold Chisel louder than before, door closes, the music is muffled, and I'm alone.

For a brief time.

"You all right?"

Animeid has positioned herself on the end of the bed, close to where Nicholas had pushed, shoved and waved his willy about.

"Yes," I say. Still don't move a muscle.

"Ol' Nick's not a particularly good shot with his pitchfork, is he?"

"He was drunk."

"He'll get his."

"I doubt it."

"How could you like someone like that?"

Close my eyes. "I don't know."

"He's a jerk."

"Then so am I."

The past. That's all it is. A dead currency. She runs fingers over the stubble of the buzz cut on her scalp, feeling the occasional scar, counts five different ones, each with their own story.

I'm staring at nothing, even though before me stands a gaily painted menagerie with an entrance that's a clown's gigantic, gaping maw.

Once did a school project on this amusement park, back in Year 7 while I was still at Gardenview Central.

Luna Park had been initially developed by an American showman named James Dixon Williams, who later returned to the States to help set up film studio Warner Brothers.

The place opened its doors in 1912, and looked like it had retained exactly the same amusement rides and attractions for seventy-four years — just continuously painted over and dolled these up to make them look new.

Anyway, I'm staring at Luna Park from a nearby public park, even though before me stands nothing I actually see.

Don't know when I become aware that there's a little black dog sniffing my leg. Little dogs were my soft spot, even if this example wasn't particularly cute — its face squashed in, pink tongue hanging out of the left side of a foamy mouth.

When I kneel over to pat the tiny beasty it jumps all over me, spattering clothes with fresh mud. End up laughing my head off on my back, while this terror ruins my wardrobe.

"You've made yourself a friend."

I recognize that voice.

Instantly sit up, attempting to brush off mud, joy forgotten. In the same moment sham a greeting.

Clair squats beside me with her own tentative smile. She's wearing clean jeans and a pink windcheater, and there's a leash dangling from her hand. Don't think I've ever seen her dressed so casual.

"Is she yours?" I ask, now diplomatically attempting to keep the dog at bay.

"He. Yes. Meet Jiji." Looking me over, the girl appears horrified. "Oh no. I'm so sorry about the clothes. He can be a real devil."

"It's okay — that was funny. French bulldog?"

"Mm-hmm. I thought you two would've met before."

Clair has made herself at home beside me on the grass.

"No." I shake my head. "Never actually been to your place."

Considering this for a moment, Clair shrugs. "I guess not. It must've been Hannah who met him. So, you're going in there?"

I realize she's pointing to Luna Park.

"No. Just window shopping."

"Window shopping? *Hah.* Funny."

Why is it, then, that Clair looks so damned sad? Having spiralled the leash around her right arm, she stares at it as her head sinks a fraction.

"You all right?"

Her eyes turn to me.

"I was wondering the same thing. About you."

I'm about to lie — it's standard procedure — but something in this girl's expression stops me. Clair and I have always been like-minded spirits, even if we shared a minimum of words. If anyone's going to understand anything, it will be her.

"I'm in trouble," I finally admit.

"I know."

"You do?"

"How long have you been mistreated?"

Again the fib gets caught in my throat as truth slides past, but I'd never heard The Problem called that before. Makes me feel like a stray about to be rescued by the RSPCA.

"Is it that obvious?" I ask.

"Nobody can be as accident-prone as you pretend to be."

"I guess." I study the undulating, whitewashed tracks of the Big Dipper ride. "A long time. It's been a long time."

"Your dad?"

"My brother." At that point, I somewhat violently shake my head. "But he's not the point. He's not the reason I'm moping round here today. Not really. I mean I'm used to *that*. I live with it. No, something else happened. There's this guy. My brother's best friend Nick. Last night, he... Well, what I'm trying to say is that Nick — *um* — I don't know. He tried doing something. To me. You know?"

Clair stares. Meanwhile, I notice her dog Jiji is licking his private parts.

"He *sexually violated* you?"

The girl almost spits out the two words 'sexually' and 'violated', and the reaction makes me remember she's from a very devout Christian family. How could I be so stupid?

"No, no," I assure her. "I mean, well, the arsehole tried but he didn't succeed."

Doubted this lame assurance was a success, since Clair continues to ogle.

"I swear I'm okay. Just sitting here thinking about stuff. I'm fine."

"Are you sure?" Clair finally manages to utter.

"Yep."

"Oh well, then, good." Just like that, Clair has a sunny expression on her face. "If there's one thing I've learned at church, it's that God created the majority of the human race for the specific purpose of damning them to Hell. But while God willed eternal damnation for some people, He also reserved salvation for others. We're all destined to go where He chooses no matter what our actions here."

Wasn't sure I agreed or entirely understood.

Sounded like my friend was trying to make me feel better — saying none of this was my fault — but, in the same breath, was she excusing Nick and Patrick's actions as well?

Predestination my foot.

Clair has gotten back to her feet, uncoiled the leash, and clips it to Jiji's collar. "Well, I must take this bad boy home," she announces. "I'll see you on Monday. And remember — you can talk to me any time. I hope you know that."

"Sure."

"You do?"

"I do. Thanks."

After the two depart across the lawn in the direction of the footpath by Lower Teslanade, I find myself gazing at that gaily painted menagerie again — seeing absolutely nothing.

Sad, I guess.

The following Tuesday, Saint Valentine's Day, I received a pink envelope that was pushed beneath the front door. There were beautiful drawings of passionflowers and red apples on the envelope, which smelled of fuchsia.

My heart skipped.

When I opened it, I found a card bearing a pastel-coloured picture of a young woman with long brown hair, dressed in a simple white robe.

She also had a halo about her head.

On the back I discovered the card was printed by the Catholic Trust, the painting by an artist named Giuseppe Brovelli-Soffredini, and the sitter was someone I'd never heard of: Saint Maria Goretti.

Making for a peculiar Valentine's missive.

Once I opened the card, however, things became clearer courtesy of big block letters.

HAPPY VALENTINES [*sic*] DAY YOU FUCKING FREAK!

The woman had used herself as bait — tossed off the rags to stand straight-backed, some kind of nonsensical pride in her posture, in the middle of the showroom floor downstairs. Surrounded by mannequins equally naked, littered like the slain troops of an Amazonian army — limbs missing and body parts without obvious owner. She'd shivered in the humidity as the soon-to-be-dead man approached, couldn't see his eyes beyond the opaque black visor under a metallic helmet, but knew well enough that they'd be washing over her, ogling, just as Archer crept up from behind, wordlessly grabbed the man's helmet, and twisted it to the right.

Snap-o.

Next day, Wednesday, I scored a black eye courtesy of Patrick's fist.

Batting slump my brother might've been in, but he could still throw a decent punch. Hit me so hard I first bit my tongue, and then bruised the coccyx when I struck terra firma.

Swam there in yellow stars aplenty.

I'd stood up to him for a change after he threw opinionated weight about, argued a trivial point (knew I was right), so he turned round and clocked me.

Hadn't seen it coming, though I should've guessed. Probably got blindsided by the recent good behaviour.

Through one fuzzy eye (my left, full of tears, since I had the right covered with my hands) I observe Animeid fluttering about him, squawking, already cottoned on that she can't help me. Finally pick myself up, hunched over in a defensive posture, still clutching my face, can sense Patrick hovering behind me.

As per well-trained custom I make up a story on the spot, tell him without looking his way. That I've been stupid, spinning a flashlight like a baton, and the thing has hit me in the right eye.

"Yeah, okay, that sounds reasonable," I hear my brother say. "It's your own fault anyway. I told you — don't you ever fucking speak to me that way again. I'm your brother. You know nothing. *Nothing!* Do you get it?"

All I get is that he's becoming angry and irrational again.

"Yes. I know. I'm sorry. Really sorry." The pain is settling down, thank God, and as I cautiously ease off fingers I have the beginnings of proper vision again. "What should I put on this? A steak?"

"Ice," Patrick announces, switching to charming and helpful. "Come on, then, Butter Fingers. Let's get you sorted out."

After getting home under an hour later, Dad believes the yarn. He also praises Patrick for quick thinking with the ice — but then insists on taking me to the local hospital anyway.

"You never can be sure about these things," my father assesses en route as he drives. "You might have given yourself concussion. Tossing torches. Really. You need to grow up."

The hospital staff know me fairly well by now, and as I check in one nurse cheekily deposits two cents about the clumsiness of adolescent girls being some kind of infectious complaint. "We might have to isolate you," she laughs.

The doctor was a young, reasonably handsome guy with salt-and-pepper-coloured hair and I'd never met him before. Name of Christopher Stein, whose merest glance causes me to blush. Anyway, this medico acts more circumspect.

After carefully checking the eye, he then goes through my file.

"Has the elbow healed properly?" he asks, holding up an x-ray of my left arm. The real reason I'd finished with tennis.

"Sure," I say.

"Any stiffness?"

"Sometimes. But it's fine."

I notice as he moves on to another x-ray, this one showing my right tibia in all its hairline-fractured glory.

The doctor is no longer looking at me. He's staring through the glass partition of this observation room, straight over at my father in the waiting room.

"Do you like horror movies?" he inquires.

"Old ones are fun."

"All those supernatural vampires, ghouls and bogeymen." Dr Stein then shakes his head. "The only real monsters are people." I can hear him exhale, long and loud and somehow sad.

"He thinks your father is doing this to you."

The announcement came from Animeid, who's positioned herself beside me. All three of us are now watching Dad, who obliviously flips through an ancient copy of *Vogue*.

"I'm clumsy," I say.

"Really?" The doctor glances at me. "You know you can report these things."

"My father isn't abusing me."

"Then who is, Mina?"

Animeid makes to punch my shoulder but there is no contact. "Just tell him and be done with it," she mutters.

"Nobody." I shrug. "It's all my own fault, I should be more careful."

Next morning, I had purple-and-blue bruising and a right eyelid that partially refused to open — no amount of cover stick was ever going to hide this trophy.

When I rock up to school, students I barely knew stare. There are commiserations from others, and Nicole laughs out loud —

asks if I'd been chasing parked cars.

As we enter 12E at 8:26 Sarah sidles up to pose the question I'd hoped to avoid: "What happened to you?"

I field the spinning-torch fib, a well-oiled device by this stage, one in which I dissed my own clumsiness and made light of the injury — and yet I can perceive she doesn't believe me.

"Who did this?" she demands instead. Anger right there in front of me.

"Me. I told you."

"Don't you dare lie to me," she responds, voice low in order that the other students taking their seats around us will not hear. Her left hand reaching up, Sarah almost touches the purple-and-blue region. "Jeez, Mina."

"It's nothing. Really." I gaze at her, conjure up a smile in spite of the pain I feel in my face and deep inside. "Only me being Mizz Clutz." I spin away from her then, and purposely collide with my own chair. "Ouch! — See?"

I hear Sarah sit behind me.

Keep my face impassive as I look straightforward at Mrs Williams while she calls our names — wasn't sure that Sarah believed me and know that Angelika, to my left, would at this angle be unable to see my prize.

Until art prac in a couple of lessons' time.

What on earth were they on about? What could they do thereafter? And why the Hell did she remain with these sorry excuses for humanity?

When that class started, Angelika surprised me.

I whizzed over from English lit, head down and fringe over my face, but could hear the girl hot on my tail. She followed me into the art room, chattering away like there was nothing wrong with my face. The fact I didn't pay attention to what she said made us relatively equal.

Anyway, a few minutes after the bell everybody starts getting out brown squares of linoleum and slapping them onto the big table we share in the centre of this room. I notice most people have almost finished.

Me too — was up half the night after getting back from hospital, hacking away.

Luckily had rediscovered tools under the bed. One red, plastic handle that had ten different blades, my favourite being the #1 that gave a fine cut — perfect for plumage. I used it almost exclusively this time.

Still have a few feathers to finish and the text to etch. Half asleep and yawn aloud, making Miss Vicks look over from some internal debate.

"Good God, Mina, what happened to your eye?"

I feel everyone stare anew and silently curse the woman. Before I can respond in more diplomatic fashion she has a hand up to silence the effort.

"Do you mind if I take a photo? The colours are beautiful."

When Miss Vicks decided to take a picture there was no stopping her. Having whisked out the Pentax 35mm, she reels off six shots from extremely close to my face.

"Done," she announces, winding the film. "Now, back to work."

I don't need encouragement. This is the escape I crave. So focused on my task that I shut out everybody in the room. Can hear bits and pieces of conversation, perhaps even snatches from Angelika steered my way, but I lean in close to my lino block, digging, scraping — and certainly not communicating.

Yes, this was a portrait of Animeid.

Something from inside our head, Miss Vicks had requested, and Anim deserved the attention.

I define a statuesque, if skinny girl; arms outstretched either side, the body coated in intricate feathers, the head surrounded by a wild halo of hair, and the face — blank. I know it'll come out as shadow when I print. Go so far as to cut her name beneath, exactly as she'd written it on the mirror those months ago, with the N, the E and the D back-to-front, like the bird-girl was semiliterate.

So tired, I don't think to reverse the name for the printing process.

I slap the lino with black Zephyr Block Printing Ink, put A3 paper on top, compress that with a dry rubber roller, and finally prise off the page.

Flip this to look at a slick, black print — still wet — on the table before me. Rove down from the dramatic hair, awry, through the orderly feathers and patches of naked skin, to the name.

Sitting clearly under the girl is the word 'DIEMINA', in caps.

Possibly I blanch — I've got no idea and wasn't in any fit state to pay attention to myself. The letters on the lino block are all I now see; perfectly legible in spite of the fact I'd forgotten to reverse them. Animeid had done that already, courtesy of a mirror.

Die Mina.

God, it was so damned obvious. She even left me clues. Was I stupid?

No one else could be allowed to see this. No way.

I grab the paper, screwing it up, toss the thing into a nearby recyclable bin. Take out the red plastic handle, attach my #5 cutter, and dig huge divots in the linoleum across the writing and the girl.

Don't quite know when I realize I've continued cutting right on off the lino — have travelled up my left arm. Stop what I'm doing; inspect the damage, feeling detached and somehow free of pain as blood starts to run across the skin, falls to the floor.

"Good God," Miss Vicks exclaims for the second time that day. "What's happened now? Mina? Your arm—"

"It's okay," my voice is saying, sensationally calm and collected like it's discovered a new form of autopilot. "Cut myself, but I'm fine. Silly me. Just need to give it a rinse. May I go to the toilets?"

"Of course you can! Don't you need the first-aid kit?"

"I'll rinse first, and then we'll see. I'm sure it's fine."

Honestly?

I feel my head is stuffed full of cotton wool, rammed in tight with a shoehorn, and someone's been liberally dressing the stuff with liquid Panic.

You'd never know it from the weirdly calm monologue I offered up, acting so blasé you ought to have me gift-wrapped and send me home to mother. Not that I have one, a mother, knowledge lurching with an enormous shadow now over everything.

Ol' reliable (the fringe) has fallen over my face, interweaves with a sense of detachment, of being on another planet.

Didn't need to see the walking route from art class to loo.

The toilets here are old — original cisterns installed when the school was first built in the 1930s. A space dark, damp and mouldy since it's lacked direct sunlight for fifty years. Russian-green tiling climbs the walls, buckled in places, with the random tile amiss. The linoleum covering the floor — appropriately a shade of mildew — curls up at the corners, breaks ranks at the seams.

I detour directly to a basin, ignoring the collateral damage. Wash my wound beneath cold water. Deeper than I thought, hurts like all hell. Yet somehow I find myself grateful for this pain — grateful to embrace the shabby thing. Able to ignore the festering sore right behind my eyes.

Dim it may've been in the bathroom, but once I push back the bangs, tuck hair behind my ears, I find myself before a mirror. Dusty, dirty, one that lost its lustre two decades before, but a mirror all the same. With a reflective surface.

I can see the anguish etched there into my face, like someone's used lino-cutting tools to prove their point. Am horrified by the sight, let my guard down, and now it comes seeping out. This has happened before, but always at home — closeted away in my room, out of sight of anybody.

Not here, I beg myself. Not now. Someone will see. No. *Please, God, no.*

I'm shaking all over; panting for breath, clench fists as hard as I can. Glare at myself in the looking glass, pleading and challenging both at once.

Not *now*.

Tension in my arms causing more blood to come a-gushing from the cut. It tumbles across skin, spatters over the floor, splashes the sink, redecorates my uniform.

A sensible part of me says it was my responsibility to clean this up, to do so quickly. Another rails and screams and bludgeons my senses. A third? She's right now laughing in my ear, just like Anim, about how pathetically over-the-top the second part is behaving.

I lean on the bloody sink in front of that hideous reflection, shaking all over, battered by vying complaints, suggestions, grievances. Anger simmers most beneath the lot, along with the gem of an idea that maybe I should've dug deeper. Maybe I should've done more damage, finished it. Easy enough to go fetch the lino-cutter, or break the glass before me and slice/dice with a handy shard.

So, obviously, any pretence toward composure was a thing of the distant past when Angelika chose to stroll in.

I catch her in the mirror early, her face over my shoulder, and in those wide brown eyes I see she's absorbed my accidental soap boxing of vulnerability, insanity, pain, anguish, and whatever else had overloaded frazzled senses.

The eyes stare initially into mine, and then run over the bloodstains on my dress, across the sink, to the floor. A comingling of shock and horror simple enough to read there.

I can't cope with that.

Having the madness inside me, hinted at by family and medicated once by doctors, hangs awful enough. Can't bear someone else seeing it, someone I actually like.

So I try not to see at all. I shove the heels of my hands into my eyes, pushing so hard it hurts, trying not to cry.

Precisely the moment Angelika surprises me.

She takes my hands in hers, easing away the fingers so I can see her up close and caring. Gently places my face on her right shoulder, close by her neck, in order to reach around and gift a hug — right there in the world's ugliest bathroom.

Hanging stiffly, arms at bay, trying not to share any more blood and partially frozen stiff by the mere notion of this show of affection, I realize I'm doing exactly what I tried most not to do — bawling my eyes out, overwhelmed by new emotions I've never before caroused with.

Even above the stupid, self-indulgent din I hear Angelika say, "Don't worry, it's okay," in the sweetest, most undemanding tone I think I'd ever encountered. "Everything will be okay. I promise. I promise."

How could I not return the embrace?

Hug her back for God knows how long, until the old terrors return, flitting across panicked mind, mocking weakness, and sanity reasserts. I push out of her grip. Hold up hands — a warning — to keep this girl at bay, since I can no longer look her in the face.

"I'm fine," I say, battling to get my breathing back in-line. "Fine." Still can't look at her. The kind of compassion I so recently witnessed would kill me now. "Just don't touch me."

"Mina—"

"I'm *fine!*"

"I believe you."

"Okay." Turn a circle, dumbly looking at the amount of blood about.

"Okay," I hear Angelika mirror. "Even so, I think you need

stitches."

"I'm fine. I told you."

"Not doubting you there, hon. But I don't think anyone has the miraculous healing power to fix an injury like that. You're losing a lot of blood."

Finally I have the strength to look at her from beneath my fringe, stifling anger.

"Okay." I wipe my eyes and snotty nose with the sleeve that isn't bloody. "Just don't you come near me, all right?"

Angelika actually smiles, albeit abstractly. "Fear not — I'll steer clear. Lots of practice. I'll go get Miss Vicks."

"One other thing." I actually feel light-headed and perch myself against a tiled wall.

Angelika has stopped in the doorway. "What is it? Are you okay?"

"No, I mean your uniform. It's a mess too. I'll make sure my dad pays to get it cleaned."

The girl glances down at her dress, as if she'd never noticed it before. "No need. I kind of like the shade it is now," she mutters, before speeding off to the art room.

Same day, another doctor — on this occasion a middle-aged quack with short, silver hair named Marissa Stirpe or Stirrup; I miss hearing it correctly since I'm so wrapped up in fainting just as Miss Vicks and Glenda Matlock hand-deliver me to this nearby clinic over on Steady Street, minutes from Mac.Duagh.

Once I revive she ushers me into a secondary room.

"Black eye as well. You're really in the wars, aren't you?" the doctor comments by way of small talk while sewing up my left forearm —four stitches' worth — and she sticks in one extra needle for a hefty shot of antibiotics.

Most of the time, I was barely there. Had a raging headache, skin felt clammy, the world wasn't as straight as it should be. I completely zoned out.

Even so, undercutting such bliss, I vividly recall what Angelika had seen in the bathroom. Could imagine the story getting round school like wildfire and by three p.m. everyone'd know what a loser or freak — couldn't decide which best applied — I really was.

An hour later, once I've partially recovered my wits, Miss Matlock chauffeurs me home in the passenger seat of a red Studebaker Commander Starlight. I brought along a bandaged limb, the usual souvenir. School had contacted my father and he is home to meet us, an abstract picture of concern.

We head straight to the lounge room, me deposited for safe-keeping on the brown leather sofa, surrounded by cushions, while Dad and Glenda begin a chin-wag on our check-design armchairs.

Having outlined my 'accident' with the lino cutter and the subsequent medical treatment, Miss Matlock ends by sliding a large envelope across the coffee table. I wasn't sure if it contained receipts, bills, a prescription, or a message of dire warning, but nowhere in the short conversation are the words 'self-inflicted' used.

Dad rubs the thinning black hair up on top of his head, looks tired.

"All these accidents," he grumbles, and then p'raps thinks better, sits up straight, and smiles at me. "You're a lucky girl."

"There's one more thing." This is the first time I've said boo-hoo since I went to the doctor. Guessing I must feel marginally stronger.

"What's that, sweetheart?"

"We need to get two uniforms dry-cleaned — mine and Angelika's."

Miss Matlock thinks about this but shakes her head. "I wouldn't know about that. I wasn't there when the accident occurred — Victoria brought Mina to my office."

"Fine, whatever the case."

Dad leans forward to toy with the sealed envelope on the table.

"Can you ask Miss Perks to pass on our gratitude? To this girl, I mean — tell her family we'll pick up the cost?"

"Certainly can."

"And hats off to both of you as well."

"You're welcome. We all care about Mina."

Glenda hops up with surprising vigour given her age, says swift goodbyes, and leaves.

I pretend to be asleep when Dad returns to the lounge room after seeing the woman out. He stands beside the couch, me watching him through mostly closed eyes so he won't know I'm awake and peeking. Pray that he'll reach over and pat my head like he used to do when I was a child, but he cut physical contact out of the equation a long time ago — I don't know why.

After a long while Dad leaves the room without any sign of affection.

I have no idea where Patrick is. Hope and pray he's dead somewhere, being snacked on by feral hounds.

During the night while I slumber (on and off) downstairs on the couch, Animeid puts in an appearance. The lamp is still on, over in the corner, but it gives off very little light — my visitor resembles a Balinese shadow puppet hovering above.

"Seems you have someone else to look after you now," Anim says in a voice pushing grumpy — but grumpy was how she always sounded. Nothing new here.

"I don't know what you mean."

"That girl. Angelika. With the K."

"We just met."

"Still."

"Have you been spying on me?"

"Does it matter?"

"No," I sigh as I lie there. "I know your real name now."

"Took you long enough."

"Anyway. All you do is criticize me. At least she gave me a hug."

"I can't," Anim mumbles, wrapping herself in wings. "I'm just like your dad."

Better to go it alone. Better. But where? Why bother? Nothing left. Even the rags embalming her were on a fast track to disintegration.

She feels itchy — probably this has less to do with the old hessian sack she'd appropriated as a camisole than the fact she hadn't showered in an age. The last time was a dousing under a water cannon alongside a dozen other people. Freezing water that knocked her back into a wall and dislocated the left shoulder.

She tugs the sack round and rips it at the front, in order to be able to move the neck more freely (as well as scratch a bit), but realises she tore it too far and now you could see her sternum bulging through thin skin above a shrunken breast.

I took Friday off school.

Missed the second half of *The Birds*, didn't want to write any more, and so to compensate I dug out VHS tapes of *Horse Feathers*, *There's No Business Like Show Business* and *The Masque of the Red Death*.

Gorged on Campbell's tomato soup (mixed with half a can of Pura milk), along with fruit and nut chocolate and salt and vinegar chips, while envying Vincent Price's voice, Mitzi Gaynor's legs, and Groucho Marx's fake moustache.

Might've forgotten all about the eye but my arm throbbed like buggery.

I took a couple too many painkillers, which left me vague and anesthetized, a feeling I actually enjoyed. Hid in my room pretending to be asleep (again) when first Patrick, and then my father returned.

Skipped out on dinner, woke up early Saturday and left the house to go have breakfast alone in Ackland Street.

After some self-indulgent eggs Benedict and two cups of strong coffee that make me feel far better than I should, I pay the bill and head in the direction of Sarah's place.

Maybe she lives just twenty-five minutes away on foot, but I can count on one hand how many times I've visited in the three years we've known one another.

Also isn't part of the relationship we share to drop in unannounced.

Should've called first, but the first few phone boxes I pass have been vandalized, a red phone is being used, and then I forget all about depositing twenty cents to forewarn the girl. Next thing I'm waltzing up the garden path to a double-storey house painted chocolate-brown, with strawberry-red fixtures.

Instead of my best friend, it's Sarah's mother who answers the white door.

I don't know her first name — called her Mrs Murray — and she has no idea how to label me. Scrutinizes my black eye and the bandaged arm in its sling, followed by the footwear I'd dared lay upon their coir doormat.

I suppose these particular shoes made her breathe a fraction easier — not ruby slippers, but expensive Italian ones Dad'd brought back from a business trip to Milan.

"Can I help you?" Mrs Murray asks, following upon said inspection.

"Um. Is Sarah home?"

"You're a friend?" Mrs Murray's voice has suspicion written all over it.

No, I'm Sarah's archenemy Kid Pathetic.

"Yes, I've been here before — we *have* met. I'm Mina, in Sarah's class at Mac.Duagh."

There was always the possibility she thought me some kind of defective vampire and was hesitant to invite me in, but she shot down this theory (in flames) via her very next sentence.

"Oh! Oh, of course, well then, of course you may come in.

Sarah, dear!"

The woman shouts this over her shoulder in a tone at once joyfully melodic, like some overexcited parakeet.

"We have a friend!"

She'd forgotten my name. Most people did.

Mrs Murray leads me along a tastefully lit passageway with hand-drawn sketches and studio portraits of family — Sarah, her younger sisters, parents, grandparents, a deceased hound with the text 'R.I.P.' engraved beneath — through to a billiards room that looks like it's been shipped over from the mother country, oak wood panel by oak wood panel.

We enter the back garden patio via twin glass doors that slide to either side. Having spotted Sarah forty metres away, black hair tied back, basking in the sun in a red and white bikini to one side of their very large swimming pool, I stupidly wave — having forgotten she's short-sighted without the prescription lenses she needs to wear while playing tennis.

"Sarah, dear!" Mrs Murray repeats. "A friend!"

Sarah partially sits up, supporting herself on one elbow. With the other arm she reaches up and removes sunglasses.

I already know Sarah has a superb body, sufficiently curved in all the right places. In this swimwear graced with white lilies she rubs in that fact like salt sprinkled on my butchered arm.

"Mina," Sarah calls back. "Hello, you."

Before deserting me on the redbrick patio, Mrs Murray inquires if I'd like a Diet Coke and nibblies. I guess the two offerings are supposed to balance out one another.

The moment she disappears through the door I wander over in my friend's direction. Now using both elbows to prop herself up, Sarah watches my approach with no expression on her face that I can see. She isn't frowning, anyway — just a partial squint because of the bright sun.

Eventually I squat beside her, close by the edge of the pool, while Sarah commences an inspection that reminds me of her mum. Using those closed Donna Karan sunglasses as a pointer, she indicates my arm.

"Ow. What the heck happened?"

"Accident." I'm focusing on keeping it mundane. Poke my finger into warm grass beside my foot.

"*Another* one?"

"I'm a walking disaster-zone. You should know that by now."

"What was it this time? That looks nasty."

"The price of art," I mutter.

Straight after Sarah rises to a proper sitting position, having bent knees beneath her, doesn't ask what on earth I'm doing here. Am glad of that.

Instead she's kick-started a monologue about the past week's activities, the ones I might've missed, especially the new Year 9 tennis club members — who were clearly hopeless.

As she speaks I remove shoes and socks, feigning interest all the while, and dip my toes in cool water.

Rolling over to face the clear blue sky, her titbits coming in a regular flow, Sarah finishes with simplicity. "So — tell me about your week, m'dear."

"Same as ever," I respond, rubbing my feet, studying toenails that need a trim. "Aside from battle scars, I mean."

Sarah sits up again, obviously restless, and this time comes a little close for my liking. "Isn't that the same as usual too?"

Feign I miss the canny remark.

"Just another of those weeks that flies by and leaves you wondering what single worthwhile thing actually happened."

Use the big toe of my left foot to prod at a floating leaf, but I then remember to flash a minor smile Sarah's way so she won't take me too seriously. Conjure up an additional throwaway question.

"And did you do anything exciting last night?"

"Mina!" Sarah laughs. "Don't you listen to me anymore? You think I babble too much?"

"No — why?"

"Why?" My friend compresses her lips, a kind of flat-line pout she does well. After that her head tilts to one side, the left. "I just finished telling you about last night."

"Huh." I think about that. Obviously autopilot was offline. "Really?"

"Really."

"Was it exciting?"

"No, nothing to write home about. I'd tune out too."

"Okay, then. Lucky."

"You could say that again. You're becoming such a dizzy-head." Sarah might be sighing, but she still prods me in the ribcage, something new for her.

I know she isn't being serious — I *know* that — but glare at her all the same.

The girl instantly looks away, her cheeks going red. My face feels hot too and I note some weird kind of anger bubbling away.

"Was only kidding," I hear Sarah say, an afterthought.

"I do realize that," my retort bangs back too quickly.

Have to calm myself, rediscover the numbness that usually prevails. Zen and all that meditation crap. Decide to settle on small talk.

"I saw the picture of the dog in there."

"The dog?"

"Inside your house, the beautiful golden retriever. You must miss him. What was his name?"

"I don't know," Sarah says.

"Oh, so this was someone else's dog? Your mum's?"

"No, he was mine. Or was it a she? I can't seem to remember." The girl appears genuinely perturbed.

"How about this, then. D'you remember the day we first met?"

"That's an odd question."

"From someone famous for being odd."

"I didn't say that."

I hold her eyes.

"You have before, but that's not the point. I don't think this is an odd question, and I also don't — recall, I mean. Isn't *that* weird?"

"Well, it was so long ago."

"Only three years."

"Three years is an eternity."

Meanwhile Sarah has got to her feet, heads to the swimming pool ladder, climbs into the water. Having kicked off backwards, takes a few lazy slaps of backstroke, and then dunks her head. Disappears for several seconds.

The moment I start fretting she pops back into view. Stands up, skin wet and shiny in the early afternoon sunlight. She's looking straight back at me as I sit there on the pool's edge.

"Don't you want to come in?"

"Can't." I hold aloft my bandaged arm. "Doctors are real Nazis about swimming in pools with your body-part in a sling."

"Ah. Strange, that."

"I think so too. I mean otherwise I'd hop in no worries — getting to wash the grubby bandage at the same time. Who needs a laundromat?"

"*Ew!*" Sarah looks reasonably ill. Even so, she remembers to broach the real topic on her mind, something I hope will be negated by years of practice between us. "So, when are you going to tell me what's the matter?"

"I don't understand," I lie.

"*Is* something the matter?"

"Nope."

"You sure?"

"Why should there be?"

"Well, I didn't mean—"

"What *do* you mean, Sarah?"

My friend shrugs. "I mean, that is, I kind of thought..." Voice speedily vamooses as her *hausfräu* mother carries over a tray with two tall glasses of Diet Coke and an opened packet of mint slice biscuits.

I thank the lady, which reminds Sarah to follow suit — even if she does so in gruff, forced manner. Hovering above us a few moments, Mrs Murray is either waiting to espy happiness once we tuck into said goodies, or expecting a tip. I can't decide which.

The bickies are great, but I detest Diet Coke. Stuff tastes unnatural. Still, I do attempt to look content once I take a sip. Sarah's mother has a satisfied mien, hands clasped together in front of her.

"Would you girls like anything else?"

How much do you tip a mum, I wonder?

"No." This was Sarah, and it rung final — service charge be damned. "We'll be fine, Mum. Go back inside."

"Very well." Heading toward the house, the woman calls out, "Just yell if you need anything at all. You too, Mina. There are plenty more snacks in the kitchen."

So the lady does remember my name.

"God, she's a pain," Sarah says in a low voice. Although still standing in the water, she's moved to this side of the pool, close by my soaking feet. "Such a typical suburban housewife. Nothing to her aside from the kids. So boring!"

"She looks happy."

"Really? I think she behaves like she's had a lobotomy."

"At least your mum's alive."

Silence might hang over us then, but I swear I hear applause and am sure Sarah feels slapped out.

While we whittle away precious seconds like this, poles apart from one another, I make out magpies in the next house over, a crunch as if someone stepped on a twig, a lawnmower further away. Don't know why, but I can't shake the sensation of being watched.

From Sarah's house come the very low sounds of a television. I'd almost swear this is *Neighbours*, but it isn't a weekday.

Don't know when I first notice my friend's hand on my knee. It was the left knee, closest to the pool and her right hand.

The girl looks up at me, peering past the hair I used to run interference with the outside world.

"I know about your mother."

Sarah said this in a slow, even tone. Once uttered and out in the open this way, she continues to arrest my eyes. Hers so vividly blue in this light, only slightly paler than the sky.

I have no idea what to say.

Am torn between hamming complete indifference, throwing back my head to laugh at the clouds, and/or punching this girl in a face far too close to mine. Thankfully opt for the first of these three choices.

Look at her, unfazed. "And?"

"And I'm so sorry."

"Pfft." I blow out numb cheeks, play the boredom card. "Water under the bridge."

Amazement swings across Sarah's features as she steps away from me, making small waves that radiate to either end of the pool.

"Why didn't you tell me?"

"Why? I don't know. What's the point?"

"Well — because I'm your *best friend*."

"So?" I actually pull off a minor yawn.

The girl looks still more amazed, an expression decanted into another ingredient. Horror has entered the mix.

"Mina — Mina, friends are s'posed to tell each other things like this. To help one another."

"Are they? Had no idea. Silly me."

I remove my feet from the pool and check the prune-like effect the H_2O has had upon my skin — before replacing the Italian slip-ons.

"Gotta go."

"Jesus."

Sarah is now several steps away, standing pretty much in the centre of the waterhole. She now looks scared as well as horrified. Likely amazement has scarpered.

"I don't know you sometimes."

I shrug. "Try all the time."

Anim's feathered arm has appeared and almost wrapped around my shoulders — yet it sweeps there without touching the skin.

"There's my girl," she whispers in my ear. "Tell it like it is."

"Mmm."

"You don't — you don't let anybody see inside — inside *here*," Sarah stammers, voice edgy, p'raps careering toward upset, her hand most definitely covering her heart. "Don't allow anybody to see what's happening, do you? The real Mina, right here inside."

"Oh, come on," I mutter, now irritated. "That's our little group all over, never being honest to one another because we're collectively running scared."

"God, what is wrong with you?"

"Dunno." I even have a vague smile to pretty up this quip.

Standing, I feel a sense of pride — proud for playing this game better than Sarah, one of its masters, no matter that I don't know the rules or what the game entails. Hurting people and ruffling feathers — *sorry, Anim* — was quite simply beginning to make me very happy.

And it's always good to leave on a high note, right?

"Have to go home now," I announce. "Things to do, people to see, blah, blah."

Just before I turn away I notice that Sarah has placed a second set of fingers on her chest, both hands right above the bikini. Something I also did once at the beach when a bikini strap broke in the surf.

The memory makes my vague smile turn into a grin. This is hilarious.

Sarah's face loses colour, turns ashen, and she mouths

something impossible to make out because it's hardly audible.

"Say again?" I sigh. "Can't hear you."

"You're breaking my heart."

That knocks some of the wind out of my sails.

I notice she's also breathing hard, possibly snivelling, as she turns away and dives into the water. Swims first one furious freestyle lap, and then another — faster, angrier — arms and legs churning pool.

"Obviously the strap held," Anim remarks beside me.

"It wasn't the strap, you know that. I can't leave her like this."

"You can, and you will — again and again. What, you think you're going to kiss and make up? Too late there." The bird-girl strolls over to the patio. "Coming? I doubt there're many more bridges to burn."

I relent then. Follow her out of the back yard, to the soundtrack score of Sarah's personal swim-meet.

On the patio it's Anim who lingers.

"Toodle-oo," she calls out with a strange lack of conviction. "Don't drown."

Once I get home (minus the bird-girl, who's vanished) I go straight to my room and jump on the Olivetti—

—But by eight-thirty, I needed to be in the city.

Didn't know what to wear, so I raided Mum's wardrobe — no one had had the heart yet to clean it out. Found a sequin miniskirt with the label Jean Varon, prob'ly something my mother wore in the '60s before she got married. I chucked on black tights, my pair of red Converse All Star runners, and at the last moment opted for a black t-shirt (hawking The Cure's 'Let's Go to Bed') that I'd won in a competition from WJAD FM and until then chiefly worn as pyjamas.

Having tied back hair aside from part of the fringe, I forgot earrings or any kind of make-up and headed straight to the tram stop.

March in Nede heralds with it the annual Moomba festivities that'd gone on along the Birrarung River since 1955. The name of the festival — an Aboriginal word — was rumoured to mean "up your bum" in the local dialect.

This year, the organizers had decided to kick us in the derrières a month early with this huge event dubbed the Moomba Mardi Gras.

Sponsored by one of the more prominent new commercial FM stations Radio Roo, this required the temporary closure of Swanson Street — a major thoroughfare through the city — for one night of open air music, raucous bands at various locations, new-fangled screens on which to play the latest Top 40 videos, and the overall drunken debauchery of close to a half million people.

The Moomba officials would never, ever make the same mistake twice.

Our group decision — here read Nicole's — had been to meet under the clocks at Flinders Street Station, a ridiculous one given that one hundred thousand other souls made the same plan.

Pushing, shoving and cajoling my way through inebriated people, increasingly battered and bruised, I located Clair and Nicole after a twenty-five-minute search.

Perfectly made-up, they were wearing identical multicolour, multi-tiered ruffle cotton skirts with a floral design, along with black-and-white striped, long-sleeve crop tops that Nicole pulled off with her exceptionally toned midriff, but Clair didn't.

Personally, I must've missed the fashion memo.

"Look at you," shouts Nicole above the din.

"What?"

"I said, look at you!"

"I'm looking," Clair says beside me. "And...?"

Nicole huffs. "Oh, forget about it."

I step closer to Clair, always the nicer one. "What'd you do today, Bear?"

"Nothing much. Made a cake, went for a walk, watched this drama, did a spot of gardening."

"And here I was thinking," pushes back Nicole, "that you spent the afternoon praying to Mecca."

Clair surprisingly simmers. "That's Islamic idolatry."

"Do people still use that word — 'idolatry'? Hah."

Realize this conversation's going nowhere nice, so I stick my beak back into the fray. "Where're the others?"

"Sarah cancelled." Sounding grumpier than ever, Nicole studies my footwear. "Who knows where D.D. is? We'll never find her — and what idiot cares? Let her find us."

"Shouldn't we wait?" bounces back Clair, causing a killer look from our friend.

"What — are you going to ask some dippy deity to find her? Oh God, please help us."

"No!"

"Then come on."

What happened thereafter bordered on madness.

Clinging to one another as we entered the crowd, Nicole was elbowed in the eye, my sore arm banged too many more times to count, and Clair almost ended up in a fountain. We'd planned to go to the banks of the Birrarung but were pulled in the opposite direction along Swanson Street, amidst people dancing, singing, shouting, screaming, bodysurfing, and lobbing about bottles of beer. I narrowly avoided stomping on a duck on a leash at the same time that Nicole fended off hippy fire-twirlers.

Somewhere around the statue of Burke and Wills we managed to turn a minor tide, thence heading in the right direction.

No way we'd discover Hannah in this chaos.

So it is that we eventually find ourselves at the underpass next to the river, an area closed off to traffic but rammed with revellers on foot and a Hell of a lot of ambulances. Three massive screens surround us, surprisingly playing 'The Love Cats' by

The Cure.

"Must've heard you were coming," Nicole decides in a loud voice that doesn't sound impressed.

There's a vacant gutter with a tuft of grass where the three of us make ourselves at home, exhausted and frazzled. That's when Nicole reaches into her Chanel bag to conjure up a bottle of Tia Maria and a pack of see-through plastic cups.

"Oh, you've got to be joking," Clair shouts above the surrounding noise. "No way I'm drinking!"

"Who says I was offering?" snaps back Nicole. "Everybody knows you're a Puritan."

I'm leaning forward, trying to read the label in the half-light. "What flavour is it?" I eventually ask, since Nicole looks annoyed again.

"Coffee and vanilla." The girl has poured herself a full cup, but then sizes me up while ignoring Clair. "So. I guess you want some."

Give me a coffee-flavoured anything and I'll drink it. I nod.

Seconds later I'm being handed a cup that's overflowing.

"Careful!" my bartender warns.

My experience with alcohol wasn't particularly esteemed. Had a couple of glasses of red wine with my mother the birthday before she died, and Dad allowed us a small ration of champagne every New Year.

Thick liqueur it may've been, yet I still pour the Tia Maria down my throat in about half a minute, and then lick lips. Greedily size up the bottle it came from.

Initially, Nicole looks scandalized and sweeps up her prize, clutching the bottle close, but then something resembling a crafty smile — I've seen that one before and should be alarmed — lifts the corners of her mouth.

"One more, darling?" she inquires, all innocence and ready to pour.

Of course I say yes.

Clair hasn't noticed this interaction — she's too wrapped up in video hits the size of a house.

"Don't listen too hard," Nicole says in her ear, "or they may play it backwards and you'll hear a soliloquy from Satan."

"Whatever," the other girl responds, still glued to the screens.

With a refill that touches the brim of the cup, I peer over at Nicole and the smudged make-up round her left eye. "So it's your turn to look like you've been chasing parked trucks."

I notice Clair smile even if she doesn't tear herself away from 'Kiss' by Prince and The Revolution.

"Hush up and drink," huffs Nicole.

We clink plastic chalices.

Two down.

The world is becoming a dithering thing out there, the music somewhat muffled. I blink a few times, attempt to clear the head.

Nicole has positioned herself closer. Fills my cup with panache.

"What's up between you and Sarah?" she asks.

I glance at my friend, away from the growing drink. "Nothing. Why?"

"Well, Clair said she wasn't happy when she spoke to her this afternoon."

"Really?"

"And when she mentioned you were coming tonight, Sarah cancelled."

"Oh."

"No clue?"

"None."

Nicole hands me the cup. "Here you go, m'dear."

"Ta. But I think I need to go to the loo."

"Drink up first."

Don't know when I realize that Nicole has taken me for a walk, supposedly in search of a toilet that wasn't crowded or filthy — and left Clair behind.

My brain takes its fine time catching up, and everything now seems to be swaying.

"Clair," I say, "we need to go back and get her."

"No."

"Sorry, what—?"

"I said *no.*"

Find myself pressed up against the brick wall of a shop near the station — how did we end up here? — with hundreds of people walking right on by, and all I can see is Nicole's malevolent expression.

"What—?"

"Just shut up one minute, Mina," the other girl declares in a low hiss I'm able to hear. "One single minute."

"Okay."

"You like gangster movies?"

"Um... I don't know," I admit.

"My dad loves them, especially *The Godfather* and *Once Upon a Time in America.* You're the movie buff — you must know them." This isn't a question; it's a snarl. "Well, you know what? Doesn't matter. This is the kiss-off."

"Huh?"

"You're out."

I look at her, say nothing.

"You're not one of us anymore. Got that? Unwelcome."

This time I pipe up. "But I—"

"Pfft. 'But I...' But *what*, Mina? 'But I'm one pathetic, sad little individual who's turned out to be Miss Freaky Shit'? 'Cause that's what you are. None of us liked you. *None* of us. Ever. We felt sorry for you. And sympathy has a time-limit."

"No, but I—"

"Oh, get a life. Look at you — the arm, the eye. And what decade d'you think this is? You're a shocker. An absolute embarrassment."

Don't care how drunk I am. The words are a direct hit. Mission accomplished, Nicole peels away. Disappears into the mob.

Alone. Again.

Having wrapped myself in my arms, I stumble off. Push blindly through happy people celebrating like this's the end of the world.

She'd motioned everybody to his place. They heeded without dispute, fanning out quietly, far enough away from one another to lay the trap, but still able to see each other in the darkness, amid falling water geysers that shower down from the smashed ceiling, courtesy of the torrential rain.

I'm vomiting against a dark brick wall that throbs azure.

Lift my head, somehow remember to wipe my chin, see only metres away the statue of Matthew Flinders — that explorer the nearby railway station was named after — whose plinth, beneath a bronze rowboat, has been redecorated with cans and empty beer stubbies.

The proximity of this monument means I've been throwing up on St. Paul's Cathedral.

Oh crap.

Rotating blue illumination splashes across the wall beside me, highlighting it every few seconds. A 1964 Ford Falcon police divvy van is the culprit, namely its enormous single light on the roof, but the vehicle has no occupants.

Just like those swirling flash patterns, my head is spinning, basic sensations — seeing/hearing — kind of skewed. There's an iron clamp tightened round my skull and I feel like shit, wonder if I'm going to die. Dying would be easier, easier than anything else.

Deal with that once you survive this ordeal.

Try to stand up straight, rubbing my face which is sweaty, am aware only fractionally of the noise around me.

The Mardi Gras in full swing. God knows what time it is.

Didn't wear a watch. Could turn around, look across the road at the Flinders Street Station clock tower — just don't have the energy and I'm running scared it may be after midnight. Won't be able to get home.

And now, the pièce de résistance — rain begins.

Should cover the tears I'm liberally shedding.

"Mina?"

I freeze. What, there's more to torment me? No way. I can't — won't — run into someone in this awful state.

"Hah! It *is* you, isn't it?"

Finding some cleverly hidden reserve of fortitude, I look up into a heavily eyelinered face I recognize in spite of blurred vision — it's that Liz Taylor/Theda Bara girl from the train, sheltering beneath a big, black man's umbrella and wrapped in her cardigan.

"Hello," I mumble. Wishing I could vanish on the spot.

"Margaret. Remember?"

"Mm-hmm." No sooner does this lacklustre response squeeze itself out than I keel over again, hands on my thighs, regurgitating very little except awful-tasting bile.

This girl has the gall to laugh. "Well, anyone can see you've been busy."

"Dying."

"Redecorating too, from the looks of things."

"Don't," I manage. "I think I'm going straight to Hell." That's when it dawns upon me. I glance back at her. "You changed your hair colour."

"You noticed?"

Margaret hands me a surprisingly cutesy handkerchief (it has rabbits in Gustaf Tenggren style) while touching up her gravity-defying red hair-do.

"Purple is old hat. Red's more my style — matches the train in which we met."

"Matches my shoes."

"The ones you just threw up on? Gee, thanks."

There were other people apparently, phantoms lurking over her shoulder also with brollies, but they cut only basic human shapes for me in this ravaged state.

"Who's the teeny-bopper?" some boy deigns to ask.

"A mate," Margaret says. "Sort of."

"Man, can we go now?" A female voice.

"Yeah, what's bloody well happening?" Another girl.

"Hold your horses!" — Margaret again.

Some genius lights up a cigarette close by, causing me to cough and gag, physically back to square one. I hear Margaret lay into the individual while I attempt to calm a fluttering stomach.

Around us the rain is falling lightly. Even so, I'm soaked.

"Reckon you can walk, hon?"

"God, hope I can."

"Here."

Without apparent thought Margaret offers her arm for support.

As I cling to this for dear life, we leave grass and hit slick cement. The crowd, I've noticed, has begun to diminish, but things are at a relative right angle that pushes me back toward woozy. I want to curl up on the ground, go to sleep. Never thought a rubbish-strewn gutter looked more devilishly attractive.

Margaret barks orders at someone. "Double-U — make yourself useful. Grab her other side. She's dying here. So am I!"

"Yeah, yeah, memsahib."

"Oh God," I finally comprehend as a second arm slips round my waist, "so embarrassing."

"Don't worry — think we've all been here," Margaret says.

"Some more than others," replies the voice of the additional person supporting me. A boy's voice. On my left side. Fighting grogginess, I peer up, since he's slightly taller and I'm sagging.

Take in short-cropped hair and a long fringe — better than

mine — parked over one eye. The other flaunts a glint of mischief when it chances to look back. This good-looking blond Satan is wearing a black suit jacket and stovepipe trousers, very 1950s or '60s, along with a black shirt and narrow burgundy tie.

Somehow he pulls off the ensemble.

Retreating into self-inflicted misery, I watch the litter-ridden asphalt jungle breezing by my feet.

"You really drunk," this boy checks, "or just prefer to be carried?"

"Shut up, Double-U — focus." That's Margaret, in my other ear.

"Drunk," I mutter. Think the comment needs clarification.

Having crossed the road, we're close to the station — which is crammed with the general public.

"What time is it?" I struggle to ask.

"Just after one," says the boy carrying me.

"Morning?"

"No, in the arvo — what d'you think?"

"Trains will've stopped running."

"Uh-uh. They're going all night, thanks to this silly street party."

Once we reach the top of stairs, pausing for breath and balance beneath an overhanging set of clocks, there's better artificial light to see.

Via this simple artificial luxury I first glimpse the girl with my rescuers — have no idea how I missed her before. Guess she looked nothing like her Mac.Duagh self.

And yet she did.

Angelika. With a K.

Hanging back a fraction, beyond the seriously cute boy — what was his kooky name? Dubble Ewe? Double-U? — with that entourage of people dressed in black I didn't know and couldn't see properly.

Wearing an A-line school dress, dyed black and cut way too

short above blue-and-white striped tights.

Has the warmest smile on a face otherwise so flawless it resembles white marble. Mostly. I say mostly because she has her eyes heavily made-up, nowhere near as intense as Margaret's, but still all dancing eyeshadow, mascara and liquid eyeliner, diagonal stripes that take flight from either side of the bridge of her nose and land above the ears, some of this smudged because of the rain.

Also wearing matt mauve lipstick — daring and fashionably spooky to my giddy mind.

"We're headed Northcote way," says Margaret, cautiously letting me go. "You going to be all right?"

As the other girl unfolds, Angelika slides in to my side.

Whispers in my ear. "Don't worry. I'll take you home."

Honestly? I'm that close to falling back into her arms right then and there. "Awesome," I answer.

Margaret reminds me she's still here by clearing her throat.

"Girl never listens to a thing I say," Angelika laughs. "You tell her."

"Okay. I'll be fine — now. Thank you."

Strong enough now to present this red-haired girl with a half-mast smile, along with the boy with the strange name.

"Both of you."

"Anytime." The boy winks.

"Speak for yourself," Margaret complains, even if she's also smiling. "Ta-ta."

As the group heads away, I find my left hand linked with Angelika's right. Look at her and she looks at me. Don't think I ever felt so relieved.

"C'mon, Mina," she says, brown eyes holding mine with a grip stronger than the fingers. "You've had a long night. God, I know I'm bushed."

When I awake, I'm blessed with a raging headache. Find us lying inches apart on the same mattress, in a bedroom I've never seen before.

Don't really recall how I got here — just flashes of a train ride, the rest napping with my head on Angelika's shoulder and my hand interlinked with hers.

Even now, asleep, Angelika holds my hand.

She's apparently remembered to clean the make-up from her face, and snoozes like her namesake — an angel. Calm, at peace, beautiful. Looks like the girl doesn't dream.

While I'm scared to be in this kind of close proximity with anyone, at the same time I'm so unfathomably happy. With my free hand I reach up to touch the very short black curls around one ear.

Nothing sexual about this. At all. We're both fully dressed. More a tranquillity, a feeling of absolute contentment. Or something like that. Couldn't really put my finger on it since these were brand new sensations. The only drawback?

The headache.

A sense of responsibility also kicks in — Dad will be worried.

The last thing I want to do is wake this amazing girl who's already done so much for me without my asking, so I gently unfurl the fingers, free my hand, and put my legs over the side of the bed.

The movement hurts more than I expect. I need Panadol — quick — and I notice I have specks of vomit on my pants.

My runners?

Look slowly about, and then crouch quietly on the floor. Find them tucked neatly beneath the bed.

I stand up straight; take a pained moment to examine this large room.

Her space. From the burgundy velvet drapes (drawn) to a book collection similar to mine — though Angelika's steered into the gothic territory of Mary Shelley, Bram Stoker and Edgar Allan Poe, along with Radclyffe Hall.

On a bedside table next to the sleeping girl are a half-empty glass of water, a blister-sheet of Microgynon, and the paperback of Robert Louis Stevenson's *Strange Case of Dr Jekyll and Mr Hyde*. A bookmark shows she's read about a third.

Across the walls, attached helter skelter, there are colour snapshots and black-and-white photo booth close-ups, mostly people with bouffant hairstyles and unrecognizable faces covered in make-up. I recognize my hostess in one of these, sporting the same look as the others. Big brown eyes give the game away, but in that picture she has wild black hair down to her hips.

In an Edwardian period double-wardrobe, Angelika has jammed clothes, mostly black from what I can see — since the doors are open — but also some white as well.

Next to that is another antique, a dark-stained cedar dresser covered with stacks of cosmetics, hair utensils, kooky hats, and a long, black wig on a polystyrene mannequin head.

In a collection of plastic milkcrates are vertically stacked records, while tapes are lined up in alphabetical order above my head along a picture frame skirting board that circles the room.

There's a huge poster that dominates one wall, cast in basic monochrome: 'Christian Death' this announces in bleeding typeface, a rudimentary crucifix and crossed bones beneath that.

Enough snooping.

Take one final look at the girl asleep on the bed, smile slightly, and then sneak out the door.

Find myself in a passage lined with framed photos, mostly black-and-white, of exotic locations and extraordinary people. One of the standouts being a three-masted sailing ship cutting through a raging, stormy endless ocean.

Don't smell the sea, but instead a mix of citrus and lavender.

Walk along this hallway, past a big Holy Mother Mary & Jesus planter vase stuffed full of feathers (peacock, lyrebird, ostrich, emu), an 8 mm Bell & Howell Zoomatic movie camera on a low table, and a small bronze statue on a pedestal — a young girl like one of Edgar Degas' ballerinas, straight-backed, almost boyish, holding a scimitar in her right hand and two chunky keys in the left — positioned next to a big, wooden front door.

This door has a small, inset window of colourful stained glass and a large, broken antique wagon wheel hangs beneath.

There're two deadbolts I'm luckily able to unlock without keys. Check about myself one last time to make sure I haven't woken anybody, and walk out to a chill morning that's overcast.

On the veranda wall, beside the door, is affixed a shiny nameplate that reads Portinari, while beyond the porch a huge front yard awaits.

The house, I come to understand as I walk along a footpath, duck under a palm branch, weave around a ladder next to an apple tree and glance back, is an aged Italianate number with a minaret and a crown motif set into the cement at its peak.

I open a simple cast-iron gate, hop down three steps — and find myself on an exceptionally average suburban street I don't know. Lined with elms and gums, it's devoid of traffic so I go out onto the road itself, look both ways, and ponder with a splitting migraine.

Which way is home?

Two relatively young police officers — one man, one woman — and a lady my dad's age minus a uniform are in the lounge when I arrive.

I'd been clued-in by the white, sharp-nosed 1973 XB GT Ford Falcon Coupe squad car parked out front, with its two bubble lights astride a pack-rack on the roof, to either side of a pair of small loudhailers. Had assumed the cops were off intimidating neighbours who'd lately indulged in raucous parties with loud disco music like 'Funky Town' that my father hated.

Yet here the police were, standing in uniform by our French windows, while my father talked with the plainclothes woman — dressed in a particularly plain paisley blouse — over on the couch.

The two of them, sadly not the officers, have cups of tea on the table beside a fat manila folder. Their conversation stops dead the moment I set foot on the threshold.

All four individuals look over. I stand there, injured arm in its sling and the other tucked up behind me, not knowing what to think or say. Looking like death warmed up I'm sure, am grateful I'd picked up a small bottle of Listerine beforehand.

Dad's the first to speak.

"Thank God — I was so worried about you! Where on earth have you been?"

"Stayed at a friend's."

"You could have called."

"Sorry."

"You must be Mina," the woman on the sofa interrupts us, possibly picking up on my significant exterior markers like the eye, the arm, and the inability to speak long sentences.

I nod in return.

"Sweetheart," my father says, his voice strained, "these people are here to see us. They have some... concerns."

"Yes," agrees the woman. "I do think it would be best if we spoke to your daughter in private."

"Is that necessary?"

"Quite. Senior Constable Copeland, here," she indicated the male police officer, "will take your statement, Mr Rapace. Is there some place else where we could chat with Mina?"

"What about?" I'd found my voice.

"Well, let's sit down and talk about that. Mr Rapace?"

"You should stay here. We'll head upstairs to my study."

"Fine." The woman stands, followed by my father. "Could you give us, say, a half hour?"

"Certainly." Dad peers at me, worry in his expression to bookend the strain in the voice. "Shall we synchronize watches?"

The quip falls flat. I'm the only one to smile — he loves that joke.

After the two men leave, we three girls have the lounge room to ourselves. The funny part is no one speaks for about half a minute. More surprising? I'm the one to break the silence.

"Would you like some tea?"

I've directed this question to the police officer over by the window. She smiles the smallest amount, shakes her head.

At which point the older lady again sits. "Would you like to know why we're here, Mina?"

"Sure."

"Wonderful. I'm Christina Mariell — a social worker with the Department of Human Services. That's Constable Andie Summers over there."

"Nice to meet you."

"And you." This woman Christina pats the couch, the space beside her. "Would you sit down with us?"

"Sure." So I do.

"We're here because we received a copy of this from your local hospital — all patient records for one Mina Beatrice Rapace." She points to the open folder on the table that has apparently been shown already to my father. I recognize hospital letterhead, illegible annotations, Photostatted x-rays.

"They're here to bust your dad." That was Animeid, lurking behind the couch.

"He didn't do it," I say.

"Do what, Mina?"

"What you think he did."

Christina smiles. It didn't seem a particularly honest smile, but there it was. "And what would that be?"

"I don't know." I shift on the sofa. "My arm hurts. Can I go now?"

"Give us a few minutes. Our watches are synchronized, remember?"

At that, I glance her way. "Okay." At least she has a sense of humour after all.

"Now, you do understand that doctors, nurses, police and school teachers are legally obliged to report suspected child abuse?"

I'm still looking at her. Don't nod or shake my head at that one. Guess it's the young medico that's ratted me out. What's his name? — Dr Stein.

"In this case the complaint was anonymous."

"Meaning that doctor at the hospital."

Christina shakes her head.

"Meaning I don't know. You see, any person who believes — on reasonable grounds — that a child needs protection can make a report to the Victorian Child Protection Service. It is the Child Protection worker's job to assess and, where necessary, further investigate if a child or young person is at risk of harm."

It sounds to me like she was quoting from Scripture. The words were coming out but there was no feeling in them. Might as well have stuck on a record.

"Bit of a windbag, isn't she?" Anim decides.

"Mmm."

"So shall I go on?" the woman asks — apparently having decided the 'Mmm' was steered her way.

"Mmm."

She doesn't notice my little dig.

"Well." Having placed hands together, she steeples the fingers. "What we have here is a situation that I believe falls into our jurisdiction. The injuries alone suggest this. Repeated fractures, bruising, sprains, abrasions, and so on, at least over the past ten years. It's all there, well documented. I haven't researched further back, but I'm sure we'll discover a longer history of systematic violence. Am I right to assume this, Mina?"

I look down; studying the flora that decorates a shag-pile carpet my father recently had laid over the slate flooring. Don't think I've seen it before now.

"What kind of flowers are they?" I ask, pointing with my

right hand.

"Hibiscuses," speaks up Constable Summers, for the first time.

"A hideous thing." The social worker shivers. "Anyhow, where were we?"

"Me being accident-prone," I said.

Christina ignores me.

"Now, this situation is usually attributable to one of two parents, and given that your mother is sadly no longer with us yet the injuries have continued, I think we can safely rule her out of the equation."

"Mum never hit me."

"I believe I'm saying precisely that. However, unless you can convince me otherwise," here the woman taps the folder on the table, "I intend asking these good officers to take your father in for further questioning."

"Intend to."

"I'm sorry?"

"Intend *to*. You should be using the infinitive."

The woman sighs. It's a long, ugly, drawn-out sound. "You're obviously a smart girl, Mina."

I don't take this as a compliment. The comment was a cross between sarcastic and patronizing.

"Why play dumb and put up with this — this —"

"Shit?"

"Yes. That." The woman kicks back. Studies me with an expression I cannot read.

"You can't blame my father."

"Let's leave that to the courts, shall we?"

"He doesn't touch me."

"Sadly true," agreed Anim, somewhere over my shoulder.

"Then what do you call this? And this? And this?" Christina tosses page after page onto my lap, each one defining some injury or other. She dealt them out like oversized playing cards. "For

God's sake let us help you. Stop being a coward. This man is a monster. You want him to do this to other people?"

I glance sideways at her. "*Who*? I don't exactly have any younger sisters. Or brothers."

The way I said the word 'brothers' must've sounded off. A night-light claps on in this woman's eyes as she observes me.

"Where exactly is your brother today?" She's rifling through a notebook I hadn't noticed before. "Patrick, right? Two years your elder?"

These don't seem to be genuine questions and I continue to watch the paperwork flip between fingers.

"Patrick J. What's the 'J' for?"

"James."

"Named after the father. Figures — how sweet. And repeating Year 12, I see. Any resentment there? He must've been angry to watch you play catch-up. Getting better grades too, I bet."

I bite my lip, say nothing.

Christina looks straight at me. "It's not your father, is it?"

Avert my gaze to Constable Summers by the window. Surprisingly, the police officer inclines her head.

So I turn back to Christina. "No. Not Dad."

That evening I lie on my back for a while, on damp grass in the yard, watching Anim soar and fly circles high above in the moonlight. Wish I could do that too.

Above the sounds of gurgling water and the pound of that rain, there's footfall on the back staircase, the one leading up to this level. Floorboards groan. Down the corridor, closer to the stairs, Taylor lifts his pistol. He gives the woman an awkward wink, and then aims at some place she can't see.

Taylor has a ringside seat and he's silently laughing.

40 tossed in 146 times

While I had no compulsion to ever again set foot at Mac.Duagh in front of Nicole and Sarah or even Angelika, I took the next week off school because I wasn't able to easily get there.

Spent a few days at my uncle's place in Subere, a tiny country town thirty-four kilometres east of the CBD, out near Belgravia.

This wasn't by choice.

The social worker, Christina, had interrogated me regarding relatives after my father was escorted to the local police station Monday morning.

I didn't understand the legal tsunami that swept up my brother and father both.

Dad was charged apparently because, in the state of Victoria, 'It is an offence for a person who has a duty of care to a child to take, or fail to take, action that has either resulted in harm to the child, or has the potential to cause harm.'

This is the spiel I read in paperwork Christina shoved my way when she discussed my future — or seeming lack of one.

"The maximum penalty ranges from twelve months' imprisonment to two years' and Mr Rapace may be found guilty. Do you have any immediate family we should talk to? With whom we might make arrangements?"

She got hold of my uncle Dam at his place of employment (he didn't have a home phone), made these arrangements, and dropped me off at his place since he'd come straight home Monday afternoon.

Funnily enough when Christina met my uncle at the front gate, I could've sworn I saw recognition pass between them.

The only other time I'd been this far out of Nede was to ride Puffing Billy back when I would've been about eight.

Damiel Rapace (we called him Dam) was a rake-thin, forty-year-old child who scored his own double-storey weatherboard holiday house in the country — a birthday prezzie from our grandfather — when he was twenty-five. This was a place now in complete disrepair, buried in a jungle of fern trees, stringybarks and a couple of towering ghost gums.

The old letterbox, by the entrance to a narrow footpath, had a corroded number 146 attached and was bent diagonally on its waist-high pole. The week I lived there, this had a resident huntsman spider the size of a human hand.

Out the front of the house, under overhanging tin roofing, sat hundreds of handcrafted staves interspersed with uncovered oil paintings and spray-painted boards. My uncle's handiwork, through which he tried to make a living — but Dam earned most of his cash teaching art part-time at the local TAFE College.

He had so much junk inside the house that he had to push some of it out the window in order to make space for me in one of the bedrooms. My mum, a cleanliness freak, would've fainted if she'd seen the cloud of dust that arose first time I lay on the mattress.

But I liked Dam. A lot. Mostly quiet, thoughtful and artistic, he was the complete opposite of my dad. Liked to talk about passions to anyone willing to give him the time of day, yet never pushed his opinion on anyone.

I always listened since he gifted me the same.

Anyway, here I was being dropped off like a sack of unloved potatoes, and the moment Christina drives off he gives me a hug. I try to return the service but the effort is exhausting. Completely out of practice — not that I'd ever really had experience in the first place.

Dam then leads me to a cluttered kitchen and pulls out one chair.

"A red V-back diner manufactured in Chicago," he says.

Takes me a moment to realize he's discussing the seat.

"1950s. Upholstered in burgundy vinyl, with piping plated in silver. A great diner chair for restaurants and homes with a tough fourteen gauge, all-welded steel frame that'll last for years. The comfy deep-padded seating is an additional bonus, making it a certainty to become your favourite chair."

I peer at him. "Dam, did you rehearse that speech?"

To which he chuckles. "I did. Want to road-test it?"

"So long as it stays indoors? Sure." I flounce into the chair, shift round my bum a bit, and nod. "Not bad."

"I was angling for a more glowing tribute."

"Give me time. Me and the chair're getting to know one another."

"Tea?"

"Any coffee?"

"Sadly only instant stuff that's gone hard in the jar. I think it's ancient."

"Um. Tea is fine."

"Tea it is. Earl Grey's okay?"

"Yep."

Going over to the sink and shoving a lot of dishes in order to be able to fill his kettle, I hear Dam sigh.

"So. This Christina woman tells me Jim's in with the police for questioning."

"Mmm. She told me they might keep him there for two years."

"Worse-case scenario. You don't sound overly concerned, Min."

"Still sinking in. Do you know her?"

"That social worker?"

"Christina, yeah."

"She looked familiar. Can't place it." He shrugs, and then — having switched on the gas — turns to face me. "How're you really coping?"

"I'm okay."

"You seem to be keeping your chin up surprisingly well."

I know he's concerned, and I'd never lied to Dam.

"That's the worse part," I admit. "It's like all this crap is badgering someone else. I don't care what happens. Wish I did. But I don't."

"Must be some kind of relief — concerning Patrick, I mean."

"No, same. I feel nothing."

"I get it."

This makes me look back up at him. "Do you?"

My uncle nods.

"To tell the truth, it wasn't easy growing up as Jim's younger brother — though he appears to have been more careful than Pat. Didn't break anything. I think people like those two walk a double-edged sword. They thrill to the sense of domination, bullying people, yet live in terror of being discovered. They do this because, at heart, they're weak. Why didn't you tell anyone?"

"Couldn't. I was scared."

"Fair enough. I didn't tell either, till I was twenty-one. Told Dad over beers at the local pub — the alcohol loosened up the tongue. If there was one thing Dad hated, it was bullies — did you know he ran the eastern suburbs chapter of his trade union for something like forty years? So he was seriously pissed off with Jim. One reason I inherited this place when my dad died, and your dad got sweet F.A."

For several hours after I arrived we sat together in that kitchen — since it was marginally cleaner and had more space — listening to records and chatting while we drank consecutive mugs of Earl Grey.

The music was, like Dam, eclectic — veering toward minimal, electronic, experimental-sounding.

He walked me through LP covers that included Cabaret Voltaire's *The Voice of America* (released by Rough Trade in 1980, according to the liner notes on the back), self-titled records by Yellow Magic Orchestra (Alfa Japan, 1978) and Primitive Calculators (Slow Drama/Au Go Go Records), and *The Complete Studio Works* of local outfit Whirlywirld (through Missing Link, released just this year).

The Voice of America is the one that stands out. It's bleak and crunchy, overloaded with distortion, decay and warbled sweet nothings.

The truly zany thing about living in that squalor — boxed into a ramshackle house in the middle of nowhere, with intimidating vines, rodents and insects all about — was that it ended up being the most fun I'd had in ages. For starters, spending hours circum-navigating each precarious pile of books and comics (dozens were stacked around the place), and then leafing through individual tomes that caught my fancy. Some were mouldy, others stained and torn or missing covers, but there was stuff here on just about everything.

Other times I'd spread out on the lumpy divan with a dozen cushions about me, feeling like the Queen of Sheba while I watched a flickering black-and-white TV, rolling picture and all, that switched to double vision when you turned channels to the ABC.

School was the last thing in mind and Dam never reminded me to do homework. He seemed happy for the company and hanging out, since he'd taken the week off work.

That is, until Friday morning.

In my uncle's household there was a single rule and that rule only — not to interrupt him once he embarked on an artistic binge. No sight of one until the end of the week, at which point he suddenly locked himself up in the studio. Didn't emerge at any point on Friday or the following day.

Leaving me to, *well*, me and my errant thoughts — not the best prize in the world.

I took a long walk in the evening along pitch-black streets and heard a lyrebird somewhere nearby that I couldn't see. Went into the tiny town of Subere to a takeaway where I bought fish (two pieces of flake) and chips, plus a couple of large pickled white onions, and they wrapped these in newspaper.

When I got back I placed half in an old Tupperware container on the doorstep to the studio, but didn't knock or make an unnecessary ruckus.

Back in the main house I flicked through the channels, squirming with the poor picture and a lack of choices — even Ivan Hutchinson's choice for his Friday Family Movie on HSV-7 was a fizzer: *C.H.O.M.P.S.* was basically the story of a kid who creates a crime-fighting robot dog (looking like Benji) with a circuit board tossed inside. Yawn.

By Saturday morning I'm climbing the walls.

Animeid hasn't show her face at all — possibly here we're outside her flight-range — but another girl does, one sensible enough to have caught a train, though she claims to have ridden by horse.

When I open the front door I find this individual standing there in tight black jeans, black t-shirt and black cardigan on an overcrowded welcome mat. She's also just stopped sucking on a white-and-green striped wax paper straw that leads to a 600 ml glass bottle of milk with brown stuff floating in it.

"Hi!" Angelika-With-a-K says in a chirpy voice, smile swinging alongside.

"Hey." Call it surprise that tempers my response.

"Rode here to rescue you from woop-woop."

Crossing my arms, I lean against the doorframe. "So — where's your white steed?"

"Let me think now. *Horsing* round?"

"That's plain sad."

"Agreed. I would've rung, but Miss Vicks said they didn't have a contact number."

"No phone." Could actually feel my body beginning to thaw. "Nice drink?"

"Lovely. I went to the milk bar down the hill and asked them to add chocolate Quik." Straight after the comment, Angelika sucks the bottle dry.

"They still believe in service hereabouts."

"So I hear. I sent you a card."

"You did?"

"On Monday, when I saw you weren't at school."

Have no idea why but I'm actually smiling as I still lean here — guess I do so since I'm taking in everything about this beautiful person before me.

"Oh."

"A nice one, with a picture of Luna Park."

"I wouldn't know — was too scared to go near the letterbox."

Angelika returns my look with suspiciously slit eyes but a mischievous grin. "Why?"

"Spider in it. *This* big." I have to stand up straight to hold out my arms, indicating an arachnid the size of a desk.

"Then your uncle must have a pretty huge letterbox."

I thought about that. "Actually, it's possibly more like the TARDIS — from *Doctor Who*, I mean. You know?"

"I know. Small on the outside, humongous within. So," the other girl has now crossed her arms, a reflection of my earlier stance, "are we going to continue gas-bagging out here all afternoon? Not that I'm complaining — it's beautiful weather. Or are you happy enough to invite me in? I won't bite — promise. And I certainly don't have six legs."

"Eight. Spiders have eight. And how do I know you aren't hiding any?"

"I'm the one with the crucifix, remember?"

"Oh yeah."

I gnaw at my lower lip, shyly smiling same time. Prob'ly comes across as coy but isn't intended that way.

If she notices, Angelika is kind. Patiently stands right where she has all along, but does have that same question.

"So — may I come in?"

"Oh! Sure." I quickly squeeze to one side of the entrance, yet the girl remains on the doorstep.

"You need to say it."

"Sorry? Say what?"

"Come in."

"You're kidding."

"Not at all," assures the other girl with mock indignation. "I'm a traditionalist."

"Traditional something, that's for sure."

"Excuse me?"

"You and your vampire stuff." Can't help rolling my eyes, but I do laugh. "All right, all right. Please enter of your own volition, steam, whatever."

"Never thought you'd ask!"

Still, my arm blocks entry.

"Be careful. This house can be a death-defying obstacle course."

Having hefted a large backpack over her shoulder, Angelika nods, so I drop my arm and she steps past me, over the threshold, into a jam-packed living room.

"Wow," she says. "You weren't kidding."

"What's in the bag?"

"Essential goodies — wooden stakes, holy water, silver bullets."

"Thought you said there was no such thing as werewolves."

"We're in the country now."

Having found a small area of carpet incredibly free from bric-à-brac, the girl squats down, unzips the bag, and produces Arnott's Chocolate Teddy Bear Biscuits.

"I hear they're your favourite," she says, handing up the packet to me.

"Holy cats. How'd you know?"

"Gotta keep some secrets," Angelika now murmurs, head down as she removes more of the content: Two bottles of Bailey & Bailey Heaven's Gate Moscato — "These need to be chilled. Your uncle *does* have a fridge, right?" — along with several cassette tapes, a smaller bag of clothes, one box marked L'Oreal Super Blonde, and a make-up case that has taken up a third of the interior.

I notice each of her ten fingers has a silver ring, and three sleepers are back in an ear apiece. She settles back on haunches, wearing her Doc Martens, and appraises me in return.

"My turn to stare."

"I wasn't staring."

"Then neither am I." She checks me over. "Eye is looking good."

"Cheers."

"Arm?"

"Okay."

"You're not just saying that?"

She gets me better than I realized. "Um. No. Honestly. Least it's healing."

"Cool. Now — where is it?"

"Where's what?"

"That elusive fridge we need." She holds aloft the two bottles of wine.

Half an hour later I've attempted my second guided tour for Angelika, this time of the premises (including said refrigerator), along with overgrown front and back yards. It takes more vim than you can imagine.

So we both collapse afterward in the marginally orderly lounge room.

That's when I wind out a query that's had its hook in me.

"You're a Catholic, right?"

Angelika laughs. "Don't think I ever answered the question."

"Yes or no?"

"My, aren't you pushy? *Yes* — well, my family is. Me, I'm rebelling against all that hocus-pocus."

"Yet still you wear the crucifix."

"To deter vampires. I told you."

"Anyway." I push a loose coil of hair behind my left ear. Was thinking of a Valentine's card I'd recently received. "Do you know of a saint called Maria Goretti?"

Angelika nods, but she has an unusual expression, one venturing toward grave. "I know."

"And...?"

"She was born almost a hundred years ago."

"Go on."

"What's the big deal?"

"No biggie, just curious."

"Uh-huh."

"All right, well why was she — what d'you call it, 'sainted'?"

"Canonized is better."

"Canonized, then. Though makes the people sound like cannon-fodder."

"You really want to hear this?"

"Yes, sorry."

"Not the prettiest story. Might put you off your dinner — it sure makes me ill remembering."

"I'll live."

"Lucky you."

"Count my blessings everyday. On one hand." I hold up five fingers for effect.

"That many?" responds Angelika, aping a close inspection. "Well, don't say you weren't warned."

"Duly noted."

Angelika smiles — marginally. "Maria Goretti was an Italian virgin-martyr. You know what that means?"

"The virgin or the martyr?"

"Both."

"I know. Pretty obvious."

"Right you are. Well, she was also one of the youngest canonized saints."

"How old?" I ask.

"Eleven."

"Wow, that is young."

"Which was when she died from multiple stab wounds inflicted by an attempted rapist after she refused to submit."

That painting on the card. A dead eleven-year-old.

"Mina? You okay? You've gone pale."

"I'm okay. Just sad."

"It's a sad story. Most saints have awful bios. The Catholic faith is full of horror stories, sadly most of them not perpetrated by well-intentioned if often deluded martyrs."

I look at her again. "If your family's Catholic, how do they put up with the poster on your bedroom wall?"

"Huh?"

"The one that says 'Christian Death'."

"Oh *that*! That's just the name of a band. I'll tell you something funny, though — you know the name of the lead singer? Roz Williams."

"You're joshing? Like Rosyln?"

"Exactly!"

We burst out laughing, effectively killing the morbid moment.

"That's unreal," I manage, wiping my eyes.

Angelika has taken to watching me like a hawk, her laughter reined in. "Now you sound like them. Sarah and Nicole."

The comment slaps me, miring further mirth.

"Have they said something?"

"About you?"

"Mmm."

"They don't talk to me, remember?"

At this point Angelika rises, scuttles through junk to the kitchen, makes some noises, and returns with a bottle of wine and two ceramic mugs.

One of these has Tink on it, a pint-sized character in a green Peter Pan outfit (I know this because *Princess Knight* was my number one cartoon when I was a kid), the other an off-white beige thing that likely is stained that colour rather than intentional.

She wipes both cups with a dirty tea towel illustrated in Scottish highland tartans.

"Nice to see your uncle's growing his own penicillin," she muses. "At least the alcohol should counter any ill-effects."

"I don't drink."

"Really? Then what d'you call last Saturday night?"

"Stupidity?"

"Okay." Angelika has already uncorked the bottle and poured. She hands one cup, the one with the anime angel, my way. "To stupidity — long may it reign. Go on. Be a devil. I pinched this from my mum's wine rack and she swears by it."

Of course I take a sip. This wine is tart but fruity — far better than the Tia Maria.

"Not bad?"

"Not bad."

"Don't get too excited."

"I'll try."

"Now, is there a stereo in the house? I'd go looking, but I fear I might become lost."

"You need to cart about a machete," I agree. Point over to the curtained space beneath the TV. "Under there."

"Is it safe?"

"No spiders I know about."

"Can I play something?"

"Sure, so long as it's not Whitney Houston."

"Nope."

Angelika holds up a Maxell cassette with tiny writing on it I can't read even at the short distance between us.

"PiL — live at the Seaview Ballroom, 21st December, 1984."

I shrug. "Is that supposed to mean something?"

"Hopefully it will," Angelika says, having drawn the small

curtain, checked for bugs, and inserting the tape into an Onkyo cassette player. "Public Image Ltd — John Lydon's band after the Sex Pistols broke up."

This sounded familiar. "Think I read about them."

"They're not exactly obscure knowledge, especially in the British press. Anyway, this is from their live gig at the Seaview Ballroom in St. Kilda — a place I'm going to take you to tonight."

She pushes play.

And thereby plays me.

Have no idea how she convinces me to undertake the chore I do next.

Spending two-and-a-half hours in an attempt to learn (from scratch) how to master basic make-up techniques — and, after that, extending this rushed know-how into the excessive style she and Margaret slap about their eyes.

"Still don't see why you can't do this," I say at one point, having lost hold of the memory of when I actually agreed to the idiocy.

"You need to teach yourself."

"Why?"

"Everyone does — that's what nurtures individualism."

"Huh," I grumble. "You make it sound like some kind of silly tribal initiation ceremony."

"Well, I won't always be here to act out the role of underpaid beautician."

"Slave driver, you mean."

"Even slave drivers earn a salary."

"Still."

"You don't have to do this."

"I don't *want* to."

"Then why are you, Mina?"

I nut over this, lose the thought, and shrug. "Because you told me?"

To which the girl sighs. "You don't always have to do what

40 tossed in 146 times

people say."

Not that this stops me.

All the while I worked I was supposedly also being educated — here read drilled — in music by the likes of PiL, Bauhaus (just one song, 'Bela Lugosi's Dead'), The Birthday Party, Siouxsie and the Banshees, Cabaret Voltaire again (an up-tempo release called *Micro-Phonies*), The Smiths, Sisters of Mercy, Soft Cell (two tracks, 'Tainted Love' and 'Sex Dwarf') and, yes, Christian Death.

Joy Division the girl skips.

By turns encouraging, cajoling and critical — in that exact order on both fronts — Angelika lazes on the settee next to the stereo, my Queen of Sheba position, sipping at wine.

My intake is more significant and possibly accounts for a third of the time wasted in front of the full-length mirror I'd dragged out of some dusty corner.

One time I ended up resembling a panda, on another occasion something painted by Picasso.

"Very 'Weeping Woman'," Angelika surmises.

Meanwhile, I continuously mistake which song is by who as my personal deejay shoves in, stops, ejects, and hits fast-forward and/or rewind.

Eventually my hacking away at cosmetics and musical ineptitude appear to bore Angelika.

She relinquishes the music, stops watching my wayward artistry, and goes instead to grab that packet of L'Oreal Super Blonde I'd seen earlier on.

Shows it to me in the reflection, a sparkle to her eyes.

"You were saying you liked your blondes."

I stop dabbing with a cotton bud. "When?"

"Last Saturday, on the train. Half asleep and raving about drop-dead Hollywood starlets — Lana Turner, Jean Harlow, Veronica Lake. Other people I can't remember."

"That does sound like me," I admit.

"Right?"

"But didn't I mention my idols Brigitte, Louise or Mitzi?"

"Maybe. Can't remember."

"Louise was never a blonde."

"God forbid. By the way, you missed a bit — there." The other girl points to stray mascara, but then grabs another cotton bud to do the rescue work. "You also said you wanted to change your hair," she says while wiping.

"I was drunk as a skunk."

"More than drunk, you were hammered."

"My point."

"Exactly." Angelika sits back to survey my face. "Going to have to start again."

"Can't you do it for me?"

"Better to learn how to do it yourself, young grasshopper."

"Whatever."

I wipe most of the gunk off, becoming annoyed.

"I don't even want to go. Can't believe I let you convince me. I'll stand out like a fly on rice with or without shit on my face. I don't belong."

"Who belongs anywhere?"

"Easy for you to say."

Now I really was furious. I toss a pile of cotton buds, balls and tissues into a plastic bag, tie a knot, and toss it across the room. Lose sight of the thing in a ramshackle, darker area of my uncle's living room.

Angelika has watched its departure. "That time capsule over there will one day puzzle archaeologists."

"I don't care. This is ridiculous."

"Are you angry at me, the bag or yourself?"

"Can I pick on all three?"

Angelika surprises me then.

Comes from behind, kneels, wraps arms about my neck. Her gaze finds mine in the reflection and somehow deflects the fury. Don't know how she does it — I'm just not angry anymore.

"You don't have to come tonight. Or ever. Certainly not because I say so. But I think you need fun," she says, close by my ear. I feel her breath there.

"I'll come."

"Because I say so?"

"Because I want to."

"Good." She kisses my cheek, sits back. No triumph on her face — more satisfaction. "Nice to know you don't feel corralled."

I catch her eye in the looking glass. "I wrote about you once."

"Really? Some diary scratching — 'Met this flaky new girl at school'?"

"No. A story."

"A story?"

"You were the hero."

"There's a change. When can I read?"

"Are you joking?"

"Don't think so. Why?"

"Nobody reads my stories."

"Nobody?"

"Well, nobody I like."

Angelika has a smile she's trying to repress. "So I *can* read it."

"*No!*" I stare over my shoulder with disbelief.

The girl stares back, narrowing her eyes. "Well, that's unfair, dashing hopes."

"I can't remember giving you hope."

"Oh, well, why bring it up if you're never going to let me take a look?"

"I don't know."

"Neither do I."

"Shouldn't've brought it up at all," I say.

"Amen."

This is when the other girl again holds aloft that box of bleach, like she's advertising the product on the telly.

"So, anyway, moving right along — I'm sick of having black hair. Going to bleach away for blonde-bombshell status. You're welcome to join in the silliness."

Which accounts for the fact that two hours later — after I put finishing touches to make-up I'm finally kind of happy with — Angelika drags me to the bathroom with a disposable towel (one of Dam's, since I figure all his discoloured, threadbare numbers are disposable).

She's already done with her hair. This was a mix of orange, yellow, beige and silver because she'd gone directly from black.

Turning on the shower, the girl admits we're long overdue washing mine, which does no end of good for my confidence. In the process of rinsing out the bleach I end up with bleeding eyeliner and mascara that spirals down my cheeks.

Once a bucket of water — with a diluted substance called magic silver white — is poured over my head, the remainder of the make-up job is pretty much destroyed.

"Going to have to redo your eyes," Angelika says, while roughly towel-drying my hair. I hear her laugh after I give out a groan. "The make-up bit gets easier. Soon you'll be able to do it in forty-five minutes flat — Oh shit."

I pull off the towel. "What d'you mean, 'Oh shit'?"

Angelika pushes sheepish. "Maybe we left the bleach in too long?"

Wiping grime off the bathroom mirror, I stare at myself. I have a platinum halo that glows under the naked 100-watt pearl globe. "Jesus. *That's* white."

"You think?"

"Verily."

"Also next best thing to jelly texture-wise. Maybe take a couple of days to get back into better shape, but till then there's not much we can do with this except tie it back. Um... I think I murdered your fringe too. Oops."

One reason I ended up with all surviving hair brushed

sideways, left and right, into tight, snowy braids that defied gravity either side of my head.

Looked like Pippi Longstocking — an effect Angelika decided to enhance by stuffing hidden pipe cleaners inside the braids, and then hairspraying the lot.

"I have handlebars," I mutter, once I start reapplying make-up.

"Oh good. Gives me something to hang onto — hold it! That reminds me... We now need to employ our secret ingredient."

"There is one?"

"Yep."

"I'm not going to regret this too, am I?"

"Doubt it. Hold your horses."

"Them again?"

The other girl delves into her black case, rummaging through canisters, bottles and flasks, and then holds up a squat glass jar of something whiter than my hair.

"Ta-dah — professional foundation greasepaint, as used on stage."

"What are we s'posed to do with that?"

"Put it on our faces before we do the eyes."

I stare at her, horrified. "I'm not intending to indulge in any theatre-sports tonight."

"Mina, clubbing is all about theatre."

"Really? I'm thinking we'd be better suited to a circus."

"Pithy," Angelika deadpans. "You want to give The Bearded Lady a shot? — I'm sure I have hair tonic somewhere. And here I was convinced you liked your effective disguises."

"Oh for goodness' sake, just get on with it."

At least she does this job for me — I wouldn't know where to start. Using a sponge, she has the foundation covering both our faces and throats inside five minutes.

I blink a few times, praying none of this gets in (and stings), but upon viewing Angelika I forget my woes and instead guffaw

— she looks like a marble statue with spiky, piebald hair.

Having already started marking out her eyes with a grey pencil, the girl side-glances my way.

"Belaboured make-up first, merriment second," she grumbles in a manner not unkind. "We're late. Besides, you should see yourself. Zounds."

Ninety minutes later we pack up everything and rinse out two empty wine bottles. Unlike my encounter with Tia Maria I feel light-headed, silly — and happy. Likely the company and the music helped.

I'd kept a glass of wine for Dam. Covered it with Gladwrap and stuck the cup in the fridge. It's about six p.m. The make-up and hair took the better part of five hours, aside from a quick peanut butter sandwich we scoffed down for lunch.

Ad hoc mathematician that she is, Angelika has calculated it'll take two hours to get into the city, and another hour to St. Kilda. Time to have another speedy snack and a drink, she says, before heading to Locomotion, or Loco — the name of the night at the Seaview Ballroom.

This idea now terrifies me.

Number one, going to a club like this, and number two, rocking up with white handlebar hair that has wires in it and would likely blind somebody or attract errant lightning.

My face, beneath this improvised antennae, is deathly pallid, my eyes done up like Nefertiti to match the prominence of those brows.

I'd even drawn in a teardrop beneath my left eye, something to mark my own touch, but when I looked into the mirror all I saw was pretension and poor draftsmanship.

Still see it now as I take one last glance in the looking glass.

Apply some purple lipstick while I'm tempted to go run and scrub off all of this crap. I mean, I don't even have a fringe to skulk behind.

"You don't need one anymore," Angelika says, leaning beside

me, like she read my mind. "The face is mask enough."

As we leave, I write a quick note to Dam letting him know where we've gone.

Don't know if he'll be annoyed or find the letter before I come home — there's every possibility he'll be stuck in the studio for another few days. I heard his record was a week straight.

Wondering about the best location to leave this missive in all the chaos, I decide upon the television — place it partially on top, with the note itself dangling over the screen. Obvious enough, but I need a paperweight.

Right nearby is a heavy-looking hardback so I grab at it, and as I place it on the TV I notice the title, *Catholicism & Saints for Dummies*. Wish I'd seen it before — would've meant I didn't need to quiz Angelika.

"Ready, Pippi?" she asks, behind me.

"Ready as I'll ever be."

"Then saddle up."

"Oh God," I groan. "Think I've had enough of the horses to last a lifetime."

The ride into the city from Belgravia, aboard a 1960s Blue Train, was bizarre.

Kept forgetting what I was wearing, tried to rub my eyes on countless occasions (stopped every last moment by my companion), and wondered why people stared before I remembered what we were wearing.

Dark outside the carriage but brightly lit within.

Every time I glanced at Angelika, found I had to force myself not to laugh. I mean, she was drop-dead gorgeous so far as I was concerned, but also didn't look real — with those large, dark brown/black irises occasionally reflecting the light she came across as less human, more *Blade Runner* Replicant.

Halfway through the trip a group of boys — mid-teen, rough-looking bogans — got on at Box Hill. One of them hung over the back of his seat ogling. Obviously was multi-skilled since he also fielded a running commentary to his mates, basically defining our appearance in brave new words.

Since Angelika was wearing a simple burgundy, velvet dress with tights and high-heels while I had on stuff I'd borrowed from her — a short black skirt, Joy Division black tee — I had to wonder if this juvenile hoodlum was more impressed with our heads, or my legs.

Before we left Angelika had given me a wrapped present. "Early birthday," she announced.

Inside was a pair of sensational tights, from Japan the girl told me. Clear nylon on the thighs, but with black cats enveloping my calves and knees.

"Ooooo!" calls out the boy down the carriage, a wavering yodel like the beginning of a 1950s B-grade horror movie. "The Bride of Frankenstein! Dum-dum-dum-dum!"

"You get used to it," Angelika says, looking bored. "Which one of us do you think the kid's referring to?"

"Have no idea. I just wish he'd get the film references straight — Elsa Lanchester had much longer hair, piled up like an afro'd beehive." I blow out my cheeks, and then sigh. "Then again, I guess we're all guilty of labelling."

"Time: T minus 3 minutes."
    "Service Module, third stage S&A arm permit to close."
    "Closed."
    "Friedrich Lang Space Centre, third stage S&A armed."
    "Armed."
    "Propellant 1, vehicle fuel tank press open."
    "Open."
    "Fuel umbilical purge to open."
    "Open."
    "Space Centre, vent 1 heater control exit."
    "Exit."

"Space Centre, vent 2 heater control exit."

"Exit."

"NSC reports spacecraft is go."

"*Die Frau im Mond* spacecraft is go."

"Friedrich Lang Space Centre—FTS bat one and two heater controls heaters off."

"Off."

"Prop 1, pressurized first stage LOX tanks to relief."

"Pressurized."

"Propellant 2, top first stage LOX to one hundred percent levels."

"Up and down, 100 percent."

"Time: Ninety seconds."

"Space Centre, hydraulic external power to on."

"External."

"Time: Eighty seconds."

"Range Control Officer, report range go for launch."

"Range go for launch."

"*Die Frau im Mond*, you're go for launch."

(Captain Aire & Commander Rapace in unison) "Roger."

We pit-stopped in the city for a couple of refreshments.

Place was called the Fat Black Pussycat. According to my tour guide (yes, we'd finally swapped roles) this was a famous Nede jazz club — and Angelika inspected their wine-list to the dulcet turntablist sounds of Herbie Hancock's 'Rockit'.

Hastily ordered two flutes of Bollinger champagne as well as a beaten-up aluminium ashtray.

Angelika puffed away on cigarettes like a chimney and yet, on one occasion, made a dry remark about how smokers annoyed her. Later, during the second drink, the subject turned on a slippery dime to pretention — and before I knew it the girl raised eyebrows and was pointing out herself as prime example.

Both moments, and others, coerced me to laugh, but while indulging in the second round I inhaled bubbly the wrong way

— had never guzzled the stuff before — making me cough, hack and splutter. Actually, the hack likely came from second-hand smoke I was breathing in.

The cigarettes my friend chose were called Churchman's No. 1 and they came in a rectangular, green and gold cigarette tin with a hinged lid.

"I smoke these because of the insanely cool collectors' cards you get in each pack," she confides with a lipstick smile that this time sits sincere rather than intending to split my sides. "Each has a full set of fifty Churchman cards and 'tis my ambition to own them all."

Dangling the cigarette from the corner of her mouth, Angelika reaches into her small handbag and produces a handful of cards tied with a rubber band, at the same time that the speakers belch Louis Prima crooning 'If You Want to See Some Strange Behaviour (Take a Look at Man)'.

"These are the pièce de résistance — the 1935 Well-Known Ties, Second Series."

I slide my glass to one side to gape at the surface of the table as the girl first wipes it dry and then spreads several cards with, yes, a full-colour neck-tie in the foreground along with the English public school it belonged to cast in a background of monochrome.

"Ah. Ties. Wow. You're right."

I'd say I'm astonished.

That's when Angelika sweeps out the cigarette in her right hand and fixes me across the table. "Says the girl who collects comic books."

She has a lopsided grin while swirling that cigarette in the air in a slow motion stop-start that mirrors the opening repeat loops to Miles Davis's 'Pharaoh's Dance', and before I know it I'm laughing again.

Whenever I did laugh, Angelika's eyes sparkled and she'd keep the commentary flowing until she had me hysterical.

Everything combined to compliment the surreal flavour of the moment: our ridiculous Halloween make-up, madcap hair, the expensive drinks, and the steady flow of jazz-related tunes that bent barriers.

I don't know what the other people there thought of us.

We were hardly jazz-heads but the place was a low-key affair patronized by locals who rarely lifted fixed gaze from the heads of their beer.

On the next train, from Flinders Street to St. Kilda, I lean my head against the window and gaze into a passing blackness I fail to actually see. A story is formulating, and when one does it's difficult to drag myself back to reality, no matter the circumstances.

In my mind, astronauts Aire and Rapace exist minus make-up and alternative fashion palette.

They're dressed in futuristic metallic/plastic space suits possibly designed in the 1970s by comic-book artist Jack Kirby in screwball cahoots with Keith Wilson, the space suit designer on *Space: 1999*, and Hardy Amies — same job for *2001: A Space Odyssey*.

Angelika and Mina's outfits are matching gold.

Minus helmets (wearing a tight skullcap apiece the same colour as their space suits), the two are strapped side by side in the command module. Since lift-off they've reached an altitude of sixty-eight kilometres at a speed of 6,164 miles per hour, and the G-forces have them pinned.

"*Très* ouch," astronaut Mina decides.

"Nothing exciting to flap over," astronaut Angelika — her commanding officer — says over the intercom. "I'm going out for another check. Over and out."

"How about coming in for a swim?"

That's when I realize Sarah is one of four fellow space-travellers in the seat behind Angelika, dressed in a flight suit coloured metallic-blue, and it dislodges me from self-indulgent reverie.

Having taken my preoccupied silence in stride, Angelika has out a small mirror to double-check every millimetre of her face and then attack her eyes with a futuristic eyelash curler, swaying train carriage be damned.

Without looking she remarks, "You've left some of your forehead on the window," and upon turning I spy a white smudge on the glass there. "Give me a moment, and I'll fix it up."

The Seaview Ballroom was in fact recent window-dressing for the once-venerable St. George Hotel, originally established in 1856 on the corner of Fitzroy and Grey Streets opposite the train station. The huge four-storey replacement building — later constructed in 1880s boom-era Nede — was of a Renaissance Revival style, with a circular corner tower and a turret.

Cornices, pilastered bays and a balustraded parapet punctuated the whitewashed exterior. I'd been past the place plenty of times — took the tram this route to get to Ackland Street and Deveroli's — but never before set foot inside.

The building smacked of faded Victorian glories, was likely home to alcoholics, junkies, other intransient, homeless people — and looked like it'd collapse at a moment's notice or a mistimed step.

When we arrive at about eleven o'clock, there's a queue around the corner, most of these prospective patrons dead ringers for the kind of people I expected to live here — and we hear a muffled doof-doof-doof from somewhere above.

Straight away, Angelika nabs my hand and leads us to the front of the line, by a deep entrance portico.

"What're you doing?" I ask in a low voice. "This is cheating."

"I call it blagging. Look like you own the place," she whispers back.

"Will they even let me in with these antlers? We're underage."

"Course they will. Get that sultry pout of yours happening."

"*What* pout?"

A brunette girl at the door, standing next to a six-foot-wide bouncer who until now had been busy taking cash and stamping arms, waves us over. She's done-up in a black, silk lace dress showing ample bosom, with make-up and long false eyelashes on her face making my effort seem like it was nothing.

"Love the look, sunshine," she says, following the course of my braids from far left to far right. "Come on in."

"How much is it?" I'm asking Angelika, but the doorgirl shakes her head.

"On the house."

The two of us squeeze past disgruntled customers and enter the building over a mosaic floor, past marble wall panelling and people dressed in torn jeans, stockings, motorcycle jackets and archaic ballgowns.

That's when the real noise hits, above the chatter.

"This way," my new friend says, still leading by the hand if not the nose — up a set of wide, marble stairs, squared Corinthian pillars, beneath a chandelier. On the second floor it's more crowded, dark, and the music drowns out virtually everything.

Turns out this is the dancefloor, a huge space with bracketed ceiling beams dividing the room into windowed bays, though the windows had been covered over, offering no scenic view. Anyway, a haze of smoke blankets all.

Across the floor before me tenuous silhouettes pogo to a fast, punkish song with lyrics about being too inebriated to copulate.

"Welcome to Loco," Angelika shouts in necessarily loud voice close by my ear. She also hands over a glass of white wine — where'd she score that? I hadn't glimpsed a bar — and then is gone. Vanishes into the swirling artificial ether like a ghost.

Leaves me standing there, lonely, wondering what I should do.

"Hello, you."

This voice surprises me from behind, so I swivel and come close to taking out Margaret's left eye — she cannily judges antennae trajectory and ducks beneath it.

"Think you need a license for those things," the girl grouches in a voice I only just catch above the musical din.

"Hey," I say.

Not sure how to continue, so I raise my glass in salute. Usually this comes across debonair in movies but in my case it's plain awkward.

Margaret looks the same — same cardigan, same skirt, same boots, same eyes — but is wearing a different t-shirt (this one says 'Red Lorry Yellow Lorry') and her hair's a shade of cerulean blue. Without further hesitation she reaches over and hugs me in front of everybody.

"I had no idea you came here."

"First time," I manage. Find it hard to breathe since she squeezes so hard, I'm overwhelmed with embarrassment, and desperately trying not to spill wine.

"You look great." The girl has unshackled me to lean back and appraise my hair. "Wild."

"The blue looks cool."

"Matches your shoes?"

"God. I'm so sorry about that."

"Hey, it was funny. You here with anyone?"

"Angelika," I announce.

Surprisingly, this girl hardly reacts — she looks distracted and I don't think she's heard.

"Me? I lost my date," she shouts while peering through smoke. "Listen, I'll be back, but just in case — it's cool to see you."

She kisses my cheek and does the same thing as Angelika. She vanishes.

I'm beginning to wonder if I'm stuck in some kind of revolving door, where people are desperate to escape my clutches.

Meanwhile the music has switched from the sound of someone throwing up to British singer Danielle Dax.

All around these people laugh and chatter and give each other embraces, no idea how much that means to someone who's missed out on basic human contact — aside from fists and wayward sexual organs — most of her life.

So I finish the glass of wine, force myself to enjoy the tingly sensation it imparts, and head off in search of the bar.

Once I find that, I'm stuck waiting for quarter of an hour (no queue jumping this time), order two glasses of white without being asked for ID, and head to a convenient corner where there're marginally less customers.

Hear the muffled pounding of 'Sex Dwarf' by Soft Cell on the other side of Victorian masonry.

Having gulped down one drink, I set the empty glass on a low, crowded table, and try to take fine time with the second. Fat chance. Think I bought it for Angelika, but I have no idea how to find her and am incredibly thirsty. Figure I'll make my escape after I finish this drink — am on edge, feel like a sore thumb, over-tired.

Wine finished quicker than Speedy Gonzalez, I perch that glass with the other, steady nerves, and beat my hasty retreat. Join the flow of pedestrian traffic headed downstairs, try to be as innocuous as possible by not blinding a single soul.

Since the denizens of this packed staircase resemble a zoological garden of styles, I like to believe my snow-white aerials and me are not so obvious. Heart pounding much faster than the languorous sounds of 'Bela Lugosi's Dead' above, I know I need to flee quickly but this is impossible to squeeze through. Taking one step at a time, two flights in half-darkness feels like the journey of a lifetime.

Closer to the bottom than the top someone pushes me and I virtually collide with two girls heading up. They have fresh, clean faces I actually know: Clair and Hannah. We stare at each other for a handful of seconds, time enough for my fool's paradise — that they wouldn't recognize their Mina beneath the face-paint and bleached hair — to crumble.

And then the throng shoves us apart again.

Have no idea what the girls are doing here. Loco is the last place they ought to be, but I guess the same rule goes for me. Am in such a hurry that I almost trip over another girl's wedding dress.

Head straight into the bar downstairs. At least I think I'm downstairs. By this stage I'm so confused and overwrought that I have no clue where I might be in this labyrinth of a mansion. Will admit to being freaked-out — don't want anyone I know seeing me like this, couldn't stand the gossip to be all over school.

But there's a counter and a bartender so I order myself another wine and hover close to a wall where the music from above is less oppressive.

Did they make me out? No idea. Hannah had that oblivious look she always wore, but something in Clair's eyes, a glimmer, smacked of recognition.

Then again — did it matter and do I really care? Wasn't this a cheap thrill I felt? The girls looked completely out of place, at least I had on camouflage. Anyway, have my head down now so no one will again be able to see my face. Just in case. Guess I forgot about the landmark hair.

"Here you are."

Margaret pushes in front of me to lean against torn wallpaper on plaster.

"Thought I recognized the feelers. I'm starving — you wanna come and grab something to eat?"

That's when I realize exactly how famished I am too, a sensation stronger than my racing heart. In fact the silly organ jumps in the back seat.

"There's somewhere open at this time?" I ask.

"Yep, just round the corner."

"Thought you lost your date."

"He can find me. C'mon."

She takes my hand and tugs me through a horde by the entrance, so that in moments we're passing a long queue, patches of vomit on concrete, and two semi-conscious junkies in the gutter.

Head into a glaringly bright Seven Eleven, an oasis in this urban sea of decrepitude, thereafter to rove the aisle of chocolates. While I drunkenly covet a Mawes Bar, forgetting what my appearance might look like in this kind of illumination, Margaret decides she's desperate for a hot dog.

Start to tuck into the nougat, soft caramel and milk chocolate bounty I just paid for, waiting for Margaret — who's busy asking the cashier behind the counter whether he has cheese sauce. His negative response causes her to swear profusely.

The combination of what Margaret uttered draws my attention, and when I look up I see two shapes beyond her, worrisome ones that rummage through nearby fridges.

"Uh-oh," I say in a low voice. "Metalhead bogans — all the way up from Frankston, I should think."

"*Ahh.*" She hardly bats a false eyelash.

The guys choose that moment to turn about. Both young yet haggard, fourteen pushing forty. Expressions that remind me of pictures I'd seen of Java Man. Empty eyes above tight mouths that turn into unbalanced sneers once they spot us.

Pretend I haven't noticed and gaze at a suddenly enticing ceiling. Still, I can make out Margaret taking her time, searching pockets to pay for the hot dog, while the boys the other side of her snuffle and grunt.

"Fuckin' freaks," one of them eventually slurs.

I look at Margaret. She looks at them. They glare back.

"Oi, love ya hair," the other boy announces. "Gedda haircut, maybe."

"Fuckin' haircut." His companion giggles.

"What's your problem, dickhead?" responds Margaret, hands planted on hips and money forgotten.

I can't believe she's done that. Tell her in my head to shut up and leave.

Don't think the bogans can believe it either — laughter stifled, they glance at one another for moral support.

"Well?" Margaret demands.

That's when I toss two dollars onto the counter, don't wait for change, take hold of the other girl's arm and tug her out of the store.

A final shout — "You fuckin' freak sluts!" — bird-dogs us onto the street.

"Fuck you!" Margaret yells back, as she fights against my grip. "You fucking losers! ... Let me go!"

"Leave it be," I urge, somehow hanging on. "Eat your bloody hot dog and forget them. Those arseholes aren't worth the trouble."

She breaks free and storms off down the street, deserting me by the convenience store window. I look back inside, observing the two boys with furious looks on their faces — now jostling each other in uncoordinated fashion.

Just before running to catch up with Margaret I can't resist poking my tongue out at them, and then I skedaddle like the wind.

"Owe you a drink," Margaret has decided, even if she's still fuming.

I let her take me back to Locomotion, Clair and Hannah be damned. Besides, I need to say goodbye to Angelika.

The place is more crowded than before, bumper-to-bumper clubbers, overheated and smoky. Having drowned myself in two more drinks, we head upstairs — which takes about a half hour to accomplish. Along the way I lose grip of Margaret's hand and find myself pressed up against yet another wall, a mob of people I don't know surrounding me.

A perfect time for squealing, distorted wall-of-noise guitars and percussion to erupt from nearby speakers, nearly deafening my ears, while a new burst of smoke-machine smog swallows the place.

"Jesus and Mary Chain," a male voice yells close by. "C'mon, let's dance!"

An arm wraps round my waist to pretty much drag me onto the crammed dancefloor, assailed by that racket from all quarters. The clientele here are bopping, jerking, swaying — never once colliding — but I'm hardly one of them. I stand there amidst the calculated mayhem, scared stiff, and turn about to face my newfound captor.

There he is right in front of me, eyes closed, bouncing in mad abandon to the music. Dressed in a black suit with stovepipe trousers, blond hair on his head and narrow, burgundy-coloured tie flopping in different directions as he jumps.

Margaret's friend with the unusual name — the one who'd helped carry me to relative safety at the Mardi Gras — and right now he's blissfully unaware of my petrified state.

The clamour subsides, to be replaced over the soundsystem by David Bowie's far more melodic, wistful 'Heroes' — a song I actually know since I think I told you my dad owned the LP.

Double-U, or whatever his real name is, has stopped rebounding and opened devastating eyes to look at me. Don't know when I realize he's stepped closer, has arms around my waist, and we're swaying together in time to the song.

While I fret I might set foot on his toes, he leans closer.

"You look different," he's decided.

"Do you actually remember me?"

"Course I do."

"Or d'you often put arms round complete strangers?" My cheek surprises me, even if this boy takes the comment in his stride.

"Ahhh, but I've had my arm around you before."

So he does remember. "Just the one."

"Like a first date. On the second, you get two."

"Last week I couldn't exactly say no."

"If I remember correctly — you couldn't say much at all."

It's a joke, a stupid one — I know that — but I feel my cheeks burn beneath the foundation, and I need to get those arms off. Pushing my fingers behind, I manage to separate us.

"Sorry," he says, and I can tell he means it. "I didn't mean to offend you."

"Who says I'm offended?"

"Aren't you?"

"Not offended — not really."

That's when I make *my* move. Step closer, arms encircling his waist. It's like we're in some kind of slo-mo other place, the sound of the music drops several decibels, and everyone around us is a blur framed by a strobe machine.

"You look like an evil school kid with those pigtails," the boy tosses my way.

"I *am* an evil school kid." My chest hurts and I can barely breathe — but can't remember ever before feeling this excited.

"How old exactly?"

"Seventeen. Too young?" My right hand daringly brushes past his bum as I gaze up at him.

"Old enough."

Another song makes its presence known inside this crackpot cocoon. The drums and percussion kick in first, minimal and sporadic like a dysfunctional hospital ventilator. Seconds later the guitar riff winds in, followed by Ian Curtis' verbal drone.

'She's Lost Control.'

Busting loose from this boy, peering at the ceiling from beneath a fringe that no longer exists, I drift back across the floor, mesmerized, get bumped by people.

My song.

Mixed feelings.

Squeeze closed my eyes, heart in mouth, old terrors roaming nearby.

Other arms embrace me from behind — force me to look around. It's Angelika, finally back, leaning in close.

"Joy Division," she sighs. "Why aren't you dancing?"

"I'm scared."

"This is *your* song. Own it. Jesus, don't let boring inhibitions get in the way."

Angelika snuggles in close, arms wrapped around me, a warm cheek pressed against my left ear, and I lean back into her.

"Won't you ruin your make-up?" I mumble.

She laughs softly in return. "Fuck make-up." Then she lifts my arms. Forces me to move. I'm sucking in my lower lip, teeth holding it there, but gradually thaw. Relax. Smile.

"Who cares about anyone else? He's not here, Mina. Nobody can hurt you. Understand? There's only you."

She's so right.

The fears abate, scarper. Ian's voice washes over, claws away cobwebs. I know this song too well — have played it a hundred times. Every single key is my ally. Simple enough to again shut eyes, willingly this time, let the music run its course, and embrace it in return.

Her hold gone, I understand Angelika has done another runner, yet this time I fail to care. Feel someplace else, liberated. Me alone, married to the bliss that is this song.

And when the song finishes, slain by something I don't know that shatters the illusion, I discover Double-U still there on the dancefloor, a metre away, an easy grin on his face, hands covering ears.

"You dance beautifully," he shouts, above flaying noise.

Not knowing how to take the remark — yeah, *right*, guess he's taking the piss — I sham not having heard. Easy in the circumstances. "What?!"

"I said — Ahh, forget it! Do you like this song?"

"Not really! I think my ears're bleeding!"

"Drink?"

"Love one!"

Surprising me, this boy takes a turn grabbing my hand to lead me off the dancefloor. "Be careful with those blunt instruments of yours," he calls back just as I nearly impale someone with my hair.

"What was *that* song?"

"Boyd Rice, alias NON — 'Rise'. Acquired taste and the guy's a bit of a Nazi. If you're going to go for noise, I'd recommend Einstürzende Neubauten or this Japanese guy Merzbow."

At the bar I obtain another wine while Double-U orders a Heineken, and then we push through the crowd to a small table over by a broken window that lets in one very welcome breath of fresh air.

"Think I was half-fumigated and my brain melted," I say, gifting my partner a grin. I also get more daring — lean into him while holding my drink.

The boy laughs. I like his laugh.

"You have the best dimples when you smile."

"I *have* dimples? Had no idea." I shimmy closer, a kind of bravado I never thought possible.

"Let's face it." The boy also dips near. "You're severely cute all over."

"Severe being the key word?" My nose touches his, ever so gently. "Sounds like punishment."

"Definitely punishing enough."

"Funny. I never thought of 'cute' having a brutal edge."

"The things we learn."

This is the moment he kisses my mouth. Perfect timing, as gentle as the nose tickle. Like he knew the score and didn't want to ruin my lipstick.

I gaze straight into his eyes, blink slowly for a few seconds, feelings running riot, and then I grab hair to pull him close — kiss back harder, make-up be damned.

When I wake up the next day, Sunday, it's early afternoon and I'm alone in our empty family home.

Surprisingly not hung over, but the eyes sting and my mouth feels raw.

Haven't washed off make-up and thus resemble a demented clown when I spy myself in our bathroom mirror. Recoil at first, horrified, wondering whom this crazed stranger might be. Once realization comes home to roost — the crazy is me — I'm by turns fascinated and appalled by this cosmetic explosion.

My hair is another matter. The antennae are buckled, bent and haggard.

As I tear at strands of bent-up braids to remove the pipe-cleaning wire, Animeid puts in an appearance over by the doorway.

"You have fun last night?"

"Sure."

"Anything special?"

I throw the last pipe cleaner into the bin by the bathtub. "I met a boy."

"Oh, whoopee! What's this charmer's name?"

"Double-U."

"What kind of name is that?"

"Hungarian, if you must know."

Animeid's next sentence is suspicious — "Are you messing with me?" — but I don't care either way, since I turn on the shower, throw off stinky clothes, and hop in.

"Anim?" I call out while lathering up soap. "Do you ever moult?"

"How's that?" she responds from the other side of the shower screen.

"Moult — you know, shed feathers."

"I know what moult means. Why?"

"Just curious."

"You *are* weird."

After about ten minutes I hop out and get changed into a light cotton frock that's liberating even if it is a cutesy lilac. Wander the house, inspecting the emptiness, and venture into the back garden. The air is chilled.

Up in a cloudless sky flies an advertising blimp. The jingle on the side of this vessel declares 'The World is Yours!', which means nothing to me. Surprisingly there's no corporate logo. Can hear the buzz of propellers, become bored, go back inside.

After consuming a late lunch of rye bread and melted Swiss cheese, I returned to my room, stuck on the portable TV, and kicked back to watch a rerun of '60s comedy *Hogan's Heroes*.

Didn't pay attention, except perhaps to Colonel Klink's outrageously bad German accent. My mind drifted to Angelika, and then to Margaret — hadn't seen either before I left the club — but mostly, of course, a certain boy took pole position.

Double-U.

He'd been such a gentleman. Didn't try to go too far. When I told him I had to leave, he took me outside and waited there on the street until a taxi arrived. Me in his arms, my face pressed against his chest.

"Gentleman — Pfft."

Animeid had made herself at home, lying beside me on the bed, her face — dark and mysterious as ever — almost as close as Double-U's had been the night before.

"You believe that crap?" she mocks.

"I do."

I sit up then to place the Olivetti in front of me, along with A4 paper, *Roget's Thesaurus*, a fat encyclopaedia that's twice as heavy as the typewriter, and a book coveted by my dad — all about weapons and aircraft from the First World War.

"In fact, I'm inspired to write a story. You can go to Hell."

"Oh, I've already dropped by there. Nothing it's cracked up to be."

I do believe my first bona fide blunder of the war was when I shot a goddess between the eyes.

Unforced error number two came into play the moment I took note of said mistake. Having yanked up my goggles, I perched in the seat of my plane, stunned. With my head turned around, searching for her descent, I obviously wasn't looking where I was going, and the next thing I knew I'd collided slap-bang up the arse end of a 530-foot dirigible.

The propeller of my Sopwith Pup punctured the rubberized cotton fabric, the nose went in, the biplane shuddered, and then we hung there, conjoined in the clouds several thousand feet up.

The name *L.19* was written in big gothic letters on a ripped flap that waved above my head, and beneath that "Kaiserliche Marine".

I'd buggered a bloody zeppelin.

Hence, it wasn't long before the Huns on board started taking pot shots at me, having positioned themselves on an iron trellis built into the rear-engine gondola. They were so close I could see the rifles poking out — standard issue 7.92 mm Mauser Gewehr 98s — but the dunderheads were such poor marksmen that I continued to sit there, strapped into my open cockpit, unharmed and reasonably unfussed.

Eventually I got tired of the fun, games and projectiles. I unholstered my Webley Mk IV revolver to fire off three rounds in return. The soldiers ducked for cover. Then I glanced around, wondering what the devil I should do.

"You know, that hurt."

I peered over the side of my aeroplane, past the words 'Sea's Shame' that my batman McPherson had stencilled onto the canvas fuselage, to the jutting-out wooden wheel frame beneath my Pup. What I discovered alarmed me far more than the pointy-headed fools only yards distant.

Winged Victory, or whomsoever this was, hung there one-handed. In her other hand, the left one, the woman was armed with a trident and shield, and on top of her head she wore a centurion's helmet that was at an accidentally jaunty angle — probably because it had a couple of dents in it, courtesy of my machine gun. Platinum hair poked out from under the hard hat, and this fluttered in the breeze. Her emerald-green eyes, however, remained fixed on mine. They were anything but flighty.

"So, are you going to offer assistance? Or would you prefer to sit there and gawk while those men continue shooting?"

"Can't you fly?"

"Do I look like I have wings?"

She had a point. There was nary a feather on her body.

"Why doesn't she have any feathers?"

This was Animeid — she'd been peeking over my shoulder while I typed.

"I don't know. Maybe she plucked them."

"This girl sounds suspiciously like you."

"Whatever. D'you mind? I'm busy."

There was nary a feather on her body.

"She's younger than me, too."

"Who is younger?"

"Your Winged Victory."

I certainly hadn't expected things to turn out in this squalid manner — they'd started out innocuously enough. There had been heavy fog the evening before, when a fleet of zeppelins took advantage of the cover to bomb a string of inconsequential towns in the West Midlands.

The next afternoon — today — one of the intruders was spotted over the North Sea, which explained away my current mission flying a spot of reconnaissance. Having flown out from Freiston Airfield in Lincolnshire and spent the past frigid, unproductive hour in empty skies, I'd decided to return home to a jolly good cup of warm cocoa, with a shot of Dalmore whisky, when directly ahead in my flight path — in the midst of a bank of clouds and silhouetted by the setting sun — I spied Winged Victory.

Before I could think, I was triggering my Vickers machine gun, the woman tumbled, and I crashed. This surely smacked of something of a feat.

"I do wish you would desist with the Winged Victory nonsense," called out my unwilling passenger, as I unstrapped and leaned over to give her a hand. "She's Greek," that voice nattered on, "and, dare I say it, has no arms and lacks a head."

A bullet whizzed close by my ear. "Would you stop that?" I yelled, directing my words at a stout sergeant in a greatcoat and a rather dangerous Pickelhaube spiked helmet. "Can't you see I'm busy?"

The man lowered his rifle to act sheepish. "Es tut mir leid!"

"Not a problem. Be a good fellow and go fetch your commanding officer."

At least the gunplay ceased. I encircled the woman's wrist with my gloved fingers and proceeded to haul, although I had a bugger of a time. I barely managed the exercise, what with the heavy armoured trinkets and her Amazonian stature — at about six feet, she was at least as tall as me, and had broader shoulders.

Finally, she propped herself up behind the cockpit, powerful, stark-naked legs straddling the canvas for balance. While I'm hardly one to gush, the woman's face was something precious — a pert mouth, strong eyebrows, magnificently bewitching dimples.

"Is there a way down?" she asked, while I rudely stared.

"You mean to terra firma?"

"No, I mean the moon."

"Ahh, you're joking."

"Bravo." She breathed out in loud, overdramatic fashion, apparently annoyed. I suppose I would be too, if I were god-like and recently gunned down by an overzealous aerialist. "Now, about getting off..."

"I think we're stuck until this zeppelin lands. I heard the Huns have introduced a device called a parachute, but we haven't anything like that in the Royal Flying Corps. I suppose you could jump. You are, I take it, some kind of deity?"

The young lady held up a majestic chin. "I am. I have been worshipped by people since the Pritani, well before the Romans invaded Britain two thousand years ago, and in all that time nobody ever shot at me before."

"Hold on. If you really were some kind of patron saint-cum-goddess, why didn't you kick the Spicks back to Italy?"

"We choose not to interfere in human affairs."

"Well, that's bloody convenient. Why, then, do you bother lugging about the military gear, and what's the story with the Roman helmet?"

"It belonged to Julius Caesar. I liked Gaius. After he invaded, he named the island after me, Britannia. Claudius I loathed — he had no respect for foreign figureheads — but Hadrian was marginally better."

"Oh, I see. Britannia. Of course."

"Britannia? Wouldn't Australiana be more appropriate? Or Brigitta — you know, that frustrated angel from the film we saw, *I Married an Angel*?"

"You're worse than me," I decide.

"Oh, I see. Britannia. Of course. I do apologize for the Winged Victory bon mot. I'm known as Wilks. Might I call you Brit?"

Since I was leaning out of the cockpit, I felt something tap my buttocks.

"Are you forgetting the trident?" the woman reminded me. Thank Heavens; she resisted using the sharp bits. "Britannia shall do nicely. If you're searching for something earthier, you may call me Frances. I prefer Britannia."

"Speaking of earth — given that you're a god, well, I would venture to guess that jumping will not be a problem."

She looked down through the clouds and I would swear I saw a grimace. "How high are we?"

"About three or four thousand feet, the last time I checked."

"Then it's a problem."

"You have height restrictions?"

"Something of the sort." Britannia shivered. No wonder, since she was wearing only a light shift of linen material that barely came down to her thighs, and the woman had a lot of cold metal pressing against her.

After I took off my leather coat, I reached across to place it on her shoulders.

"What are you doing?"

"Attempting to be a gentleman."

"Well, stop it. I reside on a completely different plane. I don't feel the chill. Put the blasted thing back on."

"Right you are." It was my turn to play annoyed as I buttoned up the coat. "Anyway, I thought Britannia was a nymph of some kind."

"Hardly."

"And aren't you supposed to have a lion? What were you doing, prancing about on top of a zeppelin?"

"Trying to help — you looked like you were going to fly straight past, so I decided to intervene."

"Against your better nature?"

"I do that sometimes. These people dropped bombs on my native soil. I was cross." She smiled. "I left my lion at home."

Touché.

I resisted a spot of laughter, and again instead looked over the side of the aeroplane. I decided the sea was closer than it had been only a quarter of an hour before. "We're losing altitude."

"Quite possibly it has something to do with the giant hole you ripped in their side. Gas must be escaping."

"True — which means we'll end up in the drink in the North Sea, not the best idea in February. It's probably around forty degrees Fahrenheit this time of year."

I heard somebody discreetly cough nearby.

There was a new addition to the open window of the gondola. With the monocle, a Luger 9mm in his hand, the soft hat and pencil-thin moustache, this man was a stiff-necked caricature of the German officer class.

"I say, Englander, my name is Kapitänleutnant Wilhelm Klink."

"Charmed, I'm sure. Flying Officer 'Wilks' Wilkinson, 287 Squadron, RFC, commanded by Major William E. Johns."

I heard him click unseen heels as he bowed. "We are currently throwing excess baggage into the sea in order that we might gain some height and make it to the continent. Your blasted flugzüg — your aeroplane — is not helping matters, Herr Wilkinson."

"Sorry, Herr Klink, but the crate is here to stay. Your men shooting at me has not been much fun — it makes it difficult to come up with a viable plan."

"Well, you are the enemy."

"There is that. But tell you what; I have a woman here with me."

Klink adjusted his monocle. "Ja. Quite the fräulein."

"Eyes off, Fritz."

"My apologies." While he inclined his head, Klink's stare remained affixed to my hitchhiker. The man was incorrigible.

"You know, I always envied you English your Britannia. The Americans have Columbia, even the Italians have their mundane Italia Turrita, but we Germans... ahhh, we are sadly lacking in the allegorical personifications."

"Er... yes." I frowned. "Once the balloon— "

"Zeppelin. This is a zeppelin, not a balloon."

"All right. Well, once the zeppelin gets lower, Britannia and I will bail out, jumping into the sea and thereby lightening the load up to two hundred and eighty pounds."

"I beg your pardon," the girl behind me grouched, "just how chubby do you presume me to be?"

"Well, you are six feet and wearing all that armour."

"Pfft."

"At least she says her 'pffts' well."

"Shhh."

Klink rubbed his chin. "To tell the truth, I am more concerned with the aircraft — not that I do not appreciate the gesture."

"Every little bit helps, am I correct, Kapitänleutnant?"

"Ja, Ja, in getting my crew safely home."

"Then we have a deal? Toss me a lifesaver, there's a good fellow."

I hadn't counted on Klink lobbing the contraption so damned hard, and I can't fault the officer for accuracy — the lifesaver struck me on the forehead and, being unstrapped, I fell straight out of the plane.

I recall nothing thereafter, until I came to in darkness in the shallow water of a cove. I was saturated, half-drowned and mostly frozen. Flashes of memory — a flapping dirigible, the burlesque German officer, Britannia in a dimpled helmet and very little else — played a merry jig across my mind and I deduced that an aeroplane crash and a bump on the skull must have conjured up the whole fiasco. Since I had no plane, I could only assume I'd ditched at sea.

Turned out, I was on the coast of northern France.

A helpful farmwoman named Marianne, who carried a rowdy rooster tucked under her arm, got me safely to British lines. While she spoke no English, this woman was remarkable for big brown eyes, her height — she towered over me in her Phrygian cap — and an impressive stamina, since she never tired once during our ninety-mile hike.

Two weeks later I discovered myself back in Blighty, at company HQ. I was informed by my commanding officer, Major Johns, that a zeppelin earmarked L.19 had in fact gone down in the North Sea, with a loss of all hands, and he was putting the kill on my record sheet.

"Jolly good show, old chap," the major decided as he shook my hand.

So. There was a balloon. But what about the balance of the featherbrained dream? I returned to my quarters and allowed McPherson to mix up a drink. I continued seeing the girl's face in the sights of my Vickers, right before I pulled the trigger, as I stood first in front of the fireplace and then wandered over to a bay window. It was dusk outside.

"Restless, sir?" McPherson inquired as he handed me a tumbler.

"Vaguely." I bowed my head. Was she dead too? Or was she some figment of an overactive, semi-concussed imagination? "I think I'll hit the sack, old man," I decided. "Take the evening off. Sally forth and enjoy yourself."

I trudged slowly up the staircase with the drink between my fingers. I felt inconceivably dismal. Probably, it had to do with touching God — or, in this case, a goddess — and losing her. Never good form to do that kind of thing. One might as well try manhandling the sun.

When I entered my room I switched on a lamp, and straight away noticed the Corinthian helmet on the desk. It had been hammered back into shape. Next to it — slouched unmajestically on my favourite leather armchair, with her feet up, sans armour, and showing far too much leg — was someone I recognized.

"You."

"Me." She straightened up, stretched her back, and smiled. "You recall that that my name is not Winged Victory?"

"I do seem to remember that. It was a Victorian fancy — and, to be honest, I thought you didn't exist. That you were only up here." I tapped my right temple, but this acted as the woman's cue to stand up and slip out of the miserly frock she wore.

"Perhaps you should put down your glass?"

I realized I was spilling the drink, and did as suggested.

Britannia stood before me, without even her shield, her head at an angle, green eyes close, platinum hair framing her face, and I realized she pipped my height by two inches.

"I like you."

"Where's your trident?" I responded. I had no intention of accidentally sitting on the bugger.

"It was on extended loan — now returned to its rightful owner." I could feel her cool breath on my neck.

"Shield?"

"Beneath the bed. You're stalling."

"Not at all. I believe you said you didn't interfere in human affairs."

"Nobody ever shot at me before. C'mere."

It was evening when I finished the silly boys' own yarn.

"Why did you kill off the German officer?" Anim complains while getting to her feet and stretching wings. "I liked him."

"Dramatic effect."

"Thought it was supposed to be a light-hearted comedy?"

"Life always has its dark twists — you know that. Doesn't matter how happy you might be."

I remember to check the post-box. Unlike Dam's, ours doesn't house a spider so I'm not at all cautious when I do so.

Amidst a flood of junk mail there's a large, carefully sheathed gift in there — which winds up being junk of another kind.

No postage stamps, no postmark, no return address.

Wrapping paper covered with large orchids that in colour were bright golden, but the back sheath white, barred with lines of black, and in the exact centre of each flower's pouch there is a single black spot shaped like a great ape. Overhanging brows, the deep recessed eyes, the surly mouth, the massive jaws — everything.

This bizarre flora is so old-fashioned it reminds me of something from an Allan Quatermain romp. Probably would sit well in the story I typed out earlier.

There's a tiny card with an elegant 'M', which I turn over, finding no message. Guess it's for me since no one else in the house has a name starting with that letter.

Inside is a book on the Vish Kanya — women whose blood was so poisonous to others, they were used as political assassins during the Indian Mauryan Empire (322 to 185 BC).

Squeezed into every second page are pictures of voluptuous,

half-naked statuettes and stills from old Indian films.

Story goes that the girls were made lethal by exposing them to toxins from a very young age, this practice referred to as *mithridatism*. While many died, those that did not developed an immunity and their bodily fluids would be poisoned — hence sexual contact made fatal to other people.

So I learned for the first time as I flipped through pages.

The development of a 'venomous vamps' culture passed on into folklore, an archetype explored by southeast Asian writers resulting in popular poisonous literary characters, mostly women, in Sanskrit texts.

I close the book, sigh.

Another unsubtle message — no doubt from my Valentine.

Half an hour later I hear another television, the one in the room beneath, so I leave Anim to descend the stairs.

In the lounge room I glimpse Tony Barber hosting *Sale of the Century* before I notice my dad on the couch. Haven't seen him in a week. He looks older, sadder, but allows me the benefit of a smile.

"Hello, sweetheart," he says.

Makes not one remark about the bleached hair.

"Would you sit down a moment?"

"Sure, Dad." I fall into the armchair across from him. Tuck my feet up on the cushion beneath my thighs — something guaranteed to annoy — but he doesn't notice.

"How is everything?" the man asks.

"Okay. You?"

"Fine, fine."

I'm already trying to hide behind a fringe that's no longer sufficient. "So," I venture, "what's going to happen?"

"Too much." He leans forward, pushing the tops of his fingers together, perhaps struggling to find the right words. "I'm sorry," he finally says.

"It's okay."

"No. It's not. I understand that now. Patrick…"

Trailing off, Dad looks away.

For a moment I think he's absorbed himself back into his favourite TV game show, but at last he speaks again.

"The Court has suspended his sentence — with a steep good behaviour bond I had to pay, plus a strict regimen of community service. Also anger-management classes, meaning it's going to be impossible for your brother to find the time to focus on HSC. He's going to suspend his studies, find work."

Tragic, I think. Feel and say nothing.

"Pat can't come home. The authorities — that Christina woman, I'd say — have seen fit to slap a six-month restraining order on him. This means he won't be allowed within fifty feet. Of *you*. So I've found him a place to stay, a small bedsit, a nice place in Camberwell. I paid the rent in advance for the full six months."

"You're forking out a lot of money for him."

"Patrick says he'll repay me."

"And you?"

"Me?" He looks over.

"The police, the Court."

"The Court let me off the hook."

"I'm glad. I never wanted you involved."

"I am your father. Always was going to be involved."

I could tell he blamed me — for my brother, if not for his own thankfully abridged legal tussles. For everything that'd taken place.

Don't think Dad deliberately thought along these lines, but the blame/shame was there to read in an occasional glance and in the silences between us. Possibly he blamed himself as much. I don't know.

"For twenty points," Tony Barber enthuses over on the telly. "For twenty points, name the American country music singer famous for 'I Will Always Love You' twelve years before Whitney Houston's version of this song."

"Dolly Parton." Dad and I both say it at the same time.

For my sins, the Court ordered I attend twice-weekly counselling sessions.

That Monday I bit the bullet — and went back to class.

Couldn't do much with my hair so tied it back in a simple pigtail. Arrived five minutes late, during the calling of the roll, and the room went silent.

"Sorry I'm late," I say from the doorway.

"No worries." Mrs Williams nods. "I'll mark you as present. Come on in."

Both Angelika and Sarah's desks are empty, looking barren to me as I sit down and face front. Can feel Clair to my right but don't glance over. Take out a notebook instead and start writing bits and pieces. At least I appear busy.

"Mina. A word, if you wouldn't mind."

Having finished the roll, Mrs Williams marches me out into a corridor now empty, and she closes the door to our class.

"Dear, I quote here the rules of this school: 'No make-up is allowed — hair must be in a neat style and should be in a natural hue.' Do you understand?"

"The key word being 'should'."

"Beside the point. We have to abide by these regulations, must never bend them or anarchy will reign."

"No make-up here," I say. "But Nicole's always sweating under a truckload of foundation."

My teacher's reaction here is a curious one. Her eyes dart to the door of the next classroom, 12D, which is also closed.

"Please. That's 12D's concern — you are mine, as is your hair. And Nicole has some... skin problems." The way Mrs Williams says this makes me frown, can't say why.

But it's also when I decide, on the spot, to play the card.

Wouldn't say I'm proud as I do so, but I don't feel morose either.

"Ros, I have problems too. Mum. My brother."

Her glance tells me she's heard already about Patrick.

"I'm just so confused," I act up, actually getting teary, "that things like this — colouring my hair — help make life somehow, I don't know, bearable. Can't explain it. I'm so sorry."

"Shhh," Mrs Williams croons, my best friend now. "Don't you worry about a thing. I'm sure we can smooth it over with the principal."

As I watch her mouth work these words, I keep thinking about what Angelika had mentioned.

"Excuse me, Mrs Williams — Ros. Have you ever been in a rock band?"

That brings a strange mistiness to the woman's eyes.

"You know, I did once entertain the idea. In high school, younger than you. My best friend and I went so far as to agree upon a name: The Sleez Sisters. Sadly, I can't play any musical instrument and my voice is far better a tool in class than on stage before hundreds of groupies. So, no."

Once I return to the room to sit down, our teacher resumes her place on the platform up the front.

"Girls," she says, wringing hands in unusual fashion, "our last item on the agenda this morning is some distressing news I would prefer not to discuss — but Miss Cook has requested all classes be informed."

The room is so silent you could hear a feather strike the floor, not that one did on this occasion.

"I know some of you are very good friends with Nicole Milton next door in 12D. Over the weekend, on Saturday night, a fire broke out at Nicole's home."

Wild whispering ensues. Though I try to keep my eyes front and centre, focused on Ros, I notice none of the whispers come from beside me, where Clair sits. Looking over, I find my friend deep in silent prayer.

"Girls, shush — shhhh. Be quiet! Nicole is fine, but she was taken to hospital with burns to ten percent of her body. While her condition is serious, the doctors there expect her to make a complete recovery. Fortunately the rest of the family escaped unscathed — we've had word from Nicole's parents John and Eve that she's doing as well as can be expected. Anyhow, we'll be putting together a group card from 12E. Clair, dear — I'd ask Sarah but she's been absent these past few days. I know how precious Nicole is to you also. Would you mind organizing this?"

"Sure."

The response surprises me. Flat as a tack, lacking the usual colour I'd expect from Clair.

Much as I want to turn again to her, give the girl my support, I can't. Am paralyzed in this same ineffective position peering straight ahead like any good student. And for Nicole? I feel nothing.

"Mina?"

I home in on my teacher again. "Yes?"

"You'll need to drop by the teachers' room after we're finished. I'm sure you have a fair amount of homework to catch up on."

After the bell rings, I hole up at my desk waiting for everyone to leave before I dare do so.

Once I pack books into my bag and leave the room, Clair is standing on the threshold. She's clutching a purple folder to her chest, with a rectangular sticker attached that reads 'PREDESTI-NATION!' in big, bold letters and beneath that, in smaller ones, 'no ifs or buts'.

"Missed you," she says. Can tell she means it, but have doubts.

"Really? Thought I didn't matter. I've been blacklisted."

"I don't listen to everything these people say."

I smile at that.

"Terrible news, though, about Nicole."

Now I'm looking away. "I guess."

"You guess? Mina, it's horrible. No one deserves that."

"I know." I blow out cheeks, looking past her. "I have to go. Got a million things to do, and God knows how I'm going to get on top of everything."

"You'll be fine. You're *way* smarter than me."

"Oh sure!" We both laugh — a shared, ongoing joke. "Okay, have a good lesson."

"You too."

When I knock on the door of the teachers' room, Mr Osterberg answers.

One eyebrow raises as he takes in the sight of my hair, but otherwise it's same as usual — except I notice the staff here are listening to 'Another Brick in the Wall, Part 2' by Pink Floyd. Wasn't that an anti-teacher rallying cry?

"Glad you came," Mr Osterberg says while rustling me over to his desk, which is jammed with books and messy paperwork. "You're probably wondering about the song."

"A little."

"Well, we were all oppressed kids once."

I nod, say nothing. Can't think up anything of worth — I mean, how do you respond to that?

"Anyway, we're organizing speeches for tomorrow, part of the end-of-year assessment."

"Tomorrow?"

"That's right, Mina. *Mañana.* So you have your work cut out."

"Can I get an extension?"

"Surely you jest?"

"Um... no."

"Zero chance, sorry. Wouldn't matter if you were dying."

Card-playing time again. "Or family falling apart?"

The teacher looks straight at me.

"You're one of the bright ones, I don't care what your home

life is like. I have great faith. I think you'll find the task relatively easy and it's better to get this over and done with."

"I understand." Not really, but still.

"Good. Don't you want to know the topic?"

"Oh. Uh-huh."

"This one's a freestyle affair — basically any literary topic that catches your fancy. I've secured us two consecutive periods, but you're going to have to scramble to put something together by tomorrow. We'll have a projector, so come in early in the morning and get together some transparencies. Grades will be based on volume, eye contact with the audience, attitude, originality, and visuals. Each student has up to five minutes — and you'll get better marks if the speech is given from memory or improvised. Jimmy knows you'll roll with the vibe."

Before he stops waffling, I twig what I'm going to do.

A comic book I have, an original one from 1942 that Dam gave me when I was twelve — and I'll need a pair of my mother's spectacles.

Speech day.

I set myself up beside the overhead projector with its large box containing a lamp and the loud fan to cool it.

Slide my first transparency over the glass before switching on the machine. Tweak the adjustment wheel to move the lamp towards the Fresnel lens, creating better focus.

After that I place on my nose Mum's prescription glasses, so anything more than four feet away is lovingly *out* of focus — meaning the rest of the class including Clair.

Already know Angelika and Sarah have again pulled sickies. Disappointed as I may be regarding the former, I realize I'm grateful the latter is out of my hair — am sick of Sarah's prying. Both girls will be spared the sight of me all nerves atop a podium.

Anyway, I have the word 'VILLAIN!' projected behind me in big, hand-drawn cartoon letters.

I made this myself last night, having traced the font from a cover of *Tales to Astonish* and making up the 'V' to match.

"Time, Mina," announces Mr Osterberg.

Time it is.

A sea of washed-out heads before me.

"Hi, everyone," I start out. "Okay, so I'm Mina and today I'm going to talk to you about a different kind of literary storytelling, something you won't find in Broadway plays or between the covers of your Joe Average novel. I'm going to natter on a bit about comic books — something higher-browed types might call sequential art. And to give you a better insight, I'm going to focus on the lamest comic-book villain — ever."

I remove the VILLAIN! graphic and slide on a projected image of Australian actor Vernon Wells, looking spiffy in a sleeveless chainmail vest and Village People moustache, dog tags dangling from a thick silver necklace.

The look makes me smile.

"Not surprisingly when it comes to comic books, there are dozens to choose from. Same goes for cinema — hands up anyone who remembers Bennett from last year's Schwarzenegger flick *Commando*? That's him here. In particular, the man's comeback when Arnie utters 'I'll be back' — Bennett's cutting response being 'John... I'll be ready, John.' And that's it. Jeez. Anyway, where was I? Comics, that's right."

I switch projector transparencies to a pointy-headed Impossible Man, two frames snatched from *Fantastic Four* issue 11 (1963).

"The litany of flabby monikers and so-called skills include the Impossible Man. This was not a villain per se, but an alien who first showed up in *Fantastic Four* in the 1960s and has popped-up occasionally thereafter to plague other Marvel titles. Then there's Captain Boomerang — a fellow Aussie who made his debut with 'villainous' boomerang accoutrements on the cover of *The Flash* issue 117, drawn by Carmine Infantino in 1960."

Need to stop for a moment to regain my breath — have barely

inhaled during that particular monologue. Having changed images from this Flash cover and ensured the new one is in proper focus, I lean forward on the desk.

"There're lots more where these people came from, such as Tweedledum and Tweedledee — no, not the dynamic duo from the pages of Lewis Carroll, but hardly-arch-fiends Dumfree and Deever Tweed who bounced about Batman and Robin thirty years ago in *Detective Comics* issue 74. Actually, DC was a leader in its day for lame-arse villains. Others include the Fiddler — murderous violins, anyone? — along with Codpiece. No words there are necessary. But Marvel Comics and its predecessor Timely also had their share: Lady Stilt-Man, Gin Genie and Asbestos Lady for starters."

I change the image to a girl in a red V-neck tunic, yellow hot pants and blue boots, with long, wavy brown hair and a silver helmet shaped like a bullet.

Joy.

"But the worst comic-book villain ever? Funnily enough, the final choice I made is a character that wasn't conjured up by either major American comic-book sweatshop, DC or Marvel. Up here you see Bulletgirl, a golden age comic-book heroine, from the 1940s. The daughter of a police sergeant and girlfriend of Jim Barr — a.k.a. costumed crime fighter Bulletman — Susan Kent made her debut as Bulletgirl in the April 1941 edition of *Master Comics*, issue 13, through publication company Fawcett — the people behind Captain Marvel."

A slide projection of this comic's cover now occupies the space over my shoulder. It shows Bulletman and Bulletgirl flying through the sky as another character, Minute-Man, knocks out Adolf Hitler.

"Oh, by the way, she's not the villain I'm talking up, and neither is Adolf — but I'm getting there. Give me time. After discovering her boy's secret identity, Susan basically adopts the same drug-taking regimen — killing germs and toxins in the blood; creating great strength — and gets her own gravity-defying helmet. Thereafter she starts socking it to cheap hoodlums. While reading into Bulletgirl further, I stumbled across the January 1942 *Bulletman* issue 3, with art by Mac Raboy of *Flash Gordon* fame and Bob Rogers, though it's unclear who wrote the script — possibly Otto Binder. Regardless, it's hard to believe they jammed sixty-four pages, only fourteen of them actually a Bulletman/Bulletgirl adventure, into the magazine for a measly ten cents."

Cue projection of this cover, the most worn-out one, with a tear along the spine. Wish I'd taken more care of it.

The title (*Bulletman*) is made up of a font composed of cartridges, while the two Bullets (man/girl) victoriously soar together out of some scary-looking fireworks.

"In this month's exciting instalment, our heroine flies solo to investigate the murder of distant relatives. Meanwhile, bowler-hat-wearing gangland boss Bugs Jonker nabs one of these cousins. Nope, Jonker's not the scoundrel we're set to focus on, despite the silly name — hold your horses. Turns out Jonker is less kingpin than lackey to Lightning King — an individual in an orange boiler suit, with a beehive keeper's basket doohickey on his head and gloves that look like they were nicked from Lon Chaney, Jr. when he played The Mummy."

This is the moment I put up the first frame of our villain, a drawing from behind, as he enters the fray declaring 'I'm Lightning King!'

"This archfiend's opening lines would do Bennett — from *Commando*, remember him? — proud: 'Prepare to die, Kent! Kent, Kent, Kent! ...How I hate that name!' Yawn. He does lots of jabbing into people's chests to accentuate his tired point, but Bulletgirl has followed her cuz into the dragon's lair and busts up the gangsters' pistols."

The next projection displays three consecutive frames of our heroine beating up mobsters, breaking a gun, and the chief villain's reaction.

"This is where Lightning King gets down and dirty — and pre-empts the language of *Scooby-Doo* villains thirty years later. 'Stand back!' he commands, 'I'll take care of this meddler!' And of course he fails, electricity charges and all, but while Bulletgirl is dazed and confused the rascal makes good his escape."

Next is another triple-framer that shows precisely this riff in the action, although the third frame is faded and the ink has run, due to mould the issue copped over the years.

"He then goes on a killing spree of anybody bearing the family name 'Kent', a little like Arnie terminating all the Sarah Connors of the world in *Terminator* — including electrocuting one of the Kents down the phone line from his candlestick telephone.

"Why the Kents? Thought you'd never ask. Well, on page seven we get the traditional villain's soliloquy, and I wish to God I could call this one classic. Ends up the man in the basket is one Professor John Willoughby, and 'Twenty years ago the Kents of Kentucky tried to finish off our feud by killing all Willoughbys... just because we burned down the Kent plantation. But they failed to get *me*! And now I'll blast down all the Kents on the face of the earth, with my wizard control of lightning!'."

I stick on a close-up of Lightning Man with a skull-like face beneath the basket.

"Sadly, I swear I'd tuned out before it was over and I'm sure Prof Willoughby's victims felt the same, even if they were about to be fried by an over-excessive ten million volts of electricity. Which is precisely when Bulletgirl, this time accompanied by her paramour, bursts through the door — overleaf on page eight, of course. While these projectile twins produce their own cheesy repartee over the course of six panels, Lightning King again scores kudos for the best banal remarks. 'Stop them!' he shouts. 'They're spoiling everything!'

"It's odd, then, that Willoughby wins this round. He knocks out Bulletman while Bulletgirl escapes to go fetch the cavalry —

but she's promptly kidnapped along with her police-officer dad. They *are* Kents, after all."

The last two-frame projection shows Bulletman lobbing a spanner.

"Meanwhile, Bulletman breaks out of a completely unguarded cage to discover how exactly Lightning King gets his mojo... from cables leading out of a power station. Obviously the man packs a set of seriously long extension cords. Simply snapping the wires defangs him, giving our hero free-range to knock about the diabolical rotter, until Prof Willoughby grabs the wires, recharges — and is promptly dispatched by an accurately lobbed wrench.

"Thus a spanner destroys everything. 'Electrocuted,' says Susan's cop father as he inspects the charred corpse. 'Well, he got his own electric chair a little ahead of time.' Which tows the old literary line that crime doesn't pay. James Bond would've had a better quip, I'm sure. Something like 'shocking'. But this was twenty years before Sean Connery got discovered."

I switch off the projector, look out over a vague sea of grey A-line dresses, faces with mouths ajar and expressions stunned.

My head hurts from wearing the glasses but I don't dare to take them off.

"Any questions?" I remember to ask.

Silence prevails, followed quickly by lukewarm applause from Mr Osterberg.

"Well — that was certainly original," he concedes, standing to usher up the next student.

After school that day I wanted to go find Angelika's house — she hadn't been in class since the weekend, but I didn't have a phone number and had failed to take note of her address when I stumbled out nine days before.

Anyway, once I got home around four I was distracted by a brief message my father had attached to the board: 'W[?] called', it said, followed by a seven-digit number. I leapt onto the telephone, dialled, and waited a few seconds — was beginning to suspect no one would answer when there was a click, and I heard his voice.

"Hello."

"Hello," I thankfully remember to say.

"Margaret?"

"No!"

"Then this must be Pippi Longstocking."

"Do you even remember my real name?"

"Not Pippi?"

His chuckle sounds vaguely empty over the line. Am about to terminate the conversation when he stops me.

"Don't hang up!"

"Why not?"

"I wanted to invite you out for a drink."

"I don't drink."

"Ahhh, we're off on that tangent again."

"No, really. I'm underage. You shouldn't be encouraging me." I've started sketching Double-U from memory, but he's bundled up in an old-school pilot's cap and scarf.

"That's why I was thinking coffee. Or tea?" Now he doesn't sound so cocky. "Or an ice-cream spider, if that's more up your alley."

"How old do you think I am?"

"Seventeen. Right?"

"And how did you get my phone number?"

"You gave it to me — remember?"

"No." I pause for effect, and then relent. "Coffee's fine. Is it decent?"

"The coffee...?"

"Mmm."

"Yeah, it's really good, actually. Trust me."

"Okay. Where should we meet?"

"D'you know the Brigantine Café in St. Kilda?"

"Soon will — once you tell me how to find it."

I'm grinning so hard it actually hurts. Thank God I'm on the phone, taking notes, and this boy doesn't get to see the idiocy.

Ninety minutes later I'm outside this browbeaten coffee shop on Carlaisle Street, awaiting my first ever date.

Had been in such a rush I left on my school uniform and tied back the hair with a cut-off strip from a pair of black tights. Applied excessive make-up to the eyes, if nowhere else, yet this still took me an hour.

Oh yeah, did put a quick layer of powder on my face so it wouldn't come across shiny or sweaty.

Mask back on, I hope Double-U may be better able to recognize me — yet I have doubts nagging.

If the guy was stupid enough to be interested in me, maybe he suffered eyesight issues? Or more likely these issues went deeper. One of those people who's a seriously poor judge of character, definitely.

So I stand there on the kerb debunking the boy and myself as dusk settles over everything, while I pretend to watch passing cars and the beautiful colours in the sky.

That's precisely when a young pilot waltzes by.

I'm talking World War One era — all leather flying hat, goggles and scarf — looking like Double-U as I'd imagined him in my story. Staring after him, I therefore miss my real mark crossing the street.

"You often gawk at complete strangers?" he asks.

Startled, I swing about and strike my forehead against his bony shoulder.

"Ouch!"

"Serves you right for perving."

"Wasn't perving," I say, rubbing my skull.

"Hmm."

I take him in, then.

Look up to the gorgeous face that reminds me now, in partial daylight, of a young Sean Connery — if he'd bleached his hair, I mean. Likely this impression is helped by the archaic suit and thin tie (this time a classy moss green against obligatory black shirt) and relatively thick, dark eyebrows that complement mine.

I desperately want to be back inside his arms again, held tight like last Saturday night, but I'm terrified he's since re-evaluated things.

Decide upon a cunning plan.

Stop rubbing my head, lean forward, allow myself to fall into his arms — hoping he'll remember to catch me. Saw this manoeuvre once in a classic Hollywood movie, though I can't remember which.

Of course Double-U snags me in time. "Say — what's with all the swooning?"

"Nothing." All the same, I snuggle close and have hands on his lower back. "Just nice to see you."

"Feinting, then. Huh." He endeavours to keep some distance. "You didn't sound so eager on the phone."

"I was playing coy."

"That's what they call it these days?"

"Apparently."

I steel myself inside, a trifle more confident in his hold, and wink up at Double-U — something he'd done to me when I was incapacitated the night of the Mardi Gras. Eye for an eye and all that jazz.

He almost drops me onto the footpath. "So... coffee?" the boy then says in an uneven tone.

"Please."

Double-U escapes from my clutches, swings open the flywire door to the Brigantine Café, and stands aside with an inclined head.

"Ladies first."

"My, you're open-minded," I decide as I breeze past.

Inside are a dozen tables, all of them curious geometrical shapes like triangles, hexagons and parallelograms — there's not a square, rectangular or circular surface in sight.

"Triangle?" I ask.

"Triangle," he agrees.

I choose a red triangle since it's the smallest and will go best with my hair — the other triangle is canary yellow — and the table is configured like the letter 'A'.

Once I pull out a chair I smile, since I recognize the style.

"Ahh. Nothing like a '50s V-back diner manufactured in Chicago."

"That's what these are?"

"You didn't know?"

"Never thought about it before." The boy looks unsettled. "Thirty years old, huh? Are they safe?"

"Live a little. Same vintage as your clothes."

I have no idea where the verbal window-dressing came from, let alone the newfound ability to fire off half-cooked repartee. In the course of mining for a personality, p'raps I've stumbled across a new seam of power, albeit stolen — a little bit of Angelika, a smidgeon of Margaret, and the furniture know-how of my uncle?

And while I may feel like a thieving magpie, I don't care a hoot. Someone's lifted an anvil apiece from both shoulders.

Watching him stabilize his seat and make sure it wouldn't suddenly collapse, I have my elbow on the triangle, chin in the palm of my hand. I'm calm, happy and words are accumulating on the tip of one very unruly tongue — who is this person?

"All settled yet?" I ask.

"Who recommended this place?" The boy has a frown, studying the ancient woodwork and linoleum all round.

"You did."

"These chairs were ten years old when I was born."

I decide he looks cuter while flummoxed. "Anyway. What kind of coffee would you like? My shout."

The comment finally reels-in undivided attention.

"No way — I asked you here."

"You can buy the second round."

He looks dubious. "We're having seconds?"

"Don't know about you, but I will."

"Okay then."

"Flat white? Cappuccino?"

"I'll go with an espresso macchiato."

Having stood, I gaze down at him with respect.

"Nice choice! Think I'll have one of those as well."

I pick up my tiny purse to venture over to a counter that has a large, primary-colour mural of body-less heads (wearing striped party hats) in rowboats.

Above this rests a formidable-looking XZ-12 coffee machine — all stainless steel, black plastic knobs and bulb diode lamps — across the back of which (facing patrons) has been stuck a religious note from Ezekiel 23:37, 'Blood is in their hands, and with their idols have they committed adultery.'

Around the machine is a cluttered array of anodized milkshake flasks, coffee cups, glasses and dishes; cutlery stashed in dirty plastic buckets, herbal teas and creased/stained baby photos.

There is a woman behind this barely functional mess, an attractive lady in her thirties with a prominent mouth that's a vivid smear of matt-red, jet-black hair tied back in a kerchief that's red with white polka dots. Perhaps mimicking the chairs in the place, she has a V-shaped fringe just above provocative blue eyes. Dressed in a tight white shirt with a red apron over the top, and I notice tattoo-work poking out from under both rolled-up sleeves.

This woman would fit right at home working an aircraft factory in World War Two.

"Hello, love. School's out?"

"I guess," I say, surprised by the comment till I recall I'm still wearing uniform. "Can I have two espresso macchiatos, thanks?"

"Coming right up — take a seat and I'll bring them over. Which table?"

"The red, A-shaped triangle, over there."

"Ahh. Okay, I'll look out for the eyes."

"Thanks." I hold aloft my purse. "Pay now?"

"Pay when you leave."

Order made, I whiz back to our table to soak up more Double-U. He appears relaxed regarding the seating arrangements and watches me sit down with a smile.

"Hello, beautiful."

"Hello, you young ruffian."

"No problems over there?"

I fix him with heavily made-up eyes. "What, with the illustrated lady? I'm not entirely stupid. I *can* order stuff."

"There's a relief," he laughs.

"Here you are, darlings," the coffee shop lady is announcing as she places a tray on the triangular table between us. "Two romantically identical macchiatos."

Places one of these before me and the other in front of my tablemate.

"Ta, Bettie," he says.

Tray now safely tucked under her left arm, the woman has taken a tiny pad from her centre apron pocket — just below sizeable boobs.

"Can I get you kids anything else?"

"Think we're fine for now."

The waitress lingers beside the table and I can tell without looking that she's inspecting me.

"This is the latest?" her voice asks in toneless manner. "Bit young, isn't she?"

"Bettie."

Double-U sounds annoyed, so I glance at him. No. Less annoyed, more embarrassed.

"I get it — Beak out and back to the grind!" Bettie announces in a voice far too sweet as she waltzes back toward the open-air kitchen beyond the counter. She has a waltz to die for.

Double-U blows out loud, slumped over, his face stuck disconsolately in both hands, elbows on the table either side of the coffee. "Don't know why I brought you here. Stupid."

Of course I can't help myself. I'm still seeing the edges of trapdoor tattoos. "Who is she?"

"She's Bettie."

"Yeah, I did catch the name," I say, trying hard not to inject sarcasm.

Worse yet, I instantly picture the woman in a bed with this boy, without any clothes aside from a C-cup Wonderbra. So much easier to conjure up her bare skin — Double-U's nakedness remains an elusive thing — and my imagination has a field day with the ink work: A multicoloured dragon coils morphing into a collection of green, blue, black and red flowers on her shoulder blades, which then makes way for a three-headed hellhound.

Sighing again, Double-U sits up straight.

"My wife," he says. "Bettie is my wife."

"Oh." That has me sitting up too. I remember the baby pictures over on the counter. "Kids?"

"None."

Double-U has concealed himself behind the palms of his hands, has the fingers twisting through his long blond fringe.

"I'm so sorry," I hear him mumble. "I should've told you. Never should've brought you here. God, I'm so stupid."

"Well, which one is it?"

The boy stops rubbing and sneaks a peek. "Huh?"

"You should've told me you were married, you should've masked the fact, or you're just plain dim?"

This comment causes Double-U to appraise me anew. He

drops hands to the table.

"You know, you remind me of a wild animal on the cusp of self-destruction."

"Is that an attempt at a compliment? Sounds more like you're dissing me."

Likely he's immune to my newfound 'charms' — and I suspect he still hasn't remembered my name.

"If I were dissing you, sunshine," the boy says, serious now, "I would've gone with *Hell-bent* instead of on-the-cusp."

"Oh. Big difference." I've started unwrapping a small packet of sugar cubes.

"It is."

"Let's not split hairs."

Pop a cube into my mouth, on top of the tongue. It starts to dissolve straight away, sugar overtaking every other taste.

"Why do you act this way?" Still serious.

"None of it's real," I finally enunciate once my mouth isn't quite so busy. "Nothing. It's all just sham theatre."

"I'm not so sure it's an act."

I relent then and shrug. Old habit, remember? "Okay, okay. I don't know. Keeps the demons at bay."

Double-U nods. "Fair enough." He watches Bettie as she serves another customer. "So, anyway, now you know. About me."

"I do."

His eyes return to mine. "So what happens?"

"She's older than you." Don't intend this to be a question, but he treats it as one.

"Yep. Twelve years. Was never an issue."

"For you — or her?"

"For me. She had... concerns."

"Think I can see why."

My mind squirrels beneath the icy veneer.

I'm in love and the arsehole is married — even has the gall to take me on our first date to his wife's café. What the Hell was with that? Said spouse is pretty and has tattoos, but she's past her prime. Not that this matters. He's gorgeous and bound to another woman, one so old-school sexy you could pin her up on the side of a B-29 bomber.

One thing stands out: *I'm in love.*

I know that now. Think I knew it the morning I woke up last Sunday.

God, I'm an idiot.

"Let's go," I say.

Can see in his eyes that he believes I've made my decision, the date is over, and we're finished. Probably he's had experience. Even so, I delay a few seconds, making him wait while I finish coffee, stand, and pull on my school blazer.

Already making his resignation speech. "I hope we can be friends. I hope this doesn't affect things between us."

I walk straight up to him and kiss the boy's nose. That ends the prattle. Again feeling the watchful Bettie over by the cash register, I slide my right hand into Double-U's left.

"Walk me home," I suggest.

Next morning, Wednesday, I had an early-bird appointment in the city.

The offices were on the third floor of the Collinwood Chambers Building at 110-114 Collins Street, a place of dark pink bricks and pale yellow fixtures equal parts inspired by Elizabethan and Medieval Gothic architecture.

As I say, the appointment was pencilled in early (7:30 a.m.) so I could spend forty-five minutes getting my head examined while Dad treated himself to a tasty breakfast at the nearby Windsor Hotel.

After that he'd give me a lift to school, meaning I only missed the first period.

My father was the one more nervous beforehand. Woke us at five, shoved me into the shower, and I was forced to wear something discreet (school uniform was perfect) along with Mum's favourite chocolate-brown beret that (mostly) covered my platinum hair.

Subversively added some cherry-coloured lipstick since otherwise my face was a blank canvas dominated by black eyebrows. Went along with the sham mostly because I was off the planet — kept thinking about the evening before with Double-U.

Wild abandon hugs, kisses. His jacket and shirt off, him on my bed, as I investigated every available millimetre of this gorgeous boy's chest, tummy, sides, shoulders, back, throat. And he didn't miss.

The memory took my breath away most of the trip into the city — until we arrived at 7:25.

Listed on a polished brass plaque outside the entrance were four physicians, all shrinks, under the business name Bethlem Royal Hospice: Drs Lyman Sanderson, William Chumley, Hugo Hackenbush and Pamela Pearl.

Doc Pearl was my girl, nominated by the Children's Court to give me a well-earned dose of counselling.

Her redheaded secretary Nicky Marotta (the lady had a cheap plastic nameplate on a tiny desk) ended up being the aunt of my friend Clair — I'd met her once before at a Mac.Duagh school fête. Don't know whether the woman recognized me since we hardly shared a word as she shooed me into a large room lined with bookcases.

There was a much bigger desk there, pressed up to one corner, with an insipid Ken Done print above that — all Sydney Harbour Bridge and Opera House.

Didn't take long to find a white, upholstered chaise longue and a one-man armchair opposite one another either side of a low, innocuous table.

As for Dr Pearl, this was a fortyish brunette with long, frizzy hair that took up several inches of space either side of her head. Wearing blue, thick-frame glasses and a white lab coat over a herringbone Harris Tweed suit, she sat behind the desk, face down, assembling a file I guessed was mine.

"Take a chair, Mina," she says without upping periscope.

I gravitate to the armchair but somehow she notices. Maybe sonar.

"Try the white one."

"Can't we trade?"

"Not today."

So I sit and test how soft the sofa is — not bad. Goldilocks might be happy.

A memory flashes by (Double-U again, raining kisses on my neck) and, just in case I've blushed, I look down at the floor. There's a zebra rug there I hope isn't real, atop frigid tiles.

Feeling less embarrassed, the memory repressed, I check out the rest of the room.

On the dozens of shelves that surround me I find not a single interesting tome. Only books on medicine, therapy, theory and case studies.

"Do you treat one another?" I ask while making myself comfy on that white couch.

"Pardon?"

"You doctors — if you get depressed, d'you check in to the room next door and hop on the couch? You know, help one another."

"I'm sure if ever we have issues, the door would always be open."

"Liar," Anim announces from a convenient perch on the windowsill. Didn't know she'd come along for the consultation.

Having finished the file, Dr Pearl sits in the armchair with that folder, a notepad and a mug of coffee within easy reach. I wasn't offered any of these things.

"So you're Mina," the woman decides.

"And you're Pamela."

"I am indeed. Put your feet up. Make yourself at home."

I stay right where I am — sitting on the side of the sofa, shoes steadfastly glued to that striped rug. "My dad hates me putting feet on the furniture."

"Really?" The woman swaps drink for pad. "How do you feel about that?"

"Is this part of the test?"

"Not a test. A chat."

Of course Anim lets me know her opinion. "It's a test."

"Mm-hmm."

The woman smiles.

"Mina, why do you think you're here?"

"I don't know. Because of my brother?"

"You're not sure."

"No, I *am*. I just like throwing about my opinion as a question."

"Interesting." The woman leans over and writes something.

"Careful," Anim warns.

So I clear my throat. "I was being glib."

Pamela nods. "I know you were." Placing the notebook on her lap, she leans back and stretches like a sun-drenched cat. "May I ask you a question in return?"

I glance round the office, smiling slightly but suspicious. "Isn't that why we're here?"

"Is it?"

Now I frown. "Is that the question?"

"No, no. Merely warming up."

"Sweet," says Anim over at the window, parting flimsy white-lace curtains. "You're royally screwed, M."

"The question," Pamela poses while tapping her chin with the end of the fountain pen in her fingers, "is this: Why do you think your brother Patrick physically abused you?"

"Don't know — shouldn't you ask him?"

"I prefer asking you."

"Why?"

"Well, to start with, I'd venture that you're more interesting."

"Pfft."

"Seriously. Boys Patrick's age, also older ones, are usually quite stupid."

"Okay."

I slide out of my shoes and place feet up on the sofa. Something silly — let's see how interesting she really thinks I am.

"When I was little, I used to think Patrick hurt me as punishment for killing my pet tortoise."

Doc Pearl takes a nip. "Punishment from a higher authority, you mean?"

"Like God? — God no. I mean, I was only four at the time and this was an accident — didn't know the difference between a tortoise and a turtle."

"I believe I still don't," cuts in the good doctor.

"Turtles're the ones that swim. Tortoises are land-lubbers like us."

"Well. We learn something new every day. Please continue."

"Sure. At the time — I was four, remember—?"

"You already said." I guess this was Animeid's turn to interrupt.

"So I did." I laugh.

A mistake.

Causes the doctor to peer my way. Biting lower lip, I shrug and plough right on.

"Anyway, *I* didn't know the difference back then. Had a pet tortoise named Touché Turtle — further confusing the issue, I guess."

"Named after the cartoon character."

I'm impressed. "You know him?"

"I do. My son was an avid fan. Please, go on."

"Okay. We lived in a different house then, one with a large swimming pool in the back yard, so I took Touché out there and launched him into the water."

"What happened?"

The other woman has put down pen and looks riveted.

"Well, he sank. Depth-charged straight to the bottom. That part of the pool was a metre and a half deep. No one else was home and I wasn't allowed in. An hour later, Touché still hadn't budged from his position — which is when I figured out tortoises weren't the swimming sort."

"That's awful."

"Like I said, it was an accident. I didn't know."

"Even so." More notes flow.

"Think you have a black mark against your name," my pesky housemate decides, billowing the curtains back and forth because she's bored. "Prob'ly a card-carrying member of Animals Liberation."

"Then that should make *you* happy," I'm lashing in return before I know it.

"Oops." That's Anim.

Pamela posits nothing. May have stopped writing but is transfixed — doesn't shift a muscle. Her gaze is focused on the zebra rug where my shoes were.

"There's someone else here," she finally voices in a soft tone.

"No." My response is anaemic. Against better judgment, I change mind straight after and come up with something truly stupid: "Can you hear her?"

Regret saying it straight off — this woman couldn't hear or see Animeid.

"I don't need to." The good doctor raises surprisingly kind eyes to meet mine. "But I'm correct, aren't I?"

I sigh then.

"Yes. I have my very own Harvey."

"Shhh," warns that erstwhile guardian angel by the window.

Pamela apparently hasn't heard my comment correctly or is confused. Definitely doesn't register Anim's warning.

"I'm sorry, Mina — you have your own what?"

"My own Harvey. You've seen the film?"

"Well, I'm not certain. Which film?"

"*Harvey*."

"This doesn't ring any bells."

"1950 — James Stewart, based on a famous play. Guy has a best friend no one else can see. A six-foot, three-and-one-half-inch tall invisible rabbit."

The woman slides spectacles down her nose and looks over the frame.

"You have an invisible bunny for a friend?"

"No, I've got a bird-lady."

"A bird-lady." Pamela jots this down.

I notice Animeid shaking her head. "Dumb, telling her."

"Shhh."

Sitting back, Pamela assesses the situation anew. "Was that shush intended for me, or your feathered friend?"

"My friend. Only she's not really my friend."

"*Aw*, thanks." Animeid might currently be hamming up a swoon, but I get the feeling she's also pretending to be Sarah — since feathered hands are firmly laid upon her breast. "You're busting up my heart."

I ignore the beast.

"What colour is this bird-lady?" asks the doctor.

"Does it matter?"

"Might do."

"Okay. She's black."

"Matt or gloss feathers?"

"Glossy."

"When you say black, what shade?"

"Like liquorice."

"Jet black." The pen is scratching wildly. "I assume she rather resembles a crow."

"Actually, more like a raven."

"There is a difference?"

"Apparently. Though this one acts more like an old magpie."

Anim says nothing. Has turned her back to us to stare out our third-floor window just as Dr Pearl turns a page in the notebook.

"Tell me about her. This bird-lady."

"Where do I start? — She does have a name."

"Yes?"

"Animeid. That's 'Die Mina' backwards, by the way."

"Very interesting."

"I call her Anim for short."

"Does she object?"

"Not thus far."

"Is she with you all the time?"

"Not always. Anim visits on a regular basis, though she refuses to tie herself to any particular schedule. I know she's not real but she's overbearing and I can't seem to shake her. Like you guessed, she's here right now."

Pamela raises her head again. "Where, exactly?"

"By the windowsill."

"What's she doing over there?"

"Before she was annoying, but now she's ignoring me. Enjoying the view."

"Well, it *is* a very good view. One reason for the exorbitant rents."

Anim huffs. "These quacks're being ripped off. All I see is traffic."

Of course I don't translate.

There's no point — can already imagine what Dr Pamela Pearl is thinking. Something I've thought for years.

My throat is surprisingly dry, so I clear it, and then sink back into the softness of this sofa. Wish I had coffee.

"Is this what you people call schizophrenia?" I ask.

"Not quite. What you're describing tends toward dissociative identity disorder —laymen often mix them up. I could be in error, however. This may be something far simpler to treat. But you've suffered an ongoing trauma for years, Mina, and I'm not surprised there's damage here."

Having turned abruptly, I see Animeid is angry, visible facial features or not — her feathers stand on end.

"The old cow is calling me *damage*?"

It takes a lot of effort to keep my trap shut.

This is the moment Dr Pearl produces a big blue pill, something that looks like it would weigh down a horse.

"I'm going to prescribe Elysium, three tablets daily with meals."

"You really call it Elysium?"

"Mm-hmm. The registered trademark for Swiss health-care company Pfizzer-La Roach. Or are they Swedish? I can't seem to remember. Anyhow, there are caveats. I'll need to see you twice a week over the next few months in order to monitor progress. This medicine helps reduce depression in some D.I.D. patients, but antidepressants must be taken only under expert guidance as some of them have side-effects. Any change in behavior due to the effect of medication must be monitored consistently."

"Is it dangerous?"

"No! Safe as houses. Let's see if we can't conquer the problem together."

"Conquer Anim?" I have to clarify this, fear in my heart.

"Conquer the disorder. You do know he's not real?"

"*She*."

"She, then."

"In your bin," my bird-girl mutters, now beside me on the sofa, the toes of one bare foot following the course of a zebra stripe. Still bristling.

I cautiously, surreptitiously, stretch out my hand — out of the other woman's sight — and touch Anim for the first time. Her feathers and skin are cool.

"I know," I say.

C57-D predates T-47

— jumping for the windowsill as someone barges through the doorway behind, and take a leap as a bullet whistles past my ear.

Two storeys aren't as easy as they might sound.

Haven't busted my spine or anything that drastic but looks as if I've crunched some bone in the right ankle at the end of the drop — heard it snap when I landed — and the pain is blinding.

Even so, I hobble along an abandoned, rain-washed city street in some kind of panic, unable to put decent weight on the busted foot but refusing to stand about — anyway just as agonizing — to be used as target practice.

That's when someone hollers behind me.

"Stop where you are —!"

Don't catch the full warning, only the beginning, but this sounds urgent and convinces me to pull up stumps. I duck for cover; try to deflect the pain, focus askew.

Quicksilver intercuts of a kiss, a slap, a gift. A blue pill, a black feather. Someone swimming, another writhing.

" — girl. C'mon. I need you. Now."

Straight away, somehow I feel warm and cold all at once — ankle agony miraculously amiss.

Is that possible?

Whiff burning vegetation along with the stench of likewise aflame plastics and fuel.

Opening eyes, I see the fires responsible.

Littered everywhere, scattered between skeletons of trees alight and torn sheets of melted/twisted metal that stretch out into the distance.

I appear to be lying flat on my back in a forest on compacted ice, possibly having attempted to make snow angels.

Sounds like fun. Wasn't I being shot at?

No idea.

Night-time, I'm outdoors, it's hot and cool at the same time, I partially choke on those noxious fumes, and someone is leaning over me. A shadow, one impossible to define properly in a pall cast by the dancing orange pyre — though I do see this is a shade dressed in metallic blue that refracts said light. The colours are intense, particularly the blue suit and the fires.

"What happened...?"

My voice shams someone else's, mostly croak, followed by a seizure of coughing that seriously hurts my chest.

"There, there," says the hoverer's voice.

Don't know why, but both tone and content irritate me.

"What happened?" I repeat, firmer this time — inducing the shadow to cut any crooning.

"We crashed," she says. Simple, if insufficient. Crashed?

For a moment I figure this should be Dad above me, that we've pranged his precious antique BMW, except that the voice is a woman's, one I think I recognize. Trouble is I'm dazed, confused, seeing stars, can't figure out a stupid thing.

Keep it simple. As.

"Who're you?"

"This again?" My sight-unseen attendant in blue has her own hacking cough — probably because the smoke is thicker now — and then she clears her throat. "Sorry. Murray, sir."

I squint, trying to discern her face better. So close, yet I can't make out a single feature. It's like everything there has been erased. "*Sarah?*"

"Got it."

"Hey. Long time, no see."

"Not so long."

That's when I realize that the stars I'm seeing are real. They fill the night sky, above and beyond the glare of fire.

A crash.

"We were in a car?"

"Not exactly — no wheels. Our ride had wings."

"Wings."

"Remember?"

No. I don't remember. At all.

"What happened?" Am still trying to sort nonsense from, well, other nonsense. Easier to start at the bottom rung and work my way up through this folly.

"What's the last thing you recall?"

"Nothing." Except avoiding bullets, but that already feels like another life.

"Look around, sir. We crash-landed."

"Crash-landed *what*?"

"The ship. Come on — think, sir. We need you."

"Why d'you keep calling me sir?"

I grumble this aloud; annoyed that nothing at all is sinking in — even the twinkling stars refuse to budge from my brain. And this person is not the Sarah Murray that should be here according to recent diggings in an apparently distant past. Trying to think clearly, I realize I can't.

"Are you being sarcastic?" I tack on, bewildered.

"Nup. We don't have time for laughs."

"I'm thirsty."

"*That* I can help with."

She's kind enough to bring a drink to my lips in spite of errant grumpiness and complaints.

"Sip," the woman commands. "Not too much."

My throat feels less like sandpaper. "Thank you."

"No worries, sir."

"Mina. I'm Mina."

"I know."

Exhausted, I close eyes.

The darkness, I realize, has no end, with the straight lines of nearby spotlighted tree trunks abruptly swinging to diagonal, and I'm lazing in inky darkness. A white pinpoint appears. Wonder if I should hike toward that, retreat in the opposite direction, or stay right where I am. But the light's getting bigger and there's a current now, dragging me that way. Treading water, I'm indecisive, shooting pains speaking nonsense from my elbow.

And suddenly — awake.

Sitting up on the side of a plasti-steel cot, cords and wires hanging from places all over a half-naked body.

An extremely elderly nurse is unstitching the devices, pulling them out, rolling them up. The woman has a pert mouth with thin lips and zero expression on her face. It's like looking at another wall.

"Feeling better?"

I stare at her. She has on a starched white uniform over a frumpy frame but I know that voice, in spite of the time difference. Sarah.

"Vaguely," I say.

"We need to bring you up to speed — about the ship."

A ship?

I fence away inane thoughts of passenger liners like the *Titanic* and *Britannia*. While this woman looks vintage enough to have been a passenger on either vessel, the Sarah I know was born in 1969.

"Where am I?" I think to ask.

"Hospital."

As the nurse tucks everything into the top drawer of a stainless steel cabinet on wheels — in yawn-inspiringly dithering fashion — I feel dizzy. Have to lie down again, and I guess pass out.

"*— You still with me, sir?*"

Back on the ice instead of a cot. Fifty percent baked, the other half frozen. Allowing my eyes to wander from scrunched-up tinfoil props that're scattered all about, I peer up at my hostess.

Wings. This younger Sarah I can't see properly said something about wings. Not smokestacks. No bright red lifebuoys or icebergs.

Certainly this looked like something that'd once been a fuselage, a lot of scrap metal now, and some of the flames were blue — a good indicator of burning rocket-propulsion fuel.

I check myself then and there. How do I know this stuff?

Memories seep through the cracks: A cramped cockpit, a countdown, and lift-off. What was the vessel's name? Something German, an unusual moniker for a space vessel.

Die Frau im Mond. The Woman in the Moon.

Blinking generates flashbacks of military and aeronautics training, something to do with handguns, zero gravity and centrifugal forces.

These make me reel to such an extent that the world this time banks vertical, and I stumble forward — spread out on my front this time rather than the back, beneath me a cold stone floor partially covered in straw.

I appear to be wrapped in a drab chemise-and-shawl combo, legs hidden beneath a long skirt made from scratchy woollen cloth. Feel at my head — a cap there holds back the hair — while cottoning on that I'm in an ill-lit space, surrounded by people behaving unfriendly. The raised farming utensils are the giveaway, along with the manner in which they glare down, all distrust and hysteria.

Leadlight windows, the only source of illumination beyond the heads of this crowd, reveal an equally menacing sky.

Pull myself into a sitting position, refocusing on the angry mob, just as a leather-bound book bangs down between me and another person I discover kneeling a few inches away.

Black hair over the face, bits of straw in it, same archaic Puritan dress-sense as me, and a broken broom nearby on the slate flooring.

For a moment I believe this is Angelika.

A large man in dark garb and a booming voice — possibly a priest — corrects my error.

"Sarah Murray," he directs her way, snubbing me. "What evil

spirit have you familiarity with?"

"None," the girl responds. She hasn't moved a muscle. Voice sounds a million miles away, down an unreliable telephone line.

"S," I whisper, grasping at her hand, but she pulls it free.

Her fingers then fall over this hardback lying on the floor, and it causes the agitated chatter around us to taper off. Everybody's staring at the one point and I join them. Look down at the girl's hand covering the lower half of an ancient, mouldering *Malleus Maleficarum* — *The Hammer of Witches*.

"S."

Reaching over to part the curtain of midnight hair, I find a terrified, pale-looking Sarah, seventeen again, exactly as she'd looked in the swimming pool when I reputedly broke her heart.

"Have you made no contract," Big Man, Big Voice demands, still speaking through me like I'm not there by his feet, "with the Devil?"

"No."

Sarah finally looks to me, blues eyes pleading for something — but what? Help to escape these people? Some kind of release?

"Can't help you," I tell her; equally afraid of what I begin to realize is happening. A kangaroo court. This is a witch trial. "I'm so sorry."

That's when she surprises. Forgets her fear or is brave, and smiles.

It's the smile, I think, that incites these townsfolk.

One of them, a tall, blonde woman with a bonnet down over her eyes, pushes through and all too quickly raises a farming hoe with which to strike. I lunge between the attacker and attacked, expecting the blow instead, squeeze shut my eyes.

Open them again when I realize I'm not going to die.

A companion has joined the woman with the hoe and together they're dragging Sarah, who's limp, through double doors. Jumping to my feet I shove through the others here in hot pursuit. Upon fleeing the building, I enter a muddy town square of some sort, wooden houses framing the space, a cart and horse to one side.

Everything washed out, bordering on sepia, the horizons to all sides unclear, murky. Am overwhelmed by the smell of urine and rancid foodstuffs.

Spy those women from behind, crouching over something near a trough.

They're busy slapping away with paintbrushes frequently dipped into a substance black and sticky in a steel drum too modern for this period. This has the words 'Nede City Road Construction Authority' stamped on the side.

Closer to me is a hessian sack full of feathers, the feathers black.

Anim, I remember in that moment — where is Animeid? — and then I think I faint.

Come to on my feet in another place entirely.

Look around. People and horses are gone, Sarah has vanished, and I'm dressed in my school uniform — standing before a double-storey house slap-bang in suburbia.

Chewing my lower lip so viciously that there's blood (again) in my mouth. Stock-still on brownish-black bitumen, left hand holding my right elbow behind my back.

The sky is overcast, slate-grey, threatening a downpour. Can't begin to fathom how long I've been standing in this spot.

Don't know how I got here, no clue what I'm up to, but I do recognize Angelika's house — an Italianate manor with the moniker Portinari, a minaret and crown motif set into cement high above the name, and an apple tree out the front.

No traffic at all. Zero people. The sounds appear to have been sucked out of the place. It's bitterly cold and I have to wrap arms around myself.

Think I imagined all this. Thought I was going mad.

From further down a street lined with elms and gums a girl approaches. She's possibly eight years old, with long, straight black hair, dressed in a white pinafore. Doesn't look cold. Behind are two old ladies almost the same height, bent over and difficult to see properly since they have on black nuns' habits, with dangling rosaries.

This minor entourage stops before me.

"Are you coming in, dear?" the girl asks, looking straight up with a smile, like we've met and already become best mates.

"Not sure."

"Well, don't stay out all morning — you'll catch your death."

The ancient nuns titter, covering their mouths with veined, parchmenty old hands as they do so.

"Who are you?" I conceive to ask.

"Beatrice. What a silly question. Come," this girl says in commanding tone, eyes sparkling as she turns toward the house, "I'll make you breakfast."

"Hang on — *you'll* make *me* breakfast?"

"Stranger things do happen."

"When?"

"All the time."

So I follow the party up three steps, past a simple, cast-iron gate, along the footpath. Duck under that palm branch; weave around the ladder still propped up against the apple tree. Figure this must be Angelika's younger sibling, though she never mentioned one.

Find myself alone in a passage lined with framed photos, mostly black-and-white, of exotic locations and extraordinary people.

Hear kitchen noises somewhere further inside the house.

Walk along the hallway, past the big Holy Mother Mary & Jesus planter vase (emptied of feathers) and the smaller Degas-like bronze statue now holding a scimitar in her left hand and one chunky key in the right.

This eight-year-old is in a *Home Beautiful* kitchen, one I didn't bother inspecting last time I was here. She's rummaging through a fridge far too large for her, while the sisters seem to have scarpered.

Crossing arms on my chest, I stand in the doorway and lean against the frame.

"Don't slouch, dear," the girl says without looking over.

This forces me to stand up straight. "You're not my mother."

"No? There's a shame."

Don't think she's listening.

"You're a kid."

"So're you."

"Twice your age."

"Debatable." This girl Beatrice stops what she's doing in the refrigerator and peers over. "Scrambled or poached?"

I stare in return. "Eggs?"

"Mmm."

"I like poached. Can you do that...?"

"Easy as. Eggs Benedict, right?" The kid winks at me.

My favourite dish — the devil she knew. Still, will have to work harder since I like to believe these days I'm not so easily rocked.

"Sure."

"Listen to her," the girl mutters while tucking a carton of eggs and a bottle of white vinegar under her arm, "feigning indifference."

This does make me smile. "By the way, my middle name's Beatrice."

"Mm-hmm." Having closed the fridge, my miniature chef turns away from me. Because of her small hands, she takes one egg at a time from the carton and carefully lays these on the counter.

"Who are you?" I ask. "Really?"

Silence, aside from utensils and ingredients being arranged and eggs cracked.

"And where's Angelika?"

The second question causes the girl to look over her shoulder.

"Don't you know? Thought you'd have figured that out by now. Go on, then — breakfast can wait."

Sadly, I never get to try the chicken eggs. Wake up instead with goose bumps.

Where is—

"— Angelika?"

"Who?"

It's the shadowy science officer/navigator from the crash-landed spaceship — I somehow remember this was Lieutenant Murray's occupation — instead of that evil courtroom scene or the leftfield kitchen encounter.

This officer has taken a hiatus to cough again into gloved fist and after that rests back on her haunches.

"No Angelica here," she tells me.

I do now remember, however, that there were other passengers.

"Where's everyone else?"

The woman looks away. "The initial blaze caught Lieutenant Milton's side of the hypersleep hangar before the crash. She's in a bad way."

Nicole? — Had no idea she was with us, but move right along. "And Angelika?" The meaningful absence.

"Again — who?"

"The captain."

"You're the captain."

"No, I'm not."

"Yes. You are."

"Then... she's gone?"

"Like I say, I don't know what you're talking about, sir. Maybe it's your head."

"My head?"

The remark shoves me closer to shrill panic, especially after feeling my skull — there may no longer be a Salem chapeau but the blood I see on my fingers has replaced it.

"What's wrong with my head?" Am thinking farming hoe.

"Easy there, you're okay, you just banged it up some in the crash. She'll be right."

Angelika — forget the head.

"We have to find her."

"This Angelica again?"

"With a K."

"Chief, I keep telling you — believe me, there's no one else."

The woman now places a hand on my shoulder. Reassuring or restraining, I'm not certain which.

"Not anywhere here. Only Lieutenant René and Ensign Satana back in the orbiting mother ship, but I haven't been able to raise them."

Clair and Hannah too?

"Or," I mumble to myself, "she's somewhere in this pyre."

In my mind I can already see the charred corpse and skull, black and defined in orange/red flames, mouth ajar, nothing left to recognize. Awful. I nearly vomit. Pull myself together, trying not to fret.

"Okay. Okay. So where are we?" I ask, determined to rise above the useless. Another me kicks into gear. "Do we know?"

"We do. According to instrument readings right before the ship came down, we crashed on Ice Planet Goth."

"They got that right. Where exactly is this dump?"

"In the Alpha Aquilae star system. I'd say about a billion-billion miles from where we ought to've been."

Ice Planet Goth? Alpha Aquilae? Hypersleep hangar?

While I did not get any of this mumbo jumbo, some words hung ambiguously familiar. Placing any one of them in this frazzled state, however, was next to impossible.

This causes no end of dread, so I try sitting up — only to find I can't succeed there either. Everything spins.

"Easy now, Commander. You've got a busted rib, possible

concussion. Still, lucky to be alive. We both are. Milton too. *Maybe.*"

My companion is now gazing at another shape I hadn't noticed, an unmoving body two metres away that's covered with a blanket. A red-sleeved arm is poking out but it also remains inanimate.

"She's alive?" I ask, seeing no proof.

"She's alive." Sarah sounds dubious.

"None of this makes sense."

"Nice you noticed. Orders?"

"Huh?"

"Orders. You're the boss of this fast-sinking ship."

News to me. This is ridiculous.

I again endeavour to pull myself to a sitting position, only this time round the woman helps. Can now see that my gold pressure suit's torn around one leg and my waist but is otherwise intact. Just wouldn't be able to prance about in a vacuum anytime soon. Neither of us is wearing a helmet anyway.

"I'm guessing the atmosphere here is breathable."

"Thus far." Lieutenant Murray busies herself checking the rips in my suit and attempting to gaffer tape these. "Haven't ruled out possible side-effects, however. Or we could gradually be poisoned. No way of knowing till it happens. We lost everything in the crash."

"How about emergency rations?"

"Was able to salvage a med-kit and food supplies to last a couple of days. As I say — everything else is gone. Apart from this."

She slides an object across melted ice, a parcel in charred, decorative paper that looks familiar (all large, golden orchids) and has a small card attached, boasting a picture of a knife. Inside this card is a short message, 'Happy Birthday, Cap'n! Respect, Satana & René', and once I tear open the present I discover a precious white ballet tutu.

"Useful?" asks Sarah.

"Hardly."

At least I can see the woman a little better in the light cast by a nearby fire.

Most of her head is covered with a blue, vinyl skullcap-based system of a mike and headphones, only the face naked to the elements. There are smudge marks on one cheek, a cut on the chin, and she has a look that bleeds fear and consternation, both under control.

Even so, I make out features like the cherubic mouth, cast in a face at least ten years older and harder than it should be.

"You?" I say. "Are you hurt?

"A few scrapes and abrasions, but otherwise joyfully intact."

I shake my head, one very silly attempt to clear it. Makes my neck ache more.

Realize I'm partially saturated inside the spacesuit, probably by melting snow thanks to the surrounding flames. But at least these're keeping us warm since the ventilation garment beneath seems to be out of action.

"Do we know if there's any intelligent life on this world?" I check.

"Not intelligent per se."

"Go on."

"The Krell — primitive sub-humans."

"Instruments told you that?"

"Only the name." Sarah visibly shivers. "No, I've seen the buggers already. In the woods about a half klick away, apparently terrified of the blaze but curious all the same. Ugly bastards — green, huge heads — and they're a hostile, deadly crowd. I worry about what they might do once the fires die down."

"Cannibals?"

"I think these 'people' will tuck into anything with a pulse — since the conditions on this planet aren't exactly conducive to an idyllic vegetarian lifestyle." Lieutenant Murray allows herself a chuckle. "Not really cannibalism if they eat us anyway — we're a different species."

"There's a point. Weapons?"

"Them, or us?"

"Both?"

"They have clubs, so far as I saw. Not sufficiently developed to've graduated on to the projectile sort, but all we have are our nails and a pair of binoculars."

"You're forgetting the tutu. Oh, well. Anything for a barrel of laughs." A thought, yet another worrying one, occurs to me. "D'you think they have the captain?"

"This again? *You're* the captain."

"Oh. Right. What happened to our munitions?"

Murray nods at the conflagration. The fate of most things useful aside from leotards. "In there, somewhere."

"Blast."

"Were a few of those too while you were unconscious." The officer looks me in the eye. "So what happens now, sir?"

Memories flood through, and the right words to say. "Standard procedure."

"Is that the best we can expect?"

"Probably."

"Standard procedure, then?"

I attempt a shrug. "If we're incommunicado for more than twenty-four hours, Unit 5 will send one of the rescue vessels stationed on Ganymede."

"Those old crates?" The woman sits back. "So we'll be waiting forever."

"Unless we end up on some ethnic menu."

"Or René and Satana get off their arses to help."

Tentatively, I place my right hand on my chest and softly push. Yes, there's the pain, but it's nowhere near as sharp as a busted rib ought to feel.

"The other thing I salvaged," Murray says. "A few doses of Elysium."

I've latched straight onto this word. "Elysium."

"Gave most of it to the lieutenant there, that's why she's so out of it. Was shrieking and tearing hair before that. Anyway, we had enough left over to give you a dose. Will be wearing off in three or four hours, though, and there's no more. Sorry, chief."

"No apologies necessary — you've done everything while I caught up on beauty sleep. Thank you."

Murray inclines her head.

Force myself to sit straight, chemical and physical lethargy be damned, and scan our surroundings afresh. Time enough to wallow later in self-pity and confusion.

"So, we have a job to do. Stay alive."

"Easier said than done."

"So they say. All right, first step we'll need to find arms." Surprise myself by the way in which I take charge. "If the Krell are toting blunt wooden instruments, then we'll settle with metal ones. Any long pieces from the wreckage will do, preferably with a jagged tip. Second, we'll have to find shelter. Once these fires go out, I doubt this is a hospitable location — weather-wise or in terms of defending our position."

"What about Lieutenant Milton?"

"Can she walk?"

"Out like a light."

I nod at that. "Okay. You say I've got a few more hours of Elysium in me? I'll carry her."

"Sir, we'll take turns."

"Uh-uh. Thanks, but no. I need you to defend our backs in case the Krell attack. You're in better condition."

That uttered, I lurch up to my feet and sway.

It's again Lieutenant Murray who supports me. She has an arm encircling my waist. We gain a better perspective of the crash site — there're fires burning in the darkness up to a kilometre away. A bitterly cold wind fans smoke through the black skeletons of trees with no vegetation on them.

Fuck it, Angelika — where are you? Are you okay? Are you alive?

End up blowing out my cheeks, dismayed. "Jeez. We sure pick our vacation spots."

That's when the pounding explosions erupt — depth charges dropped from somewhere above.

As we struggle along with a limp, unconscious crewmember between us, buffeted by shock waves, Lieutenant Murray glares heavenward.

"What the Hell does she think she's doing?" she rages beside me. "Damn you, Satana, you'll kill us all with your friendly fire!"

Which is the moment a concussion round knocks me off my feet.

Find myself stumbling in jeans instead of a spacesuit along a long, narrow corridor made of wood, with soft matting on the floor, sliding doors to the right.

Hear something that sounds vaguely like a guitar twanging away, very Japanese in style.

Beat a quick path to one room that has the door ajar, see two people kneeling either side of a squat table, indulging in a tea party — a geisha chatting with a handsome if dishevelled man in a trench coat — but they look busy and I keep moving.

Find a balcony, step past discarded clogs, emerge into a sun-drenched place. Warmer, barren — a strange children's playground looking a hundred years old.

Now I stop to ogle.

Here is a seesaw with a rotted plank of wood that'll never again carry kids. Over there are four busted swings with rusting chains. Next to that a slide made from old cement. Cowboy movie tumbleweeds roll about courtesy of a stiff breeze, while in a sandbox full of mud blooms a collection of swaying Venus flytraps, each the size of a football, snapping at empty air.

Bullshit.

There's no rhyme or reason to the set-pieces here — am forced to puzzle if I've wound up either in a surrealist film made by Luis Buñuel or (far more likely) some hack is splicing together stock footage borrowed from low-budget horror maestro Ed Wood.

Worst part is that this hack appears to be me, yet I can't find the means to escape our ready-made reel.

Each turn taken propels me through some new, invisible trapdoor — or back through ones I've already traversed — bouncing from one scene to the next with assorted friends as bit-players. Can't remember how I first set foot onto this rollercoaster, unable to quite fathom what's real and what is not. Am playing for time when I have no idea if time actually matters.

Which is why, here, I refuse to play ball. Stay right where I am in the middle of this dusty ground and stare at my feet — which are clad in red Converse All Stars. Try to focus on what's afoot (no pun intended) inside my head instead of the fiction before my eyes.

Why is it so hard to think? How come I slip so easily into each scenario, embracing the moment, forgetting who I am?

Think. Cue: Spotlight.

Mina. Seventeen. Schoolgirl. Loser. Unloved. Pitied, maybe. Laughed at, certainly. But is this combination all that I am? Hadn't Angelika accomplished anything? Animeid?

I blink several times, realize I'm crying.

And what about Sarah too? — though I never appreciated that before.

Fluttering behind makes me think instantly of Anim. In spite of determination not to participate I swirl about — to find hundreds of crows on the swings, the seesaw, and on a broken-down set of monkey bars.

All studying me in silence, until they raise their wings — as one — and a slew of black feathers consumes everything.

Change of scenes. Anew.

Inside a place just as awful if completely different, wading through rubbish, broken furniture, torn-up linoleum and the stench of mould. A window ahead is huge, twice my height, with the glass chiselled out; fly wire ripped and flapping, and rain beating through. Don't need all that space, require only a couple of centimetres to check the devastated world two storeys below.

I tumble through that space.

Land on my feet in softness.

It's three a.m. when the clock on the tower of the Second Empire style South Nede Town Hall, next street over, strikes two — off-gong for the first time in 106 years of wound-up local history.

This is when I know things are amiss.

That, and stumbling over a corpse.

The snow on this quiet street is knee-deep, its powdery glory a thing of the past. Bottom half of the stuff is freezing hard and diabolically slippery, while the upper layer has turned into dirty slush.

Since when did it snow in Nede?

Never that I remembered — accounting for my inexperience trudging through this gunk, and no wonder I haven't counted on a dead body being deposited in the mix.

When my legs get tangled up in stiffened limbs I fall forward, arms sinking in up to the elbows while a white-and-blue set of fingers pokes up round my nostrils — someone else's left mitt, sticking out of the snow like an albino spider in periscope-mode.

Of course I jump backward, kicking old ice all about and banging my head on a metal street-sign pole.

As I stabilize myself against that pole, rubbing the back of my skull, I stare at the body that's partially surfaced. A middle-aged man, the ballast of any clothing amiss, his skin — like his hand — white and blue. Pink splotches, dried blood and tear marks around the throat are all I can make out in poor light.

Stop massaging my head, allow fingers to linger there, twisting hair between fingertips. Not sure what to do. It's not every day one trips on stiffs in small city snowdrifts — or they find you.

Especially when the dead body belongs to your father.

Cover my face, about to scream, but this is torn out of my throat.

There's a soft breeze, a whisper that's supremely gentle. Drifting on its current, floating above ground, sight unseen. There is some kind of movement nearby, impenetrable in the blackness. Can't see anything at all. Must be dozing, and this surprises. Since when did I lucid dream?

Straight lines abruptly zigzag like ragged lightning bolts, and an instant later vanish.

Am swimming in inky darkness.

When the white pinpoint again appears, confusion if I should head there or retreat in the opposite direction, but this spot's getting bigger and the current is headed that way. Treading water, underwater, I'm indecisive, can't breathe — shooting pains speak nonsense from my ribcage.

Suddenly I'm awake.

In a large, old bathroom, five doors to toilet cubicles behind me. Am leaning on the sink before a dirty mirror. Dim it may be, but when I push back my bangs, tuck hair behind my ears, I find a reflection I hardly recognize.

Happiness etched there, like someone'd used lino-cutting tools to prove their sunny point.

The cheeks with a dimple apiece, either side of a smiling mouth. Thing is, I can't control it, cannot stop grinning like an idiot.

Horrified by the sight, wanting to tear down that stupid face, now the real stuff comes seeping out — literally leaking from the pores of my skin, from my nostrils, mouth, ears, tear ducts: Something foamy, frothy, that closely resembles saliva.

Not here, I beg myself. Not now. No. *Please, God, no.*

Cover eyes with my hands to push hard against the slippery wetness, and then finally drop the fingers.

Am blinded.

The glare is overbearing and I can't see a thing for several seconds.

Once vision does return I realize the culprit is the sun and I'm looking out over a grand, wooded valley without trace of civilization.

Standing atop a green-grassed cliff, drenched in that sunlight, close by several unclaimed bodies in chainmail and armour, much blood spilled, and a whole lot of buzzing flies.

Horror hops in the back seat — this sight terrifies me.

A sword, a mace and a double-edged axe lie on the grass near my feet, as does a leather pouch, a whalebone corset with serrated strings, and a bejewelled tiara. Brightly coloured flowers decorate it all.

When I peer over the edge of the precipice I spy a man's body below, crumpled up, bent at entirely wrong angles.

No sign of any other.

Beautiful day for a stroll on a battlefield location. Angelika still nowhere to be found, Sarah also A.W.O.L.

Predictably, things go topsy-turvy, just like that place at the top of the Faraway Tree in Enid Blyton, and the world is now upside down.

I dangle in our backyard, hanging from the clothesline beneath a billowing Daisy Duck skirt, my favourite when I was four.

Pointlessly bawling while my skull pounds, something passes close by, having fallen from above. I cut the snivelling to look below and spy it there — skewering a lump of dog dung, this object now stands to flagpole attention.

A liquorice-coloured feather several inches in length.

Fade out, like in old movies.

Come to in a cave of some sort — tiny, dark, dead cold.

A small fire fights for a last, fitful gasp on frozen ground before me. Otherwise it's pitch black in every nook and cranny. The sounds appear to have been sucked out of the place.

I rise to a sitting position against an uneven rock wall. Pain in my chest unbelievable, my head failing to deal with important things like balance and depth of vision.

Even so, I see no one is here and I still hear fuck all.

Murray and Milton clearly gone, at least so far as the tiny area of light is concerned. I make to call out but end up keeled over, coughing and heaving. Bile trails from my mouth to the ground but I don't bother wiping it.

Try instead raising hands to fiddle awkwardly with headgear. Slide back the vinyl skullcap and attached circuitry. Blonde hair tumbles loose. Over my eyes. A seeming safety there in this God-forsaken place.

Push to my feet, hunched over so I won't bang the head on a deceptively low ceiling, venture along this tunnel to an opening and a lighter, brighter place — where I find Lieutenant René and Ensign Satana seated on watch.

How and when did they get here?

Mouth a different question. "Where are the others?"

"Gone," says René. "There's only us now."

Shove straight past them, out into the open, hear Satana's voice behind me.

"Captain, where're you going?"

"I have to find them." Got to find Sarah, Nicole, Angelika, me.

"Don't leave us!" shouts René — not that I'm listening. Refuse to look back.

There's a blizzard that blankets everything.

Not sure when I swapped my gold spacesuit for a set of skimpy, silver armour covering little, but I don't feel the cold. Hair waves about my head as I plough forward through snow up to my knees.

Step over grey objects I soon realize are the corpses of men, wander past stray body-parts and dismembered horses, kick aside instruments of an ancient war now abandoned.

Suspended in a nearby dead tree is the carcass of a fallen aeroplane that once had two wings. These had been sheared off and lie nearby, canvas flapping in the wind. On the side of the old aircraft are the words 'Sea's Shame'.

There's a trench, also covered by a thick bank of snow, into which I slide.

A circle of soldiers kneels at the bottom playing poker.

Some of them wear those classic old World War One Brodie helmets and long greatcoats British and ANZAC troops got about in, but one individual has on a brown leather jacket with sheepskin collar and a flying hat, goggles carelessly pulled back. All eight are seated on wooden ammunition crates.

None of them notices my approach because they're frozen stiff.

Dead for hours, if not days.

The pilot has a potentially killer hand held before glassy eyes — an ace, a king, a queen and a jack, all hearts.

I recognize this gentleman straight away.

Kneel before him, dust some of the permafrost from his face, push the stiff arm with the winning cards aside, and lean in to embrace him. Tears gush from my eyes to be instantly frozen on the cheeks. Haven't cried this much since Hadrian sliced my country in two.

Never should've let him go.

Eventually I ease free of the dead pilot, kiss a frigid forehead, and walk away. Make a slow ascent up the side of the trench, through a coil of rusted, twisted barbed wire and an unmanned Vickers machine gun that has icicles hanging off it.

That's when I meet the natives.

Find myself surrounded by a dozen green grotesques — huge celery stalks with cycloptic eyes and four arms apiece. We look at one another for an age before they react, howling, pointing sticks my way.

I fall to my knees in a snowdrift. Await a killing blow — if, indeed, I can be killed. Expect it's possible on this alien world.

No friends, no lover, nothing.

Hands then grasp me, arms wrapping round the torso, and I'm being lifted into the sky above those huge, leafy heads and the primitive spears that wave in frustrated, hungry anger.

Snowflakes swirl about as I crane my neck.

See her. My saviour.

A great wingspan of black attached to a girl clad in only midnight feathers.

"Animeid," I laugh aloud, even while starting the waterworks all over again.

She peers down as we ascend into angry clouds. Can't make out her face, only scowling shadows.

"The meds, Mina!" shouts this girl above the sound of a swirling gale and wild yelps from somewhere far below. "You need to flush the evil stuff!"

$1 \text{ rad·s}^{-1} = 60/2\pi \text{ rpm}$

Huh?

Someone's apparently ripped out this sweet rescue scene and shoved in another less attractive.

The colours're all different; the dimension of the space tighter, it's night-time instead of late afternoon, am no longer winging it, and the cast has multiplied.

All at once I keel over in my new sitting position, hardly the same as flying, and I'm coughing like crazy.

"Meens, you okay?" someone is asking as they whack my upper back. Not hard enough to be Patrick — besides, this is a girl's voice — but still hurts.

"Will you stop that?" I mutter. "Not helping."

The coughing subsides, precisely when I burn my right index finger and see a wilting cigarette in my hand.

"What the Hell?"

Promptly swap the butt's position so that it now sits between the tips of my thumb and index finger, meanwhile searching about for somewhere to lay the evil thing. The plate of soggy-looking fried chips on a nearby coffee table? Perfect.

But not for everyone.

"Oh man, that's my *dinner*," another voice groans.

Least now I can pay proper attention.

Look up from a lumpy, threadbare couch that's sagging in the middle. See the complainer standing nearby in a living room of some sort — this is a bedraggled stranger in a dishevelled jacket with long, wispy beard and dreaded hair, and a huge frown.

Of course I recoil. Was hoping to see Double-U's nicely kempt good looks.

"Who're you?" I ask.

Long Hair, Long Beard raises one eyebrow and stands back to study me, apparently more irritated. "This again? Makes me wonder who the real stoner is."

My couch rocks and I realize someone is sitting beside me — the back-slapper.

"Memory of a sieve," this girl says as she leans forward, and I'm looking at Ingrid Pitt, circa *The Vampire Lovers*, only younger. I hardly recognize her since she's without any make-up. "Mina, Danny Murphy. Danny, Mina Rapace. Blah, blah, blah."

I'm staring. "Margaret."

"Omigod, the kid remembers *some* things!" Harsh as it sounds, Margaret smiles and tussles my hair. "What're we going to do with you? Hmm?"

Slowly peering around I see two other people, a girl and a boy with matching black leather motorcycle jackets sitting cross-legged on the floor between two large stereo speakers. Most of the furniture here (aside from the couch, two armchairs, two bookcases, the coffee table and a tall lamp on a crooked chrome pole) appears to have been rejected by the Brotherhood of St. Laurence.

There's a giant, partially torn poster over a boarded-up fireplace — a classic, washed-out still from the 1920 German silent horror film *The Cabinet of Dr Caligari*, the one in which somnambulist Conrad Veidt carries hapless Lil Dagover under one arm.

I'd never previously set foot in a room such as this.

Still struggling to come to terms with the fact I'm no longer being hauled to safety. Nor in a coffee shop, flirting with a boy I like. No rocket ship flight, corpses, dystopian future, witch trial or vacant lots. Can't shake the sight of my father and the boy I adore — both dead.

"Um... Where's Double-U?" I finally dare to ask.

Having already lost interest, Margaret flicks through a copy of *The Face* sitting on her lap. "In your room, right where you left him."

"*My* room?"

"Der."

Long Hair, Long Beard — Danny? — has started sifting through battered chips and ash on his plate.

"Oh man," he whines a second time.

I stand up, feel weighed down, and look at my feet. See that I'm wearing heavy, six-hole Doc Martens identical to Angelika's, along with a shredded white ballet tutu and black stockings with runs galore. Since when did I dress this way?

Docs. Angelika.

Flashes of her, an older (but wiser) Sarah, my murdered dad in the snow, and — again — Double-U's frozen pilot doppelganger dance a jolly jig across my mind.

"Upstairs. Second door, the green one."

I glance down at Margaret, who now has a four-litre winecask of Stanley Shiraz Cabernet on her lap. When did she switch accoutrements?

"Huh?"

"Your room, in case you forgot. Looking pretty vacant there."

"Oh. Thanks."

"Anytime, dear."

"And you owe me some hot chips," pipes up Long Hair, Long Beard.

This house appears to be of 19th-century Victorian construction, since the ceilings are high, cracks pepper the walls, and there's decorative work around light fixtures.

Venturing through the loungeroom door, studying everything to ensure that this time it was real, I find a flight of steep stairs in the hallway. Take one step at a time in case this route suddenly collapses.

"Hey."

Double-U is perched on the landing at the top, looking down from beneath his blond fringe. Not frozen to the spot at all. He's in his regulation Anthony Sinclair suit and there's a quizzical expression planted on that gorgeous face.

Astonishingly happy, I'm all set to change pace and bound up the remaining steps to jump into his lap, but the boy's dour look deters me.

"You're not taking your medicine anymore?"

He's holding aloft an empty, rectangular packet of Pfizzer-La Roach's Elysium.

Don't remember doing this, but somehow know what happened. "I flushed them."

"Is that wise?"

"They were messing up my head." I reach the boy, sit down next to him.

"Didn't seem that way to me."

"You're not inside my skull."

"Jesus, Mina."

"You learned my name," I mutter. Lean against him, placing my head on his shoulder. "Are we together?"

"Unless I missed something."

His arm comes over my shoulders. My forehead is blessed with a quick peck from his lips.

"How long?" I ask. Then, aware the question might come across bizarre or at the very least insensitive, I add: "Exactly? I always get dates mixed up. Want to be sure."

"Exactly? Three months last Tuesday."

Three months? I've lost three months?

"Five-oh-three p.m., to be precise. That was the time we met outside the Brigantine — and you discovered my dark and dirty secret."

"Bessie."

"Bettie. You make her sound like a dairy cow."

I hear him laugh, a sound that makes me ridiculously chirpy in spite of other concerns.

Quarter of a year. Making the current month May. No wonder it's chilly.

"Are you happy?" I'm rubbing the palm of my hand alongside

221

the boy's inner thigh.

"What do you think?"

"I don't know. Think you need to show me."

Gently taking hold of my cheeks, he kisses my mouth. A short manoeuvre that proves the point, even if his growth is a little rough.

"You need to shave," I tell him.

"And you need to take your medicine."

That's when I ease away. "Why?"

"You *know* why."

Narrow my eyes. "Pretend I don't."

"Mina, Doc Pearl says this is important. To help you."

Feeling anger now. "How d'you know that?"

He shrugs. My trick — deflecting things. Sorry, it's not going to work.

"I said how do you know about that?"

"You know."

"I don't."

"Mina. The session we had — you, me, your dad, the doc."

Double-U's lost his mirth and studies my face at the same time I scour his. Can see concern inscribed on the surface and alarm bells deep inside.

"Um... You don't remember?" he mumbles.

"I remember."

Liar, pants on fire.

Have no idea if I'm wearing any make-up or have eyes done, but I do know I have no fringe to hide behind — and yet I don't need it. Look at him and I know my expression is calm, passive, relaxed. The anger and fretting and confusion are safely boxed up beyond that. Time to deal with them later.

Double-U does surprise, though, when he picks me up, like I'm no weight at all, and carries me across a threshold that has a green door just as Margaret described. Heads straight into a large room with a double bed in the centre.

"Put me down, you show-off," I pretend to demand. "This is very undignified."

Unceremoniously tosses me onto the bed, scrambles atop, and has his hand beneath my mashed-up tutu to pull at catches holding the stockings. Black hair tumbles about my face — black?

"You're so bloody sexy," he says during the struggle — a comment that causes me to burst out laughing.

This apparently maims the moment.

The boy slumps on his back beside me, a loud sigh ringing out, and he stares up at the ceiling.

I look at his face mere inches away. Of course I can't resist — last time I saw him he was dead. Flipping over, I sit astride this boy's crotch, gazing down.

"Wild," he decides, but I cut off any future inane observation once I push my mouth against his, scratchy as it is, fingers roving about in a desperate attempt to locate the buttons of suit jacket and pants.

A belt with a large skull-and-crossbones buckle is off and tossed across the room when Double-U reverses our position and now has my nylons rolled down, tutu and undies lassoing my knees.

Have hands all over his bare bum, and he's just about to push into me, when the boy's face is unceremoniously scratched out — like someone got a coin and scraped away the silver latex covering on a scratchy lottery ticket.

My fingers stop clawing.

He's still trying to find his mark when I shove him away, have backed-up to the wall by the bed-end, and I'm sure I'm wide-eyed as all Hell. For a moment, just a fraction of one, the face I saw there wasn't Double-U's but a combination of Patrick's and his best friend Nick Shahan.

"What is it?" the boy asks, back to himself, alarmed. "Did I hurt you?"

"No. Not you. I'm so sorry."

"What is it?"

"Just me."

Sighing again, Double-U is already yanking back his boxers and trousers. "This is why you need to take the medicine."

I watch him get dressed, still against the wall. "Was I different?"

"You were normal."

Double-U is on his back and snoring.

I get up, naked, intending to switch off the overhead light but linger before the rectangular mirror attached to a wardrobe with a busted door.

Yes, my hair is black now, shoulder-length, mostly stuck up and frizzy. Damaged, I reason, from too much hairspray, chemicals and teasing. I also have two bleached lightning-bolt streaks either side of my head — *now* I look like Elsa Lanchester.

This mess encircles a face overly pale. Guess it's winter, so understandable to a degree. I'm thinner, too. Notice my childhood freckles have vanished.

Wearing simple eyeliner and mascara in thick rings round the eyes rather than the Nefertiti look, but one of the rings has smudged down my cheek. Eyebrows still thick but shaped into arches, three sleepers piercing each of my ears.

Cut the preening to pull on a nearby black cardigan, one with a hole in the right elbow and that barely covers my bum. Survey the space.

Our bedroom — the boy's and mine.

Read the signs that it's partially his.

There's a Gillette safety razor and a can of Perfect Potion Wild Lime & Veteran Shaving Foam along with Issey Miyake after-shave on a shelf near the door, while on the desk sit hair pomade and musk-scented roll-on deodorant I'd never touch.

My personal touches are new ones mixed with old — in the

bookcase, balanced precariously atop a copy of *The Complete (Illustrated) Sherlock Holmes*, one stray blister pack of the pill (same brand as Angelika) and a small plastic bottle of Pandora Plus Codeine painkillers.

An antique, dark-stained cedar dresser that's covered with stacks of cosmetics, hair utensils, tampons, batty hats, and a long, black wig on a polystyrene mannequin's head.

In a collection of plastic milkcrates are vertically stacked records, his and hers from the looks of things. Cassette tapes line up in alphabetical order above my head along a picture frame skirting board that circles the room.

A poster is on one purple wall for Nitzer Ebb, a band I don't know (but possibly discovered in my three-month hiatus), along with a bigger one on the opposite side of the room for Christian Death — just like Angelika's. Next to a large banner depicting a white and red helicopter on a black background, with the numbers 242 at the top and 'They're coming down for you!' written appropriately enough along the bottom.

Also, a long, thin handbill advertising a London gig for the Jesus and Mary Chain — definitely Double-U's.

I open each drawer in a small pine chest of three of them: Containing boxer shorts, mostly black but also a pair with Teenage Mutant Ninja Turtles, along with cotton socks and vintage sets of braces to hold up Double-U's suit-pants.

Beneath my bare feet we have a ghastly, threadbare carpet covered in pansies and cigarette burns. I assume some previous tenant must've been colour-blind since two of the walls are painted slime-green and the other two a garish purple I think I already mentioned.

The broken wardrobe appears to be mine.

Black clothes aplenty poked full of more holes than Swiss cheese. The only things not mistreated are a long velvet dress that'd reach my ankles and an antique white, lace wedding dress.

At the bottom of the closet rest two sets of newish Doc

Martens (a pair of cherry-red six-holes and another pair that're black fourteen-ups), a pair of lace-up pointy-toed boots, and my red All Stars.

Another red object, my Olivetti, is stuck under the desk. It has a layer of dust. Apparently I haven't been writing.

Brought some books and postcards, but must've left most of them, along with the comics, at Dad's place. No pictures of Brigitte, Louise or Mitzi or a Hollywood blonde bombshell anywhere to be found — but there was a framed/tamed still from Jean-Luc Godard's bold, jump cut *À bout de souffle* (1960).

It's between a small, hand-drawn bill celebrating the Australian Anarchist Centenary Celebrations, and a glossy flyer for a Treasures of Pharaoh Rama-Tut exhibition at the National Gallery.

After glancing again at the mirror, and then *À bout de souffle*, I locate scissors stuck in a plastic container with over-large safety pins. This time use them (the scissors, not the pins) on my hair instead of mutilating defenceless materials.

Cut off everything until it's about an inch in length, allowing the rest to fall onto the ugly floor. Successfully cover some of the pansies.

Once I finish snipping, I lay down the scissors, take a small amount of my lover's pomade. Rub it through fingers, and use them to ruffle up and adjust my remaining hair until it sits and looks, in the reflection, roughly similar to Jean Seberg's pixie cut in *Bonjour Tristesse* or Mia Farrow in *Rosemary's Baby*.

So I've found her — even if my eyes are green instead of brown.

By my feet, peppered with snipped black hair, is the distressed-look white tutu I'd been wearing earlier on.

Intending to be neat, I pick this up, shake it, and notice something small attached to the inside lining.

A custom clothing label. Name there?

NICOLE MILTON.

That's the moment I change into something else and head for the door.

I'm standing before a vacant lot in suburbia.

Chewing my lower lip so hard that there's blood (yet again) in my mouth. Stock-still on brownish-black bitumen, left hand holding my right elbow behind my back.

The dark night-time sky is cloudy, threatening a downpour. Can't begin to fathom how long I've been standing in this spot. Don't know how I got here, or why I know this is where Angelika's house once stood.

No traffic at all. No people about. The sounds appear to have been sucked out of the place.

The vacant lot is huge, with overgrown tufts of weeds. Looks like nothing has been here for years.

I stayed up the rest of the night, occasionally toying with my newfound shoddy habit: Churchman's cigarettes. Wondered briefly where I put the collectors' cards, or if that really was Angelika's obsession — a side of myself in many ways a complete stranger.

Thought of Nicole, Sarah, and Clair. Dad, Mum, my brother.

Ruminated most about Animeid and how much I missed her. She'd saved me, of that I was certain. Don't know how she did it.

So far as Angelika-With-a-K was concerned, I had only to peer into the looking glass — and that hung queer. She'd been well on the way to becoming my best friend and I'd fooled myself.

After opening the window to clear the air, the morning delivered up new concerns.

Bright and early, I searched for my school uniform (without success) for over an hour. No sign of the thing in this brave new bedroom.

Being May, Mac.Duagh Girls' High School would've switched to the winter ensemble of tartan green and red skirt, school tie, long-sleeved shirt, black tights or knee-high socks, green jumper, charcoal blazer, and our school scarf.

As I say, I couldn't find any of these things.

So I end up nudging Double-U, who hasn't moved a muscle all night and still sleeps on his back in the nud.

This process takes quite a few shoves along with a firm elbow in the ribs, at which point the boy grunts and shifts to his side. I lean in close, wondering whether I should kiss his hairy face or go grab the Gillette.

"What?" he mumbles, eyes screwed shut.

"Are you going to shave today?"

"What?" A grumpy look passes across the features. Fascinating to observe.

"You have whiskers."

"You woke me up to tell me that?"

"Actually, no. I'm looking for my uniform."

Double-U rolls to his other side, still bothered. "For work? Thought you got changed at the hotel."

"Work?" I find myself sitting beside him on the mattress. Am afraid to ask, but realize there's no choice. "What about — *um* — What about Mac.Duagh?"

That cranks open the eyelids a smidgeon.

"You quit."

"I quit." Something further out of leftfield than any other recent windfall, and that was saying a lot.

The boy pushes himself onto one elbow, yawns, and then pulls the doona about him. "*Brrr* — cold."

"Why? I forget."

"Why'd you quit, you mean?"

"Yes."

"Oh, man."

"And that means...?"

"It means if you took the meds I wouldn't have to rehash every bloody thing."

"Indulge me."

"Okay. Sure, sure, whatever. You're taking the rest of the year off — going to find yourself, work out some issues, do Year 12 properly in '87, et cetera, et cetera. Remember?"

"By work out issues, you mean *working* — a job?"

"You moved out of home. Money doesn't grow on trees. Jesus, we've been through all this. I feel like a broken down record, Mina. I just woke up. Fuck."

"If I'm such a pain, hon, you could always go back to Bessie."

"Told you, it's Bettie." Eyelids open a fraction more and he stares at my hair. "Wow. That's short. When'd you cut it?"

The job I'd taken on ended up being a breakfast waitress for a forgettable half-star hotel in the city called the Château Nede — rising and shining with heavenly exuberance at five-thirty, four mornings a week.

At least they apparently didn't hassle me about the hair, but when I ventured in this particular morning without a clue as to what I should be doing I think I gave a fright to the elderly Japanese and American tour-groups in the restaurant area.

These were people in a foreign city desperate to tuck into bacon that was overcooked, waterlogged scrambled eggs, and hash browns with the consistency of cardboard, being served by a member of staff who kept confusing tea and coffee, bearing the natural pallor of Morticia Addams.

Don't know how I last three hours in the place.

At the moment, however, I'm 'home' again — this rundown double-storey terrace place I share in St. Kilda with Double-U, Margaret, and Long Hair, Long Beard... who is, apparently, Margaret's latest flame.

Turns out this Danny person was a born-again hippie like Miss Vicks, only much younger — a surprising choice in partners for Margaret, who had a tendency to be volatile. P'raps he was calming? The guy yearned to be a vegetarian yet constantly attacked slabs of red meat whenever he smoked too much dope. Hence most of the time.

Danny had dirty-blond, dreadlocked hair and a thick beard

that was partially grey. Forever wore a black suede jacket with tassels on the sleeves and a tight pair of black jeans that were stained and appear bonded to his flesh. The only items of clothing he ever changed were his t-shirts, his socks, and (I pray) his underpants.

A lover of Nede indie thrash bands like God and I Spit on Your Gravy, Long Hair, Long Beard hated what he dubbed the 'foreign, politically unsound' music I generally listened to — and constantly badgered whenever that was played.

The guy was a brilliant artist, however.

He'd spend hours (like he's doing right now in the lounge) hunched over his fat sketchbook on the floor, doodling bizarre people who belonged to an apocalyptic, post-nuclear world.

"These little guys are going to take over the planet," he told me earlier, after I got home from work, exhausted, and crouched to see what he was doing.

An hour later, cradling a large glass of Margaret's cheap cask Chablis, I'm tackling lumps on the couch. Listen to Danny's pencils scratch across paper. Smell his spliff from the other side of this spacious room.

Double-U's at uni and Margaret at her part-time hospital-cleaning gig, so the place is dead quiet.

Having surrendered the battle with the sofa I take my drink upstairs.

Sit on the bed, drag out the typewriter, give it a quick polish, and ponder. The words most definitely do not flow. I can't think of a thing to write.

So I throw on a cassette, a bootleg recording of a new LP by The Smiths, *The Queen is Dead*. Tape starts at the song I love right now, 'There Is a Light That Never Goes Out'.

Makes me smile, but Morrissey's vocals always do.

I didn't know Danny, and despite apparently living together for three months my only memories of Margaret were short vignettes from when we first met, meaning I hardly knew her at all too.

Wasn't sure which page Double-U and I were on, since he seemed to be irritated by everything I now did.

Needed some escapism without dropping chemicals that ripped out my life, writing wasn't working, and I realized I missed my comic books — felt like I hadn't perused them in an age.

Same time, I wanted to see my dad to ensure he was okay.

Guessed he'd now be living all alone at our house and wouldn't object to some drop-in company. I had a key still but I didn't call. Figured Dad would be at work anyway.

When I get there around six o'clock in the evening the place is dark.

The BMW isn't in the garage.

Switching on the hallway lights, I go to the kitchen and unveil two bottles of Bollinger that'd pretty much bankrupted the meagre savings in my purse. Decide to open one now, so put the second bottle in the fridge, locate a couple of champagne coupes in the cupboard above the sink, unfoil the bottle and pop the cork.

Fill up one of the glasses and take a swig. Yep, the bubbles *do* get a tiny window of opportunity to tickle my nose.

I head upstairs, leaving the bottle behind but having topped up my glass.

My bedroom smells off-colour, like it hasn't been sufficiently aired. I pull aside the Moomin curtains, and then crank open the window. Return to the bookcase, turn on the lamp to illuminate things, and start taking out comic-book 'zines.

Pausing with *2001: A Space Odyssey* issue 2, price thirty cents, publication date January 1978. A split cover, classic '70s Jack Kirby rendering of a woman's face, half-cave girl and half-astronaut. The subtitle reads 'A Fiery Female Makes the Centuries' Trip — From the Caves to Eternity!'

Don't know why this particular comic grabs me right now.

Anyway, I place it carefully on the bed along with my 1950s Steve Ditko treasures, the '40s adventures of Bulletgirl and Miss Fury, the November 1973 Kitchen Sink Press reprint issue of *The Spirit*, featuring P'Gell.

Collect together some records I'd forgotten — surprisingly this included the seven-inch of 'She's Lost Control'. Look at the Suzi Quatro cassette tape and decide better to leave that here.

Finally, I kneel down to dig beneath the bed.

It's dusty there but I want to collect together some of my writing to see if I can't enkindle the old imagination again.

Had no idea I'd piled in so much paperwork.

I take out a stack of A4 about ten-inches high. Flick through the top pages, hardly recognizing anything written there. Most of this was freestyle, kind of pretentious stream-of-consciousness bunk, but some pages did have structure, and there was dialogue squeezed in there as well, reading like a stage play without directions.

One page has the following riff:

"Hi!"

"Hey."

"Rode here to rescue you from woop-woop."

"So — where's your white steed?"

"Let me think now. *Horsing* around?"

"That's plain sad."

"Agreed. I would've rung, but Miss Vicks said they didn't have a contact number."

"No phone."

"So I sent you a card."

"Really?"

"On Monday, when I saw you weren't at school."

"Oh."

"A nice one, with a picture of Luna Park."

"I wouldn't know — was too scared to go near the letterbox."

"Why?"

"Spider in it. *This* big."

"Then your uncle must have a huge letterbox."

"Actually, it's possibly more like the TARDIS — from *Doctor Who*, I mean. You know?"

I know. Small on the outside, humongous within.

On the page beneath are unrelated, handwritten notations that range in size from large to words you'd need a magnifying glass to read. None of it makes sense.

Sitting up, I whisk the glass of champers off the dresser and take a sip. Drats — almost finished. I'll need to go top it up, but exploring the back-catalogue is proving to be more interesting than I expected.

I bend over again, pull out an open cardboard box with another stack inside. Discover there, also, a long black feather next to a pair of tailors shears.

Take the feather out and hold it up to the lamplight, puzzled, barely able to breathe.

Don't know when I become aware that someone is standing in the doorway to my room. I assume this to be Animeid, and have a silly smile on my mush, as I look straight over. Lose the smile instantly. This is not Anim.

It's Patrick.

Like me, he's changed in three months. Dressed in a violet Violent Femmes tee with the sleeves cut off and a shapeless pair of grey tracksuit pants. Bare feet, hair nowhere near so groomed. Face looks thinner, hollow around the cheeks.

But a cellared version of the same old rage decants itself through pores to ride his expression, and I can smell stale alcohol from three metres distant.

"You're not supposed to be here," I say, while carefully sliding the comics and paperwork in a safer location under the dresser.

My brother says nothing. I get to my feet to face him.

"The restraining order."

"Fuck the restraining order." The way in which Patrick barks 'fuck' is sufficiently agitated to cause spittle to fly.

"Patrick."

His eyes tell me he's close to old tricks. "Fuck the restraining order," he repeats, in a calmer voice that worries me more.

"Patrick," I repeat. A warning, I guess, though it sounds weak.

"I live here. You don't."

He's so quick and well-practiced that he has me flat on my back before I know what's happened.

Pinions me to the floor with each of his knees on one of my shoulders and his butt deposited on my tummy. Leaning in close, mad grin on that tired-looking, unshaved face, my brother begins crooning an old favourite.

"I found a cocoon that a caterpillar made, fastened to a leaf, hanging in the shade. She barely had room to wiggle or wag — like me zipped up in my sleeping bag."

Then comes the encore, the lovingly strung, frothy saliva across my face.

Attempting to invade all available orifices like ears, nostrils, and my tightly closed mouth. The eyes he allows to escape spittle since part of the never-ending joy was allowing his victim to witness this travesty-in-motion.

"I found a cocoon that a caterpillar made, fastened to a leaf, hanging in the shade. Dum-dum-dum."

As I watch his freckled face thirty centimetres away and that taut, white mouth puckered up for another strafing run, surprisingly I don't wince.

"Patrick, stop."

Makes him finish louder and more tunelessly — *"A cocoon that a caterpillar made, hanging in the shade!"* — before clearing his throat to gather up an almighty grot from the deepest parts of his gullet.

In moments this will be gifted my way.

Calmly, no rush, I reach underneath the dresser with my right hand, grab hold of the tailors scissors, and smile despite all the foreign drool on my face.

Patrick stops gargling up a special brew of the stuff. Licks his lips.

"What're you smirking at, you pathetic bitch?"

My smile expands. "This."

Before my brother can move, the ten-inch blades are up and open and placed either side of his throat. I have one hand on each handle of the shears — ready to snip.

"Actually, I'm wrong. I should say *these*."

"What—?"

"Scissors are plural. My mistake."

Patrick's eyes slowly bulge as he becomes aware of his predicament. Takes longer than I'd like, so I give a soft jab and the right point slightly punctures the skin on his neck.

The way in which my brother yelps and jumps back across the room, holding his throat while a trail of saliva hangs from his chin, borders on comedy — but I'm angry rather than amused.

Get back to my feet, wiping stray slobber from the face, continue to point scissors in the prick's direction.

"So where's your braggadocio now?" I demand to know.

He doesn't answer, just stares at me, all upset and mouth gaping. Looks like a goldfish, surrounded by a halo of Hollywood blonde postcards attached to the wall. Clutches at the tiny scratch mark on his neck like he's copped a life-threatening laceration.

This makes me more incensed and I end up poking the shears closer to his face.

"Do that again — touch me again — and I'll cut off your dick." My eyes flash briefly down to his nether regions. "Understand?"

Silence, aside from panting.

"Patrick." Now I stare at him, head tilted to one side. "Do you understand?"

"I — Bloody Hell. Hell."

My brother backs up three more steps, over the threshold and into the passageway. Looks well and truly terrified. If I suddenly stamped my foot, I bet he'd faint.

"Who *are* you?" he asks. "What's got into you?"

"I grew a backbone. Now get out."

One flick of my head and he scarpers back to his room, slams the door.

Once that's done I exchange the scissors for the champers, salute empty air, and drain what's left.

Look at my right hand, holding that glass, and notice it doesn't tremble or shake. At all. Nothing like my heart.

Put down the coupe, flex fingers, and breathe out loudly.

Thank you, Anim. Thank you.

When Dad gets home at eight I behave like nothing's happened.

He seems happy to see me though I can tell less than impressed with the way I look. Warns me that Patrick has moved home, to which I feign mild surprise.

Find out that my brother has also quit school, given up all sports, and now works full-time as a packer in the Brockhoff Biscuit factory. Obvious to me Dad's disappointed both kids have proved such failures, but he keeps the disappointment under a leash.

We order in pizza (Hawaiian, my preference), at which point I unveil the second bottle of Bollinger that's been hiding in the fridge. While I pour two glasses, I hear Dad shuffle behind me.

"Are you allowed to drink? With the medication, I mean."

"I stopped taking it."

"Why on earth would you do that?"

"Why on earth would you insist I stay on something that deadens the senses?"

I turn about, all smiles, like we never had this discussion. Hand him his glass and bang mine against it.

"Cheers."

The two of us end up drinking the whole bottle, and watch a light comedy (*Mother and Son*) on the telly together.

Dad remembers to check his watch a couple of times.

"Can't imagine where your brother is," he says towards ten o'clock.

"Dad, I worry about him."

"Why, sweetheart?"

I shrug. "Patrick does tend to run with scissors." Stop myself from looking up at the ceiling toward my brother's room, and certainly don't laugh.

"He's had a hard time."

That comment snares me. "Really."

"You heard his best friend's gone missing?"

"Nick?"

"That's the one. Nicholas." Dad looks peeved. "The police had the gall to act like Pat was somehow responsible."

What was it with all these disappearing people?

"Must be the history of violence," I decide.

On the late-night bus trip to Flahan the vehicle is thankfully mostly empty.

Sitting up back, Walkman on, I work my face fast — skip the facial scrub to instead cover everything with a mask of foundation greasepaint and ivory powder that spills onto the seat beside me.

Slap on stuff in time to beats by Front 242 and Sisters of Mercy.

Had a lot of music to catch up on over the past nine days since my return from the kaleidoscopic Ice Planet Goth, or wherever the heck I'd been. Skipping out on school meant I gained more time to perfect make-up — or at the very least cut down the time this took to apply.

With a mirror in hand, I hurdle pencil work and use liquid eyeliner instead to outline the arching shape from nose to temples, but have to fix uneven lines since we keep hitting bumps and lurching around unnecessary corners. Try to disguise the mistakes with grey and silver eye shadow along with my vacuous, spiralling tear on the left cheek.

Must be ironic since I find it so hard to cry in the real world.

Employ thick mascara and eyelash curlers to finish the job — and pray it'll be dark enough in the club to get away with this butcher's work.

Tease short hair with a comb and a lot of hairspray that causes the driver to complain — surprised it took him so long — and finally hop out at Commercialized Road as headphones rattle to 'If There's a Heaven Above' by Love and Rockets.

Sometime during my three-month chemical purgatory, Locomotion (and the St. George itself) had been shut down, so the clientele moved ship to a new club, Soho in Flahan.

Being the last day of the working week meant this particular night was called Black Friday.

I'd been with Margaret and Double-U the week before, met people apparently my friends — like Kedra, a super-cute fifteen-year-old who claimed to have fairy floss hair, a bronze-blonde collaboration into which she'd tied several flowers. Then there was Mateo — a Pole with dangerous metal spikes sewn all over his motorcycle jacket, sounding when he spoke just like Schwarzenegger doing the Terminator — and Messerschmitt Twins Gavin and Frank, who got around in identical German SS uniforms with jackboots and were members of local band Beijing Au Go-Go.

Others including Swedish sisters Karin and Viveka (one platinum blonde, the other ebony brunette), another stunner named Kristina who had nose and lower lip both pierced above a sublime white wedding dress. Trish, Sharon, Avon, Maria, Aggie,

Carl — couldn't believe I'd met and liaised with so many individuals while honeymooning in la la land.

Tonight, supposed to meet Margaret and Kedra here before midnight, but rock up at five past, taking off headphones to swap The Smiths for Man 2 Man Meet Man Parrish.

Everything here is painted black — the entrance, the door, the walls, ceiling, speakers, and bar.

Parts of the floor are viscous black linoleum and other sections sticky black carpet. It's gloriously dingy (which suits my hack make-up effort), a smoke machine is in constant use, and there're ultraviolet lamps scattered about.

A familiar black-clad, gaunt-faced horde moves around the confines of this artificial inner sanctum. Girls with white faces, long velvet dresses and multicoloured hair hover near a dance-floor while bouncing about on it are boys with Mohawks and personalized motorcycle jackets, or done-up like members of The Cure.

'Male Stripper' vanishes into someone yelling, "Where is the youth?" ('Youth' sounding more like 'yoof') and a fiendishly fast synth pattern — this is 'Murderous' by Nitzer Ebb — just as I reach the halfway point in a tardy queue, attempting to buy a drink.

Instantly give up on that fool's mission and race out to the dancefloor amidst huge plumes of smoke and a strobe making me dizzy. At one stage I collide with that Polish guy Mateo who's leaping about like a hyperactive frog, and we share a brief, knowing smile that this is one of the coolest tracks ever conceived.

Once the onslaught's over I head to a toilet full of both sexes reapplying make-up before a huge mirror. One of these Margaret. When she notices me in the dirty reflection she gifts a wink made meaningful by excessively long false eyelashes.

"Good to see you made it, Meens."

"Sorry I'm late. Got held up at my dad's place."

"All okay on the home front?"

I smile to myself. "Think so now."

"Cool."

"Kedra?"

"In the dunny still, taking sweet time." Flicking her head toward one of the three cubicles, Margaret blows out her cheeks. "Kid must have a cotton candy machine hidden away in there."

"Now you're making me hungry."

"I make *myself* hungry. Kedra, you hear us? We're hungry!"

"Coming!" someone shouts back.

Out of my bag I take a box of cosmetics and push this onto the crowded sink.

"By the way," Margaret continues, "been meaning to tell you — either someone's casing our joint or I have a stalker."

Am in a desperate attempt (with eyeliner and cotton buds) to correct the balance of my right eye. "How d'you mean?"

"Some tall kid in a baseball cap and a hoodie." Margaret slides lilac lipstick across her mouth. "Seen her a few times this week, hanging outside our place. Today she followed me here."

"How do you know this's a she?"

"How? 'Cos I knocked her down out on the main street." Having puckered and blotted her lips, the other girl smiles too. "Pretty blonde thing that ran like a hare."

I picture Sarah, a girl I'm fairly sure I haven't spoken to since that poolside argument almost four months before — but she's a brunette. Still, that means nothing. People in our circle swap hair colour left, right and centre.

"Weird. You've never seen this person?"

"Nope. But could be any of these buggers right here — I wouldn't recognize a single one without the house-paint." My housemate has motioned to the toilet patrons around us. "Anyhow, bet she has a sore chin."

"You hit her?"

"I'll say."

Margaret elevates a right fist that's currently graced with a long black cocktail glove reaching up past her elbow.

"She was creeping up behind me so I turned around and punched her one. Bam!"

Three days later, Margaret's stalker took revenge.

"Least I reckon it was her — same cap and hood, but this time I didn't see her face since I had blood pissing all over mine."

Margaret was in the midst of a rant in her hospital bed, several stitches holding together a long cut from her cheek, just beneath the right eye, to the neck about three centimetres above the collarbone.

She said the painkillers made ranting possible. Before that she could barely talk.

Double-U, Danny and I provided an audience to focus on, and after a lot of swearing combined with plans of revenge and agitated soap boxing by Margaret, we pieced together what'd happened.

Earlier in the evening, on the way home from work, Margaret had been jumped by two people who hid in a laneway. One of these attackers, a shorter one dressed in black, held her from behind while the other — the one Margaret said she recognized — twice swung a white-handled kitchen knife.

First time making only a hole in their victim's sleeve, but the second time slicing flesh across the face.

Right now she might be grandstanding, but Margaret looks pale and there are dark rings about her eyes that are (for once) not make-up related. The nurse told us before we entered that she'd lost a lot of blood between the scene of the assault and surgery.

"You know the best thing to come out of all this?" Margaret declares, looking at each of us in turn, blazing a challenge I have to admire. "I'm going to have the coolest goddamned duelling scar."

Don't ask me why, but I keep thinking of Sarah.

Yes, I'm certain this assailant isn't her, yet there's a niggle at the back of my mind that wants to know where exactly she is — what's become of my former friend.

Possibly this is the fault of the bizarre dream sequence I had while on Elysium, in which Sarah figured heavily.

Next day, when I ring her mother, Mrs Murray breaks down.

Tells me no one has seen Sarah since she went missing in February.

The Murrays filed a missing persons report with the Victoria Police, her photo and case had been showcased on TV program *Crime Stompers*, and the family finally hired a private detective, someone called Art Miller.

"Mr Miller never found a trace," says Sarah's mum, in a shattered tone.

"No letter?" I ask softly, stunned by this news. "No note?"

"Nothing. The police believe she ran away from home. But why? She was happy — wasn't she? You were her friend. Wasn't Sarah happy?"

"I don't know," I admit. I really didn't.

This is the point when Mrs Murray throws me a doozie.

"The sad part? I had such hopes that she spoke to you about what might have been troubling her. Said *some* thing. You were the last person to see her, Mina. When I called her in for dinner that evening, Sarah was gone."

After dropping in some tapes for Margaret, along with my Walkman and the latest issue of *The Face* — since she was climbing walls stuck there in that hospital ward — I came home and went straight up to my room.

In retrospect a magazine called 'The Face' hadn't been the smartest idea, given Margaret's injury. I hadn't thought at all. She'd stared at the cover a while with a mighty scowl, and then looked over pristine white bed sheets in my direction.

"You've got some cheek, Meens, giving me a 'zine with a name like this."

Realization kicked in, making me hit my forehead with the ball of my hand.

"Crap, I didn't think — I'm sorry!"

Margaret, however, had a lopsided grin that favoured the left half of her face, the side without stitches.

"Oh come on, hon!" she said. "You think *I'm* serious? 'Cheek'... get it? Just continuing the silliness. Gotta laugh."

Now, however, as I mentioned I'm home and have been sitting on the end of the double bed I share with Double-U for something like four hours.

Haven't moved except to occasionally scour my reflection in the small wardrobe mirror. Appraising the mouth, the chin, the ears, the hair, the eyebrows — and especially the eyes. Wonder if it's possible. I know I've had issues. An imaginary friend or two.

That's why they stuck me on Elysium.

When my boyfriend gets home he throws his bag onto the bed beside me, asks, "What'd you do today?" and pecks my forehead.

After no response he pauses.

"Everything okay, sunshine?"

"Not sure."

"Want to talk about it?"

"You mightn't like it."

"Try me."

"You'll think I'm crazy."

"I already think that."

I look up at him standing there, hovering as he unbuttons his shirt, and say nothing.

"Joke," he adds.

"Sure."

"Look, just tell me."

"All right." Glancing at the mirror again, I steel nerves. "Do you think I'm capable of killing someone?"

The boy's initial laughter surprises me.

Like Margaret earlier in the day, Double-U has a subsequent grin, although his expression is straighter.

"You were right about not liking it. Still, what can I say? Everyone is capable — of killing someone."

"You think so?"

"Mina, you have to learn that people, *all* people, are potential monsters."

I remember Dr Stein's words at the hospital. Lean forward, thinking. "You're the second person who's said that to me."

"Great minds think alike."

"Great minds don't cite clichés."

"Which part was the cliché?"

"The second. You should've stopped with Part One. More enigmatic." I breathe out noisily, get to my feet — and then fall back onto the bed. Several hours' inaction has consequences. "Ow! Ow! Pins and needles!"

"Karma."

That comment makes me slit my eyes in his direction. He's taken off his shirt, I see a brief flash of smooth, pale skin, and then a black turtleneck jumper blocks the view. Comfortable now, Double-U sits beside me, takes my left hand, and massages the palm.

"Mina, getting back to your original question — why?"

"The killing thing?" I gaze now at the floor, studying the ugly carpet. "I don't know. Just curious."

"You haven't had any... ideas?"

Something about Double-U's voice makes me aware that he's afraid. "Are you scared of me?"

"No. Course not. But the reason Bettie and I separated was because she had problems. Violent — she could be violent. And self-destructive."

"Why don't you divorce her?"

"What, and marry you?" He laughs.

This time I don't join in — "Is that such a bad idea?"

—Which abbreviates his leg of the laughter. "Um. No."

"Then why is it funny?"

"I have no idea. Sorry."

"You're still in love with her."

"Umm. *No*."

Shame he doesn't sound convincing.

Now the pins and needles have eased off, I march straight from the room and head downstairs to the kitchen — probably some kindling left in the brain from astronaut training school drill exercises.

Break open Margaret's winecask to squeeze out a big glass. Lean against the sink while pouring half the contents down my throat. This stuff's pretty brutal, but does the job.

Even so, am rattled.

Not about the marriage quip. That was nothing more than a dumb joke and I'm glad I made Double-U feel bad about it. It's clear now that he's still in love with his wife. This hurts, but I'll live.

No, I'm rattled about every possible other thing in this world.

Fuck it, Anim — where *are* you?

I think about returning to Dr Pearl, for all of about five seconds.

After that I'm miffed with myself for having entertained said thought. Knew she'd stick me straight back on the meds and I'd lose another three months.

Or more.

No, I had to tackle this thing myself.

Trouble was, what particular 'thing' was I on about, let alone up against? Looked like support and/or understanding would be difficult to rustle up even from yours truly. Self-trust had gone seriously astray — going it alone may have been something I'd gotten used to over the years but these days I wasn't sure I actually knew who I was.

Did I have the right stuff to kill somebody? Or was I capable of hurting others? Both without memory of having done so?

While eighty-odd percent refused to believe I had this kind of homicidal chutzpah, an element of doubt lingered — that remaining twenty percent or so. And a fifth of a possibility was enough to be concerned.

Next day I end up going back to Dad's.

Thankfully in the afternoon the place is empty, so I have free range to brew strong coffee and smoke a cigarette in the kitchen, and then head up to my room.

Dive under the bed to pull out thousands of sheets of paper in stacks and disarray, dusty, decorated by hair and crumbs and an unspooled cassette. I blow over it to remove most of these baubles.

Having reasoned that there might be clues here, mostly regarding my mental state, I see straight away that there's no reason to the filing system.

Let out a discordant whistle.

Do I really need to do this?

Honestly and truly want to gauge how mad I might be? See the hallucinatory tête-à-têtes I believed had happened laid out in sparse, typewritten courier font across white paper? Smudges of ink and liquid paper, scrawled annotations in pencil or pen?

Oh, for God's sake, shut up — I have to believe in myself.

Aside from my writing there're two separate piles of folded newspapers (mostly *NME* along with new local street press weekly *Beat*) and magazines (*The Face, i-D, Future Hip Hop, Dark Angel* and *Dolly*). On top of the papers stack is an opened feature article on Cabaret Voltaire, several pages' worth, published in *NME* in 1980.

There's also a black, vinyl padded storage case for cassettes, which I decide to open. Find inside tapes with names on them like 'Alt. Mix, 1986', Bauhaus, The Birthday Party, Siouxsie and the Banshees, Sisters of Mercy, Soft Cell, Christian Death, Cabaret Voltaire, Yellow Magic Orchestra, Primitive Calculators, Whirlywirld, The Smiths, and — yes — PiL live at the Seaview Ballroom, 21st December, 1984.

Mine? I don't remember. I guess this is.

And then I notice.

One of the photocopying paper boxes I use for storage — it has a broken seal.

I'd copied James Bond (think this was in *Dr No*) and planted a cotton thread between the lid and the side of the boxes here, tiny and inconspicuous since the threads were also white.

So who had been here?

Patrick or Dad? Possible. Animeid? ... She asserted that she couldn't physically touch things, though she had flattened that mouse last year. Off-her-head me?

Entirely plausible.

I open the box, scrutinize the top page. Another dialogue, minus stage directions:

"How long have you been mistreated?"

"Is it that obvious?"

"Nobody can be as accident-prone as you pretend to be."

"I guess. A long time. It's been a long time."

"Your dad?"

"My brother. But he's not the point. He's not the reason I'm moping round here today. Not really. I mean, I'm used to that. I live with it. No, something else happened. There's this guy. My brother's best friend Nick. Last night, he... Well, what I'm trying to say is that Nick — um — I don't know. He tried doing something. To me. You know?"

"He sexually violated you?"

"No, no. I mean, well, the arsehole tried but he didn't succeed. I swear I'm okay. I was just sitting here thinking about stuff. I'm fine."

"Are you sure?"

"Yep."

"Oh well, then, good."

A thought occurs — might I not have been simply transcribing real conversations, rather than creating them inside my head?

Like that idea much more.

The page beneath jumps to an entirely different situation, filing system well and truly damned.

It's handwritten, awkwardly so.

"Hey, saw your light on, thought I'd drop in. Unfinished business."

"No."

"C'mon, don't be like that. Mina, Mina, Mina."

"No."

"That's not what your eyes said downstairs. Was it? Know you dig me. Hey? What's not to dig?"

Nick.

Close my eyes, remember that horrible night of Patrick's party, and then think about what Dad said. About my brother's best friend having vanished, just like Sarah had gone missing.

Margaret attacked, Nicole burned.

And who was it that'd really reported my brother to the authorities?

Sure, chances were none of this related. Just a bunch of random incidents and a lot of bad luck. Maybe that was my particular mojo: Bad Luck Girl, or even better Miss Fortune. That had a ring to it.

Me with no memory of any of these events — yet not exactly off the list of suspects.

Beneath page two inside this box is a miniature coffee table tome on venomous vixens (the Vish Kanya). Don't remember putting it there. Thought I'd tossed the offensive thing.

When I raise the book, a torn piece of floral paper falls out.

Pick this up, read three words.

'From Nicholas Shahan?'

This time, not my longhand.

I don't recognize it. And why the question mark? I *know* the book is a heavy-handed message from Nick.

On the flipside of the small note 'Shahan' is stricken out using a red biro, and different anagrams jotted down (HANSHA, ASH-HAN, SHANAH, ANSHAH, NAHASH), the last one circled.

So who's responsible for this memorandum? That a doped-up Mina had adopted a different set of hieroglyphics hung possible, but I doubted it.

Okay, so now we had a mystery. Or not. Either way, this pushed me off my own case.

Cautiously, I open the book. Don't want to tread back here, but no choice.

Inside the front cover I find another two pages of that flowery paper (pink tulips on baby blue), this time folded but intact.

The contents are more effusive, again in the hand I don't recognize.

[PAGE 1]

Rappaccini's Daughter: Short story by Nathaniel Hawthorne, published 1844. About Giacomo Rappaccini, medical researcher in medieval Padua. Grows a garden of poisonous plants and coerces daughter Beatrice to tend this flora. Result? She becomes resistant to the poisons, but in the process becomes herself poisonous to others.

Traditional story of a poisonous maiden traced back to India, and Hawthorne's version has been adopted in contemporary works.

Giacomo is the Italian version of James. Mina's father's name is Jim.

[PAGE 2]

The family name Rappaccini is possibly derived from the Italian/French noun 'rapace' meaning 'bird of prey', or the French adjective 'rapace' meaning grasping or rapacious.

Rapace = Mina. Family name.

Middle name Beatrice. Implications re: Dante's Divine Comedy, or back to Hawthorne?

First name symbolism = Mystery. Central character in Stoker's Dracula??

Well. Disturbing.

Who's been deconstructing me in such obscure fashion? *Me*? Or was this Nick's writing? Makes sense, given the association with the Vish Kanya. Or nonsense, more like it.

I remember Nick's Valentine's card; know I hung onto that because I'd wanted to find out who this Saint Maria Goretti happened to be.

Sitting on top of a pile of Christmas cards and letters also beneath the bed.

'HAPPY VALENTINES DAY YOU FUCKING FREAK!'

Compare the caps, the Fs, Rs, Ps, Is and Ts. They're sufficient. The styles of writing on card and note are completely different.

There aren't more missives inside the book, so I have no further clues. Could go through the piles of paperwork but decide this will be sad rather than enlightening.

Got to pursue a different course.

I go and open the window, part the Moomin curtains, and lean out. Gaze into the yard while I take out a cigarette and light up with a flimsy red disposable. That brief moment of fire makes me think.

I drag in on the cigarette. Yep.

Decide on the spot that I need to talk with Nicole.

Since the accident Nicole had taken up residence to the rear of the sprawling suburban mansion in which her family lived.

She'd adopted habits that had more in common with Miss Havisham in *Great Expectations* and Gloria Swanson in *Sunset Boulevard* — a dictatorial diva rehashing past glories who never leaves the house.

Even arranging this visit proved difficult.

I spoke on the phone first with the father, John, followed by Nicole's mother Evelyn for close to half an hour, which is how I gleaned these details regarding Nicole's brave new lifestyle. Much of what I said to the harried and saddened parents amounted to lies.

I intimated that Nicole and I had been the greatest of friends at school, but I'd been abroad for several months and, having freshly returned to Nede, was desperate to see their daughter.

After forewarnings and a vigorous cross-examination I apparently passed, no mention was made of Nicole's actual best friend Sarah, and we scheduled an appointment for one o'clock next afternoon.

Sunday.

Thought about inviting Clair along (moral support and all that jazz), but knew she'd be at church.

Having learned from previous experience dealing in other people's parents, I dressed with a vague sense of decorum — had little on my face aside from lip-gloss, a smattering of mascara. Put on Mum's beret and wore a simple black, sleeveless dress.

Had never visited Nicole's place before.

The rambling front garden was a refugee from better days — overgrown, close to dying — and blue tarpaulin wrapped the lower, right-hand Edwardian façade, obviously the area damaged by fire. I wondered why it hadn't yet been repaired.

Evelyn Milton, when she answered the grand front door, squinted in the sunlight and looked unwell. I could see Nicole in her face, but this woman had a much nicer nature, albeit reserved.

She ushered me inside to a spacious dining room with a crystal chandelier, sheets covering most of the furniture like mansions you see in British period-piece cinema.

I was offered a choice of drinks that numbered more than all the fingers on my hands. Ended up going with lime cordial, as this was the one that stuck.

Admit to being nervous, to you not her.

Was here under great pretence, they had opened their house and refrigerator to a phony, and I had no idea what Nicole would now be like.

After delivering the cordial, Mrs Milton has an announcement.

"May I check your handbag?" she asks.

"Sorry?"

The woman looks at me then with such pain in her sad eyes that I hand over the bag without further thought.

"It's the tabloids," she says, unzipping my bag to peer inside. "*The Truth* has been particularly vindictive ever since the accident. Given that John is a famous man, they're after any and all gossip regarding his poor daughter."

Apparently satisfied there's nothing dangerous like a recording device inside, the woman zips the bag shut and passes it back.

"Just last week we had a reporter disguised as a plumber. Awful business."

Am glad I thought to leave cigarettes at home — had doubted anything involving a naked flame would be welcome here.

"Are you prepared?"

"Prepared?" I echo, making it a return query.

"For the scarring."

"I think so."

"Try not to overreact."

Now I'm really wondering what to expect.

Ros told us Nicole had burns to ten percent of her body. Was she wrong? But the more I thought about it, the more I realized that ten percent was a significant portion of the human body.

I follow Mrs Milton along a hallway to the rear of the huge house, and there we take a left turn down another, darker passage. Come to a closed door painted over with purple passionflowers.

She knocks.

The response from the other side is terse. "What?!"

"Dear, Mina is here."

Silence.

"Nicky, darling? Did you hear what I said?"

"I heard you."

"May we come in?"

Silence.

"Honey?"

"Fuck! All right!"

In spite of inadequate light I do see the reaction to these words of Nicole's mother. She tenses up, the jaw quivers, her eyes look close to tears.

Even so, she pushes open the door, allowing us entry to a room that's large and fractionally shadier than the hallway.

Little in the way of furnishings — a barren desk sporting a battleship grey, double-speaker ghetto blaster and a lamp with an ugly tartan cover, empty bookcase, a cabinet with an array of medicines and creams. The portable fan in the corner of the room keeps this space cooler than it is outside, and I shiver.

Straight after, spot a figure seated on the single bed in the centre of this space.

Hair is tied back in a ponytail. Wearing a cream, roll-neck submarine jumper — her right arm inside the jumper, with the sleeve pinned up to the shoulder.

While her throat's hence covered by the jumper, I can see the puckered, pink-and-red blotched skin that leads from the right side of her chin to the forehead and partially erases the hairline there. Her right eye must've been lucky. Remarkably similar placement to Margaret's injury — but far worse.

Nicole looks at me; head arched to one side, saying nothing.

"I'll leave you two girls to get reacquainted," Evelyn suggests, but neither of us speaks as this lady makes to depart.

Once the door softly closes again, Nicole exhales air in loud fashion.

"Mum told me you were coming."

"I kind of fibbed."

"I know. She said."

"She knew?"

"She didn't. I did."

"Did you tell her—?"

"What a pack of lies it was? Why should I?" The other girl chooses this moment to awkwardly turn away. Seems to have a problem doing that. "Why're you here, Mina?"

"I wanted to see you."

"Gawk, you mean. You want a closer look?"

She does that stiff swivel again, back to me, and pulls down the neckline on her jumper.

"See? Goes all the way down to my hip. I'm wondering how long it will be before my parents closet me away in some travelling freak show — anonymously, of course. Can't tarnish the family name. Oh and don't forget to tell everyone at school. They can buy a ticket apiece."

I won't lie further here and tell you I wasn't tempted to 'gawk', as Nicole put it. But I do resist.

"Hard to sell tickets. I'm not at Mac.Duagh anymore either."

The other girl has no response.

So I amuse myself by walking over to the main window, which has a closed, Japanese-style blind. Obviously expensive. Toy with the pull-cords.

"Please — don't open that."

Look over my shoulder at the girl crouched on the bed. Can barely see the burns from here, given the shadows.

"Wasn't planning to."

She has her left hand up inside that roomy jumper and scratches at something. Feigns nonchalance. "Just in case."

"Should you be scratching?"

"No." Continues to do so regardless. "Drives me mad sometimes."

"I can imagine."

"Don't give me that bullshit. No, you can't."

"Have you left the house at all?" I ask.

"Since I returned from the hospital?"

"Mm-hmm."

"Are you kidding?"

"Not I know of."

"No."

"You need to."

"Don't want to."

"You need to," I repeat.

"I can't, Mina."

Having stopped scrubbing, the girl leans forward in order that I may better again see her face.

"Look at me."

"I am." This is when I leave the window, return to her at the bed, kneel on the floor, and take hold of the girl's left hand. "I see *you*. Nicole."

She turns aside. Can now tell this process hurts. I observe the twitch in her neck muscle.

"You're the first person to visit," I hear her say to the blank cream wall next to the bed. "No one else did. I stopped waiting. Realized it was my fault no one came."

"You have your parents."

"They drive me crazy. You know, neither of them can bear to look at me?" Nicole's eyes swing back to mine. "Not like you're doing. Hideous, isn't it?"

"No."

This comment makes her grumble.

"Don't lie to me. I'm not my mother."

"All right." Still hanging onto the fingers, I get up and sit next to her. "You have you."

"Oh yeah, I've had a lot of me over the past few months."

"Appreciate it."

"Are you for real? You know what kind of person I am."

That comment makes me smile.

"Okay, fair enough. Sarah never came?"

"Never called either."

"You know she's been missing four months?"

Very gradually Nicole looks back at me. Very slightly shakes her head. "No."

"You've heard nothing?"

"No."

The other girl lets down the iron barrier that's been there as long as I've known her. She's peering at me with worry and concern tied together.

"She isn't... She's all right — isn't she?"

"I don't know. God, I hope so. I'm going to try to find her."

"You always were her friend."

My turn to push dismissive. "No." Shake my head. "I wasn't."

"She's still lucky to have someone like you." Nicole carefully looks me up and down and the left cheek flutters, like she's repressing a grin. "In spite of outlandish dress sense."

"I tried to dress down."

"And you almost succeeded."

Placing my hand very carefully under Nicole's chin, away from the injury, I lean in closer. "We're all lucky. We have one another."

Am surprised with the reaction this causes.

Nicole squeezes her eyes closed, and a tear runs down the left cheek.

"You're wrong."

"Why?"

I'm thinking this reaction has come about because zero so-called friends have bothered putting in a house call — and end up being wide of the mark.

"I never told the police. Couldn't," Nicole says in a shaky tone. "But I saw someone through the flames, outside my window. I saw the face of the person who did this to me."

For a horrible instant I believe she's going to denounce me, or perhaps even Sarah — who's been unaccounted for since the conflagration.

This girl's left hand grips mine with unexpected strength.

"It was Hannah," she whispers, looking stiffly to either side like she expects another firebomb. "It was our Hannah."

The girl looks terrified — know this because I am too. Hannah?

Very carefully I place Nicole back on the covers of the bed, and then lay down next to her. Say sweet nothings in a gentle tone, platitudes that mean little. Hold her tense left hand until it relaxes and she slips into sleep.

For an hour after I remain in that position, thinking about being here when she awakes but deciding against it.

Finally, I sit up.

Hannah. D.D.

No.

Why?

Realize I need to get desperately drunk. This is all too much.

Soho on a Sunday night was called Block Party and it specialized in funk, R&B and hip-hop. In other words the antithesis of what I usually listened to. But I was smashed and desperate to lose myself, to blot out everything — no matter what the tuneage.

Barge right in past the doorbitch, doing what Angelika once told me to do (look like I own the place) and inebriated enough not to care. Gallop upstairs to throw myself into the warming pyre of a familiar club if unfamiliar sounds.

Being still dressed in the tidy black dress and beret, sans make-up, I detour around a couple of boys busy mimicking upside-down helicopters and head to the bathroom.

Fix lipstick in the mirror (shade: Chanel Rouge Allure Laque

#75 in Dragon, borrowed from Nicole) beside a bunch of suicide blondes with sensational bodies clad in miniature, jungle-pattern crop tops and skirts.

After that I go grab a straight Corona from the bar — screw the lime — and down the contents before ordering a second round a minute later.

Have already consumed two or three screwdrivers at a cheap bar round the corner, plus a 500ml bottle of Gordon's Gin on the bus ride to Flahan.

Obviously can't trust the senses.

Music here is all off-kilter drum patterns with a rap over the top — sounds like they're wailing 'Here is something you can't understand, Oh I could just kill a man', something like that — with these psycho-beta voices beneath that make for a song loaded up in subtleties and nuances beyond me in this state.

Slow, staticky, with some kind of horn over the top, three or four different rhythm structures jammed into one track.

I end up being wide-eyed and blown away.

So I bound over to the DJ booth, lean in to the man there who's carefully cueing-up.

"What is this?" I shout into an ear free of headphones. "I love it!"

"Cypress Hill," he yells back.

"Never heard anything like it."

"That's the funny thing. Hang on a minute, will you?" I pick up he's British by the way in which he drops the H in 'hang'. Makes him sound like Michael Caine.

This man crossfades into the next song, pulls the previous record off the second turntable, and then passes it to me.

"See the date here?"

In the centre of the vinyl there's the usual round label (this time a yellow one), with details like the name of the band (Cypress Hill), the title of the record ('How I Could Just Kill a Man') and the record company (in this case Ruff House, Sony and

Columbia — I couldn't tell which one was responsible). But there, on the left-hand side, was the date: 1991.

"Huh," I muse. "Five years early."

"Weird, huh? I've been seeing these discrepancies a lot lately."

"You'd think major companies like Sony would have copy-editors."

"Right?"

I hand back the record, which he slides into a red sleeve and places in a large, metallic record crate.

"I'm surprised these people got away with the sample — did you hear it? Hendrix, 'Are You Experienced?' — but it works a treat," the man shouts my way. "Kosher hip-hop, the real deal. There's also another sample in there from 1945, New York City Mayor Fiorello LaGuardia reading comics on-air. I have that record too, very rare."

Don't know why I linger. Think I'm as mesmerized by the spinning twelve-inch on the other platter as I am with the musical nuggets this guy tosses my way.

"You have good taste," I hear him comment, so I glance up.

The DJ was wearing a navy blue Kangol hat. "And we look like bookends," he observes.

Sounds like one of my poor attempts at a joke, so I have to laugh.

"What's your name, kiddo?"

"Brigitte," I fib.

"As in Bardot?"

"Mm-hmm." Knows his movie stars too.

"Cluey Clive. Clive Campbell." Reaches over the partition to shake my hand.

I place his age in the early thirties. Has on an oversized hoodie top bearing 'B-Boy Records' across the front — looking like it was snatched from factory-siding graffiti — along with chunky DC runners and parachute pants a lot baggier than I'm used to, pockets aplenty and a proud Members Only tag on the thigh.

Not the best-looking guy in the world, rust-coloured hair and eyebrows with a chin rather lacking, but this Cluey Clive had confidence and charming crinkles at the corners of his eyes.

Winds up his set to make way for the next DJ.

This was a young, edgy boy with thick-rimmed glasses calling himself DJ Preach N Teach, according to a quick waffle on the microphone.

Having finished and packed his box, Clive lays a hand momentarily on my hip, presenting me a drink card with the other.

I do notice the wedding ring there.

"Be a doll and get me a Crown, will you? You can have whatever you like."

When I return with carbon copies of the same bottle, Clive has left the DJ booth and is gasbagging in the ear of his replacement Preach N Teach.

There's a sticker on this new DJ's box, one I've seen before: 'PREDESTINATION! No ifs or buts'. Figure he must attend the same church sewing circle as Clair. I should check, but doubt I can clearly enunciate Clair's name in this state.

"You know that commercial song 'Walk this Way'?" Clive's already saying into my eardrum as he relieves me of one of the beers.

"With the long-in-the-tooth rock band? Aerosmith?"

"That'd be the one."

"Think everyone's sadly seen it — the video on *Countdown* or *Video Hits*."

"Well, Brigitte, the song playing now is off the same Run-D.M.C. album *Raising Hell*. This one's far, far better: 'It's Tricky'. Hear the sample? 'My Sharona' by The Knack. This kid spinning now has taste."

Don't know what it is about the way he speaks and the tips

he's passing on, but I find myself enjoying the attention even while the alcohol makes my head increasingly fuzzy.

Have no idea what to do with the Crown Lager in my hand, but I certainly know I shouldn't drink it.

When Clive moves in closer and says, "You have charming eyes," I realize — somewhat dimly — that he's moved up the food chain from breaks to body parts.

Smile absently at nothing as his fingers move across my cheek and down the neck. Feels like he's a million miles away, but I'm not complaining. The other things are more distant, the things I've come here to escape.

Hustles his lips against mine, our hats collide, and there're fingers groping at the material around my left breast.

I casually push myself free to attack the beer I vaguely remember in my hand.

Cluey Clive and I end up tipping back the bottles in unison, shades of that game at carnivals — the one with the balls and rotating porcelain clowns with their mouths wide open — and he has his arm now around my waist. The music, all obscure sampling, bass heavy beats and scratching, seems muffled.

So I look up at his face, try to focus; find myself laughing that oxidation could affect hair as well.

The man's flicked back his Kangol hat, has a jolly grin, and when he shoves his mouth against mine the tongue nearly jerks down my throat.

I cough, making him think I'm going to throw up, so he evacuates fast. This guy had obviously never read up on gag reflexes.

Have my head down, confused.

All I can hear is that erratic music, machinegun lyrics currently debasing women. Don't know what I'm doing. Need another drink since I seem to have finished the Crown.

Place my arms round Clive's neck, intending to ask for more of the drink card, when I peer over his shoulder. See Double-U staring from the bar. His eyes collide with mine far too briefly, and then he turns and leaves.

It's well on the way to sunrise but still mostly dark when Double-U returns to the house.

I've been sitting on the doorstep above the small flight of stairs for hours now.

Felt like I couldn't go in — being seated outside on a frigid night dressed in nothing more than a minimal one-piece, slowly sobering up, was fit punishment.

Skull thumping with pain, eyes scratchy-dry and likely bloodshot, lips partially cracked — well, I imagine I looked like Hell and that's the way it ought to be.

Someone's awake inside the house. Don't know who, probably Danny. Playing The Boys Next Door album *Door, Door*, with Nick Cave currently crooning 'Shivers', appropriate to me in this state and this time of morning. My heart really is at its knees.

The overhead light flickers, a collection of moths circling. Half a dozen motionless cigarette stubs perched on the step below. I should hide them, but don't have the strength.

Instead, I watch Double-U struggle to park his yellow dolly 1971 Holden Kingswood on the other side of the street.

Have a passing fancy to kick him out of the driver's seat and finish the job — license or not. At least irritation was a superior dram to this paralyzing combination of dismay, shame and regret.

Having locked up and checked both directions for traffic, Double-U crosses over, steps through the gate, slowly makes his way up the staircase — and passes by me huddling there. Says nothing. After unbolting the door he stands on the porch and I suppose he's staring down at me.

Keep my face between my legs, peeping through bare knees at the slowly brightening horizon.

More footfall tells me he's gone inside, and then the door closes.

Minutes later the boy's back.

Behind me again, the sound of keys sliding back into a suit pocket.

Still can't face him. Still can't talk. Shed just three or four tears that tumble down onto the concrete. They're hardly enough. I know that.

"So," he says in a grave tone.

Cover my face with hands and listen very carefully to his breathing. I can hear it even above the sounds of early morning birds.

"I love you," I finally manage to push through.

Hear him sigh, long and drawn-out.

"Do you? I just don't know anymore."

"I do."

"Nothing makes sense."

"I know."

Have no strength to force more dialogue.

We remain in respective positions for a while, but as the sun begins to poke above nearby roofs Double-U sighs again, walks past me with a bag of belongings tossed over his shoulder, and leaves.

I withdraw fingers long enough to observe as he looks both ways, gets back into the car, starts the engine, drives off.

Blinking several times, sad beyond belief, I mumble, "I'm sorry."

Straighten my back; stretch the muscles along my spine and in the area of the shoulder blades. Push back at hair too short to need such attention. Pick up the beret beside me, place it on my knee. Look out at a wonderful morning with a blue sky.

"Eggs Benedict," I decide aloud.

Only way I'll ever feel alive again.

Squares Ending in 5

I never saw my father again. Alive, I mean.

Eyeballed him atop a square slab at the mortuary after being summoned to ID the body. His chest was caved in when he slammed his BMW into the brick wall of our garage.

Being a vintage jalopy it didn't have any of the new safety features.

Constable Andie Summers and a fellow female cop I didn't know hand-delivered me the news, and then gave me a lift to the hospital to do the inspection.

Afterward, the two officers shuffled me upstairs to the cafeteria to talk about things for an hour or so.

Constable Andie did most of the talking for a change, while her partner took notes. Diplomatically, I must say, brought up the issue of my relationship with my father.

The other cop occasionally glanced under her serious brow as she wrote, concerned perhaps because I hadn't shed a single tear. Not that I didn't care — I just didn't have it in me to cry.

Dam traded places with the two women when he picked me up. We hugged for a while in the hospital's foyer before going to grab a beer.

The funeral was three days later, the weather miserable.

Something black wasn't a problem, but locating an outfit both formal and intact proved impossible in my wardrobe. So I plundered Mum's clothes — which were mothballed in tea chests in the garage, next to blackened brickwork and broken glass.

Located another knee-length, sleeveless number, slid into cheap tights and low-heeled Lovmee Ingénue slippers, didn't care if any of this sat together well. Also stuck on a pair of my mother's Wayfarer sunglasses to cover not puffy eyes, but the fact I still couldn't cry.

Felt like I was in a daze as I straightened Patrick's tie before we left. Surprised him by lending a supportive grip when he broke down at the chapel.

Was in turn surprised when Clair showed up towards the end of the service and placed an arm round my waist. Found myself thankful for the gesture and put my head on her shoulder. Was so tired.

"You'll be okay," she told me, softly patting my back. "God is with you."

I very much doubted that but appreciated the suggestion.

She came with us back to the house for the wake, an Irish affair my uncle organized at which most of the people got raucously drunk and sang things like 'Danny Boy' and 'Back Home in Derry'.

Dam conducted these ditties while getting crimson in the face. He hadn't noticed or perhaps didn't care that Patrick retreated to his room straight after we got home.

Being a teetotaller, Clair made a stream of cups of — yes — tea while I guzzled hot toddies with her in the kitchen. Respected my preference to remain mum and keep conversation to a minimum.

She also played janitor, cleaning up after our rowdy relatives and Dad's mates.

"It was Hannah," Nicole whispers, gripping my hand with surprising strength.

At the end of the evening, once everyone has gone home aside from Uncle Dam — who's anyway unconscious in the front seat of Dad's open-roofed Simca Gordini, cradling an empty bottle of Michael Collins Ten-Year Single Malt whiskey — I drink a dozen glasses of tap water in the kitchen while Clair waits, jacket on.

When I can't stomach anymore I turn back to my friend.

"Thanks for everything, C. Don't know what I would've done without you."

"Anytime. You going to be all right?"

"Mmm." Not sure I sound all that convincing, so I decide to change topics to something more pressing. "We need to talk properly. About Nicole — and Hannah."

"What is it?"

"I don't know, not yet. Can't think straight today. Let's talk about things tomorrow."

Clair must note the serious intent to my voice, even if other senses are swimming, and takes deft control.

"How about Deveroli's, for old-times' sake?"

Haven't been there in months and am not exactly keen on a return visit, but at least the girl hasn't suggested the Brigantine round the corner from Deveroli's — where Double-U's wife works.

"Sure."

Clair has out a pad, writing a note. "Twelve okay for you?"

"I think so."

"Then 'tis a date." The girl tears a page out of the pad and sticks it to the fridge with a magnet. "Just in case you forget."

That makes me laugh as I escort Clair to the front door.

"Don't worry — I won't forget. If I do, coffee's on me for life."

"Then you really do need to forget!" The girl chuckles in husky fashion. "Ciao."

After closing the door and deadbolting it, I step into the garage to place a blanket over my uncle's prostrate form. Then trudge upstairs. Head along the passage to the last doorway, gently knock.

Hearing no answer I try the knob, which gives, and I push.

In the dark I make out 8-bit pixelated words ('GAME OVER') filling the screen of the TV, along with my brother lying on his front across the double bed, still wearing the black suit (our father's) and a pair of headphones on. There's a cartridge beside him that reads *The Legend of Zelda*.

Don't want to disturb things too much, so I cross the room and switch on his small lamp.

He's awake.

When Patrick looks at me, pushing the cans down to his shoulders, even in the soft light it's obvious he's been bawling his eyes out.

"You all right?" I ask.

"Don't know. He's gone. What are we going to do?"

"You'll stay with Dam."

Patrick examines the floor, nods. "And you?"

"I have my own place. Anyway, get some sleep. Dam's out like a light downstairs in the garage — won't be leaving till tomorrow, and he's going to be in serious pain. You can get a lift, maybe even better drive him. I'll sort things out here."

"How do you hold it all together?"

"Guess I had practice." I reach over, softly squeeze his cheek. "Listen to what Dam says. And try not to beat him up."

In the morning I put on a strong batch of coffee and toast four slices of raisin bread.

Take a couple of minutes by the sink, staring at my vague reflection in the kitchen window — "What would you do?" I ask — before I hear the pop-up.

Slab real butter (Christmas Star brand) onto the toast since I know Dam hates margarine. Pour out three mugs of coffee, leave them black, and place a small jug of milk and a jar of Black Bear honey on the big tray.

Head into the loungeroom to find my uncle has shifted some time during the night from the car to the couch, but clutches at the same blanket.

He's awake, groggily watching the on-screen shenanigans of Porky Pig being driven to distraction by Daffy Duck in some ancient Warner Bros. staple.

I can smell the alcohol across the room.

"Jim and I loved *Looney Tunes* when we were kids," Dam says as I place breakfast before him. Takes up a queasy examination of the condiments before him, but keeps talking. "No tea?"

"Sadly, none in the house. Clair finished it all yesterday."

"Your friend who cleaned."

"That's the one."

"Can you thank her for me?"

After I nod, Dam's eyes return to the telly.

"You know, your dad and me used to go to the Gardiner Picture House every single Saturday, watch the cartoons and a feature. Childhood tradition and all that."

He has tears on his cheeks, so I grab some Kleenex to wipe them away.

"Thanks, Min."

"You're welcome."

Once the cartoon winds down I tell him my plan regarding Patrick, and Dam agrees straight off. Knew he would.

And there was one more thing.

"You know about Dad's safe upstairs?"

"His pride and joy? I do."

"We have bills to pay, and that's where he kept his cash — you know how he hated banks."

"One thing we shared in common," Dam says, chancing the coffee. "Never trust a banker. That's our father speaking. We listened. Nice coffee, by the way."

I smile, can't wait to tell him.

"Kopi luwak. Made from coffee berries scoffed down and defecated by a jungle cat."

My uncle's reaction is, however, nonplussed.

"Well, it comes out smelling like a rose."

Pausing mid-bite of raisin bread, I look over. "Boom-boom," I mutter, a fraction peeved. "Moving right along, I need the combination to that safe. Do you know it?"

"Yep, I do." Dam drains his entire mug.

"And?"

"The combination's easy — your birthday."

"*My* birthday?"

This surprises.

Does it mean my father truly cared? Or was it a date he regretted and could never forget? I prefer to believe the former, but sadly have another problem.

"I can't remember when my birthday is."

"That's fine. Come closer."

Dam whispers the answer in my ear.

He may have finished the coffee but doesn't go anywhere near the toast.

Once he nods off a short time later I take the cups and dishes back to the kitchen, seat myself at the small table — Dad's favourite spot — and listen to the TV in the next room. Can tell it's now switched to *Video Hits* since I hear Donnie Sutherland jabbering away.

Sitting there with elbow on the table and face in the palm of my right hand, I get to thinking. 'Ruminating' as Stan Lee might've put in 1960s Marvel comic books.

Sadly the topic is not such fun.

Wonder what's wrong with me — why I haven't been able to properly cry for either of my parents.

When I look up between fingers I spy the note on the refrigerator, the one Clair had stuck there the night before, with details of our twelve o'clock.

Only now, in the light of day, do I see the design of the notepad paper.

Pink tulips on baby blue.

I get to Deveroli's early. First one there.

Wearing a tight pair of black jeans with holes in the knees, my Docs, and a large black shirt that once belonged to Double-U. Minimal make-up so I shouldn't scare too many people.

Step past the electricity pole with its seven Ps, note the new addition of an oval sticker with the simple word 'if?'

Upon entering the restaurant/café, a waitress examines me a little too warily and deigns to seat me at a lonely table — close to the big front window but over one side where I'm not obvious. I order an espresso Romano and indulge in a quick cigarette.

I'd ditched the Churchman's to take up with another called Eve. This brand had a picture on the front of a girl surrounded by flowers, looking like a poor man's Barry Windsor-Smith designed her.

Guess I liked them because of the flowers on the cigarettes themselves, and the silly, stop-start slogan:

'Hello to Eve. The first truly feminine cigarette — it's almost as pretty as you are. With pretty filter tip. Rich, yet gentle flavor. Women have been feminine since Eve. Now cigarettes are feminine. Since Eve. Also with menthol.'

Margaret would tear these words to shreds.

Having stamped out the pretty cigarette halfway through, I secret the ashtray onto the next table, finish coffee, suck on a couple of Fruit Tingles and ask the waitress for an orange juice.

Remember that time I met my friends here the weekend before school started.

A lifetime ago. What on earth'd happened to us?

Take out paperwork I got from the funeral home.

Still can't believe how much it all cost. Turn over one sheet to start jotting notes — fiction rather than figures. Vignettes really, for a possible story. Anything is better than thinking about the cost of burying my father.

Get tired of doing that too and instead sketch the waitress.

Above the sound of Marilyn Monroe singing (somewhat out of key) 'That Old Black Magic', there's the tinkle of a little bell.

Once I look up, Clair waves from the entrance.

She's wearing vertical-striped red-and-black stirrup pants

beneath a spacious red t-shirt hanging off one shoulder, and has her tiny black dog Jiji under one arm.

Hannah — six centimetres taller, dressed in a belted, oversized purple top with baggy sleeves — has hold of the other.

Both girls approach and, after she places a large, covered white basket on the floor, Clair sits at the table opposite me with the dog on her lap, and then she smiles.

Hannah sits between us, on my left and Clair's right.

"Brought you an apple," this girl announces, parking on the table a perfect red example of the fruit. "Sorry to hear about your dad."

I peer from the apple to her, wishing Clair had come alone. Endeavour to mask any emotion other than offering up a return smile.

"Thanks, D.D."

"Could your hair get any shorter? You'll catch your death once winter kicks in."

Nice timing with the quips. "I'll have to wear a warm hat, then."

Am refolding receipts and expenses to tuck into the bag I have beside me. At the same time mulling over what Nicole told me about Hannah. The small detail of Clair's notepad paper — pink tulips on baby blue.

This is the moment Clair chooses to lean forward and speak for the first time.

"We couldn't chat yesterday."

I shrug. "I know. Caught up in all that. I felt brain-dead."

"Have you been hearing the reports about the Chernobyl nuclear power plant mishap? It sounds awful. They say radiation will cover Europe."

"Really? Haven't kept up with the news," I confess. Not for three months.

Clair's tee has the word 'GOD' on it in big, bold, black capital letters and for a silly moment I wonder if she likes Danny's favourite thrash band of the same name. Then I remember this is Clair we're talking about.

"Meanwhile," she's saying, "the French keep performing nuclear tests at places like Muruora Island, in our neck of the woods. Where will it all stop?"

"What's to hate?" Hannah interjects, also leaning forward. I notice the taller girl's wearing bulky, extravagant earrings that touch her shoulders. "If we all get to glow in the dark, we'll save money on street-lights."

Clair nods, only a fraction, her next sentence directed to me.

"You didn't mind me bringing Hannah along?"

I swallow the fears. "Course not."

"So — everything in consideration — how's my Visha Kanya doing today?"

This last comment doesn't just snag my breath, it slaps my face. I blink quickly, feeling two sets of familiar eyes upon me that I suddenly don't know at all.

Suspicions had apparently nothing on reality.

"What'd you call me?"

"I'd say you heard just fine. More soon. Now, I'm thirsty."

Straight away, Clair's called over the waitress and is ordering two milky flat whites, along with an orange-pecan muffin — she's all bubbly, a little shy and charming. Can tell the waitress appreciates her presence here more than mine.

"Love their muffins," Clair tells me, observing her order head to the kitchen.

Meanwhile I have to wrestle with the previous remark.

"It was *you*? You did it?"

"Me?" This is a picture of innocence.

"The book," I stumble on, now unsure.

"What book?"

"The one about those Indian poison ladies," Hannah is whispering in her ear.

"Oh, that one! But don't forget the Valentine's card."

This causes me to stare straight at Clair. "I thought—"

"You thought the sender was Nick Shahan."

Huh? — "Wasn't it?"

"The mind boggles!"

Clair twists her mouth to one side, apparently considering something troublesome, and then she sits back and relaxes.

"There are times I wish I could fib, all in the name of carrying a joke. Yet we must think in these very moments of Psalms 120:2, 'Deliver my soul, O Lord, from lying lips, and from a deceitful tongue.' Amen."

My uncomprehending look causes the girl to roll her eyes.

"Yes. It was Nick."

"But how do you know about him, about — what —?"

Patting her pooch, Clair now lets out one of trademark husky laughs, this one seriously lacking mirth.

It's Hannah who speaks. "Are you stupid?"

"Shhh, H."

Clair has placed a finger to her lips.

"It's not nice to call people things you don't like being called yourself. Mina, doesn't Luna Park ring a bell?"

"Luna Park?" I struggle to remember said meeting — feels like so long ago. "I didn't — I'm sure I didn't tell you much about Nick. Did I?"

"You told me enough. I fished some of the rest out of you while you were off with the pixies. Elysium works better than a truth serum. Isn't that right, darling?"

She kisses her dog's nose, and it licks her face in return. I feel marginally ill.

"See this?" Producing a silver house key identical to mine, Clair holds it aloft just beyond my reach. "This helped me to investigate the rest for myself."

"Is that the key to my house?"

"Uh-huh."

The house. My room. My writing. It all connects now — the

book with the notepaper in it. Pink tulips on baby blue.

"Clair, how do you have my key?"

"One thing at a time. We don't want to get confused."

"I never gave you my key."

Hannah takes this as her cue to chortle. "Never? How do *you* know, Mina? D'you actually remember anything from the past few months? I seriously doubt it."

Right then I feel agitated instead of confused. Prefer the sensation.

"Are you two in this together?"

Clair pockets the key. "In what together, dear?"

"Well, for starters — what exactly did I tell you about Nick?"

"Enough."

"Oh, come on. That's ambiguous."

"He admitted the rest."

"What 'rest'? When?"

"The book, the card. The fact that he attempted to *sexually violate* you. That man was a devil, a stain on society."

I experience a flash of Nick on top of me, headbanging to Suzi Q. A stain on music too. Shake my skull a fraction to clear it of claptrap. Cling to the use of 'was' — past tense. The foreign correspondence in my room must've been Clair's handwriting. And the shuffling of Nick's surname.

"What does 'Nahash' mean?"

Clair appraises me anew. "You found my notes."

I nod.

"Where did I leave them?"

"Beneath my bed."

"That was careless."

Contrasting my recent head movement, Hannah shakes hers upon hearing this confession.

"You left stuff in her room? I can't believe it — you've been harping on my back about being careful."

"Mina won't say anything. Besides, there's nothing substantial in there."

"Nahash," I repeat, interrupting them. The circled anagram of Shahan.

"Ahh, Nahash. The evil serpent that appears in Genesis 3 in the Garden of Eden."

Clair's back to her old tricks lining up cutlery and dishing out theological nuggets.

"As for 'Nick', well that's simple. Another name for Satan, isn't it? Old Nick."

Part of me, deep inside, wants to take this seventeen-year-old and shake her hard. Find out where the real Clair is hiding. But a better part of me realizes this is the real Clair. I'd been friends with an imposter.

"You spoke to him?"

"Old Nick?"

"Nick. Yes. Nick Shahan."

"Oh, we had a candid conversation not that long ago."

"When?"

"The day we talked about his sordid little activities and the consequences of same."

I have to repeat this question a third time. "*When*?"

The urgency makes Clair sigh.

"Not important. Just know it's all sorted out. I've been looking after your back. While you were off on your journey of self-discovery — by this, I mean painting your face like a short-sighted harlot, wearing op-shop apparel, and kissing boys already in wedlock — well, I've been busy fixing things."

Stunned, I glance at Hannah. She's moved on to filing long nails.

Clair laughs out loud, and then covers her mouth, a naughty schoolgirl caught in the act — which I guess she was.

"Like I fixed your father's brakes," she confides. "That was easy. Just asked *my* dad the mechanic how to do it. Hypothetically-speaking, of course."

"Clair's a whiz with a wrench," appraises our blonde school chum, mid-inspection of the cuticles.

This denouement makes me close my eyes.

"Why...?"

A single word, so hard to ask.

"Too many reasons. The man was guilty of adultery before your mother died — remember? Couldn't keep his trousers on after that either. Bad role model. And the vanity with the cars? *Please*. Worst of all, he was responsible for what your brother did all those years. I know they let him off, but he *was* responsible. Should've noticed. Should have stopped your pain. So he had to pay the piper too."

"God." Dad.

"That bugger's not here right now," pipes up Hannah. "I do believe he's on vacation."

Huffing at this, Clair punches her neighbour's arm — hard.

"Ouch!"

"Hannah, how many times do I really need to tell you? Enough with the irreverential chatter."

"It was a joke."

"Hardly funny. You know people used to be stoned for that kind of humour?"

"Jeez."

I say nothing — but I remember.

My father reading to me when I was in bed with bronchitis, aged six. Our favourite Little Golden Book *Pantaloon* — about a mischievous black standard poodle coveting a job as a baker. The fingers of Dad's hand stroking my hair, the sound of his voice wavering between characters.

And then I remember Nicole's more recent, more desperate grip, and the words she whispered close by my ear.

These girls. These girls destroyed everything.

"You set fire to Nicole's room."

The taller, skinnier of the two claps hands together with

apparent glee, and then aims at me like an archer prepared to unleash her arrow.

"Bullseye! Mina Rapace, kid genius! Who gave you the first clue, Nancy Drew?"

"I can't believe this."

"Get used to it. Even funnier... You know you've been skipping about in Nicole's best ballet tutu? To shame."

Hannah has one of those whinnying laughs like a horse. We always figured it was amusing before. I now don't.

"You souvenired it?"

"The tutu? Was hanging on the line."

"And gave it to me," I realize — even if I have skewed memories.

"For your birthday."

This is too much. The only thing I can come up with sounds inane.

"I don't get it."

"What's not to get? — Not that hard. Jeez, Mina, Nicole's always been a cow. Always saying I was stupid. I *did* work out what 'D.D.' meant, by the way. Der."

"Helps that I told you," adds Clair. "But H is right — Nicole got what she deserved. She constantly picked on me for my weight and religious ways, and on you too, remember? For pretty much everything."

"I didn't think about killing her."

"Are you sure?"

Animeid rubbing two sticks beside Nicole comes back. "Well, I didn't act on it."

"That's because she had you beneath the heel, constantly grinding. What a beldam, no tears there. Remember the Moomba Mardi Gras? I followed you two when you wandered off. Typical, the way I was forgotten — but then I witnessed what she did. The final straw."

"So you hurt her?"

"No, silly, the plan was to kill her — vengeance is mine; I will repay, sayeth the Lord, all that. To my mind she got off pretty light."

"Anyway," tacks on Hannah, "the acne scars are the least of her worries." Again that whinnying laugh.

The vile quips and Good Book homilies hurt my head almost as much as a growing understanding of the insanity of this duo. Seated in a mundane venue with two mad women I recently called friends, both of whom are confessing to horrendous crimes like this is fun, everyday gossip — what on earth should I do?

"Doesn't it say in the Bible," I manage, "that it's wrong to do that? To kill people? Isn't that a sin?" Clutching at straws I may be, but am desperate.

"Is it?" Hannah, for one, looks worried.

But Clair — the specialist — is having none of this.

"Not at all. We're validated by the cause undertaken. There're always essential caveats, especially in the Old Testament, otherwise evil would hold sway over the good. I mean, look at the book of Ecclesiastes, which tradition has it King Solomon wrote at the end of his reign. Ecclesiastes 3:1-3 tells us that for everything there is a season... Including a time to kill. And then there's my favourite in Exodus 22:18: 'Thou shalt not suffer a witch to live.' Precisely. God encourages us to take the fight back to the Dark Forces."

"Kind of like in *Star Wars*," says Hannah, happier now.

"There's definitely something off about this place, sinister, haven't you noticed?" Clair goes on. "Man's heart might be evil, but here I worry about our very souls. Depravity, lust, idolatry... When a person like you or me is lost, incapable, how is it possible to choose or desire God? In all that bears on salvation or damnation, we have no genuine 'free will' but are captives, prisoners, bond slaves — either to the will of God, or to the will of Satan."

Confusion or not, Clair lost my attention a long way before, somewhere close to mention of King Solomon.

Stupid.

Me — not Hannah or Clair. Was never going to make inroads on the theological front and by doing so I'm playing by their rules. I eye the door as another patron enters the place, ringing Tinkerbell's little bell. Want to bolt from the edge of this abyss, and yet something pins me to my place.

I have to know.

"We are born again not by our own will," Clair rails on while Hannah camouflages a yawn, "but God's will; God grants that we believe—"

"Clair," I cut in out of necessity.

"What?"

"Did you hurt Margaret too?"

This interruption has made Clair frown. "That housemate of yours? I doubt I've ever met a likelier candidate for the Antichrist."

"Violent arsehole too," recalls Hannah, rubbing her jaw.

"Language, sweetie."

"Arsehole? That's nothing special."

"Still."

"Are you kidding, Clair? Arsehole's piss-poor."

"Hannah."

"I reckon God occasionally lets his hair down and resorts to a potty-mouth."

Clair bristles. "Hannah, zip it."

"Well, I could go for much harsher words, like fu—"

"Shush!"

I don't follow their absurd, seesawing commentary. Am only vaguely aware of the change of music to '70s rock from Blue Öyster Cult with '(Don't Fear) The Reaper', along with the sounds of someone frothing milk for a cappuccino or latte and people the next table over talking up the weather.

Unfinished, needing to know more, I clear my throat above

all this.

"Yes?" Clair suddenly asks, annoyed with me instead.

"What about my brother?"

"Your brother? Oh, I see, you mean reporting him to the authorities?" This time Clair shakes her head. "Sadly — No. That was Sarah. She beat me to the punch there."

Sarah.

I close my eyes.

Think of the girl swimming in the pool. The furious anger in those strokes. Her hand before that, resting on my thigh. The genuine concern in her eyes.

The best friend I'd pushed away.

For a moment, the tiniest of moments, Clair glances at the basket by her feet. But then she turns all attention to the French bulldog. A scratch under his chin and ruffles his fur.

"Where *is* Sarah?" I ask. "Do you know?"

"Oh, chilling out somewhere." Hannah sniggers.

"Don't worry yourself," her friend adds.

I look straight over the table to the girls. "You do know."

Although shaking her head, Hannah squeezes out, "Yes."

"Were you angry at her too?"

"Sarah?" Clair asks.

I nod, apprehension gripping.

"Well, you know what? I was angry with her the most. Actually, maybe anger is the wrong word. What should I say instead? *Um* — she was trouble. With a capital T."

"A very big one," agrees Hannah. "The T, I mean. Bigger than a T-bone steak."

Stare at them both now; a semblance of comprehension winging my way, hardly painting up a pretty picture. Cover mouth with my hand, horror running riot — yet still study the other girls, burrowing for clues.

"Don't stare," mutters Clair. "Didn't your mother tell you it's rude?"

I prise fingers off my lips.

"Clair. Hannah. What did you do?"

"Tell her what we did, tell her what we did," hyperventilates Hannah.

Clair sits back, more circumspect. "Give me time, H."

"Why? I'm getting hungry — we haven't got all day for these announcements. You promised me din-dins and I hate Deveroli's food."

"I haven't forgotten." Clair's eyes hold mine even while she chatters with her friend. "Patience. Be patient toward all men."

"And girls, right?" Hannah decides. "Because I'm guessing you're quoting that Bible stuff again, and those people never mentioned girls."

This forces her companion to glance over — "All right, all right!" — before swivelling back to me with further words of wisdom. "Did you know Sarah was reading a forbidden text, the *Malleus Maleficarum*?"

"What?"

"Don't lie — I saw her with it!" Hannah pounces, like she's burst into a courtroom to make a damning statement directly to the judge.

"No doubt trying," continues Clair, "to attract other young girls with enchanting stories from that evil book."

Now I'm frowning so hard it hurts.

"Both of you — stop. Please stop. What planet are you on? Sarah borrowed this *Maleficky* book —"

"*Malleus Maleficarum.*" Hannah, not Clair. Surprised she remembers the name. I couldn't.

"Whatever it was called," I bustle on, "she borrowed it from the library since she was researching a project on witches in the Dark Ages."

"Nonsense," says Clair.

"It was a prescribed text. Her teacher Mr Hopkins recommended it."

This causes the short, plump redhead to think. "Oh."

"Oh?" Her response in turn makes my blood boil. "*Oh? That's all you can say?*"

"Tell her the other bit," Hannah says, inciting Clair to nod.

"What other bit?" I cut in.

"I saw her touch you."

"Huh?"

"Here. On the thigh."

She pokes my stockinged right leg under the table.

"Like you just did?"

At that, the girl blushes. I swear Clair's face is redder than the apple on the table.

As for Hannah, I see an absurd grin planted on her face, like she's been privy to something risqué.

"I was there," Clair backpedals in a soft voice, "watching, when you paid a visit to her house four months ago. By the poolside."

"You were spying on us?"

"I saw her touch you. I saw you renounce her advances."

"I didn't renounce advances — I was being a complete bitch. And she wasn't *making* advances. What're you talking about?"

"I saw her touch you," Clair repeats. "It was an obscenity. She was trying to seduce you in that Hansel and Gretel house of theirs."

By now I'm beginning to feel like I'm in one very poor Z-grade horror movie.

"Clair, she wasn't seducing me. She was trying to be my friend. Couldn't you hear the conversation at all?"

She emphatically shakes her head. "I was next door. But I know what I saw."

"You saw wrong, hon. You saw wrong."

"Doesn't matter what you say. You'll say anything."

This was going in circles, mirroring a demented carnival merry-go-round.

"You're still under her spell, even after..." Clair bites her lower lip and sits back, a sheepish look on the face. "Anyway, doesn't matter what you say. I proved it."

Before I can insert a single rattle-brained word, the girl all of a sudden leans forward, elbows on the table, hands clasped together between them, an excited expression chasing off qualms.

"I'd made a witch cake," she says.

"You made a witch cake." My voice has flat-lined. What was it I said to Hannah at Deveroli's that other time when Nicole was present? The silly joke? 'Where's Sarah?' Hannah had asked. 'Busy with witch stuff,' I'd answered.

Clair doesn't wait for a drum-roll.

"And what's a witch cake, you ask?"

No, I haven't asked. Am still coming to grips with the disclosure and my possible culpability.

"Is it delicious?" squeezes in Hannah.

"Hush, sweetie."

The other girl pouts.

"To create a witch cake, you get a hold of the pee of people thought to be under the spell of this witch, and then you mix it with rye meal, making a little patty. You feed the patty to a dog, and Jiji here gobbled it up."

Yes, I felt more ill than ever. "Whose pee did you use?"

"Whose do you think?"

Don't bother asking how she got it — she had a key. Besides, this girl wasn't going to allow me time to badger.

"Because some of the powers the witch uses to cast a spell on afflicted people comes out in their pee, when a dog eats the cake it hurts the witch, causing her to cry out in agony."

Jiji is again licking his owner's face and she sniggers.

"Oh, you naughty devil. Anyway, I fed the witch cake to Jiji just after you left Sarah's house that day, and seconds later she stopped swimming and cried out in pain. A witch — you see. And I knew what I needed to do."

I'm speechless. Nothing comes to me. Which century are we in?

"There. Now *you* know. Pretty obvious." She sits back, stretches her back and cracks fingers.

"You think Sarah's a witch," I now manage to say.

"Think? I knew. I'd proved it."

"You can't prove anything with superstitious home remedies."

If I didn't know better, I'd say Clair's feelings were hurt.

"Oh, forget about it. I moved on."

"Me too," adjoins Hannah.

"Then, why —"

"Why *everything*?"

"Yes."

"I was angry. Yes, I think that's the right word now."

Clair finishes her coffee and waves at our cups.

"You want another? My shout."

"Yes, please," says Hannah.

"Not you, dear. Mind the weight."

"*My* weight?"

"You're the model."

"But you promised me a meal — your shout."

"I do think Proverbs 23:2 put it nicely: 'And put a knife to your throat if you are given to appetite.' A green salad should suffice."

"Bending that rule was fine when you scoffed down the pastry this morning."

"That wasn't a pastry, it was a scone — and I only ate a third. My little Jiji demanded the rest, the little gutz. Where was I? We were talking about coffee. Mina, you're up for one?"

After I nod, numbly, the girl beckons over our waitress to ask for two more sadly weak coffees, just her style. And then, obviously having been reminded of food, Clair starts tucking into the muffin.

Hannah watches this tableaux like a starving waif.

"Anyway," Clair continues while looking back to me, crumbs stuck to a corner of her mouth, "as I was saying, I was angry. Was I saying that? I think so. No, more than angry, I was furious. This monster had to be stopped, even more than the Patricks and Nicks of the world. I had to protect *you* from harm."

"No."

"No?" Hannah snorts. "What does *that* mean?"

"What does it mean?" I feel dazed. "It means I'm sorry. I don't know what to say."

"Well, you don't ever need to be sorry," says Clair. "Wasn't your fault. Sarah had you in her thrall. Pining and doing whatever she told you, all 'Yes Sarah, no Sarah, three bags full, Sarah' — it was downright pathetic. Never allowed to turn a fraction of that attention to me. You all treated me like dog poop, scraped me off your shoe. Didn't even notice the smell."

"I did," Hannah reassures her.

"For that, I suppose I'm grateful."

Clair turns toward the window and craftily rolls her eyes so that only I will see the gesture. Gives the dog the last half of the cake while Hannah appears crestfallen.

Accepts both coffees from the waitress and slides one my way.

"But then? You start to go psycho on us, listening to wee little voices inside your head. You think I didn't notice? You think I'm stupid like—" Clair again briefly glances at Hannah "—like some people? I'd heard about this condition at church. That's what our minister John Cotton refers to as a 'disease of astonishment' — when people experience strange fits, talk to themselves, try to harm themselves. All the symptoms I saw before me, in you, evidence of manipulation by the dark arts and of witchcraft. A hex."

"I'm so sorry." I really am. Sorry for the madness I'm hearing.

"You keep saying that, but I don't think you are."

Squeeze shut my eyes again, overwhelmed.

"I mean it. I am."

"Well, there's simply no need. Everything that's happened — all of it — has been done to help you find your salvation and deliver you from the evil of this world."

The husky laugh I once adored simply comes across as screwy.

I'd failed. Everything. Maybe if I'd opened my eyes and looked around, some of this mightn't've happened. But it did because I was such a selfish, self-centred jerk.

"Why?" I finally manage to ask.

"Because you're special."

"Right."

"You are."

Scrutinizing Clair on the other side of the table, I shake my head. "No. No, I'm not. But you're insane."

"I don't expect you to understand. I can't explain it, you just are. When I look at you I see an angel all set to fly. The devils of this world have tried their best to stunt your growth, but once you discover your wings, you'll soar. It was my task to protect you and help you find them."

"Mine too," Hannah says.

I'm more confused still. "Your wings?"

"No, the mission. Both of us had one together. Helping you."

"Our destiny." That was Clair.

"Unreal, right?" Hannah woops and claps hands, causing our waitress to give her an annoyed look from over near the counter.

Hardly matters. I need to work at control of breathing, move on from shocked and appalled. Have to get a grip, Mina. But I can't.

"Why...? *Why* me?"

"Well, God told us."

"Told Clair at any rate," Hannah corrects her confederate, "and she passed on the message."

I run fingers along the edge of the table, studying the natural knots in the bevelled surface. Find it somehow calming.

"How exactly," I next ask, "did he tell you?"

Clair's voice, chirpy and simple, drags my attention straight back.

"He rang."

Wood forgotten, I'm staring at her. "He rang."

"Mm-hmm."

"What — he called you collect?"

"No, silly. The Lord doesn't need to worry about earthly things like telephone charges."

"So... he paid for the call?"

"I suppose."

"Clair, if you're God — why use a phone at all?"

"Who cares?" Hannah interrupts. "At least the guy didn't stoop to writing a letter."

I'm distracted by this comment until I realize it wasn't an intended joke, giving Clair time to whip the baton from her partner.

"Anyway, the gist of the conversation came down to a simple matter: You. Cursed from birth, persecuted by family and friends. We had to free you in order that you could fulfil your destiny. We're here to show you the true path."

"How? By scaring me half to death?"

Am not as flip as I sound.

Actually running scared. These people are madder than mad. But I have to barter with them, forage out the truth. The world needs to know exactly what they've done. I need to know.

Have also cottoned on exactly where to go now. That note inside the textbook on poison girls from the Asian subcontinent — what was the waffle mostly about?

Dysfunctional families.

"The story by Hawthorne," I say, gathering together pieces to which I hadn't previously paid all that much attention. "What was it? The one with that girl Beatrice."

"You're talking about 'Rappaccini's Daughter'?"

"Yeah, that's the one."

Clair nods, a picture of eagerness. "Groomed from birth by her father to become poisonous to other people and all possible future suitors. Cursed by her own family."

"With a surname that might or might not be related to mine."

"Exactly. And Beatrice is the same too."

"While 'Mina' you're not sure about, except it's a character name in *Dracula*?"

"That's right." Crossing her arms, Clair looks triumphant.

"Fiction," I tell them both. "Hawthorne's story was a work of fiction. So is *Dracula*. And the Vish Kanya are probably also a myth. They're not true stories."

"Your point being?"

"Think I just inferred. And I hate to tell you, but I'm not some ill-fated, corset-bound maid stuck up shit creek without a paddle."

"We beg to differ."

"Sure you do."

"Why are you so angry?"

Have to temper myself. "I'm not angry." Don't spook these girls. Keep them talking. "I'm trying to understand."

"Sure you are. By the way, this is for you."

Clair's sliding across a box-shaped object, about six inches across and four inches deep. Trussed up in the very same floral wrapping paper that'd garnished the Vish Kanya tome when it arrived in the mail.

Meaning this must have been Nick's — so how had Clair come by the paper?

"What is it?" I ask, glaring at the present. "Another textbook full of sweet nothings?"

"Listen to you."

Having placed the dog inside the basket at her feet, Clair again slumps on her elbows and gazes across at me.

"You believe you've worked everything and everyone out, become cocky with your newfound inner strength. The witch might be out of the picture but this presents us with the real danger — don't you properly read those comic books? With great power comes greater responsibility. In James 4:6 we're told 'God is opposed to the proud, but gives grace to the humble', and remember what happened to Thor when he forgot humility? His father Odin taught him a lesson in the stuff. Where'd you think you were — the Garden of Eden?"

"I have no idea."

"Never did," observes Hannah as she checks her watch.

"And, what, you think this narrative's all about your journey of self-discovery? That you're the only one allowed to surprise others?"

Clair now tut-tuts.

"It got far more interesting — bit-playing third parties coming back to bite you on the bum. You need to be more careful, let the Devil take the hindmost. I won't always be here looking out for you."

"Me too," says her accomplice. "I like the biting part."

"It's not the biting I have a problem with. You can't believe what you're doing is right. I can't believe you do."

Clair chooses this moment to toss in something she's apparently been thinking all along — and it relates to a sticker I once saw on her school binder.

"Mina, any thought we possess or mindful deliberation we experience was all previously decreed, to be brought to pass exactly as God predetermined it. Making Hannah and I merely His instruments."

"Instruments? What — so you can now go grab a two-pronged twig and start divining fresh victims?"

Feel like I'm divining my own face, rubbing it as I am with hands, smudging foundation and mascara, but discover nothing of worth. Only horror, like I already mentioned.

"All right. All right, so you're doing what you were programmed to do at some stage in — I don't know — evolution or creation or whatever you want to call this. What happened to free will? The conscious decision to do what you believe is right?"

"We're doing what we think is right," insists Clair.

"Hurting others."

"Doing the Lord's work as it was ordained by Him."

"And ready to be damned by your own God in the process?"

"Every social wrongdoing is decreed and happens according to God's infinite wisdom. As the robber is decreed to rob, so the executioner is decreed to kill — all for God's pleasure and infinite wisdom."

"That's bullshit, Clair. Absolute crap. I can't — I won't — believe it. What you're doing is just plain wrong. Hannah — you can't believe this."

Throughout the latest to-and-fro the other girl has been staring into space, twirling a coil of blonde hair around one finger. She looks at me now with a blank expression.

"Which part?"

"Any of it."

"Nah, it's fine. I like the fact I'm not responsible. Means I can get away with murder and say it wasn't really me; it was some other guy — the top dog up in Heaven — controlling everything. Sweet."

"See?" says Clair. "The girl has a brain."

I'm unaware if there's intentional sarcasm, but Hannah seems to hear this too.

"Gee, thanks."

Here's where I kick back my chair with disgust and start fiddling with the packet of cigarettes I've produced from my bag — other people be damned.

Hands are shaking. Concentrate. Don't give them this — you've given enough. Don't let these evil people see how befuddled you are.

"That's a disgusting habit," Clair mutters.

I don't care. "Is, isn't it?"

Hands have already stopped quivering as I light up an Eve with its pretty floral arrangement. Muster strength from this simple process. Channel Margaret and glare over the glowing red cherry at my two neighbours sharing the table.

Drag in on the cigarette, a necessary evil, think up a silly quip.

"Not so special now, I guess."

Their silence is all the answer this deserves.

"So," I further muse, having exhaled a plume in Clair's direction, "correct me if I'm wrong, but according to you some greater power decides what we're going to do. Whereupon you blindly string along with it, destroying other people's lives in the process."

"No. You're perverting my words." She coughs slightly.

"Frustrating, isn't it?"

Leaning back in the chair, one of my legs crossed over the other, I almost fool myself that I'm not scared. That I've grown an element of attitude to gift-wrap the backbone.

"So why all this? I mean not the violence — that's plain madness and I get it. Kind of. Actually, not really. But why all the grandstanding today? The true confessions?"

Clair nods, waving in front of her face.

"We wanted you to understand why we did what we did."

"And if I don't?"

"Oh, but you must!"

"You know what, girls? No. *No.* I'm not going to stand for that."

"What're you going to do?" Clair wags a finger my way. "You can't fight God."

I screw up my mouth, a kind of bemused reaction. "Think I can fucking well try," I say straight after.

This causes Hannah to groan.

"How come she gets away with potty-mouth, and I don't?"

Enough.

Time to go.

Am in the middle of gathering things together but my former friend Clair hops up first, standing a safe distance from the cigarette smoke, and mimics the same sweet smile she granted when they first arrived.

"We'll be off now."

"Must you?"

"I promised Hannah dinner. You can come if you like."

"Go to Hell, Clair." Having sat back again, I wave. "Toodle-oo."

"By the way, don't open the prezzie till after we've left."

My turn to simmer. "Why should I open it at all?"

"Oh, curiosity's a wonderful thing. When you do open it, I want you to think of sweet justice and an evil, fornicating best friend of your brother's."

"Nick."

"And next on the shopping list might be a philandering husband."

My world lurches, even if I refuse to let her see that. "Double-U." Take another drag on the cigarette, holding onto Clair's eyes for dear life.

"Let's not name names," she says.

Rising to join Clair, Hannah screws up her nose — I'm not certain if this is a result of the smoke or because she's being cheeky.

"Spoils the moment," asserts the tall, blonde girl. "But this Double-U really does need to get a real handle. Think I'll give him one. Carve it into his forehead."

After they've left and the bell on the door has stopped ringing, I stare at this present on the table a long time.

Know what I should do — haul it into the nearest rubbish bin. If the contents're anywhere near the book or the card, they'll hurt.

But Clair was right about curiosity.

I stamp out my cigarette in a nearby ashtray; hear a song I

don't like (Sheena Easton's 'Sugar Walls') on the in-house soundsystem and make the call.

Unwrapping carefully as well as warily, I find a large wooden box.

This has a sliding panel on top, so I push this across — and a live cane toad hops out. Red-brown in colour, size wise about eight centimetres from snout to vent, skin dry and warty.

I know I shriek. Sorry, but the creature's ugly as sin.

The waitress also screams, bringing over the chef who carries a handy meat-cleaver. When he sees what's still inside the box, however, he quails too. Drops the cleaver and rushes to the sink to throw up.

Seeing this reaction, I'm terrified but have to sneak a peek. Ignore the toad, which seems content to squat there on the table cloth, and look into the wooden container.

Find male genitals in there, partially eaten — by the toad, I guess — with pubic hairs still attached.

I end up being taken to police headquarters at Rustle Street in the city, interviewed on the second floor by two plainclothes cops who seemed determined to get the truth out of me — in their minds this being the fact that I was the perpetrator, having castrated some poor, unsuspecting boyfriend.

Was left to twiddle thumbs in an empty corner office that had very little to keep me interested. The work desk was barren aside from a half-full John Wayne mug stuck on a pentagram coaster, and the walls equally lifeless with only a couple of sun-bleached wanted posters with mug shots, their names (Simon Peter and James Zebedee), and the Crime Stompers number beneath.

I felt stunned. Worried about Double-U, but otherwise couldn't seem to put two sentences together inside my head.

A while later they transferred me to the third floor, where three other officers asked exactly the same questions as before.

Could tell they didn't believe my answers, and this nurtured a new sensation — one in which I seriously considered reaching across the table to punch them out, and then take matters into my own hands.

Once I'd repeated the story ten times over — all about Clair and Hannah, along with Nicole, Margaret, my dad, Sarah, and the danger to Double-U, as well as the victim to whom those genitals most probably belonged — I was visited by someone I knew: Constable Andie Summers.

At the time they'd left me solo for another quarter of an hour so I pinched one of the cops' cigarettes (a brand called Paul Jones in a blue box with a naval commodore on the front) and was busy searching my pockets for a lighter. Hid it behind my back when she entered.

Soon as I see her face, though, I relax and bring the ciggie into the open.

"Constable Andie," I say, with some relief even if the woman wears that typically impassive face.

Still, this makes her point to the lapel on her shoulder. "Senior Constable now."

"Wow. You got promoted."

"This week."

"Congrats."

The police officer has fixed her gaze on my cigarette. "You going to light that thing or play with it?"

I pretend to pat myself down. "No matches."

"Here."

Andie takes something out of her waist pocket and slides this across the table to me. Once her fingers depart I find an ostrich skin-covered Zippo cigarette lighter.

"Classy," I decide.

"Not mine. Borrowed it off a low-life I busted last week. Keep it."

"Don't you need this for evidence or something?"

"We have enough evidence. Go on then."

I flick the wheel and the lighter flames on immediately. The cigarette turns out to be stronger than I was used to.

Breathing out loudly on her side of the card table, the woman loosens her tie and looks at me again.

"You really got yourself in some shit, Mina. More than usual, I mean."

"I know."

"The only way you're going to stop the run is by seizing life by the horns — don't let this happen to you."

"None of it's exactly in my control."

Narrowing her eyes, Andie stares me down. "Then make it."

My mouth tight, I incline my head. Yes.

"Anyway," the woman goes on, "we've been trying to track down your uncle."

"Thanks."

"And we're looking into your friend Double-U, but without a real name it's kind of tough. Do you at least know his family name?"

That was when I realized I didn't.

"His wife Bessie — *um*, Bettie — works at the Brigantine Café in Carlaisle Street in St. Kilda, if that's any help."

"Maybe. I doubt we need to worry."

I lean forward, alarmed. "What's happened?"

"Thought you might like to know that we *did* go pay a call on your friends Clair René and Hannah Satana earlier this evening."

"Evening? What time is it?"

Senior Constable Summers consults her watch. "Just before twelve."

"God, that means I've been here about ten hours." I glance at her. "Sorry. Go on."

"No worries. As I was saying, we visited the girls."

"And they denied everything." My heart had vanished ages before.

"Not exactly."

I continue looking at the police officer but say nothing.

"Satana confessed to the whole caboodle. Never have seen someone so willing to give up the goods — we couldn't shut her up. Allegedly, she did the killing but René orchestrated everything."

"What did Clair say?"

"Refused to offer any statement. Simply smiled. We had a search warrant — reasonable grounds for believing that there may be evidence related to an indictable offence. In her father's garage we made a disturbing discovery. There were a half-dozen sealed oil drums, and one of them contained a corpse, male, chopped up in pieces, missing its vital parts."

"Nick Shahan."

"We don't know yet, given the state of the body. Approximately the correct age but dental records need to be checked, next-of-kin notified and interviewed. The Coroner's Office is looking into the details now. And there was a second body."

These are the words I really do not want to hear.

"Neatly folded up in a foetal position in the freezer. Looks to've been drowned, chlorinated water in her lungs, but also there was an injury to the back of the skull. We believe this may have been caused by a garden hoe that was inside the freezer. The victim was naked but — bizarrely — had been tarred and feathered before being placed in the unit."

Her.

"I've been in the Force five years. Never seen anything like it. Neither has the chief — a veteran of two decades."

"You think it's Sarah."

"Again, we won't know for a few days."

"It's her."

"Possibly." The woman looks to the side, at nothing, lips a tight line on her face. "There was something else we found."

She delves into a white Coles shopping bag and pulls out

another sheath, a clear plastic one, wrapped tightly around red swimwear graced with white lilies.

"They're Sarah's," I say.

"You certain?"

"She was wearing them the last day I saw her."

The police officer nods, like she knew that all along.

"Where are they now — Clair and Hannah?"

"In the lock-up with their parents present, being read rights by the chief."

"Andie?"

"Mina?"

"What colour were the feathers? — Sarah's feathers, I mean."

"What difference does that make?"

I hold up my right hand, but I can't look the officer in the eye. "Humour me."

"Black. They were black."

Am at home, my empty family nest.

Only other survivor, Patrick, isn't here since he's decided to stay indefinitely with Uncle Dam down in Subere.

Me? Am in my father's room, dealing with his safe.

This is a blanket-covered brute positioned next to the old man's office bureau — his large IBM AT computer dwarfed by the iron neighbour.

The safe also sits beneath a dangling, 1/48 scale Sopwith Pup biplane that's suspended to the ceiling by fishing wire. This wire looks suspiciously similar to the one once used by Patrick to string me up to our Hills Hoist in the back yard.

After removing a pile of unmarked floppy disks, when I unveil the safe I'm surprised to find the thing looks like it was made in the last century. Old and corroded, with the words ACME SAFE CO. along the bottom of a chunky, clunky door.

The combination Dam gave me works perfectly.

Find inside wads of cash, most of these containing the new,

greyish blue one-hundred-dollar notes with Douglas Mawson on them. Had no idea Dad squirreled away so much money.

There's also a dark-brown, stained cedar box on the lowest shelf. Another wooden container. I let out a sigh — hope this one doesn't contain wildlife. No gonads either.

I flick a brass catch and lift the lid to a sea of royal blue velvet — upon which sit twin polished nickel 9mm Star Model B pistols, each with a mother-of-pearl handgrip.

"My God, Dad. Where did you get these?"

About to put the box back into the safe when something stops me. Instead I lift the pistols, one in each hand, and test the weight.

But don't know how to use a gun.

Learn, I hear someone say.

An hour later I'm tossing things into a charcoal duffel bag: In a hard folder the January 1942 *Bulletman* (issue 3), *Science Fiction Space Adventures* issue 12, *Miss Fury* issue 7, and *2001: A Space Odyssey* issue 2.

A couple of paperbacks (by Robert Louis Stevenson and Radclyffe Hall) and the hardback of *The Count of Monte Cristo*.

Little Golden Book *Pantaloon*? Check. Mum's chocolate-brown beret? Yep.

A few bunched-up pairs of black tights, undies, socks, two bras and a cardigan with a hole in the elbow. Toiletries pouch and make-up box too, though I presume the latter will now be mostly pointless.

Stick in two guns, a packet of cigarettes, the ostrich skin-covered cigarette lighter and a lot of cash.

Basil Brush I sit atop my pillow. He can stay to keep watch on the house.

Decide to leave records behind. The vinyl's too heavy, cumbersome, and in many respects no longer required. I don't have my Walkman — it's still with Margaret.

Then I change my mind. Take the comics out. They've already had their time and place.

I go grab a large brown envelope from the secretaire in Dad's study, stick on what I hope is more than enough stamps, and address it to Uncle Dam. Slide inside the comics along with a short note thanking him for everything. Tell him how much he means to me, and say goodbye. Lick and seal the flap.

Also write a postcard to Margaret, with something intentionally provocative — a toddler picture of Prince William. I know it'll set her off. Tell her to keep the Walkman and that I'll shortly send cash to cover three months' rent. Address it to the hospital where she's still staying, and end the message on the back with a lipstick kiss.

The third piece of correspondence I write to Nicole, a simple one saying that the people who hurt her would now be punished. Inside the envelope I place a tabloid splashing on the arrest of the two girls, clipped out from this morning's *Sun News-Pictorial*.

Don't bother composing anything to Double-U.

The evening before I'd gone back to the Brigantine (took a wide berth around Deveroli's) and harassed his wife — said Double-U was still in love with her and they should get over stupid things like pride. Doubt she recognized me, or simply didn't remember. Whatever the case, she lost her temper and ordered me out. But when I peeked in through the window a few minutes later I saw her on the phone, one hand placed on her chest and a huge smile riding that red mouth.

I ought to write to Clair and Hannah, let the girls know I forgive them, but this is impossible. I don't. Have yet to forgive myself.

This will take time.

The final thing I insert into my duffel bag is a black feather I once found beneath the bed.

You're going?

I stop. Smile. Can almost sense her behind me. God. I've missed you.

"I'm going," I confirm, not looking back. "Have to — you know that. There's nothing here for me now."

This's the moment I finally cry.

Double over — weeping, I think, for Mum and Dad, for Nicole, Double-U, my brother, Margaret, and the madness of Clair and Hannah. Spare a few sobs for Angelika and my lost innocence.

Most of all I wail for Sarah and Animeid, no matter if one ever really was the other outside of my mind.

Wish to God I had a second chance to gift a hug to them.

I have unseemly snot hanging from my nose and make an unholy riot.

Don't know when the fit subsides, but sometime before dawn I go to the bathroom, wash my face, and scrub off ruined make-up.

Peer at my naked face in the mirror. Enough narcissism.

I'm not going to bend to any more stupid rules, and predestination can go jump. Maybe can't change what's already happened, but I'll sure as Hell try to prevent things like this occurring again.

Time to leave.

The highway, usually a major thoroughfare, is devoid of traffic. Having pushed the envelope and card into a post-box near my house I come straight here.

And wait.

Two pairs of vacant tram-tracks, a row of ghost gums either side. The only thing travelling hereabouts is the stream of condensation from my nose. Everything slick and shiny from overnight rainfall.

Curiously, no sound of birds but the smell of that rain combined with stale exhaust.

I peer both ways, shivering from the cold, and wonder if I'll be here all day. Dance a little jig to keep myself warm, something that'd horrify Mitzi Gaynor.

The first vehicle I see — a World War Two era, canvas-backed General Motors Model CCKW lorry — is in surprisingly good condition even if it looks like it should be in *The Great Escape*. Has the license plate 'JJZ-109' stuck on top of the bonnet, along with our state slogan (The Garden State) beneath.

When I stick out a cautious hand to hail him, the truck pulls over and its driver reaches across a leather bench-seat to open the passenger door.

This is a middle-aged man pushing sixty with a white, carefully tailored moustache and a friendly smile. Dressed in khaki overalls that look like they've been starched, a bluish grey tweed cap pulled down over his eyes. Very neat and otherwise anonymous.

"Where're you headed?" I ask, hopping from foot to foot as I rub hands together, it's now so nippy.

"Heropa."

Never heard of the place. Good. I feel the warmth in the cabin before me.

"Would you care for a lift, young lady?"

"Sure. Thanks."

Climb up, settle in with the heavy duffle bag on my lap — much of that weight caused by loaded 9mm pistols I have in rolled-up t-shirts — and clap the door shut.

"Where to?" my driver asks as we ease out into zero traffic.

"All the way."

"All the way it is. And what shall we call you?"

"Mitzi," I decide on the spot.

Although I've thawed out I don't begin to relax till we're on the rural outskirts of suburbia somewhere near St. Jude, east of Nede.

By that stage we're cruising by paddocks, vineyards, galvanized windmill towers, the odd weatherboard farmhouse or general store, old advertising from the 1930s, a fifteen-metre tall concrete merino sheep, and lots of Illawarra Shorthorns.

Sparse gum trees and bush scrub.

Have the window down, cold wind in my hair, breathing in eucalyptus and manure.

After a billboard for Royal Vendetta toothpaste there's a dark green signpost that has upcoming kilometre distances for Sidon, Tyre and Nod — other places I wasn't up on.

The driver, Stan, doesn't say much and I appreciate that.

The longest conversation is a relatively short one during which he glances over at me and deduces I'm escaping troubles.

"All this has happened before," Stan says with a knowing expression, "and it will all happen again — but this time it happened in Nede."

Wouldn't swear by it, but I'm fairly certain he's paraphrased the intro from the Disney version of *Peter Pan*.

Otherwise seems content to focus on driving as he listens to a small transistor resting on the dash, set to an AM station.

While that station is currently playing a tinny, mono version of 'The End' by The Doors, it's hardly an act of precognition — just some random song on the radio.

Ahead, on the left-hand side of the highway, is a big white sign with black letters that announce

YOU ARE NOW LEAVING NEDE.

— Except some fool has crossed out 'Nede' and spray-painted EDEN above the word in red letters that've bled.

When we drive past said placard, nothing happens.

No lightning flash, no hand of God, nor the end of reality. We continue cruising in a straight line along an open road, headed towards a vague horizon.

Don't look back.

Relaxing now into the seat I blow out my cheeks, and then smile.

Antediluvian Almanac

Aussie vernacular, places, products & people, along with music, some written matter and the odd film you might want to brush up on (or not) — in brief.

ABC-TV: Australia's national broadcaster, launched in 1956
À bout de souffle: See *Breathless* (below)
AC/DC: Australian hard rock band formed in 1973
Adams, Bryan: Canadian rock singer/songwriter
Addams, Morticia: Fictional matriarch of *The Addams Family*
Airfix: Oldest UK manufacturer of scale model kits
Anne of Green Gables: 1908 children's book by Canadian Lucy Maud Montgomery
'Another Brick in the Wall, Part 2': Song from Pink Floyd's LP *The Wall*
Antz Pantz: Bikini-brief underwear made by Australian company Holeproof. Famous for TV ad with an echidna named Rex
Argus, The: Daily Melbourne newspaper est. 1846 & closed in 1957
Australian Crawl: Australian rock band founded by James Reyne in 1978
Auto-Ordnance M1911A1: .45 ACP revolver modelled on the Colt 1911
Bauhaus: English gothic rock band, formed in 1978. Famous for single 'Bela Lugosi's Dead'
Bara, Theda: Sultry vamp & one of the more popular actresses of the silent film era
Barber, Tony: Australian game show host & TV personality
Bardot, Brigitte: French former actress, singer, fashion model & icon
Baritsu: Japanese wrestling style used by Sherlock Holmes — a typo, or a bowdlerization of, *bartitsu*

Basil Brush: Posh-speaking glove-puppet fox, star of British kids' TV since 1962

Bennett: Villain played by Aussie Vernon Wells in Schwarzenegger film *Commando* (1985)

Big M: Popular brand of flavoured milk est. in Flemington, Victoria, 1978

Birds, The: 1963 film directed by Alfred Hitchcock, starring Aussie Rod Taylor, Tippi Hedren & many fine feathered friends

Birrarung: Aboriginal name for the Yarra River flowing through city of Melbourne

Birthday Party, The: Australian post-punk outfit (1978 to 1983) from Melbourne first known as The Boys Next Door, feat. Nick Cave, Mick Harvey & Rowland S. Howard

Bixby, Bill: American actor, famous for *My Favorite Martian* & *The Incredible Hulk*

Blade Runner: 1982 sci-fi directed by Ridley Scott, starring Harrison Ford & Rutger Hauer

Blankety Blanks: Australian game show based on America's *Match Game*

Blotto: Extremely drunk

Blue Öyster Cult: American rock band first formed in 1967

Blue Trains: First steel-bodied train to operate in Melbourne, introduced 1956

Blu-Tack: Reusable blue putty-like adhesive commonly used to attach lightweight objects

Blyton, Enid: English children's scribe (*The Magic Faraway Tree* & *The Wishing Chair*)

Bogan: Aust. & NZ slang for someone of minimal education along with violent nature

Bonjour Tristesse: 1957 Côte d'Azur melodrama starring Jean Seberg & David Niven

Bonnet: The hood of a car or truck

Boys Next Door, The: See Birthday Party, The

Bowie, David: English muso best-known for 'Space Oddity', Ziggy Stardust & *Heroes*

Breathless: Jean-Luc Godard's 1960 film starred Jean Seberg & Jean-Paul Belmondo

Brooks, Louise: American dancer, actress & style icon who popularized the bob haircut

Brotherhood of St. Laurence: Organization helping poor & disadvantaged in Australia

Brush, Basil: See Basil Brush

Bulletgirl: Fawcett superhero, made debut in *Master Comics* #13 (April, 1941)

Bulletman: Fawcett Comics superhero created by Bill Parker & Jon Smalle (1940)

Burke and Wills: In 1860, Robert O'Hara Burke & William John Wills-led expedition to cross Australia from Melbourne to Gulf of Carpentaria. Both leaders died on return journey

Cabaret Voltaire: Innovative British music group est. 1973, feat. Stephen Mallinder, Richard H. Kirk & Chris Watson

Cabinet of Dr Caligari, The: 1920 German silent horror film directed by Robert Wiene

Caine, Michael: Veteran English actor, starred in *The Italian Job* (1969) & *Inception* (2010)

Carroll, Lewis: Author of *Alice's Adventures in Wonderland* & *Through the Looking-Glass*

Chaney, Jr., Lon: Played The Wolf Man, The Mummy & Frankenstein's Monster in horror from Universal Studios

Christian Death: U.S. rock band formed in 1979 by Rozz Williams, heralding goth rock

Cleopatra: 1963 film directed by Joseph L. Mankiewicz, starring Elizabeth Taylor

Clinique: Manufacturer of skincare, cosmetics & fragrances, owned by Estée Lauder

Cold Chisel: Australian rock band formed in 1973 with vocalist Jimmy Barnes

Colonel Klink: Actor Werner Klemperer hammed up this Luftwaffe commandant in 1960s comedy *Hogan's Heroes*

Colt 1911 .45: semi-automatic pistol produced by Colt from 1911

Commando: 1985 film starring Schwarzenegger & Vernon Wells, directed by Mark Lester

Converse All Stars: Canvas & rubber shoes first produced in 1917

Countdown: Weekly music TV show broadcast from Melbourne by ABC 1974-1987

Cure, The: English band formed 1976, headed by Robert Smith. Music and image helped trigger gothic rock genre

Curtis, Ian: English musician, singer/songwriter for Joy Division; sadly committed suicide in 1980 at age 23

Cypress Hill: Cuban-American/Latino hip hop group set up in 1988

Czechoslavakia: State from 1918 until dissolution into Czech Republic & Slovakia in 1993

Danielle Dax: English experimental musician, artist & producer

Daredevil: Blind comic-book superhero created by Stan Lee, Bill Everett & Jack Kirby

Davis, Miles: Hugely influential American jazz musician & composer

Degas, Edgar: French Impressionist artist famous for paintings & sculptures

Die Frau im Mond: 1929 German sci-fi (*Woman in the Moon*) directed by Fritz Lang

Dillon, Matt: American actor; starred in *The Outsiders* (1983)

Dire Straits: British rock band, formed in 1977 by Mark Knopfler

Ditko, Steve: Comic-book artist & writer best known for Spider-Man and Doctor Strange

Divinyls: Australian rockers formed in 1980, fronted by vocalist Chrissy Amphlett

Divvy van: Aussie slang for 'divisional van', police vehicle in which crims are transported

Doctor Martens: Known as 'Docs', British footwear brand famous for boots

Done, Ken: Australian artist renowned in 1980s for kitsch images of local landmarks

Dolly: Australian monthly teen magazine started in 1970

Doctor Who: British sci-fi TV programme produced by the BBC since 1963

Donna Karan: American fashion designer, creator of DKNY clothing label

Donne, John: English poet, satirist, lawyer & Church of England cleric (1572-1631)

Doona: Australian name for a bed duvet/comforter/quilt

Dungeons & Dragons: fantasy tabletop role-playing game first published in 1974

Dunny: Toilet

Easton, Sheena: Scottish singer; did 007 movie theme song *For Your Eyes Only*

Einstürzende Neubauten: German industrial band, formed West Berlin in 1980

Escher, M.C.: Dutch artist known for mathematically-inspired, oft-impossible pictures

Face, The: British music, fashion & culture monthly magazine, 1980-2004

Factory Records: Manchester-based British indie record label, started in 1978

Fairy floss: Cotton candy in Australia

Fantastic Four: Superhero team created in 1961 by Stan Lee and Jack Kirby

Faraway Tree, The: 1939-51 kids' books by Enid Blyton. At top of this tree are magical locales like Topsy Turvy Land & the Land of Dame Slap — an aggressive school teacher

Farrow, Mia: Star of Roman Polanski horror *Rosemary's Baby* (1968)

Fawcett Comics: Comic-book publishers during the Golden Age of the 1940s

Flake: Battered gummy shark sold in Melbourne (& Victoria) as fish & chips

Flash, The: DC Comics' fastest man alive

Flinders, Matthew: Navigator first to circumnavigate Australia & identify it as a continent

Flinders Street Station: Central railway station in Melbourne, opened 1854

Front 242: Belgian group est. 1981. Pioneers of electronic body music & techno

Fruit Tingles: Fruit-flavoured lollies originating in 1930s in Melbourne, Australia

'Funky Town': 1980 disco song written by Lipps Inc

Gauguin, Paul: French Post-Impressionist artist

Gaynor, Mitzi: American actress, singer & dancer. Starred in *There's No Business Like Show Business* (1954)

Ghost gum: Evergreen tree native to Australia, with white to cream and pink-tinged bark

God: Rock band from Melbourne, Australia, 1986-1989

Goretti, Maria: Italian Catholic virgin-martyr, one of the youngest canonized saints

Gutz: Greedy person (or dog)

Hall, Radclyffe: English poet/author, best known for *The Well of Loneliness*

Hammer Films: UK film company best known for horror made from the mid-1950s

Herbie Hancock: U.S. musician, architect of 'post-bop'. Early jazz musician to embrace synthesizers & funk music

Hills Hoist: Iconic, Australian-made rotary metal backyard clothesline

Hissy fit: Outburst of temper, often used to describe female anger at something trivial

Hogan's Heroes: TV sitcom (1965-71) set in German POW camp during World War II

Hoodie: Hooded sweathshirt/pullover

Horse Feathers: Classic 1932 Marx Brothers film comedy

Howard, Robert E: Cross-genre pulp fiction author. Known for character Conan

HSC: Higher School Certificate, qualification for final year of high school

Hunters & Collectors: Australian rock band formed in Melbourne in 1981

Hutchinson, Ivan: Australian film critic & TV personality from early 1960s to mid-1990s

IBM AT: IBM's second-generation 20 MB hard disk drive PC, released in 1984

i-D Magazine: UK mag dedicated to fashion, music, art & youth culture founded in 1980

'If You Want to See Some Strange Behavior (Take a Look at Man)': Song by Louis Prima — for unmade Disney sequel to *The Jungle Book*

Illawarra Shorthorn: Cattle breed created by Australian dairymen to improve herds

I Married an Angel: 1942 MGM musical starring Jeanette MacDonald & Nelson Eddy

Incredible Hulk, The: Gamma-irradiated character created by Jack Kirby & Stan Lee in 1963, made into TV series starring Bill Bixby 1978-82

I Spit on Your Gravy: 1980s punk-influenced Aussie band hailing from Melbourne

Jamón: Dry-cured ham from Spain

Java Man: Fossils discovered in 1891 in East Java, Indonesia, one of first known specimens of Homo erectus

Jean Varon: Company set up by '60s British designer John Bates — who dressed Diana Rigg in *The Avengers* TV series & may have invented the miniskirt

Jesus and Mary Chain, The: Scottish band formed in 1983 by brothers Jim & William Reid

Johnson, Brian: Second lead singer for AC/DC after untimely death of Bon Scott

Joshing: Joking, kidding about

Joy Division: Post-punk band formed in Manchester in 1976; released album *Unknown Pleasures* in 1979 through Tony Wilson's Factory imprint

Kennedy, Graham: Pioneering Australian entertainer & TV personality

Kensit, Patsy: Star of *Absolute Beginners* (1986)

Kids in the Kitchen: 1980s band from Melbourne

Kirby, Jack: Innovative American comic-book artist/writer who co-created Captain America, The Avengers, Fantastic Four, X-Men, Ant-Man & Thor

Lanchester, Elsa: English actress, starred in *Bride of Frankenstein* with Boris Karloff (1935)

Lang, Fritz: Austrian filmmaker most famous for *Metropolis* (1927)

Legend of Zelda, The: 1986 video game designed by Shigeru Miyamoto & Takashi Tezuka

Lee, Stan: American comic-book writer. In collaboration with Jack Kirby & Steve Ditko, created Spider-Man, the Hulk, Fantastic Four, Iron Man & Thor

Loo: Toilet

Lowe, Rob: 1980s Hollywood actor; later starred in *Austin Powers*

Luna Park: Name for dozens of currently operating & defunct amusement parks on every continent except Antarctica since 1903. Melbourne's is oldest still operating

***Malleus Maleficarum*, The:** 'Hammer of [the] Witches', a treatise on the prosecution of witches written in 1486 by Heinrich Kramer, a German Catholic clergyman

Marvel Comics: Started in 1939 as Timely. Responsible for *The Avengers* & other superhero titles created by Stan Lee, Jack Kirby, Steve Ditko, etc.

Marx, Groucho: Member of the Marx Brothers

Masque of the Red Death, The: 1964 British horror starring Vincent Price, based on Edgar Allan Poe

Matheson, Richard: Wrote *I am Legend* & numerous TV episodes of *The Twilight Zone*

Mawson, Douglas: Famous Australian geologist, Antarctic explorer & academic

McCarthy, Andrew: Hollywood actor, starred in *Pretty in Pink* & *Less Than Zero*

Mellencamp, John Cougar: American rock singer-songwriter & musician

Merino sheep: Breed from central Spain. Arrived in Australia with the First Fleet (1788)

Merzbow: Japanese noise musician Masami Akita

Mickey Spillane's Mike Hammer: Hardboiled TV series starring Stacy Keach, 1984-85

Microgynon: Known as 'the pill', or combined oral contraceptive pill

Midnight Oil: Australian alt-rock band fronted by Peter Garrett

Mille Miglia (Thousand Miles): Endurance race which took place in Italy 1927-1957

Miss Fury: Early female comic hero. Debuted in 1941 created by artist Tarpé Mills

Mists of Avalon, The: 1983 novel by Marion Zimmer Bradley focusing on Arthurian women

Mobile Suit Gundam: Japanese mecha TV anime series, 1979-80

Monet, Claude: Founder of French impressionist painting

Moomin: Characters in books & comic strip by Swedish-Finn illustrator/writer Tove Jansson

Morrissey: Rose to prominence in the 1980s as lead singer of The Smiths

Mother and Son: Australian sitcom 1984-94 starring Ruth Cracknell & Garry McDonald

My Brother Jack: 1964 Australian novel by George Johnston

Neighbours: TV soapie first broadcast in 1985 & country's longest-running drama series

New Order: British outfit arising from Joy Division after Ian Curtis' death in 1980. Became one of the most influential bands that decade

Nintendo Entertainment System: An 8-bit video game console released in Japan in 1983

Nitzer Ebb: British EBM group formed 1982, influenced by German outfit D.A.F.

NME: The *New Musical Express* a UK weekly music publication since 1952

Nud: Nude, naked

O'Keefe, Johnny: Australian rock & roll singer whose career began in 1950s

Op shop: Retail store run by a charitable organization to raise money

Pantaloon: Poodle with a sweet tooth applies for job of assistant baker. 1951 classic by Kathryn Jackson & Leonard Weisgard

Peter, Paul & Mary: U.S. folk trio famous in 1960s for 'Puff, the Magic Dragon'

P'Gell: Femme fatale conjured up in *The Spirit* by comic-book creator Will Eisner

Pink Floyd: English rock band, est. 1965.

Pippi Longstocking: (*Pippi Långstrump*) Swedish author Astrid Lindgren's yarn about unconventional, assertive 9-year-old with superhuman strength & wild braids

Pitt, Ingrid: Actress known for work in horror in the 1960s & '70s especially with Hammer

Poe, Edgar Allan: 19th C. American writer, famous for tales of mystery & the macabre

Pollyanna: 1913 classic children's novel by Eleanor H. Porter

Price, Vincent: American actor, known for distinctive voice & performances in horror

Prima, Louis: U.S. singer best known for King Louie in Disney's *The Jungle Book* (1967)

Primitive Calculators: Australian post-punk band formed in the late 1970s

Princess Knight: Manga (*Ribon no Kishi* 1953-68) & 1967 anime created by Osamu Tezuka

Pretty in Pink: 1986 John Hughes vehicle for actors Molly Ringwald & Andrew McCarthy

Puffing Billy: Heritage steam train in Dandenong Ranges near Melbourne, Australia

Pull up stumps: Aussie expression to cease something, relocate place of abode — or die

Quatermain, Allan: Protagonist of H. Rider Haggard's 1885 novel *King Solomon's Mines*

Quatro, Suzi: U.S. singer-songwriter, bass guitar player & actor

Quik: Powdered flavouring mix by Nestlé that changed names to Nesquik in 1997

Red Lorry Yellow Lorry: Band formed in England in early 1981, lumped into gothic rock

Red Sonja: Comic-book heroine created by Roy Thomas & Barry Windsor-Smith in 1973, based on Robert E. Howard's Red Sonya. Frank Thorne ran comic book from 1977-79

Replicant: Fictional bioengineered android in the film *Blade Runner* (1982)

Ringwald, Molly: Star of John Hughes' *Sixteen Candles* (1984) & *Pretty in Pink* (1986)

'Rockit': Single off Herbie Hancock's 1983 LP *Future Shock* written by Hancock, Bill Laswell & Michael Beinhorn — feat. turntablism by GrandMixer D.ST

Rolling Stone: Mag founded in San Francisco in 1967 focusing on politics & popular culture

Rosemary's Baby: 1968 horror movie directed by Roman Polanski, starring Mia Farrow

RSPCA: Royal Society for the Prevention of Cruelty to Animals

Runners: In Australian English used for 'sneakers'

RV: Release Valve

Sassoon, Vidal: British hairdresser credited with creating the Bauhaus-inspired wedge bob

SBS: Australian multilingual & multicultural TV station founded in 1980

Schoeffling, Michael: Starred alongside Molly Ringwald in *Sixteen Candles* (1984)

Schwarzenegger, Arnold: A.K.A. 'Arnie', Austrian American actor, politician & former professional bodybuilder famous for roles in *Predator* & *The Terminator*

Science Fiction Space Adventures: 1950s-born sci-fi anthology from Charlton Comics

Seberg, Jean: American actress, starred in 1958 film *Bonjour Tristesse* & *À bout de souffle* (*Breathless*, 1960). Also famous for short pixie haircut

Second Empire style: Architectural style 1865-1880, named for Second French Empire

Sheila: Australian slang for 'woman', derived from Irish girls' name

Shelley, Mary: English writer best known for Gothic novel *Frankenstein: or, The Modern Prometheus* (1818)

'Shivers': 1978 single by The Boys Next Door banned by radio because of ref. to suicide

Simca Gordini T15s (1950): Car raced & retired at 1950 Le Mans

Simply Red: English soul band formed in 1985

Sinclair, Anthony: British tailor. Dressed Sean Connery as James Bond in the 1960s

Siouxsie and the Banshees: English punk band formed in 1976

Sisters of Mercy, The: English band est. 1977, connected with goth rock of the '80s

Smith, Robert: Lead singer, guitar player, lyricist and principal songwriter of The Cure

Smiths, The: Manchester band est. 1982 with vocalist Morrissey & guitarist Johnny Marr

Soft Cell: English synthpop duo prominent in the early 1980s

Sopwith Pup: British single-seater biplane fighter aircraft built by Sopwith from 1916

Spirit, The: Newspaper comic about masked crimefighter created in 1940s by Will Eisner & re-released in 1970s in comic-book form by Kitchen Sink Press

Star Model B: 9mm pistol identical in design to the Colt 1911 .45, manufactured in Spain

Steely Dan: American jazz rock band founded in 1972

St. Elmo's Fire: 1985 film directed by Joel Schumacher, starring '80s Brat Packers Rob Lowe, Andrew McCarthy, Emilio Estevez, Ally Sheedy & Judd Nelson

Stoker, Bram: Irish novelist best known for 1897 gothic novel *Dracula*

St. Paul's Cathedral: Anglican cathedral in Melbourne, diagonally opposite Flinders Street Station, built 1880-1891

Stuka: Junkers Ju 87 German dive bomber made combat debut in 1936

Succhi: Iconic Aussie shoe brand, famous in 'alternative'-leaning circles in 1980s

Sun News-Pictorial, The: Morning tabloid newspaper in Melbourne est. 1922, closed 1990

Sutherland, Donnie: Host of *Video Hits*

Stringybark: Any Eucalyptus tree with thick, fibrous bark

Studebaker Commander Starlight: 2-door coupe from Studebaker 1947-52

TAFE colleges: In Australia, technical & further education institutions

Tales to Astonish: Sci-fi anthology comic book initially serving as showcase for such artists as Jack Kirby & Steve Ditko from 1959

Taylor, Elizabeth: British-American actress, star of *Cleopatra* (1963)

Tenggren, Gustaf: Swedish-American illustrator of *Tawny Scrawny Lion*

Thatcher, Maggie: Horrible, horrible UK prime minister, 1979-90

There's No Business Like Show Business: 1954 musical-comedy-drama starring Donald O'Connor, Mitzi Gaynor & Marilyn Monroe

Thorne, Frank: American comic-book artist/writer, famous for work with Red Sonja

Thrush and the Cunts: Melbourne post-punk band known for song 'Diseases'

Toot: Toilet

Touché Turtle: 1960s Hanna Barbera cartoon fencer

Trilogy of Terror: 1975 telemovie starring actress Karen Black in multiple roles

Truth, The: Melbourne tabloid newspaper est. 1902. Ceased publication in 1995

242: See Front 242 (above)

Unreal: Unbelievable, but equally often fantastic

Vampire Lovers, The: 1970 Hammer gothic horror starring Ingrid Pitt & Peter Cushing, directed by Roy Ward Baker

Veidt, Conrad: German actor. Starred in *The Cabinet of Dr Caligari* & *Casablanca*

Vegemite: Popular Australian salty black spread — put on toast for brekky

VHS: Video Home System analogue recording videotape created by Victor, Japan

Vickers machine gun: Water-cooled .303 British machine gun produced from 1912

Video Hits: Long-running music show, viewed on Australian TV 1987-2011

Violent Femmes: American alt-rock band active from 1980

Walkman: Sony device released in 1979 (predating mp3) using instead cassette tapes — with chronically short battery life

Whirlywirld: Australian post-punk band led by Ollie Olsen from late 1970s

Windsor-Smith, Barry: British artist known for Marvel's *Conan*

the Barbarian 1970-73

Wishing-Chair Again, The: 1950 British children's book by Enid Blyton

Witchery: Australian store specialising in women's clothing, shoes & accessories

Witchfinder General: 1968 Vincent Price horror film, directed by Michael Reeves

XB GT Ford Falcon Coupe: 1973 Australian car adapted into the *Mad Max* Interceptor for George Miller's film

Yellow dolly: Paint colour for models of Australian car company Holden in 1970

Yellow Magic Orchestra: Japanese electronic outfit est. 1977 with Ryūichi Sakamoto

Acknowledgements

This novel was something I threw myself into (again) over about three months, a beast that ended up cutting sleep ragged and eating into my dreams — hence the celery people and oversized Venus flytraps that have cameo appearances in the yarn.

I say again because it draws upon elements of a manuscript I tossed together in 1991, and then revamped in 1993 — both versions more heavily based upon the gothic/alternative/post-punk scene in Melbourne, from 1986 to about 1992.

A round of applause to Kristina, who hung onto a copy of the '93 manuscript, mould and all, long after I misplaced mine, and footed the bill for the exorbitant postage getting it from Australia to Japan.

Further substantial thanks to my amazing wife Yoko and gorgeous daughter Cocoa in terms of support and putting up with my crazy sleeping patterns and mental leaves-of-absence while still in the same room.

A big thank you for the super image on the back cover by Japan's Sukapon-ta, along with the wunderbar frontispiece by French artist Kmye Chan — which nails the Pippi Långstrump look plus the freckles, the Steve Ditko and manga influences, and has those strings. First time I spied this painting, I thought... Mina.

Some people essential at the time in churning out those original manuscripts? Karin, Vivi, Trish, Mateusz, Gavin, Francis, Kedra, Sue, Anna, Shaun, Britt, Jen, Clair, Avon, Maria, Sharon, Matty, Aggie, Carl, Tanya, Tim, Baz, Gaz, Dominique, Georgina, Rhiannon, Laura Palmer, step-dad Tom, my parents Fée and Des, Nan, and cuz Zoe.

Subsequent mates, fellow hacks and invaluable supportive types include Fiona, Katy, Josh, Renee, John, Steven, Barbra, Shawn, Heath, Chris, Brian, OzNoir, Elizabeth, Marcus, Briony,

Lori, Chris/Tuffy, Stu K, Jongdo, Neville, Liam, Matt, Craig, Eva, Emmet, Mark, Kate, Mara, Caleb, Christopher, Matthew, John, Lloyd, Guy, Paul, Jack, Pete, Chad, Gerard, Gordon, Ryan, Bane of Kings, Greg, Ani, Joe, Kevin, Robb, Livius, Dakota, Elodie, James, Jonny, Craig, Benoit, Zoe, Bas, László, Ollie, Fliss, Dames, Paul, Alby, Devin, Danielle, Mihai, Richard, David, Jane, Andrew, Martin, Dustin, Nicole, Raymond, Patrick, Chrysoula, Bernard, Mckay, Solly, Scott, Jazmyn, Nigel, Dan, Tony, Charlee, Jayden, Falcon, Sunday, Liv, Jochem, Kriss, Katherine, Emlyn, Timmy, Seb, Rosemarie, Renee's mum, Ransley, Chloe, Wolfgang, Jason, Camille, Carl, David Aja, Walter Geovani, the Chiyoda High School girls, Yoshiko, Toshie, Hashimoto-san & the ETM crew, and Brunswick Bound book shop. As well as a huge slice of gratitude to Matt Kyme, with whom I've been doing the *Tales to Admonish* comic book — and thereby ventured into other territory trod by Bullet Gal.

Websites and magazines deserving of a nod? Dork Shelf, The Thrilling Detective, Atomic Anxiety, Books and Booze, Death By Killing, Criminal Element, Comics Should Be Good!, Word of the Nerd, Sequart, The Ink Shot, Just A Guy That Likes 2 Read, Sci-Fi Jubilee, Booked Podcast, The Geek of Oz, Loitering With Intent, The Nameless Horror, Fanboy Comics, Comic Bastards, The Founding Fields, SF Signal, Bare*Bones, NerdSpan, Rough Edges, I Meant to Read That..., Reviews by Elizabeth A. White, Comic Book Herald, A License to Quill, Geek Magazine, The Momus Report, Silver Age Comics, artsHub, Smart Girls Love SciFi, Available in Any Colour, Sons of Spade, Farrago, The Bookbag, SciFiPulse, Nerd Culture Podcast, AICN, Shotgun Honey, Big Pulp, Revolt Daily, LitReactor, The Day the Web Stood Stupid, ThunderDome, Naimeless, Black Gate Magazine, SF Book Reviews, Daily Steampunk, Shelf Abuse, Longbox Graveyard, Solarcide, Cabin Goddess, Crime Factory, Angry Robot, Bookworm Castle, Forces Of Geek, The Cultural Gutter, 8th Wonder Press, At the Inkwell, A Book A Day Reviews, Another

Sky Press and Zouch.

And it goes without saying — gratitude to the tireless Phil Jourdan and support from the posse of fellow scribes at Perfect Edge Books; slaps on the back to reader/support Maria and suave copy editor Dominic, designer Stuart, ed. Trevor, and cover whiz Nick.

Then there was the muzak, only a fraction of which made the cut: 242, Joy Division, Cabaret Voltaire, David Bowie, Christian Death, Suzi Quatro, The Smiths, Nitzer Ebb, Herbie Hancock, Cypress Hill, Miles Davis, Bauhaus, The Birthday Party, Einstürzende Neubauten, Thrush and the Cunts, Merzbow, Sisters of Mercy, Soft Cell, Yellow Magic Orchestra, Primitive Calculators, The Doors, Whirlywirld, Red Lorry Yellow Lorry, Pink Floyd, Danielle Dax, Jesus and Mary Chain, New Order, The Cure, Siouxsie and the Banshees, God and Dead Kennedys (unmentioned by name). Others from this era that almost sneaked in, didn't, but deserve attention? D.A.F., Nina Hagen, Depeche Mode, Front Line Assembly, Sugarcubes, Throbbing Gristle, Neil Young, Cat Stevens, Echo and the Bunnymen, Psycho Bunnies, Blondie, Iggy Pop, Fuzzbox, Laibach, Lydia Lunch, Ennio Morricone, Public Enemy, No, Love and Rockets, Diamanda Galas and Isao Tomita.

Also Melbourne clubs and venues like the Crystal Ballroom, Soho, Sarah Sands, Razor, Dream, The Organ Factory, Hellfire, Apocalypse, ZuZu's and The Old Greek, plus pubs such as The Punters Club, The Empress, The Champion and The Espie. London clubs? Full Tilt @ Electric Ballroom and Camden Palace, plus the Spice Of Life pub — before it was renovated.

It's equally vital to mention the comic-book art that held sway, in particular that by Steve Ditko, Jack Kirby, Will Eisner, Barry Windsor-Smith, Frank Thorne, John Buscema, Matt Kyme, Javier García-Miranda and Tarpé Mills. Not forgetting Fawcett's character Bulletgirl, Mills's Miss Fury and Will Eisner's P'Gell and Sand Saref from *The Spirit*, or titles like Charlton's *Science*

Fiction Space Adventures and Marvel's *2001: A Space Odyssey*.

There's too much cinema to jot down, but for starters think Fritz Lang's *Woman in the Moon*, Alfred Hitchcock's *The Birds*, Masaki Kobayashi's *Kwaidan*, and Robert Wiene's *The Cabinet of Dr Caligari*. Also 1950s-60s Technicolor horror by American International Pictures and Hammer Films, the great Vincent Price, fellow thesps Elsa Lanchester, Ingrid Pitt, Peter Lorre, Boris Karloff, Conrad Veidt, Christopher Lee, Peter Cushing, Martine Beswick and Bela Lugosi. Other films? *The Empire Strikes Back*, *Harvey*, *Forbidden Planet* and Disney's *Peter Pan*.

Add in a sprinkling of the gothic, oft-macabre fiction of Shelley, Stoker, Poe, Brontë and Stevenson as much as Kazuo Umezu, Shūichi Yoshida and Heinrich Kramer.

Iconic individuals, outfits and events? Stan Lee, Groucho Marx, Enid Blyton, Sean Connery, Michael Cain, Marilyn Monroe, organized religion, the Salem witch trials, Japanese manga by the likes of Katsuhiro Ōtomo, and some of the zany dreams I had while writing. Cheers to Fliss for the original inspiration with Mr Osterberg's wayward 'beatnik' poetry.

By the way, Mina's classroom rant on Bulletgirl was originally a rant I did for *ThunderDome* magazine in 2013, while her short stories originally featured in anthologies like *Big Pulp*, *Off the Record 2* and *The Condimental Op*, as well as online @ Shotgun Honey.

There're also references tucked away that hark back to my other novels and shorter yarns, and readers of those might glean some bonus extra in which to indulge. I got to tinker with tons of references and homages within the context of the story, citing things I love and/or admire that in turn complement the tale. The trick here is to deconstruct names as well as places for clues. A mirror is handy.

And hats off to the underpinning triumverate of Brigitte Bardot, Mitzi Gaynor and Louise Brooks.

'WHO IS KILLING THE GREAT CAPES OF HEROPA?'
(2013)

"Pulp fiction brought bang up to date and then slammed hard
into the roots of its own mythology."
AVAILABLE IN ANY COLOUR

"Incredibly engaging, clever and a fantastic piece of escapism
— simply super."
SF BOOK REVIEWS

"A mixed-media love letter to the golden age of comics and the
classic detective story."
JOE CLIFFORD (author, *Junkie Love*)

"Super-powered superhero literature and comic-book
goodness."
SOLARCIDE

"That this story about comics should be so similar to a murder
mystery of the Sam Spade kind is just the cherry on the cake."
THE MOMUS REPORT

"The best non-comic-book superhero story I've ever read."
COMIC BASTARDS

"Like a crazy, post-modern road trip with Jack Kirby riding
shotgun, and everyone from Stan Lee to Raymond Chandler
nattering away in the back seat."
THE THRILLING DETECTIVE

"Terrific, postmodern superhero noir."
JASON FRANKS (author, *McBlack*)

323

"Vintage pulp-dieselpunk-superhero action at its finest!"
DAILY STEAMPUNK

"Any writer who can pull twists and a mystery like that deserves recognition and a ton of praise."
ACERBIC WRITING

"Deconstructs what it means to be a hero."
DORK SHELF

"A highly stylized, retro-futuristic world."
SF SIGNAL

"Excellent."
THE FOUNDING FIELDS

"I very much doubt I'll read a better supers novel."
THE NAMELESS HORROR

"Tough stuff with a golden heart."
I MEANT TO READ THIS

"These are superheroes at their best and worst, just like Lee and Kirby intended them to be."
JOHN KOWALSKI @ WORD OF THE NERD

"One wild trip."
GEEK MAGAZINE

Heropa: A vast, homogenized city patrolled by heroes and populated by adoring masses. A pulp-fiction fortress of solitude for crime-fighting team the Equalizers, led by new recruit Southern Cross — a lifetime away from the rain-drenched, dystopic metropolis of Melbourne.

Who, then, is killing the great Capes of Heropa?

In this paired homage to detective noir from the 1940s and the '60s Marvel age of trailblazing comic books, Andrez Bergen gloriously redefines the mild-mannered superhero novel.

ISBN-13: 978-1782792352

'ONE HUNDRED YEARS OF VICISSITUDE'
(2012)

"Andrez Bergen put science fiction, noir, Australia and Japan
into a literary hadron collider."
THE THOUSANDS MAGAZINE

"Exquisite writing — incredibly touching and devastating in its
beauty by the end."
MCDROLL (author, *The Wrong Delivery*)

"By turns educational, inspiring, traumatic and humorous, this
is also one of the best books I have read this year."
FANTASY BOOK REVIEW

"A postmodern dexterity of Cirque de Soleil proportions."
FARRAGO MAGAZINE

"A terrific book!"
BARE*BONES

"Eclectic, compelling, and engaging from the first page —
the most original novel I've read all year."
DRYING INK

"A wildly enchanting journey down the rabbit hole to an
ethereal world rich with Japanese and pop culture, one which
seamlessly melds history and the hereafter."
BOOK REVIEWS BY ELIZABETH A. WHITE

"Dreamlike, and bewitchingly evocative."
THE INK SHOT

"A hedonistic, delightfully drunken tour through purgatory
and World War II-era Japan."
CHRIS RHATIGAN @ ALL DUE RESPECT

"Excellent, multi-layered writing, numerous pop culture references, the odd history lesson and a cracking great story."
READING, WRITING & NO ARITHMETIC

"This story of the afterlife is like nothing else that has come
before it. Bergen has set the standard for an intriguing,
beautiful and terrible place that leaves most of the big questions
up to
the reader."
RENEE PICKUP @ BOOKS AND BOOZE

"A breathtakingly detailed narrative."
LORI HOLUTA @ STEAMPUNK MAGAZINE

"Witty dialogues, delightful characters and a captivating story."
DARK WOLF'S FANTASY REVIEWS

"First up, a disclaimer. I suspect I am a dead man. I have meagre proof, no framed-up certification, nothing to toss in a court of law as evidence of a rapid departure from the mortal coil. I recall a gun was involved, pressed up against my skull, and a loud explosion followed."

Thus begins our narrator in a purgatorial tour through twentieth-century Japanese history, with a ghostly geisha who has seen it all as a guide and a corrupt millionaire as her reluctant companion.

Thrown into the milieu are saké, B-29s, Lewis Carroll, Sir Thomas Malory, Melbourne, *The Wizard of Oz*, and a dirigible — along with the allusion that Red Riding Hood might just be involved.

ISBN-13: 978-1780995977

'TOBACCO-STAINED MOUNTAIN GOAT'
(2011)

"An incredible novel, completely unexpected and with such a wonderfully rich and unique style that is simply mesmerizing, unmissable."
SF BOOK REVIEWS

"A cyberpunk, *Mad Max*, and Philip K. Dick kind of novel."
COMIC ATTACK

"I can say without qualification that not only is *Tobacco-Stained Mountain Goat* one of my Top 5 reads of 2011, it is one of the most creative and engaging books I've ever read — period. My mind is completely blown."
BOOK REVIEWS BY ELIZABETH A. WHITE

"Such an engrossing and visual read — with gorgeous, subtle moments in there as well."
LIP MAGAZINE

"At the heart of Bergen's novel is the love affair our author has with popular culture. This book is bursting with nods and homages to everything from Humphrey Bogart to *Mobile Suit Gundam*."
VERBICIDE MAGAZINE

"A wonderful ambush of a novel. It leads you down a well-tread path and then jumps from the brush and drags you to uncharted lands. It has been a while since I had this childlike joy at turning the page. It's an insane, hardboiled future shocker. Wow."
JOSH STALLINGS (author, *Beautiful, Naked & Dead*)

"Flows effortlessly; smart, mesmerizingly dark and difficult to put down."
VICE MAGAZINE

"A compote that mashes up a plethora of fictional frameworks into a believable, seamless whole. Floyd Maquina is ruggedly handsome and generally ruined; witty, self-destructive and self-effacing with his air of gracious defeat."
THE FLAWED MIND

"A post-modern mélange that is the most intriguing of novels — hardboiled and playful at the same time."
AUSTRALIAN SPECULATIVE FICTION IN FOCUS

"Terrific stuff, truly unique. One of my favourite books of 2011."
HEATH LOWRANCE (author, *The Bastard Hand*)

"A retro pop culturalist's dream come true — and entertaining to boot."
PERMISSION TO KILL

"A cigar-puffing, whiskey-sipping, piano-playing bar lout."
SOLARCIDE

"Destined to be a cult classic."
DEAD END FOLLIES

"Holy shit, I loved this book."
DEATH BY KILLING